PENG

Kevin Lewis grew up on the mean streets of south London. *The Kid*, his first book, chronicles his life at the hands of his violent parents and a system that neglected him. *Kaitlyn* is his first novel and is drawn from his experiences.

Kaitlyn

KEVIN LEWIS

PENGUIN BOOKS

PENGUIN BOOKS

Published by the Penguin Group
Penguin Books Ltd, 80 Strand, London WC2R ORL, England
Penguin Group (USA) Inc., 375 Hudson Street, New York, New York 10014, USA
Penguin Group (Canada), 90 Eglinton Avenue East, Suite 700, Toronto, Ontario, Canada M4P 2Y3
(a division of Pearson Penguin Canada Inc.)
Penguin Ireland, 25 St Stephen's Green, Dublin 2, Ireland (a division of Penguin Books Ltd)
Penguin Group (Australia), 250 Camberwell Road,
Camberwell, Victoria 3124, Australia (a division of Pearson Australia Group Pty Ltd)
Penguin Books India Pvt Ltd, 11 Community Centre,
Panchsheel Park, New Delhi – 110 017, India
Penguin Group (NZ), cnr Airborne and Rosedale Roads, Albany,
Auckland 1310, New Zealand (a division of Pearson New Zealand Ltd)
Penguin Books (South Africa) (Pty) Ltd, 24 Sturdee Avenue,
Rosebank, Johannesburg 2196, South Africa

Penguin Books Ltd, Registered Offices: 80 Strand, London WC2R ORL, England

www.penguin.com

First published in Penguin Books 2006
2

Copyright © Kevin Lewis, 2006
All rights reserved

The moral right of the author has been asserted

Set in 11.75/14 pt Monotype Garamond
Typeset by Rowland Phototypesetting Ltd, Bury St Edmunds, Suffolk
Printed in England by Clays Ltd, St Ives plc

ISBN 13: 978-0-141-02130-0
ISBN 10: 0-141-02130-6

For Jackie, Charlotte and Nathan, aka
'The Groovy Gang'

Part One

Part One

Chapter One

April 1976

'How much longer?'

There was an unmistakable note of panic and desperation in Peter Connelly's voice as he shouted to be heard above the noise of the wailing siren.

'Ten minutes tops,' came the reply.

'Blood pressure's dropping,' said Peter. 'Better give the hospital a call.'

In the front of the ambulance Diana Jameson jerked the heavy steering wheel hard to the right, narrowly missing a blue Mini Cooper that seemed to have come out of nowhere, then reached for the radio. 'Control, can you put me through to ST.'

She was doing nearly 60mph now, weaving her way through the late-night London traffic, her eyes tightly focused on the road ahead. A series of clicks followed by a short buzz and then a muffled cough told her she had got through to the dispatcher at St Thomas's.

'What have you got, Diana?'

'We're coming in hot. Male, eighteen months, major multiple chest trauma. Looks like a collapsed lung and torn windpipe. Pete says his BP's falling fast.'

'What's your ETA?'

'Seven minutes.'

'OK. Bring him in on bay number two. We'll be ready.'

Peter Connelly took his eyes off his patient for a fraction of a second to look at the woman and young girl – the boy's mother and sister – sitting on the red bench opposite him in the back of the swaying ambulance. Both had blank, shell-shocked faces. He was just about to say something to reassure them when the steady beep of the heart monitor suddenly changed to a single, terrifying, BEEEEEEEEEEEEEEEEEEEEEEEEEEEP.

'Shit.'

'You need me to pull over?' Diana shouted.

Peter didn't answer. The blue, pursed lips, the twitching chest muscles and the rapidly dilating pupils told him he had only seconds to act. He inserted a second IV needle into the little boy's arm, hooked it up to a bag of plasma, then ripped open a resuscitation kit.

A quick glance at the heart monitor: 36. The alarm had sounded when the boy's pulse had fallen below 40. If it dropped below 25 his heart would stop for certain and the chances of getting it started again would be almost zero. Out of the corner of his eye Peter could see silent tears running down the little girl's face as he started to prise open the boy's mouth, ready to insert the tube. It's hard enough to get it right in a hospital and almost impossible in a fast-moving ambulance when the patient already has a torn windpipe. Peter peered into the boy's mouth, deep into the shadow of the hole past his vocal cords, and shot the tube forward.

Two pumps on the air bag and the machine came back to life, pushing out a series of steady beeps. Peter gently stroked the boy's arm. 'How we doing, Diana?'

'Just coming up to Waterloo. We'll be there in less than a minute.'

Directly outside the sliding doors of bay number two a small group of nurses in short-sleeved shirts were shuffling about and rubbing the bare skin of their arms to keep warm. A moment later Dr Nathan Bishop, the lead paediatric trauma surgeon, arrived. 'Heads up, ladies, I've got a feeling this is going to be an all-nighter,' he said softly.

Pale-blue flashes lit up the night sky and the wail of the sirens grew from faint to deafeningly loud as the ambulance pulled into view. The team shifted into their final positions. There was no need for words – they all knew what they had to do and that they had to make every second count.

The back doors flew open even before the tyres had screeched to a halt. 'He almost arrested twice on the way over but I think I've managed to stabilise him. Left lung's collapsed and there's extensive trauma,' Peter explained breathlessly as he clambered out. 'I could only get the tube halfway in because the windpipe's torn.' The expanding legs of the trolley bed clattered on to the tarmac and moments later the patient came into view.

He was tiny, curled up in the foetal position and naked apart from a soiled nappy wrapped round his crotch. According to the log, Christopher Wilson was eighteen months old but at that moment he looked so frail and undernourished that he could easily have passed for half that age.

Bishop gasped – virtually every inch of the boy's body was covered with purple bruises. In twenty years on the job it was one of the worst things he had ever seen. The original 999 call said the boy had fallen down a flight of stairs but it took only a quick glance for Bishop to know that simply wasn't true. He could see the impressions left by the fingers that had been fixed round the child's throat, the deep red stains under the skin where veins had been ruptured; the circular impact marks left by the ring that whoever punched him had been wearing.

They were running through the brightly lit corridors now, Bishop barking out instructions as his fingers danced gently over the boy's body and the fluorescent tubes flashed by overhead. 'We need to get the laryngoscope in there right away. Hook up the ECG and administer epinephrine followed by an atropine drip. Come on, people, let's go.'

By the time the trolley had smashed through the

heavy rubber-edged double doors into the sterile environment of Theatre One, Dr Bishop was in the adjacent sink room scrubbing up. 'Where are the parents?' he asked the senior nurse.

'The mother, she's the one who called it in, is being taken to the family room. Daughter's going there too.'

Dr Bishop thought for a moment while using a small brush to scrub his nails vigorously.

'How old is the daughter?'

The nurse shrugged. 'Dunno. Young. Five, maybe six.'

Dr Bishop nodded thoughtfully as he inspected his fingers for any remaining traces of dirt. 'OK. I need to get into the theatre so do me a favour, ID the mum to reception so that everyone knows who she is and what she looks like. And get someone to keep an eye on her to make sure nothing happens to the other kid.'

'And then what?'

'Then call the police.'

Chapter Two

They called it the family room but it also doubled as the toddlers' play area, the interview suite and a resting place for worn-out junior doctors working the graveyard shift. The sofas were a cheerful yellow with big soft cushions, and there were bean bags and used toys and children's books scattered across the floor. The wallpaper, pastel pink with fruit and flower patterns, like everything else in the room was designed to create an atmosphere where the frightened and vulnerable felt safe and able to open up and talk freely. It didn't always work.

A young orderly stood watch in the corridor outside and shrugged his shoulders as Bishop approached; still wearing his gown and with his surgical mask hanging loosely round his neck. 'Hasn't said a word,' said the orderly. 'I had to come out to get some air. I couldn't breathe in there.'

Dr Bishop had come straight from the operating theatre where he'd spent the last hour and a half doing his best to repair Christopher's torn windpipe. He had been taken back to the ICU and was still in a critical condition. Dr Bishop's priority now was to find out more about how the injuries had occurred.

Inside the room, the air was thick with smoke. Angela sat at one end of the sofa, a cigarette hanging loosely from her lips. Half a dozen butts floated in a half-empty cup of coffee on the floor beside her. Bishop could see right away that once upon a time she had been quite striking, but that might just as well have been a lifetime ago. Today she looked as though her life had been taken away: her cheaply dyed blonde hair was scraped back into a ragged ponytail and was in desperate need of a wash, her pale skin was dry and cracked, her eyes bloodshot and puffy.

She wore a simple, slightly grubby orange blouse over faded blue jeans with worn out knees and tatty black shoes. She didn't look up, just stared blankly into space. She was lost in a world of her own.

'Is Chrissy going to be OK?'

It was a child's voice and it had come from behind him. Bishop whipped round to see a bedraggled young girl huddled up on the other sofa. She too looked like she'd been crying all night. She was dressed only in a large T-shirt, which hung from her shoulders over her stick-thin body like a giant tent right down to her knees. Her heels were resting on the edge of the cushion and she was hugging her knees and resting her chin on them. Even from the other side of the room Bishop could see the pale-yellow shadow of a week-old bruise on her cheek. A large red hand mark on her left thigh was clearly much more recent.

'Hello. What's your name?' asked Bishop, his voice soft and gentle.

'Kaitlyn.'

'Well, Kaitlyn,' he said, crossing the room and getting down on one knee so he could talk to her face to face. 'Your brother is still very poorly but we're doing everything we can to make him better as quickly as possible. You understand that, don't you?'

Kaitlyn nodded.

Bishop's eyes moved quickly as he spoke, checking the girl for signs of more serious injury. 'I need to talk to your mummy for a minute, so why don't I get a friend of mine to take you over to the canteen and see if you can get something to eat, maybe some chocolate.' Bishop glanced over at the door and beckoned for the orderly to come into the room.

'Kaitlyn, this is James. James, this is Kaitlyn. I thought you might want to show her around our wonderful canteen. Particularly the chocolate machine.'

'Sure thing,' said James, holding out his hand for Kaitlyn, who took it as she got down from the sofa.

Dr Bishop made his way to the door and held it open for the pair. As James passed him he whispered, 'Get a nurse to have a good look at her.' James nodded and closed the door behind him.

Dr Bishop glanced over to where Angela was sitting. She had not moved. He cleared his throat. 'Mrs Wilson, I need to talk to you about Christopher.' When she did not respond or even acknowledge his presence Dr Bishop moved across the room and sat on the sofa beside her. 'He's responded well to surgery but I'm nervous that there might be internal bleeding and other injuries we can't see. If I'm going to help him make a full recovery I need to know exactly what happened to him.'

Angela remained on the edge of the sofa, her body hunched forward and her eyes staring directly at the ground in front of her. Bishop noticed a tear in the sleeve of her blouse and peered into it. He could see a huge mass of dark-purple discoloration on her forearm, a classic defence wound. He looked over the rest of her. She wore no rings and the nails of both sets of fingers, though cracked and chipped, were too long not to have left marks of their own. Whoever had battered Christopher had clearly attacked her and Kaitlyn as well.

Angela sniffed heavily. Her bottom lip started to tremble and she winced as if a sudden pain had shot through her. She reached up slowly with two fingers and lifted the cigarette from her mouth, flicking the ash on to the floor.

'Angela, you know you're safe here, don't you?' Bishop used what he hoped was his most reassuring tone and placed a comforting hand on her shoulder. Angela flinched like a frightened animal. 'It's all right. I'm not going to hurt you but I just want to take a look at your bruises, make sure there is nothing more serious.' And with that he began to examine her.

A few minutes later, satisfied there were no broken

bones, Bishop spoke again: 'Would you like something for the pain?'

Angela made eye contact with the doctor for the first time, nodding slowly.

'Can you tell me what happened to Christopher?'

For a few seconds it looked as though Angela was going to speak but in the end she opened her mouth only to put the cigarette back in and then shook her head.

There was a knock at the door and Bishop looked over to see James peering through the glass window. He gestured for him to come inside. Kaitlyn followed close behind, nibbling greedily on a large bar of chocolate. Angela hardly seemed to notice her own daughter coming into the room. James signalled to Bishop that the young girl was OK, then went back outside.

Bishop watched as Kaitlyn returned to her spot on the sofa on the opposite side of the room from her mother. She continued munching the chocolate but stopped when there were two pieces left, carefully folding them back in the foil wrapper and placing them on the sofa beside her.

'Don't you want to finish it?' Bishop asked.

'That's for Chrissy.'

Bishop smiled and crossed the room, kneeling in front of Kaitlyn and keeping his voice low so that Angela would not be able to hear. 'You really love your brother, don't you?'

'Of course I do.'

'And you want him to get better as quickly as possible.'

'Yeah.'

'Then I need you to tell me how he got hurt. The best way for me to be able to help your brother is if I know exactly what happened to him.'

Kaitlyn bit her bottom lip and looked anxiously at her mother, who gave no sign that she had even heard the question. Kaitlyn took a long time to answer.

'He fell over,' she said at last.

The doctor shifted his weight so that his face was a little closer to hers. 'Kaitlyn, you know the difference between the truth and a lie, don't you?'

'Yes.'

'Well, Christopher is badly hurt and needs lots of medicine, but I don't know what medicine to give him unless you tell me the truth.'

There was another long pause. When Kaitlyn spoke her voice was soft, almost a whisper. 'I'm not lying. He fell over, he just fell really badly.' Kaitlyn turned away and as she did so James knocked on the door and gestured for Bishop to come outside.

'OK, Kaitlyn. You stay here and look after your mum. I just need to go out for a moment. And don't worry about Christopher; we're going to do everything we can for him. And when he's better, he'll get a whole bar of chocolate all to himself.'

On the other side of the door, standing just behind James, stood PC Andy Carter and WPC Sarah

Lomax. Kaitlyn could see them talking to each other as she finished off her last piece of chocolate. She recognised the two police officers – they had come to the house to help Mummy a number of times in the past year.

'They're still saying he fell but that's not consistent with his injuries. The boy took a severe beating. We've stabilised him but he's still critical, the next couple of hours are going to be crucial,' Dr Bishop said.

Carter glanced through the glass and squinted at Kaitlyn and Angela. 'I know them. Been over to her place on the Roxford estate at least half a dozen times in the last year. Her old man, Steve Brooks, likes to talk with his fists. Nasty piece of work, real jack-the-lad type. The neighbours call it in every time they hear her getting a kicking. He's had a go at the girl a few times too, the sick bastard. Guess the boy was next on the list. Mother never presses charges, though, so there's little we can do.' They all looked inside. 'Has she said anything?'

'Nothing,' said Dr Bishop. 'She's still in shock. And the little one is very defensive.'

'Hardly surprising under the circumstances,' said Lomax, tilting her head to speak into the radio attached to her jacket. 'I'll get on to Social Services.'

While Lomax made the call, Bishop pulled Carter to one side. 'I think you should have a look at the boy. There's something I want you to see.' The two men walked through the corridors making small talk on the way until they reached the intensive care unit. There, in the corner of the room, stood a large cot with a small figure inside.

Carter could only see him as he got closer. Needles had been poked into his arm, plastic tubes ran in and out of his nose and mouth, and a large strip of surgical tape had been placed over the incision the surgeon had made in the top of his chest. Most of his body was covered with a small blanket but Carter could see the deep bruises around the boy's face and neck. 'Jesus,' he gasped. 'How old is he?'

'Eighteen months.'

'Not much older than my little one. How could anyone do this?'

Both men shook their heads slowly. There was no answer.

'I think he's going to be OK,' Bishop said. 'He's a fighter. He needs a bit more surgery but that will have to wait. We couldn't do it all at once because he wouldn't be able to take it. Rest assured, we'll get him there.' Dr Bishop pulled down the sheet covering Christopher's body to reveal the circular indentations on his stomach and upper thighs. 'This is what I wanted you to see.'

Carter leaned forward and studied the marks closely. 'Looks like a sovereign.'

'I think so too. I counted seventeen of these around the body.'

WPC Lomax entered the room and made her way

over to Christopher's bed, her eyes moist with tears as she looked down at him. 'Social Services are on their way,' she said softly.

'OK,' said Carter. 'You stay here with the mum and the girl until they arrive. I'm gonna get some officers together and pay a visit to Mr Brooks.'

'What are you going to go for?' Dr Bishop asked.

'Personally, his throat. Professionally, it's got to be attempted murder.'

Chapter Three

Two hours earlier Kaitlyn had woken with a start, the sound of her mother's screams ringing in her ears. It was nothing new. Angela and Steve argued all the time and Kaitlyn had got so used to the echoing voices from the living room that she often managed to sleep right through the rows.

The worst nights were those when Steve came home drunk, high on drugs or both. Once the beatings started, Angela, only too well aware that Kaitlyn could hear everything that happened through the flat's thin walls, would turn up the television to full volume in an effort to mask her cries of pain as she collided with the walls and furniture.

There had been rows for as long as Kaitlyn could remember but they had become more frequent and more violent of late. Steve had spent so much time off his face that he had eventually been sacked from his job. He had been having a string of affairs with young girls, using his giro money to ply them with drink and drugs to better his chances. Increasingly, he only came home if he failed to find someone else to spend the night with.

Steve had finally rolled in just after closing time. His dole money had come in that morning so he had been drinking steadily all day and also managed to talk a friend into sharing half a gram of speed, which he greedily snorted up in a cubicle in the men's toilets of the Prince of Wales pub.

Christopher was crying when Steve came in through the door. He'd been crying a lot lately. Angela was doing her best to comfort him as Steve stormed around the flat, but it was a thankless task. She laid him down in his makeshift cot and rocked him gently to no avail.

'Jesus, shut that fucking baby up,' Steve spat.

'I'm trying, I can't. He's teething.'

'Then give the little fucker something to shut him up.'

'Give him what? Medicine costs money. You know there's no money. He's your son too for Christ's sake, don't you think he should come before your beer and fags?'

'You have your money, I have my money, bitch.' Angela always hated that word because she knew what was coming.

'You're not listening,' she said, changing her tone and pleading with him.

'How can I listen? All I can hear is the fucking baby. If you don't shut that fucking thing up then I will.'

'He'll calm down in a minute, just give him a minute. He'll be fine if you just stop shouting.' Angela began to rock the cot more frantically in the hope that Christopher would settle quicker.

Kaitlyn staggered out of bed, clutching the tattered

form of her favourite teddy bear against her chest. She made her way along the narrow hallway towards the living room, her right thumb planted firmly in her mouth.

Somewhere at the back of her sleepy mind was the idea that she might be able to help. There had been plenty of times in the past when Chrissy had been crying for hours and had only stopped when Kaitlyn picked him up.

The first time it happened was just a few months after he was born. Kaitlyn, excited about the new arrival, had asked her mother every day if she could hold her brother and every day her mother turned her down: 'No, Kaitlyn, you're too little, you might drop him.'

'I won't, I promise I'll be careful, really careful.'

'When you're older, then you can hold him.'

'But when I'm older he'll be too big. I won't be able to hold him.'

All that changed when Christopher started crying, seemingly for no reason. Angela tried everything to calm his screams but nothing worked. Eventually she gave up, sat him on the bed and went off to the toilet, just to have a few minutes of peace. Kaitlyn seized her chance. She dashed into her mother's bedroom and picked up Christopher gently in her arms. The crying stopped immediately as Christopher stared deeply at her, trying to figure out why her face was much closer than it had ever been, why the hands holding him felt so different.

Kaitlyn was in heaven. She loved the way he smelled, the way his eyes moved in and out of focus as he looked at her. He gurgled. Was it a laugh or was it just wind? She couldn't tell and she didn't care. It was everything she had imagined and more. She was filled with a sense of love and happiness she had never before known.

Angela came rushing out of the bathroom as soon as the screaming stopped, her pants still round her ankles. She was terrified that Christopher had somehow fallen off the bed and hit his head. Instead, she stepped into the bedroom and saw an idyllic scene: Kaitlyn cradling her little brother in her arms and speaking to him in a soft, low voice. 'Well, bugger me,' Angela sighed under her breath.

Kaitlyn looked up to the doorway, terrified. She had been so caught up in her brother's charms that she hadn't even heard her mother come into the room. 'I'm sorry, Mummy, I'm sorry, he was just crying so much, I wanted to tell him that everything was going to be OK.' She put her brother back on the bed and instantly he began crying again.

'Don't be sorry,' said Angela. 'I'm glad to have someone who can help me look after Christopher.'

And from that day Kaitlyn did. Angela taught her how to change nappies, how to check the temperature of Christopher's food, how to mash pieces together so that they were nice and soft for his mouth. Soon Kaitlyn had taken over nearly everything to do with Christopher. He still cried, but it rarely happened when Kaitlyn was around. She was happy. Her friends at school were still playing with dolls, pretending they could speak and move, and sitting them around for tea parties. Kaitlyn had the real thing. He would smile every time he saw her and she would spend hours dancing with him balanced on her hip. At night she would read to him from the story books she had learned at school until he fell asleep.

By the time Kaitlyn arrived in the doorway Steve had already hit Angela twice. Christopher was screaming and Steve was raising his voice to be heard above the noise as he raised his fists ready to strike another blow. Angela's face was contorted with pain; she held up her hands to defend herself and screamed. Then Kaitlyn screamed too.

Steve spun round and marched over to her in a menacing rage. She was trembling, frozen with fear, the teddy bear hanging by one hand. Steve's open hand lashed out, striking her bare leg. Kaitlyn screamed with pain. 'Piss off, you miserable little cunt, and mind your own business,' he hissed. 'No wonder your real father doesn't want anything to do with you.'

Steve turned back to Angela, clenching his fists as he advanced on her. 'Look what you made me do, you bitch,' he said, his words broken up by a new flurry of punches.

Kaitlyn's leg throbbed with pain and tears began rolling down her cheeks. 'Leave my mummy alone,' she sobbed.

There had been times like this in the past when she had tried to help her mother, running into the living room and begging Steve to stop beating her, but this would only make him madder and he would save his final blows for her, sending her back to bed with a bloody nose or cut lip. More than once Angela tried to protect her daughter from the worst of the violence, gathering her up in her arms while lying in the foetal position, blows from Steve raining down on her back and head with whatever he had in his hands, while she protected Kaitlyn, both of them screaming with fear.

That evening, once Kaitlyn had shouted for Steve to stop, both mother and daughter knew only too well what was coming next. Steve turned again, fists at the ready, and started marching towards the little girl in the doorway. Angela lurched forward, pushing him off balance on the way, snatching up Kaitlyn and running towards the bathroom. Steve staggered after them but got there seconds too late. Angela locked the door and fell back, pressing her weight against it.

Steve was trying to kick down the door while mother and daughter held each other tightly inside. 'Get out here, you fucking bitches,' he said, punching the door. Then he stormed around the flat, smashing plates in the kitchen, throwing furniture across the bedroom, before making his way back into the living room where Christopher lay in his cot. Angela and Kaitlyn listened in horror as the child's cries of fear turned to screams of pain. Angela began scrabbling with the lock as Kaitlyn beat her fists against the door: 'Leave him alone, leave him alone.'

Thirty seconds later the flat fell silent.

Angela ran out of the bathroom as fast as she could. Steve sat on the edge of the upturned armchair, his head in his hands, breathing hard. Christopher was lying on the floor beside his cot. He had stopped crying and was instead making a series of horrible sucking noises as he tried to draw breath. Kaitlyn screamed at the sight of him.

Angela rushed over. 'Oh God, Steve, what have you done, what have you done?' she wailed. 'He's hurt bad. He's not breathing right. We've got to get him to the hospital. Kaitlyn, go next door, ask Mrs Jenkins to phone for an ambulance.'

Kaitlyn started moving towards the corridor but something reached out, grabbed her arm and tugged her sideways. She smelled Steve's beer-sodden breath as he pushed his face right up next to hers and hissed, 'If anyone asks you what happened, you tell them he fell over. Otherwise you'll get the same as him. Got it?'

Kaitlyn nodded slowly.

Chapter Four

Paul Tobin leaned back in his chair and took another long sip of red wine from his oversized glass. 'So,' he said with a slight slur, 'what do you have in mind?'

Paul and his wife Jane were enjoying a long, leisurely meal at Giorgio's, the first Italian restaurant in Dorking, which had been doing brisk business since it initially opened three months earlier. This success was due in part to the outstanding quality of the food but also the larger than life antics of the owner, Giorgio Bellante, who made it his personal mission to ensure that dining there was like being invited into the home of a loving Italian family. A night at Giorgio's was always a delight, which made it the perfect place for a special celebration.

'I think Samantha if it's a girl and Richard if it's a boy,' said Jane, taking a sip of water from a tall glass.

'Nah. No good. Samantha will be shortened to Sammy or Sam and Richard will be nicknamed Dick. You know what boys are like. You might just as well tattoo "bully me" on his forehead for all the fun in life he'll have.'

'My grandfather's name was Richard.'

'And he was a miserable old sod when he died.'

'He was ninety-seven, he's hardly going to be

spinning cartwheels and cracking knock knock jokes.'

'Look, we're getting off the point, I'm just saying you need to think about this from the point of view of other children, not other adults. There are names that are great once you're all grown up, but a nightmare to grow up with.'

Jane put down her glass and threw both hands in the air in frustration. 'Well, I don't know. There are so many names.'

Paul leaned forward and slapped his palm down on the table. 'I've got it,' he declared triumphantly. 'Germantrude for a girl, Bungle for a boy.'

'Now you're just being silly. We're not naming our child after a character from a TV show.'

'Why not? It's a great idea, guaranteed stardom. We'll never have to work again.'

Jane sighed. 'Am I talking to you or talking to two bottles of fine Chianti?'

Paul leaned forward and lowered his voice. 'If you want me to be completely honest, I'd have to say it was a little of both.' There was a pause and Jane could see Paul's tipsy mind working overtime as a smile spread over his face. 'Can you believe what we went through and how much we spent on all that treatment' – he leaned forward a little more – 'when all you needed was a good seeing to!' He fell back and giggled like a schoolboy.

'Don't be so coarse, you filthy sod.' Jane tried to look cross but she couldn't disguise her smile.

Paul was on a roll. 'I mean, I didn't mind looking

through the magazines and all that. It was just aiming it into the tube and handing it over to the nurse that was so embarrassing.'

'So you liked the magazines.'

'Well. Yes.'

'Preferred them to me perhaps?'

'Never!'

'Yeah, yeah. Well, believe me you had the easy part. Some of the things I had to go through really hurt.' She winced at the memory. 'All those injections. Ugh. I'm glad I'll never have to go through that again.'

They had endured five painful and expensive cycles of fertility treatment to no avail and had almost given up on the idea of ever having children of their own. They had started looking into the possibility of adoption, signing up with an agency and getting through the first stages of the application process, when Jane had miraculously fallen pregnant. The doctors said it was not unusual, and that sometimes all nature needed was an absence of stress and worry to be able to take its course. Paul was delighted. He'd always wanted a child of his own, and had admitted to Jane he was relieved they wouldn't have to adopt after all.

Jane's face became serious for a moment. She sat up straight, reached across the table and cradled Paul's left hand in both of hers. 'This is going to be all right, isn't it, Paul? I mean, I know this is what we wanted. God knows we've wanted it for ever and it feels like we've moved heaven and earth to get to this point. But now that it's actually going to happen

. . . Do you really think we're ready? Supposing I'm a terrible mother? What if . . .'

Paul cut her off mid sentence: 'It's going to be fine. You're going to be fine. We're going to be great parents. This is everything we've ever dreamed of. I don't think anyone in the world has ever wanted a child as much as we do. And now we're going to have one. We're going to be a family, Jane.'

Jane's smile grew until it had spread across her whole face. 'I really love you, Paul.'

'I really love you too, Mrs Tobin.'

The older couple at the table next to the Tobins glanced over, looked at one another and rolled their eyes.

* * *

Steve Brooks sat on the living-room sofa staring at the television, the volume turned up loud to drown out the sound of the doorbell. A narrow spliff filled with the last of his cannabis was clenched between the fingers of his right hand, helping him chill from the paranoia caused by the speed he had snorted earlier. Nestled in the cushions of the sofa were the remains of his emergency bottle of Jack Daniels, which he kept hidden at the back of the cupboard under the kitchen sink.

Steve had made himself scarce when the ambulance had arrived on the estate, watching from the block opposite as Christopher was carried out on a stretcher, Angela and Kaitlyn following close behind, ever aware of his presence. He had let himself back

27

into the flat soon afterwards, drinking and smoking himself into oblivion. He knew Angela would be back sooner or later, but he had no intention of letting her in.

The ringing of the bell was replaced by a heavy pounding on the door and a woman's voice calling his name through the letter box.

'Fuck off, bitch,' he called out in a slurred voice.

'Open the door, Steve.'

'I said fuck off. Fuck off to a refuge where you belong.'

'Steve Brooks, if you don't come and open this door I'm gonna break it down.'

It wasn't just the words that didn't make sense, there was something about the voice that was totally unfamiliar. It really didn't sound like Angela at all. Steve took a long drag on the spliff and rose to his feet, steadying himself with his hands as he made his way slowly to the hallway, his bleary eyes squinting at the shadowy figures he could just make out through the frosted-glass panel of the front door. 'Angela, is that you?' his voice now inquisitive.

'Open this door right now.'

'Who the hell are you?'

'It's the police – open this door now.' The banging continued.

It was as if someone had thrown a bucket of ice water over Steve's head. Within a split-second of hearing the word 'police' he had pulled himself out of his drunken and drugged state, and was making his way to the kitchen, paranoia getting the better of him as he swore under his breath.

The ten officers outside had come prepared for a rough reception, and Steve could hear their heavy boots against the door behind him and knew it was only a matter of time before they managed to break in. The main window in the kitchen led to a small ledge from which he could jump to the nearby fire escape. If he could get down to ground level he would be able to lose the police in the warren of passages and covered walkways that made up the Roxford estate.

Steve squeezed out through the window just as the door burst open. Breathing hard with concentration and sweating profusely, he edged his way along to the fire escape and began working his way down. He couldn't help but allow himself a little chuckle at the voice of the policewoman and noise from some of the other officers searching the flat for him as he drifted down from them. He was now only a few feet from the ground and turned, holding on to the top of the ladder and letting himself drop down.

'Fancy meeting you here,' said a voice. Steve turned to see PC Andy Carter standing behind him with four other officers backing him up. Carter had a smirk on his face and was batting the thick end of his heavy truncheon into the palm of his hand, while keeping his eyes on Steve the whole time. Carter took a step back and placed his truncheon on the ground behind him. He removed his hat, revealing a close-shaven head, and undid the first couple of buttons of his tunic. Then he took a step towards Steve. 'Tell you what, mate, I'll give you one free shot. Go on, take a swing, I know you want to.'

Steve turned so that he was facing Carter head on. Steve was a big man and in good shape, but Carter was more than a match. The other officers stood back for the stocky policeman who was well known on the estate and made no secret of the fact that he had spent several years in the Paratroopers before joining the force. Brawling was in his blood.

Steve could tell from the look on Carter's face that the policeman was just dying to find an excuse to get into a fight with him. He knew how it worked. If Carter got himself a nice little black eye, he and the others would be able to beat the shit out of Steve and claim he'd been resisting arrest. And once they got back to the station every other cop there would come into the cell and give him a couple of kicks for good measure. Steve thought it through for a few seconds, then bit his lip, turned and placed his hands up against the nearby wall.

Carter let out a sigh of disappointment, reached for his handcuffs and moved forward.

He had just started reading Steve his rights when the WPC who had been banging on Steve's door and the other officers arrived on the scene, having made their way down to ground level by a more conventional route.

'Well?' asked the WPC.

'Nah, his bottle went. Only likes to pick on women and small children. Don't you?'

'Told you he wouldn't – that's a fiver you owe me, then.'

'Yeah, yeah. Just put it on my tab.'

Carter turned to face Steve. 'You've gone too far this time, Brooks.'

'What are you on about, pig?'

'While you were coming down the fire escape, I was on the radio to the hospital. Your little boy. He's dead.'

Steve's legs suddenly buckled, it was only the fact that Carter was holding on to his handcuffs that stopped him crashing to the ground. 'What!' gasped Steve. 'I only tapped him, I only fucking tapped him.'

'Nah. You killed him, Steve. Beat him to death. He died about an hour ago. You know what that makes you. Not just a killer but a child killer. You have any idea what they do to child killers in prison? Nasty business, that. I'd rather be a fucking nonce. At least then you get your own wing, bit of protection. You, you're gonna be right in the middle of it. They're not gonna take too kindly to a child killer, especially the ones who have got kids of their own. I give you two months. Either they're gonna string you up or you're gonna take the coward's way out and do it yourself.'

Steve's mind was racing. Behind him Carter allowed himself the smallest of smiles to the others as he bundled Steve into the back of the police car and slammed the door behind him. Steve was staring into space vacantly, lost in his own personal nightmare.

'The kid didn't make it, eh, poor little thing,' said the WPC, making her way to the driver's side of the car.

'The kid's gonna be fine,' said Carter softly. 'I just want to make the bastard suffer as much as I can. And besides, you heard him, he just admitted it. If I'd told him the boy was all right he would have denied it till the cows came home.'

'You're a sick son of a bitch, Carter.'

'Yeah, but that's why you love me.'

Carter climbed into the other side of the car next to Steve and took his arms in order to check his handcuffs. 'Right, let's get to the station and get you booked in. And by the way, Steve, meant to say earlier, nice ring.'

Steve looked down at the large gold sovereign sitting on the middle finger of his right hand and his forehead wrinkled with confusion as the police car set off into the night.

Chapter Five

May 1976

'When is Chrissy coming home?'

The words were spoken with such deep-felt emotion that it was almost painful for Angela to hear them. She was kneeling on the edge of Kaitlyn's bed and fighting the urge to burst into tears. She knew she had to be strong for her daughter, but this was beyond her.

Angela had taken Kaitlyn to see her brother in intensive care the morning after he had been admitted to hospital. They had gone on a second visit to St Thomas's that same afternoon, only to be told by Dr Bishop that Christopher had been transferred to Great Ormond Street and that she should call Social Services to find out more. A gruff-voiced woman on the other end of the line told Angela that Christopher had been made a ward of court and that she would not be able to see him again until an assessment had been made. That was three weeks ago and she had not seen her son or, despite dozens of desperate phone calls, heard from Social Services since.

'I don't know, love, I just don't know.'

'But he's all on his own in hospital. Why can't we

go and see him?' The questions were endless but Angela couldn't answer any of them.

Kaitlyn had been terrified when she had seen Christopher that first day. She had wanted at least to hold his little hand but couldn't even do that. He'd been lying lifeless in a large plastic box with dozens of tubes and wires protruding from his mouth and chest. The doctor had tried to explain that all the equipment was necessary to help the little boy breathe but to Kaitlyn, who could see him at eye level, it just looked as if it was hurting him. If she had been there alone she would have opened the box and taken Chrissy home where she could keep him safe.

Ever since that day, Christopher seemed to be everywhere. Once Kaitlyn saw him on the bus as she held her mother's hand on the way to school. He was up on the top deck, looking down with a big grin on his face and a gigantic ice cream in his hand. Another time he was in a pushchair on the opposite side of the road, giggling furiously while being pushed along by a large woman with hair so wild that it looked like a bird's nest.

Once she thought she saw him on television in the audience of a show about circus clowns and again the following day in a group of children in a programme about playground games, but every time he was gone before she had a chance for a proper look. At first she had mentioned the sightings to her mother but Angela had reacted so badly that she soon realised it was a bad idea and kept them to herself.

'Is Steve coming back?' This time Kaitlyn's voice was more subdued.

Angela sighed. 'He's not. He's never coming home.' She took a long draw from her cigarette. 'That's all over. We're going to have a new life without him, just the three of us. It's going to be like the old days.'

Kaitlyn reached up and gave her mum a big hug. Angela held her tightly but was a million miles away, thinking about Christopher.

'I'm sorry, Mummy.'

'Sorry? What for?' Angela frowned.

'I'm sorry I let Chrissy get hit.'

'Babe, none of this is your fault. You've got nothing to feel bad about. Do you understand?'

But Kaitlyn just couldn't believe that was true. If only she had got there a few seconds earlier, if only she had picked Christopher up and stopped him crying. Then Steve wouldn't have hit him, he wouldn't be in hospital and she wouldn't be missing him so much that it tore her apart.

* * *

The day he found out Jane was pregnant Paul had bought her a huge bunch of roses. The next day he brought home lilies and the day after carnations. Despite her protests he had continued to buy her flowers almost every day that followed and on this occasion had walked in through the front door bearing armfuls of daffodils.

35

'Where am I supposed to put those? We don't have enough vases, darling.'

'Then I'll buy more vases. I can't help it if I want to show you how much I love you.'

'I feel like I'm living in Kew Gardens. It's all right for you; you're at work all day. All I can do is wander around the house and look at the beautiful flowers you've bought me and watch bad TV. Maybe I should come back to the office.'

'No, I want you to take it easy, letting our baby grow inside you is your job now.'

'But there's so much work to be done, I should be there.'

'It's OK, I've brought a temp in.'

'A temp! That's no good.'

'I know. It's not the same. You were the best secretary I ever had! That's why I married you.'

'Cheek.'

Later that night as they made their way up to the bedroom arm in arm, Jane steered Paul into the box room they had recently earmarked as a nursery. 'I think we could build some shelves into the alcove; that would give us storage without taking up too much of the main room,' she said wistfully.

'But it's such a nice alcove, it would be better to use it for lighting or maybe even hang a picture there.'

'Darling, this is a child's bedroom, not some corporate project. Don't be an architect, be a father.

Do you think we should do something about the coving?' Jane pointed to the corner ceiling and suddenly winced: 'Ow.'

'Are you all right, darling?'

'That was odd, must have pinched a nerve or something. I just felt a really sharp pain in my shoulder. It's gone now.'

'It's probably sore from all the finger wagging you do while you're nagging me.'

'Oooh, you're asking for it. You'd better watch out. If this turns out to be a little girl, you're going to be outnumbered.'

Paul gathered Jane up in his arms, drew her close and kissed her passionately. 'Darling,' he said softly. 'We're going to have a baby. Isn't it great? I love you so much.'

'You say that now,' said Jane with a smirk, 'but how long before you're saying all this to that temp of yours?'

They had met some twelve years earlier. Paul had been a senior architect at a distinguished local firm while Jane had been a secretary, working first for Paul's boss, then with another of the partners before finally being assigned to Paul. The attraction had been there right from the start but neither was willing to make a move. Paul couldn't help feeling it was all a bit tacky to start having feelings for his secretary, particularly one whom he had seen flirting – albeit playfully – with his colleagues. Jane had reservations of her own, especially seeing what happened to some of her friends who had had relationships at work.

But the more time Paul and Jane spent together the less any of their reservations mattered. After a few secret dates it was clear the only way they could go on would be to bring their relationship into the open. Jane suggested leaving and going to work for another firm but Paul would have none of it. 'You're not getting away that easily. I don't want you to leave; I want you to marry me.' Within six months of meeting they were engaged and planning the wedding.

Paul woke to the sound of Jane throwing up in the bathroom. He looked across at the clock. It was 4 a.m. He lay still for a moment, unsure what to do. Better to wait for her to return, he decided, than rob her of her dignity by being there while she was being sick. Although it sounded horrible he'd read enough about pregnancy to know that morning sickness was generally considered a good sign and certainly nothing to worry about. The important thing was that he was there for her when she returned.

The minutes ticked by with no sound. Then he heard Jane give a sudden low groan and leapt off the bed, rushing into the bathroom. His legs still a little unstable, he tried to push open the door but something was blocking it. He shoved hard in desperation and heard a yelp of pain. Jane was blocking the door – she'd collapsed.

He pushed firmly but steadily and slowly the door began to open. He could see her leg lying awkwardly on the bathroom floor. When he finally managed to get inside she was curled into a ball. Her skin was pale and clammy; her hair was soaked with sweat. Little traces of bile dribbled down the corners of her mouth. Her pale-blue nightgown was awash with blood.

She looked up as Paul pushed the door open a little more. 'Something's wrong,' she gasped, her face twisted with pain. 'Get help.'

The first thing Jane Tobin saw when she came round from the anaesthetic was the smiling face of her husband. She had to turn away. 'Don't look at me,' she whispered, 'please don't look at me.' She felt bloated, her breasts were sore and her whole abdomen ached. She felt empty inside, her motherly instincts had gone and she knew that the baby had gone too.

'Darling,' said Paul softly. 'I love you so much.' They held each other tightly.

'I feel like I've let you down so badly.'

'Don't talk rubbish. You haven't let me down. You could never let me down.'

A shadow fell across the bed as Dr Singh appeared at Paul's side. Jane sighed long and deep. 'What happened? What went wrong?' They both looked at the doctor intently.

'You had an ectopic pregnancy. The baby got stuck in one of your fallopian tubes and it ruptured. We had to remove it, the whole thing, I'm afraid.'

Jane and Paul held hands tightly as Dr Singh explained that, even though diagnosis of ectopic pregnancies was still in its infancy, her GP should have known something was wrong because her hormone levels would have been much higher than normal.

Jane swallowed hard, then spoke, her voice soft and low. 'Is this a one-off, or might it happen again?'

'Mrs Tobin, I'm afraid to say that the chances of it happening again are pretty high, especially considering your age. You were lucky this time but the consequences of another ectopic pregnancy could be far worse. It's not unusual for this to be fatal.'

Only a tiny part of Jane's brain was listening to the doctor's words, the rest was trying to come to terms with the reality of the situation. She couldn't shake the feeling that, whatever Paul said, somewhere at the back of his mind he knew that if he married someone else, if he left her for someone else, there was a chance that he might be able to have the child he so longed for.

Paul reached over to the hospital bed, placed a hand gently on Jane's shoulder and turned her back to face him. Jane bit her lip, preparing herself for the worst. Paul smiled warmly. 'You're going to be here for a couple of days,' he said. 'The doctors want to keep you in for observation.' His smile, warm and caring as always, made Jane feel even worse, reminding her of what a great father he would be.

'Oh Paul, I'm so sorry,' Jane said, as tears began to run down her cheeks.

Paul blinked with surprise. 'Sorry for what? What are you talking about? The last few weeks have made me realise how much I want to have a family with you, how much I want to bring a child into our lives. I've been thinking, why don't we have another look at adoption?' His smile held steady.

Jane's eyes widened with surprise. 'I thought you were against that, the idea of someone else's child . . .'

'That was before. I was just being selfish. It will still be our child – we'll have a baby. All this pregnancy stuff, it's too much work. Let's get a ready-made one.'

Chapter Six

Robin Weaver felt his heart sink as he turned the corner and saw the looming towers of the Roxford estate rising up above him just a few hundred yards ahead. At first he feared the power steering had packed up, then he briefly suspected that there was something wrong with the surface of the road itself, but the way the car weaved slightly as he turned the corner told him exactly what was wrong: he had a flat tyre.

The forty-two-year-old accountant was on his way back from the supermarket, having completed the weekly shop while his wife and children remained at home. The combination of a boot full of frozen food and a flat tyre on a warm morning was enough of a disaster on its own, but what made things a million times worse was getting the flat slap bang in the middle of the Roxford, a part of London best seen at a great distance and through the windows of a fast-moving car.

The estate had been built in the early 1960s in Balham, five miles south of the River Thames. A cluster of four twenty-five-storey towers, interconnected on every fifth floor, the estate had won dozens of awards for innovation in its first few years and was seen as the dawn of a new era in community housing. Designed to be self-contained, the estate featured its own parade of shops on the ground floor, which included a newsagent, a post office, a hairdressing salon, a chippy and an off licence that doubled as a mini-mart. There was a large playground in the middle of the grassed-over area in the centre of the four blocks.

In the early years life on the estate had been pleasant enough and people were eager to move there to enjoy the panoramic views over London. But after the 1968 explosion at the twenty-two-storey Ronan Point in east London, which left three people dead, tower blocks dropped out of fashion and only those in desperate need of housing were sent there.

By the mid seventies, two-thirds of the Roxford's 2,000 residents were out of work, poverty was rife and the queues to the post office would stretch all the way out to Balham High Street whenever benefit day came round. The estate's interconnecting walkways, designed to emphasise the 'community feel', soon became a haven for criminals to hang out in and conduct their shady deals or lose the police if they were being chased. Once the scene of regular patrols, officers now only ever came to the estate when there was trouble, and then only in force. The neighbouring streets had some of the highest incidents of muggings in the capital. No one in their right mind would go anywhere near the place.

Looking around him anxiously, Robin Weaver climbed out of his Vauxhall Viva and walked round to the passenger side. The front tyre was as flat as a pancake and, judging by the deep gouge marks in the rubber, had been that way for the last couple of miles. There was a telephone box across the street but even from this distance Robin could see it had been vandalised and would be completely useless. There was no way to call his wife to let her know that he would be late. The only thing to do was to put on the spare.

He set to work quickly, opening the boot and taking out the jack, setting it into position at the front of the car and locking the handle in place. He placed the heavy wheel spanner over one of the nuts and stood on the end of it until it started to move under his weight. He loosened it a few more turns, then did the same with the other bolts. Once all four nuts were loose he began working the jack.

After a few turns the car started to rise into the air. Robin kept turning until there were a good two inches between the tyre and the ground. Another anxious glance. A few drunks and drug addicts were gazing in his direction, and a few of the estate's residents were out on their balconies, looking down on him, but there was no one close by. Robin returned to the back of the car and began the difficult task of extracting the spare wheel from its compartment under the floor of the boot. It seemed to be jammed and he huffed and puffed as he worked to free it, the whole car rocking back and forth with his efforts. When the wheel finally came free and he stood back, holding it awkwardly in his arms, Robin was alarmed to see that the car continued to move around without him.

Gingerly he stepped to one side and saw two pairs of short legs sticking out from the driver's door. 'Oi,' he called out.

The four legs shifted backwards and Robin found himself standing in front of Errol Gants and Jacob Collins, both of them just eight years old. Errol was short and heavy set, with deep brown eyes that matched the colour of his skin. A thick mop of tightly curled black hair sat on top of his head. The other boy, Jacob, was thinner, incredibly freckly and so blond his hair was almost white. His eyes were deep blue and glinted in the morning sunshine.

Robin's eyes moved to one side. The black boy had something in his hand. Robin peered closer. It was the radio cassette player from his car, trailing wires where it had been ripped from the dashboard. Robin choked in disbelief. 'What the hell do you think you're doing?'

Errol shrugged. 'What's the problem, guv?' he said with a grin. 'You take the wheels, we take the stereo.'

Robin's mouth fell open. He was utterly speechless. He couldn't believe what he'd just heard. Before he had a chance to react both boys had shouted 'wanker' in unison and begun running off towards the towering blocks of the estate. 'Did you see the look on his face?' gasped Jacob as they ran off out of sight. 'Classic.'

Rounding the side of block D, the boys had to turn sharply to avoid crashing into the tall, bespectacled woman with the black satchel who was walking the other way. As Jacob and Errol whizzed past, the woman shook her head disapprovingly and continued on her way.

The doorbell of number 1504 rang at precisely 11 a.m. For Angela Wilson, who had just stubbed out the last cigarette from the packet of ten she had opened earlier that morning, the timing could not have been better. She waved her hands frantically in the air to disperse the smoke, licked her thumb to remove a spot of dirt from Kaitlyn's cheek and went out into the hallway. She paused in front of the door, patting down her hair, taking a deep breath, smoothing down her dress and putting on her best 'happy face' before turning the lock.

'Angela Wilson?'

'Yes.'

'Margo Kane from Social Services. You're expecting me – I'm here to assess your home.'

'Please come in. Can I offer you a tea or coffee, or perhaps something stronger?'

Angela laughed awkwardly. She should have known better than to try to make a joke.

'Tea will be fine, thank you. No sugar.'

Margo Kane was a tall, thin, gaunt-looking woman

who wore her dark-brown hair in a tight bun. Her narrow eyes were hidden behind thick silver-rimmed glasses, which sat high on her sharp little nose. She wore a dark-brown jacket with a matching knee-length skirt and thick brown tights, and carried a large black satchel bulging with pens and notebooks. Her eyes flitted about the hallway as she followed Angela inside, taking in the state of the carpet, the wallpaper and making a mental note of every scrap of dirt, every imperfection.

'This is my daughter, Kaitlyn,' said Angela as they entered the living room. 'Say hello, darling.'

Kaitlyn had been promised a bar of chocolate if she managed to be on her best behaviour while the social worker was there. She sat perched on the end of the armchair in a sparkling white pinafore dress that was slightly too big for her, eyes glued to the television. 'Hello, my name is Kaitlyn,' she said, tearing herself away from the screen for a few seconds to scrutinise the new visitor. 'How do you do?'

It was a pre-rehearsed line Kane had heard many times before. Those who knew her well would know that she was smiling but to both Angela and Kaitlyn her face seemed unchanged. 'Take a seat,' Angela said. 'I'll just go and see to your tea. It won't be long.'

Kane sat on one end of the two-seater settee, which until the previous evening had been grubby green in colour. Kaitlyn had come into the living room to find both it and the armchair covered with large blue blankets. Angela had been up all night doing her best to scrub away years of filth and neglect. What she could not clean, she chose to hide instead. The flat had never looked so good and she felt proud of her efforts.

'That's a very pretty dress, Kaitlyn,' said Kane, pulling out a notebook.

'It's not mine. It belongs to Lesley. She lives two floors up. I don't really like her but Mum makes me play there sometimes.'

'I see,' said Kane slowly. Kaitlyn watched fascinated as she flicked through several pages of her notebook and began writing something down.

Angela appeared in the doorway with a large tray loaded with a teapot and matching cups and saucers that Kaitlyn had never seen before. Come to think of it, the tray didn't look particularly familiar either.

'Here we are,' said Angela, setting down the load on to a low table where the stain on the carpet used to be. Angela poured cups for Kane and herself, and handed Kaitlyn a small cup of juice.

'Before we start,' Angela mumbled awkwardly. 'Can you tell me . . . how's Christopher?'

'Christopher is doing very well. He's healing fast and is expected to make a full recovery. He's still in the ICU . . . sorry, intensive care, but he's out of all danger.'

Angela sighed with relief, looked across at Kaitlyn and smiled bigger and wider than her daughter had seen for years. 'When do you think I, we, might be able to see him?'

'I'm afraid I can't answer that question. It's out of my hands. I'm just here to make an assessment. I'm sorry.'

'I understand,' said Angela, some of the brightness already fading. 'What do you need to know?'

'Let's start with the basics. Where was Christopher sleeping?'

The question shot through Angela like a bullet. She fought to keep her composure, to keep her smile. 'You mean where *does* he sleep?'

Kane hesitated, looked up from her notepad and smiled back. 'Yes, of course, that's what I mean. Where does your son sleep?'

The pain faded. Angela felt sure everything was going to be all right. 'He's in the main bedroom with me. Kaitlyn has the other room to herself. If I'd had another girl I would have put them together but . . .'

'It's not ideal, is it? You could do with somewhere bigger, another bedroom.'

'Yes. Absolutely. I've been asking the council for months, ever since he was born. They say I'm on the list but . . . I've never heard anything. Maybe you could look into that for me.'

'Uh huh.'

It was completely unclear as to whether the response meant yes she could do something, or no she couldn't. Angela reached nervously into her handbag. 'Do you mind if I smoke?'

*

49

Prisoner RP4981 could have dealt with it all if it weren't for the smell. It was like nothing else on earth: a sickening mix of shit, vomit, rotting food, sour milk and disinfectant. It was halfway between a hospital and a sewer that left him permanently on the verge of gagging.

Steve Brooks had spent just three days at the notorious Brixton prison in south London but every moment had been a waking nightmare. Carter had been right. As soon as his exploits had become known, Steve had been targeted by other prisoners who saw him as no better than a sex offender. On his second morning, queuing up to slop out his bucket, the man behind had tipped the contents of his pail over Steve's head. Two guards had witnessed the assault but chose to turn a blind eye. At breakfast the supposedly trustworthy inmate (he had a blue band round his arm) in charge of serving up heaps of reconstituted powdered egg had spat into the portion he passed to Steve.

The attack he had been dreading came just a few hours later and Steve learned to his cost that there are few things in the world scarier than a prison fight. There is nowhere to run, nowhere to hide and asking the screw for help just makes things worse. Steve had been walking in slow circles round the exercise yard when the tall man with the shaven head and tattooed neck who had changed his name by deed poll to Meat Carver decided to pounce. One minute Steve was walking, the next he was sprawled on the concrete floor, having been punched hard in the back of the head. Within seconds he was surrounded, fists and heavy black boots flying towards his face and body at an alarming rate. He cried out in shock and pain. Out of the corner of one eye he saw one of the screws on the edge of the exercise yard. The man deliberately turned away and Steve realised he had no one to appeal to. Most of the screws, like most of the inmates, had kids themselves and the last thing any of them wanted was for prisoner RP4981 to think he could get away with what he had done. Steve felt himself being roughly turned over on to his back and the Meat Carver leaned down low over him. 'Like beating up babies, do yah?' he hissed, pulling a makeshift knife from his back pocket and holding it against Steve's battered face. 'Gonna make you sorry you were ever born.'

Other members of the gang began to signal that the guards were on their way. With that the Meat Carver slashed Steve's face, then passed the blade to another inmate who wiped it clean of prints and disposed of it in a quiet corner of the yard. Steve clutched his face and tried to get up but the Meat Carver hit him with a vicious head butt, which left him unconscious on the ground. By the time the half-dozen screws who were rushing to the scene arrived, Steve was lying in the middle of the yard, surrounded by a pool of blood.

'Break it up, come on, break it up,' said Davis, the most senior screw on watch that day. As the crowd dispersed they saw Steve. 'Who did this – Meat, what have you got to say?'

'Nothing, sir. One minute he was walking around and the next thing I saw he was lying on the floor. If you ask me, it looks like he's fallen. Fallen really badly. Ain't that right, Mooney?'

'Yes sir, Mr Davis, he just fell over.'

'Yeah, yeah, yeah.' Davis knew exactly what had happened but there was little he could do about it. Steve had it coming, everyone knew that. It was only a matter of time.

Davis shook his head. 'Let's get him to the hospital wing.'

*   *   *

High up in the Roxford estate, Louisa Briggs held her breath and padded barefoot across the living-room carpet, desperate not to wake her mother.

Vicky Briggs was slumped across the two-seater sofa at the far end of the room from Louisa, naked apart from a filthy once-white bra and knickers. Her left hand hung down to the floor, a couple of inches away from a cigarette that still smouldered in an ashtray. Two bottles of cheap white wine, both of them empty, were also to hand. A thin trail of vomit led from the sofa to the kitchen sink and a few smears remained around the edges of her mouth.

Vicky had been a big drinker all her life but it was only in the past couple of years that it had become a serious problem and begun to dominate her life. The stress of trying to deal with a personality clash with the manager of the office where she had a part-time job had been the start of it. A couple of glasses of wine every evening 'just to help me to relax' quickly turned to three, then four and, before she knew it, Vicky was unable to relax at all unless she'd drunk the best part of a bottle. Within six months Vicky had lost not only the job but every ounce of her self-esteem.

Her husband, Brian, tried to stand by her but the best of his efforts to boost her confidence only seemed to make her worse. Louisa would dread coming home from school, never sure of what she would find. Some days she would be sweetness itself, full of love and kindness. Other days she would be an evil tyrant, all too eager to lash out with her fists without warning. Increasingly, Vicky was capable of being both in the space of a single day.

Before too long Brian could stand it no longer. 'Your mother loves you,' he told Louisa one night. 'But I'm afraid she loves drinking even more.' Faced with an ultimatum of having to stop drinking or move out of the marital home, Vicky chose to leave, taking her young daughter with her.

For Louisa the change was devastating. Being popular and fitting in with the cool kids at school was out of the question, as was the idea of friends sleeping over or coming round for tea. Even if no one at her school knew about her mother's drinking, Louisa thought they knew, so she tried to become invisible.

They had spent the last eight months moving from house to house, with Louisa moving from school to school, while Brian fought and lost a bitter battle for custody of his daughter. They had never been in one place for long enough to allow any of her school friends to come round and find out the truth. Now they had a new permanent home on the Roxford, Louisa had for the first time in her life felt like she actually fitted in. Almost everyone on the estate had a problem, and most of them had problems far worse than her own.

But the new stability had done nothing to lift Vicky's mood. Instead, she had sunk even further into depression and spent most of the previous two weeks in a drunken stupor.

Louisa had almost reached the hallway when her foot crunched against an empty cigarette packet. Vicky's bleary eyes slowly opened and she stared at her daughter, fighting to focus on the tiny form in front of her. Louisa was frozen to the spot like a rabbit caught in headlights. For a few moments there was no movement apart from Vicky's head gently bobbing around as she and Louisa looked at each other. Then, as if the effort had all become too much, Vicky's head returned to the sofa and her eyes snapped shut. Louisa let out a tiny sigh of relief and continued on her way out of the flat.

Kaitlyn raced up the stairs as fast as her legs would carry her, her heart pounding hard in her chest. With

Lesley's dress bundled up in her arms it was difficult to see where she was going, but she was desperate to get the task over with as quickly as possible.

It had been less than half an hour since Margo Kane had left the flat and Angela had immediately taken Lesley's dress off Kaitlyn, given it a quick iron and ordered her to return it.

Kaitlyn was still out of breath when she reached the nineteenth floor and rang the bell twice.

Lesley's mother, Margaret, soon answered. 'Hello, Kaitlyn, so lovely to see you. Would you like to come inside?'

'I just came to give back Lesley's dress, then I've got to go straight back home.'

It was a lie but the truth was that Kaitlyn didn't care much for Lesley's family. They were deeply religious and it was impossible to spend more than a few minutes in conversation without it turning into a sermon.

'Have you heard when Christopher's coming home?'

Kaitlyn shook her head.

'I want you and your mum to know that we are all praying for you.'

'OK.'

There was a slightly awkward pause as Kaitlyn desperately tried to think of something else to say. In the end she simply raised her arms and handed over the bundle of clothing.

'Thanks. Lesley's not here right now. She's out

shopping with her dad. But you'll have to come by soon so she can say goodbye.'

'Goodbye? What do you mean?'

'We're moving away. I told your mum ages ago, she must have forgotten to tell you. She's had a lot on her mind, I'm not surprised. We're moving out of the estate. I don't want my daughter to grow up in a place like this. We're getting a house with a garden that's so big it's got three trees in it.'

'Wow.'

Margaret's voice drifted off. Her eyes looked beyond Kaitlyn, down to the courtyard area where groups of boys and girls stood on corners with clouds of smoke rising from their little mouths. 'Dexter has got a promotion at work, we've finally got enough to buy a place of our own. We just exchanged contracts yesterday.' Her eyes focused on Kaitlyn once more. 'Tell your mum I know that everything is going to work out just fine.'

'I will, Mrs Glen.'

'You take care. And don't forget to come and see Lesley. Goodbye. God bless.'

Kaitlyn walked slowly back towards the stairwell, her mind swimming with the thought of a house with its own garden and a tree where you could build your very own tree house. She was so lost in her own thoughts that she hardly saw the heavy-set girl standing on the other side of the stairwell.

She wore dark-blue jeans and black plimsolls. On top she wore a simple white T-shirt that glowed in the morning sunshine. When she spoke her voice was sharp and confident, and Kaitlyn immediately felt a little intimidated: 'Hi.'

'Hello.'

'My name's Louisa. What's yours?'

'Kaitlyn.'

'Kate Lynn?'

'No, it's all one name. K-a-i-t-l-y-n.'

'Oh. Right.'

'Do you live around here?' asked Kaitlyn cheerfully.

Louisa nodded. 'Over there,' she said, jerking her thumb towards a door with peeling red paint. Then her cheeks started to flush. 'I would invite you inside but my mum's . . . she's not very well at the moment.'

If Kaitlyn sensed Louisa was trying hard to hide something, she didn't let on. 'I thought a black family lived there.'

'Did they? Don't know. We only moved in a couple of weeks ago.'

There was an awkward moment of silence between the two as they struggled to find something else to say.

'Have you been up to the top?' asked Kaitlyn suddenly.

'No, what's there?'

'Nothing, but you can see for miles and miles. It's brilliant. Come on, I'll show you.'

Less than an hour later Kaitlyn and Louisa were firm friends. The conversation had flowed thick and fast and, while neither had said anything specific about her home life, both sensed that things were not quite as good as they might be. This drew them closer together. There was nothing to be embarrassed about. They were both in the same boat. Each would be strong for the other.

* * *

The hospital wing consisted of two long grey rooms with beds on either side. Normally there were up to four patients per room, but Steve was being kept in isolation for his own protection. The last thing the governor wanted was another death. There had been one murder and two suicides already that year and it was only midsummer.

The deep cut the Meat Carver had left in the side of Steve's face had required twenty-two stitches and left his face so swollen that he was unable to chew anything solid for almost two weeks. The nurses had told him grimly that he would be scarred for life. As his strength returned he realised he would soon be leaving the wing and returning to the main prison. The thought of another attack – it seemed inevitable – absolutely terrified him.

When a guard came to see him late one afternoon he feared the worst – an immediate move back to G-wing.

'You need to get up and get your shit together, Brooks.'

'What for?'

'You've got a visitor.'

Steve was led along the wing, down two flights of stairs and through three sets of security gates until he reached a short corridor with a line of glass-panelled offices. Each held four chairs and a small desk. Inside the first room, with a number '1' on the heavy metal door, a middle-aged woman sat on the far side of the desk. She wore a simple two-piece suit and had a large briefcase on the floor beside her.

'You're in number one,' said the screw.

'Who the hell's that?'

'That's your new solicitor.'

The guard opened the door and held it ajar so that Steve could get inside. 'Listen carefully, Brooks, this counts as a legal visit, which means that I'm not allowed to listen to what is being said. You've got total privacy. But I am allowed to watch and if I see anything that I have a problem with, I'll be in this door and down on you like a ton of bricks. You understand?'

'Yeah.'

Steve walked in through the door and sat heavily at the desk, his prison overalls itchy against his skin. He looked at the woman, who was staring with wide-eyed wonderment at the marks on his face.

Joan Kirby had spent the last seven years as a criminal lawyer working mostly with legal aid clients. At first she believed she was making a difference to the little person who couldn't afford a defence, but she had stayed in the field mainly because of her lack of ambition. She was good but the more she worked on legal aid the more she despaired. There was a lot of genuine need, but a significant proportion of her clients were a whingeing bunch of free-loading scroungers who were always feeling sorry for themselves, even when they had been caught in the act. For these people, no matter what happened to them, it was always somebody else's fault. Steve Brooks was no exception.

'Morning, Mr Brooks, my name is Mrs Joan Kirby – your appointed lawyer.'

'What happened to the last one?' Steve sighed.

'He was only temporary – I'll be your lawyer from now on.' She looked him up and down. 'I see you've been in some trouble.'

'Trouble!' Steve winced with pain. 'They fucking attacked me – twenty-two stitches and two cracked ribs.'.

Kirby asked him for the names of the attackers but Steve knew that if he gave them he would be dead within twenty-four hours. Instead, he said he was hit from behind and didn't see who attacked him.

'You'll be pleased to know', Kirby continued, 'that I've spoken to the governor and he assures me that once you're fully recovered you'll be going on Rule 43 in wing B.'

Rule 43 was a prison regulation that allowed prisoners believed to be at risk of serious harm to be segregated in a separate part of the prison. It was usually used for rapists and child molesters. Although he was relieved that he would be far safer there, Steve hated the idea of being banged up with those kinds of people.

'Can't you get me out of here on bail?' Steve pleaded.

'Unlikely. Very unlikely. I've read through the file and spoken with the prosecution this morning and they still want to go with the attempted murder charge.'

There was a pause, then Steve spoke again, this time more quietly: 'So what happens now?'

'Plea and directions hearing is in three weeks.'

'But I didn't do anything. The kid fell.'

'Mr Brooks, the ring on your finger that night matches the seventeen punch marks on Christopher Wilson's body.'

Steve didn't answer.

'There are also statements from four police officers who say you admitted hitting the child when you were arrested.'

Steve sneered. 'Bastards set me up. Told me he was dead.'

Joan Kirby bit her tongue. She had to remain neutral and objective, no matter how much of an animal her client was. 'I say we go for damage limitation. Plead mitigating circumstances. The drink. The drugs, lack of work, the stresses of home life and so on. I'll talk to the prosecuting officer and see if he'll go for a lesser charge if you plead guilty to, say, assault on a minor and child endangerment.'

'What'll I get for that?'

'Depends on the judge that day but I'd say three to five years max.'

'Fucking hell! Five years in this dump!' The screws looked round at the sound of Steve's raised voice.

'Look, Mr Brooks. I've been through this case with a fine-tooth comb. I checked every possible angle. In view of the evidence and the record of violence against' – she looked into the folder – 'Angela, Kaitlyn and Christopher Wilson, I believe it's the best we can do under the circumstances.'

'That's cos you'll be out there and I'll be in here, swinging from the fucking curtain rail.'

'I'm only here to advise you – you can always go to trial. But I don't recommend it. The jury will see all the evidence and these kinds of cases will always pull at the heartstrings. There is little defence in a case like this.'

'What do you mean?'

'I mean how on earth does an eighteen-month-old child provoke such an attack – that's how the jury will see it, Mr Brooks.' She stood up and began putting her papers back into her briefcase. 'Tell you what, Mr Brooks. Think about it. Talk to another lawyer if you want. Talk to anyone. And if you get a better offer, you go for it. Otherwise I'll see you in court.'

Chapter Seven

July 1976

The letter arrived four agonising weeks after Margo Kane's visit and hit Angela with all the force of a ton of bricks. It left her numb, sick and terrified of the future. She had expected that Christopher would be home shortly, especially as Steve was out of the way on remand. Now she had to face the truth – she was never going to see her son again.

The letter was long and full of words that she didn't really understand, but the overall meaning was clear. Social Services had decided that Angela simply couldn't cope with two children and had decided to take one of them away.

What the letter didn't reveal was just how close Angela had come to losing Kaitlyn as well. During the meeting to decide on Christopher's fate, where Margo Kane had fought hard to prevent the young boy being placed with temporary foster-parents before being returned to the estate, the question of what to do with Kaitlyn had come up again and again. Some of those present argued that the girl would still be at risk but Kane, as the only one to have met mother and daughter face to face, explained that she simply felt the bond between Kaitlyn and Angela, especially considering the way they had both suffered at Steve's hands, was too strong to be broken without causing enormous trauma. There would be regular visits to check on Kaitlyn's welfare, but for the time being she would be staying put.

'What's wrong, Mummy?'

Angela reached across and tenderly stroked her daughter's hair. 'Nothing, darling, I was just checking on you. Go back to sleep.'

It was midnight and Angela was sitting on the edge of Kaitlyn's bed, still sobbing softly. She had collected the letter that afternoon while Kaitlyn was playing around the estate with her new friend Louisa and had been suffering the consequences of opening it ever since. Now her mind was racing. Supposing something happened to Kaitlyn, supposing she had an accident or whatever. Angela would risk losing her too and that would be the final straw.

As soon as she'd read the letter she'd felt an ache in the centre of her chest and nervous butterflies that made her sick. It was a dull kind of pain she had never experienced before. It stayed with her for the rest of the day, spreading slowly until every part of her body seemed to be hurting. She had called Social Services and finally managed to get through to someone who told her the matter had already been decided and could not be changed. Angela protested until the person on the other end of the line put down the phone. She called back but no one would speak to her. By the end of the afternoon it began to dawn on her that there seemed to be no chance of getting Christopher back.

By the evening the pain was so bad it was almost unbearable and it was still getting worse. After a soft kiss from her mother, Kaitlyn drifted back off to sleep and Angela rose up and backed out of her daughter's bedroom. In the hallway she pulled her large quilted coat down off the wall, slipped it over her shoulders and stepped outside into the cool summer night.

Angela's flat was on the fifteenth floor. She moved along the walkway until she reached the stairs and then, accustomed to the overpowering smell of stale urine, she climbed zombie-like up the remaining ten flights until she was at the highest level. From there she moved to the centre of the walkway, spread her palms out on the rough, cool concrete wall and leaned forward just enough so she could see over the edge. It was a long way down and looking at the drop made her feel light-headed and dizzy. She shut her eyes for a moment, took several deep breaths and looked again.

'It's Angela, isn't it?'

She hadn't heard the footsteps. Angela stepped back and turned to see the scrawny figure of Rachel, a long-time resident of the Roxford, approaching her.

'What are you doing up here?' Rachel asked, her voice tinged with concern.

'I'm . . . I'm just getting some air.'

'Where's Kaitlyn?'

'Sleeping. She's fine.'

'What's wrong, Angela?'

Rachel wore a heavy bomber jacket and a short tartan skirt that showed off her pale, blotchy legs. It was an open secret on the estate that Rachel was a prostitute, plying her trade along Balham High Street most evenings. She was tolerated and even considered a friend by many of the Roxford women, just so long as she never touted for business too close to home.

'You look terrible. Why don't you come over to my place, have a little rest.'

'They've taken Christopher, my little boy. I'm not getting him back.'

'Bastards. Fucking bastards. What right do they have? It wasn't your fault that Steve was a complete wanker. They've got two of mine, you know. Bastards.'

'It hurts, Rachel, it hurts all over.'

Rachel, who had just finished with a regular and was on her way back to work, paused for a moment, then placed a hand gently round Angela's shoulder. 'Come on, love, come with me. You'll be all right.'

Rachel's flat was at the far end of the top floor. Once they were inside, she led Angela into the sitting room where a large leather sofa sat against one wall opposite the television and hi-fi unit. 'I'm going for the minimalist look,' she explained. 'Make yourself comfortable.'

Angela collapsed on the sofa, her back propped against the wall. Her limbs felt heavy and her head was pounding with thoughts of Christopher. Rachel sat beside her, throwing off her jacket to reveal bony arms sticking out from a ragged T-shirt. She reached into her shoe, just under the heel, and pulled out a tiny square of paper.

'What is it?' Angela asked.

Rachel said nothing but fished out a box from under the sofa cushion. Inside were strips of silver foil, a syringe, a spoon and an empty tube from an old biro. She made a V-shaped fold in one of the foil strips and proceeded to empty the contents of the little paper packet a yellow-brown powder – into it. 'It's what you need. It will take the pain away. It's exactly the same stuff they use in hospitals, just looks a bit different.'

With the foil folded into a rough half-tube shape and clasped between her fingers, Rachel fired up a lighter with her free hand and ran the flickering yellow flame along the length of the powder, which hissed and bubbled in wisps of white smoke. She placed the tube of the biro in her mouth and used her lips to move it into position. Fascinated and horrified at the same time, Angela looked on as Rachel gave a running commentary of her actions. 'You don't inhale right away. You burn off all the impurities first. Let the powder melt, let it become liquid. And then it's ready.' Her eyes glowed. 'Like medicine.'

Rachel hesitated for a moment, watching the

brown sludge become more liquid. The smoke pouring off suddenly changed colour and began rising so quickly that it almost caught her off guard. She placed the tube over her mouth and sucked in the hot air deeply. She held the smoke in her lungs for what seemed like eternity, then let it pass out through her thinly pursed lips. All the tension in her body seemed to have gone. Lazily she looked over and passed foil, lighter and tube to Angela. 'Your turn.'

Apprehensively, Angela held the foil just the way Rachel had and put the tube between her lips. Then she began running the flame along the foil and sucking in a little of the smoke. She immediately started to cough hard.

At first it was nothing to write home about. Her vision became slightly blurred and there was a feeling of relaxation. She reapplied the flame and smoked a little bit more. But as she repeated the process once more the heroin that had been racing through her veins finally reached her brain. Now she could feel it. Floating, lightness. Total bliss. There was a glow, a feeling of warmth and then she felt as if she'd been wrapped in cotton wool. She'd taken speed a few times but this was as far away from that as she could possibly imagine. With speed Angela had felt as if she had been the life and soul of the party. With heroin Angela could have been in the middle of the best party in the world and she wouldn't have cared. Then there was a feeling of acceleration. The same feeling she got when she was drunk. It was as though the world was moving faster and faster while she was standing still. Oh fuck, she knew this feeling only too well.

She stood up uneasily and started making her way to the bathroom. Where was it? Everything was coming at her and she looked dazed and giddy; the room would not stop spinning.

Somewhere on the ground beneath her she could hear Rachel's voice echoing through the room: 'Where are you going? What's wrong?' But there was no time to stop. She could feel the sickness rising within her and knew she would never make it. The kitchen was slightly closer and she dashed through the doors, but she had only just moved into the corridor when she twisted over and threw up violently.

The inside of her mouth tasted bitter, the effect of her own bile as well as the heroin itself. Her teeth felt sticky, as if she'd been chewing toffee. She stumbled back to the living room and tried to prop herself up. Rachel was now slumped on one corner of the sofa against the wall, smiling like a Cheshire cat, a belt strapped round her arm and an empty syringe falling out of her hand. Her lips were moving but Angela couldn't hear the words she was saying.

The nausea was passing now, only the feelings of gentle bliss remained. Angela felt as though she'd been wrapped up in cotton wool. She leaned back on the sofa next to Rachel and passed out, dreaming of running through fields of flowers with her children and rose petals falling from the sky like rain. She dreamed of a life away from the Roxford with a kind, caring man who loved her.

Angela drifted back home early the following morning, fuzzy-headed and full of guilt and remorse for having left Kaitlyn at home alone. As soon as she put the key in the lock the sound of tiny footsteps running along the hallway told her that her daughter was already up.

'Mummy, Mummy, where have you been?' said Kaitlyn, her eyes red and puffy from crying all night. She had woken up soon after Angela had gone out and made her way into her mother's bedroom. When she found it was empty she cried herself to sleep but woke again in the early hours of the morning to find she was still alone. Unsure of what to do she had simply paced around the flat, waiting for her mother to come home.

Angela looked down at the face of her daughter and felt as though her heart would break with the pain of it all.

Kaitlyn moved forward to give her mum a big hug but Angela backed off.

'What's wrong, Mummy?'

'I'm not feeling very well,' Angela said. Her voice was slow and deliberate. 'I'm going to go out for a walk, see if that will clear my head. You'll be all right on your own for a bit longer, won't you?'

Kaitlyn didn't have time to reply – Angela was

already heading for the doorway. 'It's good you're going to get better,' she called after her. 'You don't want to be ill when Chrissy comes back.'

Angela stopped dead in the doorway. She turned and looked at her daughter, her eyes glowing with rage. 'For God's sake, Kaitlyn, how can you be so fucking stupid? Don't you know anything? Chrissy's not coming back. He's gone. All right, you get it? He's gone. They've taken him away from me and we're never going to see him again. You're never going to see him again. Just forget you ever had a brother.'

Angela turned again so that Kaitlyn couldn't see her face. Her bottom lip started quivering as the gravity of her own words hit home. Her face screwed up with pain and tears began welling up in her eyes. She couldn't bear to think about what had happened to Christopher and she couldn't bear to look at Kaitlyn. She slammed the door behind her and made her way towards the stairwell, muttering under her breath. Now she needed her medicine more than ever.

Kaitlyn stood in the dark hallway, the bang of the door being slammed shut going right through her body. The words kept ringing in her ears: 'He's not coming home. He's not coming home.' They echoed round her head and it was as if someone had sucked all the air out of her and then placed an anvil on her chest. She collapsed to the floor, unable to move, crying, hoping that someone would make it all better and blaming herself for it all going wrong. Again the guilty feelings flooded into her mind. If only she had got there a few seconds earlier, if only she had picked Christopher up and stopped him crying. Then Steve wouldn't have hit him, he wouldn't be in hospital and she wouldn't be missing him so much that it hurt. More than anything, she wouldn't be facing the prospect of life without him.

She wandered around the flat, touching Chrissy's few grubby toys, holding his clothes up to her nose and drinking in his smell, then using them to mop her ever-flowing tears. She knew that nothing in her life would ever be the same again.

Chapter Eight

November 1976

Christopher kept his eyes screwed up tight for as long as he could, nestling his head into the shoulder of the tall, strong man who was gently carrying him into the house. He loved being held this way. He had vague memories of being pushed this way and that by a large man with foul breath who spent most of his time shouting, but the only people who had ever carried him in this soft way were the big woman and the small woman, though now his memories had faded so much that he could no longer recall their faces. Since then there had been other homes, other families, each for only a few weeks at a time, but somehow he knew this one was going to be different.

He felt himself being set down on something broad and soft, then heard a man's voice: 'OK, Christopher, you can open your eyes now.'

Christopher blinked a few times to get used to the brightness of the lights, then looked around him. It was the biggest room he had ever been inside. Bigger than the room he had had at the hospital. He looked up at the beaming faces of Paul and Jane Tobin.

'I hope you like it, Christopher,' said Jane softly, desperately trying to hold back tears of joy. 'This is your room.'

Both Paul and Jane had originally hoped to adopt a newborn child but the more they had looked into the possibilities, the more they moved towards the idea of adopting an older child.

Christopher was nearly two by the time he arrived at the Tobins'. Because of their own ages the agency had felt it would be better for them to try to adopt an older child from a problem family who would be less sought after, rather than competing with the younger, more 'adoption friendly' families for the younger, more desirable children. He and Jane had tried to look on the bright side: at least they wouldn't have to stay up half the night for the first six months feeding and changing nappies. But still Paul felt it was an important part of being a parent that he had somehow missed out on.

Jane in particular had slowly come round to the idea and had been moved by the thought of taking on a child who had not been truly loved by his own parents. She had so much love to give that she felt she would be able to more than make up for anything that had gone before. They knew little about the child they were taking on except for the fact that he had been injured and spent several months in foster homes. Paul had a few reservations about taking on a child from an unknown background but once they had met Christopher for the first time and seen his cherubic face smiling up at them, all his worries melted away to nothing.

Sitting in the middle of the nursery in the Tobin home, Christopher looked around wide-eyed. The walls were a mix of bright yellows, oranges and reds, and had pictures of racing cars, steam engines and rockets all over. The cosy bed he had been set down on had a duvet cover featuring a picture of a sleek black horse. There was a smart wardrobe and matching chest of drawers, and a large box in the far corner.

Christopher's eyes locked on the box and Paul Tobin followed the boy's gaze. 'A-ha. I see you've spotted the toy box. Well, it's your toy box, not mine, so go on.' He egged on Christopher to take a look inside.

Christopher climbed down off the bed and, with a massive smile on his face, raced across the room towards the box. It took a few seconds to work out that it opened at the top, not the front, but once he had worked this out there was no stopping him. He proceeded to take every model animal, every hand puppet, every car and truck and every stuffed toy out of the box and spread them out on the carpet in front of him.

'That's right, Christopher Tobin,' said Jane, seeing the young boy's look of disbelief. 'They're all yours. Welcome to your new home.'

* * *

Louisa was two years older than Kaitlyn but had always loved the company of younger children in the same way Kaitlyn had always enjoyed hanging out with her younger brother. The pair had played together virtually every day during the summer holidays and now, as the weather grew colder, were the very best of friends.

Louisa was good friends with two boys on the estate, Errol Gants and Jacob Collins, who were in some of her classes at school. Kaitlyn soon began hanging out with all three of them. She didn't mind being the youngest in the gang. Somehow it gave her the chance to be a little kid again and took the pressure off of having to cope with Christopher's departure and her mother's prolonged absences from the flat.

On the morning of the last Saturday of November, Kaitlyn, Louisa, Jacob and Errol stood to one side of the emergency exit doors at the back entrance of the local cinema and waited patiently, even though their hearts were racing with excitement. It took several minutes, but finally the doors burst open and a huge crowd of children came running through. In theory, the cinema frowned on people using the emergency exit after a film had finished but in practice it was a much quicker way of getting out and had developed into a habit few of the locals were willing to change.

The reason the practice was frowned upon, as Kaitlyn and Louisa had discovered, was that it gave them the chance to hold the doors open and sneak in without paying. With plenty of nooks and crannies to hide in while the audience for the next performance filtered through into their seats, the only thing they had to watch out for was making sure the ushers with their little torches didn't spot them once the movie had started. By sitting as far back as possible, they found they were able to keep an eye on their movements and duck down at the first sign of trouble. It soon became a regular part of their weekly routine and they would sneak into the cinema every Saturday morning to watch the dedicated children's programmes. The stories, which featured the likes of Flash Gordon and Superman, and always ended with the heroes in such great peril there seemed to be no way they could possibly survive, gripped Kaitlyn's imagination right from the start.

Those trips with Louisa and the others were the first time Kaitlyn had ever been to the cinema and she loved the experience. She loved the way the giant flickering screen transported her to another world where anything was possible and immersed her in the lives of people whose experiences were so different from her own. It became a way of escaping from the drudgery of life on the Roxford, but also a fantastic alternative education.

It wasn't all she learned. One chilly Saturday morning, as the gang met in the estate's playground, ready to set off for their usual cinema session Louisa, her face flushed with excitement, reached into her pocket and explained that she had something to show everyone: 'Look at this.'

Kaitlyn, Jacob and Errol looked down at the fat white tube on Louisa's outstretched hand and studied it closely. One end was slightly tapered and the other was tied off with a twist of paper. It looked a bit like a cigarette but there was no filter, just a small rolled-up piece of cardboard in the thin end.

Louisa grinned from ear to ear. 'It's a spliff. I took it from my mum's purse. You smoke it and it makes you . . . I don't know. A lot of people do it.'

'Your mum gave you that?' said Errol.

'Don't be stupid. She doesn't know. She's been up half the night making them because she's having some kind of party. She'll never miss it.'

Jacob, who'd smoked a few cigarettes in his time, picked up the spliff and sniffed it cautiously. 'Smells like dog shit.'

'You mean it smells like your house.' Errol laughed.

'Let's try it,' said Louisa.

'Sure,' they all said together.

It took a few minutes of discussion to decide that the safest place was the roof of block C of the estate. Access was supposed to be impossible but the gate and wire mesh covering the entrance had long been torn down by vandals. The long concrete roof was flat and covered with rubbish from previous expeditions. With large steel square ventilation ducts, the roof offered a good hiding place for those who needed it. It also had one of the best views of London around. On a clear day you could see St Paul's Cathedral, barges floating slowly down the Thames, the Post Office Tower and the distant hills of Alexandra Palace. All around were the wealthy neighbourhoods where houses had gardens and swimming pools, and children played in the sunshine, laughing and joking and living their lives a million miles away from those living on the Roxford estate.

Louisa lit the joint and took the first drag, holding the smoke in her lungs before coughing it back up and feeling sick. Jacob was next, then Errol and finally Kaitlyn did the same as Louisa, coughing so hard it soon hurt her throat. It didn't put them off and the spliff passed round again. As they tried to smoke more each time, the draws becoming slightly longer, they began to feel a little strange. Just as Kaitlyn was handing the spliff back to her friend for the third time, a wave of sensation suddenly crashed over her.

'You feel anything?' asked Louisa.

She didn't answer. She couldn't.

It was as if all her senses had suddenly become super-aware and finely tuned. She had been happy and relaxed when she got to the roof but now this feeling was even more apparent. Her mind felt sharp, her thoughts crystal clear. She could feel her heartbeat slowing down and a dreamy, detached sensation rushing through her body. The sounds of cars and children playing down below, the colour of the sky and the trees – all of it seemed much more vivid than before. Kaitlyn settled back and allowed the feeling to wash over her completely. Everyone in the gang looked at each other and burst out into uncontrollable fits of laughter. Tears were running down their cheeks as their screams of laughter could be heard around the estate.

'What do you think?' asked Louisa, her mouth dry after they had laid on their backs on the roof for more than an hour, simply staring up at the clouds.

'I need a drink and some chocolate,' said Errol. They went down to the sweet shop and for the rest of the afternoon they consumed chocolate and fizzy drink as never before, all paid for with the £5 note Louisa had taken from her mum's purse.

They had only been able to smoke half the joint on that first afternoon but they all knew they would do it again. Soon.

It was a combination of the drugs, the endless trips to the cinema and the close friendships she forged with Louisa, Jacob and Errol that helped Kaitlyn to cope with the prospect of her first Christmas without Christopher.

There had been dozens of times when Kaitlyn had wanted to tell the others – Louisa in particular – about what had happened to her brother, but somehow the timing was never right. There was also the fact that, no matter how many times she remembered her mother telling her that it was not her fault, she still blamed herself for her brother being taken away. She preferred to keep the pain and guilt and shame to herself and deal with it in her own way rather than have it discussed by her friends.

There were no presents from her mother that

Christmas and no decorations in the flat. Kaitlyn remembered last Christmas: even though things had already been bad between Steve and Angela, there had been a small tree and a few paper streamers hung from the ceiling. She remembered how they had all laughed when Christopher had thrown away the present Angela had bought him and instead spent hours playing with the coloured paper it had been wrapped in.

She spent most of this Christmas week at Errol's house, playing games and listening to music in his bedroom with Louisa and Jacob. Louisa gave her a bracelet, while Jacob and Errol both stole cards for her. She had to fight not to cry in front of them.

Late on Christmas Eve, as she made her way home to the empty flat, she heard happy cheers and laughter outside the estate and looked over at the lights of London from the balcony of the fifteenth floor. 'Merry Christmas, Chrissy, wherever you are,' she said softly.

It seemed to take for ever before Rachel finally answered the door. 'Have you got the money?'

Angela held up her hands, which were brimming with small change. 'Not all of it, but I've got this.'

Rachel's eyes widened with alarm. 'For fuck's sake what am I supposed to do with all that shrapnel?' she gasped. 'Can you at least change it down the corner shop?'

'I will. But can I do it later? Please.'

Rachel stood to one side and Angela made her way eagerly into the flat.

Rachel allowed herself a tiny smile. It had all been so easy. This wasn't the first time she had worked to get someone hooked on heroin, but Angela proved by far the most willing victim of her cunning scheme. She turned people on to heroin employing the same tried and tested methods her own dealer had used to get her hooked – give away the first few bags for free and then, once the addiction sets in, start to charge. A long-time junkie herself, who was only able to stave off the agonising symptoms of withdrawal by injecting four times a day, every day, the sole way she could afford to pay for her own habit was through a mixture of prostitution and dealing to others. In the early days heroin had been the ultimate high and she had loved the feelings it had given her. Now those days were long gone and she needed heroin simply to feel normal, just to be able to get out of bed in the morning.

But for Angela, still a newcomer to the world of class A drugs, heroin was everything that had been missing in her life. The feeling the drug gave her as it kicked in was like nothing she had ever known. There was no pain, no anxiety, nothing bad of any description. It was like having an orgasm while being wrapped in cotton wool. It was a feeling that she wanted to go on and on.

And then there were the dreams. The wonderful dreams where she, Kaitlyn and Christopher were all together and happy. And there was a man in her life who loved and cared both for her and the children. Each hit had lasted around three hours and each time she came round from the high and the dream she just wanted more. Some days she smoked so much that Rachel ran out and there were a few anxious minutes until her supplier, a stocky lad named Gary, appeared with a few more wraps.

Many times Angela had been so out of it that she had not even noticed the other customers coming to the door of the flat during the night, or the men that Rachel retreated into the back room with. When they reappeared the men's faces would always be flushed and Rachel would have a fistful of notes to stuff into her purse.

Angela's first night encounter with brown sugar had lasted only as long as Rachel's patience and good will. The first few times had been free but by the end of that first evening Angela had spent all of the £20 she'd had in her purse. The money was supposed to last her until the end of the week but she felt powerless not to hand it over to Rachel without a moment's hesitation.

Now, nearly four months later, Rachel deliberately gave Angela a far milder batch of heroin to smoke. After chasing the dragon twice in a row, Angela still felt almost nothing. 'It's not doing it for me, Rach. This stuff's no good, what kind of game are you trying to pull?'

'It's exactly the same stuff you had yesterday,' Rachel lied.

'Well, it's not working; it's not fucking working at all.'

Rachel held up one of her hands. 'Relax, Angela. You're getting used to it, that's all. That's what happens with heroin, at the beginning at least. Your body becomes more tolerant and you need to use more and more of it in order to have the same effect.'

'More and more? I can barely afford what I'm using now! There's got to be something I can do. I need this stuff.'

Rachel pretended to think for a few moments. 'How do you feel about needles?'

'I . . . I don't know. Are they safe?'

'They are if you follow the rules. Listen. The reason most people who use heroin seriously inject rather than smoke is that you can get a lot more for your money. If you're smoking £100 worth of heroin a week, injecting will bring the cost of the habit down to £30 a week or even less.'

'But I don't have £30 a week.'

'I'm just saying. It's a lot cheaper for you.'

'What are the rules?'

'Always do a little bit first and then wait. Then do a bit more. Don't think you can just do the whole lot at once. I know people who've OD'd just because they got locked up and they had a few weeks away from it. They come back and think they can pick up where they left off. But that's just not the case.'

'Uh huh,' said Angela.

'And when you start doing this on your own, make

84

sure that you chop the stuff up really well. Use a razor blade. You don't want to get one bit that's much stronger than all the rest.'

'Wow, you really look out for me,' Angela said.

Rachel paused. She reached over with her thin hand and touched Angela's face. 'Of course I do, love, of course I do.'

Once Rachel had finished chopping the heroin she poured a little on an old metal spoon and squeezed some drops of lemon juice on to it.

'What are you doing?'

'You have to dissolve it before you can inject it. But you can't use water. This kind of heroin doesn't dissolve in water. Lemons are full of citric acid and that works a treat. Don't worry, I've done this loads of times. I'll even go first if you like.'

'OK.'

Angela watched, fascinated, as Rachel pulled out a belt from under the sofa and wrapped it tightly round her bare upper arm. Using two fingers, she tapped on the middle of the joint again and again until a fat vein popped into view. 'I don't normally use my arms, I use the veins in my groin. The track marks don't show. But I want you to know what's going to happen so I'm doing this just for you.' Rachel took the syringe and filled it with the liquid, squeezing it a little to ensure there were no air bubbles inside. A few drops of liquid emerging from the top of the needle showed all was well. Rachel took a deep breath and gently pierced her skin, pushing the needle upwards in line with the bulging vein. Her eyes flickered slightly as the drug took effect, then she exhaled deeply and leaned back with a huge smile on her face. 'Wow. Good stuff.' Her eyes opened suddenly. 'Now it's your turn. Then I can get on with enjoying my high.'

Rachel took the belt, wrapped it round Angela's arm and repeated the procedure until she could see her vein. Then she took the same needle she had used on herself and plunged it into Angela's vein.

At first there was only the sharp pain of the needle, but then there was the same feeling she had experienced when she smoked heroin, only far more intense, far more instantaneous. It was pure unadulterated bliss. 'Oh, God,' Angela groaned.

'Now you see, now you get it,' cooed Rachel.

'Oh my God,' moaned Angela, tears of joy running down her cheeks.

Chapter Nine

August 1977

It had taken more than a year, but Steve Brooks had finally got himself transferred to Strangeways prison in his native Manchester. From his narrow barred window he could see the bright lights of the city and hear the bustling crowds moving back and forth as they went about shopping and socialising, enjoying the long hot summer of 1977.

He had hated every minute of being cooped up but at least he knew his ordeal was slowly coming to an end. He had, on the advice of his lawyer, pleaded guilty to assault on a minor and child endangerment, and been sentenced to three years. He would be released some time in January 1978, having spent only eighteen months behind bars. Most of the prisoners in Brixton had been Londoners and swore that if they couldn't get him again while he was inside, their friends on the outside would descend on him like a ton of bricks the moment he got out. At least in Manchester he felt relatively safe.

The scar on his face was not the only mark prison had left on him. On the outside he had enjoyed the odd line of speed, but the months in prison had left him addicted to heroin. Steve had discovered, much to his surprise, that it was far easier to get drugs when you are behind bars than it was on the outside. Not only that but the quality was better and cheaper than anything you could get on the street.

The drugs flooded into Strangeways stuffed into the knickers of visiting girlfriends and then passed from mouth to mouth in seemingly passionate French kisses at the start or end of visiting times. Once inside their mouths, the men would take the drugs and stuff them into the cracks of their bottoms so high that they would not show during inspection. If the drugs were not needed urgently – but they almost always were – they would be swallowed and passed out a few days later.

At first Steve was horrified. He was used to his drugs being delivered in neat white packages on street corners or in pub toilets. For a while he resisted, then he decided to try some speed. Big mistake. The increased energy and sense of paranoia the speed gave him didn't gel with the prison environment. It enhanced his sense of being trapped when what he really wanted was to dull it. It soon became clear why so many of the other prisoners took heroin and it was only a matter of time before Steve did so too.

Getting the money was hard. He earned a few pounds each week from working in the prison kitchen but had to use most of this to buy toiletries and pay for his phone calls and tobacco. On one occasion he had agreed to look after the stash of another prisoner who was expecting his cell to be searched. In the event, it was Steve's cell that was searched and the drugs were found. Both Steve and the man had gone through the most agonising cold turkey for nearly a week before they could afford to buy any more drugs. Once the suffering was over, the man beat Steve to a pulp, putting him back into the hospital wing.

As a light snow started to fall Steve looked out of the window, a roll-up clenched between his sore, cracked lips. It would soon be over, he thought to himself, he would soon be free.

* * *

Rachel threw open the door, furious at being disturbed so early in the morning having only got to bed a few hours earlier. The doorbell had been ringing for so long that she had considered ripping out the wires. Instead, she had decided to give whoever it was calling a piece of her mind. At first it seemed there was no one there, but then Rachel let her gaze fall a few inches and saw Kaitlyn looking up at her. 'What the hell do you want?' she demanded.

Kaitlyn took a deep breath. 'My mummy's not very well.'

'And?'

'She said you had some medicine that would make her feel better.'

Rachel took a long, deep drag on a cigarette and stared hard at Kaitlyn. Her face was entirely without emotion. 'You got the money?'

Kaitlyn shook her head.

'No money, no medicine,' said Rachel and began to close the door.

Kaitlyn stepped forward a little. 'But my mummy's really ill,' she said urgently, genuine concern in her voice. 'Her tummy is really hurting. She really needs the medicine.'

At that precise moment Angela Wilson was fighting through the second day of her first ever encounter with cold turkey. It was forced upon her, of course. Having spent all the money from her weekly giro and gathered up every penny of spare change from around the house, she had finally reached the point where she was being forced to go without heroin. She had heard people talk about the pain of withdrawal a few times, usually with terror in their voices, but the experience itself was like nothing she could possibly have imagined. As much of a high as heroin was, as much as it lifted her to new heights of pleasure, so doing without it sank her down to new depths of despair.

First she threw up, again and again until there was nothing left inside her and the only sound she made as she crouched over the toilet bowl was a terrible, dry, hacking noise. Then the muscles in her body began twitching constantly. Even though it was warm outside, Angela felt freezing cold. When she dared to move she could feel each and every one of the bones inside her body and they all hurt like hell. Her skin was covered with tiny goose bumps but at the same time she was sweating like a pig. All she could think about was the medicine. It totally consumed her.

Kaitlyn had tried her best to help but didn't really understand what was going on. She had placed a blanket over her mother's shivering body and mopped the sweat from her brow. She told her just how much she wanted her to get better so that they could do the things they used to do, but in the back of her mind she knew her mother had been ill for most of the past three months and that over that time her condition had only ever got worse.

Rachel looked at Kaitlyn through the crack in the half-closed door. If Angela had hoped that sending her sweet-looking daughter to beg for drugs on credit might melt Rachel's heart she was going to be sadly mistaken. 'It's ten quid a bag. She knows that. I don't want to see you again and I don't want to hear from her unless she has the money. She already owes me £50 and I can't let her have any more.' And with that Rachel slammed the door shut.

It was still more than warm enough to be outside in just a light jacket but Angela chose to visit the local Budgens supermarket on Balham High Street with its shops and Friday market wearing her heavy woollen overcoat. She moved swiftly up and down the brightly lit aisles, her hollow sunken eyes scanning the shelves for items of value.

Quick as a flash her hand darted out as she passed the shelf containing packets of razor blades. First one then two were swiftly hidden under the folds of her jacket. Angela's pace never slowed and she had to fight to keep her mounting excitement from showing on her face. Razor blades always fetched a good price on the black market and were so easy to sell they were almost as good as cash. She reached the end of the aisle, stopped and picked up a can of dog food, examining it closely as if she were a shopper rather than a shoplifter. Replacing the tin on the shelf, she risked a glance behind. And there, standing at the other end of the aisle, staring at her intently, was the store's manager. Shit! How long had he been there? Had he seen her take the blades? Angela's mind was racing. Surely if he'd seen her he would have done something about it by now, but then again she couldn't be accused of a crime until she had actually tried to get past the checkout.

She moved around the top of the aisle and came back down the other side. Sure enough, the manager had moved across too, so he could still keep an eye on her. Angela kept up the pretence of examining items every few paces but it was getting hard to concentrate. Beads of sweat formed on her brow and began to trickle down her face, a combination of nervousness and the fact that she was wearing such a heavy coat.

She couldn't risk the manager seeing her like this – the guilt would be screamingly obvious. Angela paused for a few moments, then doubled back to the top of the aisle. As she did so the manager began striding purposefully towards her, his face grim and determined. It was now or never. As Angela reached the top of the aisle and moved out of sight, she reached into her coat, grabbed the packets of blades and shoved them back on a shelf behind the tins of dog food. Then she quickened her pace and began running towards the exit.

She could hear the manager's footsteps behind her, then his voice broke through: 'Madam, excuse me, madam. Could I have a word?'

Angela kept moving but as she slipped past the checkout and neared the door two other members of staff appeared in front of her, blocking her way.

A moment later the manager was at her side. 'Excuse me, madam,' he said snootily. He was short, middle-aged with a thin moustache and gold-rimmed spectacles. His pale-blue shirt was stretched tightly over his tubby frame and dark patches of sweat were visible under his armpits. His fingers twitched with anticipation as he pointed to the folds of her jacket 'I believe you may have something which belongs to this store concealed about your person.'

Angela opened her jacket, revealing nothing but her soiled blouse beneath.

The man's face twitched with disappointment. 'I don't want to see you in here again. You're barred. Understand?'

Angela nodded.

One of the staff members held the door open and Angela went back outside into the sunshine. She tried several shops along the High Street that afternoon but the way she was dressed and her general demeanour meant she was watched like a hawk and had no luck.

Later that same night Angela Wilson cut a pathetic figure as she strolled through the filthy streets close to the Roxford estate, desperate to find some way to fund her habit. Anyone seeing her would have felt nothing but pity, but that alone wasn't enough to compel even the kindest of souls to help her out.

She had started her day begging for change outside the bank in the mistaken belief that those who had withdrawn large sums of money might be more willing to share some of it with others less fortunate than themselves.

She had picked through piles of garbage at the back of several local restaurants, looking for anything she might be able to sell. She had thought about stealing again, running into a store, grabbing a handful of goods and running out again before anyone had a chance to realise what was going on, but her legs were not as strong as they had once been and she knew her chances of getting away clean were minimal at best.

Few saw the whole story, just fleeting glimpses of what had become of her life.

They would have seen the sleek Ford Granada pull up to the kerb and an arm emerge from the driver's window, beckoning her over. Angela approached the car cautiously, bending down so that her head protruded slightly through the open window. The conversation lasted only a few seconds before Angela stepped back and began walking away, her face flushed with shock and anger.

Inside the Granada the driver pressed his fingers against his cheek in contemplation, then leaned out of his window and called out once more. When Angela failed to slow down he drove forward a few yards, mounting the kerb just in front of her. He spoke again and her pace quickened. He spoke once more and this time she slowed, turned and walked back to his open window. Once more she leaned down, listening to him carefully. Then she was standing upright again, tears welling in her eyes. She paced in small circles, bit the back of her thumb, ran her fingers hard through her hair and grimaced. Her distress was there for all to see, but no one paid much attention.

Eventually Angela returned to the window and nodded, then moved round to the passenger side of the car and climbed inside. The Granada set off at high speed.

Twenty minutes later the Granada returned, depositing Angela back at the same spot. From then on it was as if she were invisible. No one saw her walking, head held low, across the road back to the estate. No one saw the tears wetting her face as she climbed the stairs, each one requiring even more effort than the last. Finally she reached the twenty-fifth floor, moved along and rang the bell. When Rachel finally answered her face was hard. It was only when Angela held up the two crumpled £10 notes the man from the Granada had given her that Rachel stood to one side and let Angela in.

Chapter Ten

February 1979

There was a definite spring in Paul Tobin's step as he bounded up the path to his front door. It had been a good day; no, a great day. Work was going like a dream, he was at the top of his game and some of the designs he was drafting, he felt, were destined to become classics.

He glanced at his watch. It was later than he thought, he'd lost all track of time but that always happened when he was on a roll and he loved the feeling of getting lost in a world of his own. And now, to make the night complete, he was coming home to bask in the warmth of his loving wife and beautiful son.

'Where the bloody hell have you been?' Jane demanded as soon as Paul walked through the door. She was standing in the hallway, arms folded, hair dishevelled and a small red weal on her left cheek.

'My God, what happened to your face?'

'It was Christopher.'

'What do you mean? Did he hit you?'

'Not exactly. It was an accident, he was throwing

his toys all over the place and I got caught just under the eye.'

It had been more than two years since Christopher Wilson had come into the Tobins' life. He had been the answer to all their prayers and dreams, the child they would have loved to have had themselves if only that had been possible. Christopher was a child from the heart, not from the womb, and that made him even more special. Almost all the scars and marks that were the result of the vicious attack had faded away at the end of a year and, to all intents and purposes, Christopher was just a normal little boy. Even if he didn't look much like either of his parents.

Although the Social Services workers who had arranged the fostering and later the adoption agency had deliberately not provided many details, one had let slip something about Christopher spending the early days of his life on 'one of the worst estates in south London'. It didn't take a rocket scientist to work out just where that was or the kind of problems children growing up in that environment could end up with.

Paul had always believed that nurture rather than nature was the deciding factor and initially he seemed to have been proved right. In the first few months Christopher had been a model child: incredibly happy, wonderful company, sociable, loving and intelligent. The Tobins had lavished on the boy all the love they had been storing up for years and he had soaked it up. In return he had filled their lives with joy and laughter.

But in recent months Christopher had appeared troubled. Staff at the nursery he attended two mornings a week had reported that he had become increasingly aggressive towards other children. Paul had insisted on taking Christopher off to a doctor for a thorough check-up. After an extensive examination, the doctor declared that there appeared to be nothing physically or mentally wrong and that Christopher was a healthy four-year-old boy. Jane had assured Paul time and time again that his behaviour, even the aggressive stuff, was perfectly normal and, what with all the disruption caused during his earlier life, Christopher was probably just going through the terrible twos a couple of years too late.

'Where the hell were you? You said you'd be home hours ago.'

'I was working,' said Paul. 'You know we've got this big contract coming up; it's taking more time than I thought.'

'It's not good enough, Paul,' said Jane. 'You know how difficult things are. I can't do it all on my own. You need to be here.'

'But I can't do everything. I have to go to work so that you can stay home and look after Christopher. We've agreed this.'

'We agreed that you would work, not that you would never come home.'

'This is just temporary, it's just this project, it's getting in the way a bit.'

'Bullshit, Paul. You can't let it get in the way. Your family has to be your priority. You're talking about the old you, the way things were before. But everything has changed now. We have a son. Nothing is ever going to be the same again. You can't lose track of time any more, no matter how important the project is.'

'I'm sorry.'

'No you're not,' Jane snapped. 'It's like you're not even here. I bet you're still thinking about work right at this very moment.'

'Well, what am I supposed to do? Tell me what I am supposed to do.'

'You can stop shouting for one thing, you'll wake him up.'

'I'm not shouting,' Paul shouted.

They rarely argued but they had done so increasingly as the problems of dealing with Christopher had grown. Jane paused for a moment, conscious that her own voice was rising. She took a deep breath, then spoke again, keeping her voice low and calm. 'Look, all I'm saying is that if you want Christopher to be the son you've always dreamed of, if you want him to grow up to be the way we always talked about, then you need to be part of his upbringing.'

'I don't see why you can't control him when I'm not around,' said Paul, but as soon as the words had escaped his lips he knew it had been the wrong thing to say. Jane's face reddened with rage. 'I didn't mean it like that,' Paul said softly. 'I'm sorry. Let's eat, I'm starving.'

Paul reached for Jane's shoulder but she pulled back out of reach. 'You eat. There's shepherd's pie in the freezer. I'm going to bed. And I'm sleeping in the spare room tonight.'

Chapter Eleven

April 1980

The door broke easily.

Inside the living room, collapsed on the sofa, Angela woke with a sharp intake of breath as the terrible sound of splintering wood echoed throughout the flat. By the time she had moved into full wakefulness there was nowhere to go; she was surrounded.

'Hold her down, boys.'

The words had come from a man standing in the centre of the room. He was tall, stocky and totally bald. He wore smart black trousers and a matching black shirt, buttoned all the way up, which made it look as though his head was floating in the air. A single deep yellow scar sat on the front of his nose, while a pale red line ran across his throat. He was vaguely familiar – Angela could just about recall having seen him on the estate and in Rachel's flat every now and then – but she had no idea who he was. All she knew was that she was scared and that for some reason she was in big trouble.

His words had sent two burly men, one black, the other white, marching towards her. Each made a grab for one of her arms. Instinctively Angela flicked her right foot upwards, driving the toe into the black man's groin. He hit the ground like a sack of potatoes, groaning in agony with his hands clasped between his legs.

The other man had her wrist but was momentarily distracted by his fallen colleague. Angela pulled him towards her mouth, sinking her teeth into the flesh beneath his knuckles. The man let go of her and jumped back in shock, rubbing the back of his hand with the palm of the other.

The man in black rolled his eyes towards the ceiling, took two swift steps forward and slapped Angela hard across the face. The blow knocked her flat on to the sofa, made tiny white specks of light dance around in front of her eyes and left her ears ringing so hard that the next words she heard were all distorted. 'Stop fucking about. She's only a bird. Now fucking hold her down.'

The first two men advanced on her again, this time a little more cautiously. They need not have bothered. Angela was still dazed from the slap, they managed to grab both her wrists and pin her down with little difficulty. 'Who the hell are you? What's going on?' she screamed.

The man's eyes widened. 'You must forgive me. I've been very rude, haven't I? Completely forgot to introduce myself. My name is Gary. I would shake your hand but that might be a bit difficult for you right now. Maybe later.'

'Why are you doing this to me?'

'You know what you did?'

'I haven't done anything to you.'

'Haven't done anything!?'

Angela could see the rage building up inside Gary. He stepped forward. For a split-second it seemed as though he was going to hit her again, but then he calmed himself. 'Nothing? You dare to tell me you've done nothing? I'll tell you exactly what you did. You took drugs from Rachel and told her you'd sell them. Only you didn't, you stuck the whole lot up your fucking arm, didn't you? But the trouble is, those drugs didn't belong to Rachel, they belonged to me. And in my book what you've done is stealing. Nobody steals from me. That's a lesson you're going to have to learn. I've just been upstairs teaching Rachel that same lesson. Now it's your turn.'

Gary took an object which looked a little like a flat silver cigar from his pocket and used his thumb to jab at a button on one side. The blade flicked out and locked into place with a menacing 'ker-lick'.

Angela couldn't take her eyes off the knife. It had black rubber pads for grip built into each side and the blade itself was serrated, slightly hooked like the nose of a witch and utterly terrifying.

'This is beautiful, don't you think?' He turned the blade slowly in the air so that a thin strip of reflected light moved up and down Angela's face. Gary's own eyes were staring at the knife too, only he looked as though he were gazing into the face of a lover. 'This will punch through sheet steel if necessary. And what it does to human flesh just isn't worth thinking about. I could peel you like an apple with this.'

He was close enough for her to smell his breath. It was heavy with the odour of coffee and stale cigarettes. 'I . . . I can pay you for the drugs. I can get the money for you. I just need a little time.'

Gary smirked. 'How you gonna do that? By opening your legs and getting on your back? No chance, darling. I'm not prepared to wait that long.' His voice was eerily calm.

'Then maybe . . .' Angela did her best to flutter her eyelashes and look attractive, not easy under the circumstances. 'Then maybe we could come to some kind of arrangement?'

Gary threw back his head and roared with laughter. 'Believe me, you're not that great. That's the trouble with all you fucking junkies. You start off with your high morals and your virtues intact, but before too long you're out on the streets selling what you've got between your legs to make just enough to get your next fix. And once you start, you think all your problems are solved. So you let your habit get worse and worse, and then what happens? You start to look like shit. And all of a sudden the clients stop coming because no one's gonna pay good money for some pasty-faced whore who looks like death warmed up, are they? But the real trouble is that I don't give a fuck about the problems you're having.' Gary liked his speeches, he liked the power and most of all he liked it when junkies owed him money because then they couldn't get away from him.

Gary tilted the knife sideways and held it up so that the tip of it was pointing directly at Angela's eyeball. Using one hand to brace himself on the floor, he began to lean forward, propelling the blade at her, millimetre by millimetre, towards the centre of her iris. At first Angela looked on in horror, her eyes wide, but as the blade came closer she shut them tight and prayed to God to let her live through this.

She then felt the ice-cold blade being pressed against the skin of her cheek. She opened her eyes and saw Gary's grinning face completely filling her field of view. He had pressed the flat of the blade against the skin of her cheek to one side of her nose. The sensation of cold was replaced by one of increasing pain as Gary pressed more and more weight on to the blade so that it began to cut into her face. The tip bit deeper and deeper into her flesh, the skin broke and a trickle of blood began flowing down her cheek. Angela screamed.

'What's more important than money is my reputation,' Gary continued. 'If I let you get away with something like this, then everyone is gonna start ripping me off and we can't have that now, can we?'

Angela shook her head vigorously. 'Please,' she pleaded. 'Please.'

'Perhaps I should just kill you and leave your body

hanging from the balcony. That would get the message across, don't you think?' Gary stood up and removed the thick leather belt from his trousers. Then he returned to his knees, folded the belt in two and presented it to her mouth. 'You might want to bite down on my belt, dear. This may sting a little bit.'

Tears streamed down Angela's face, mixing with her blood and dripping on to the sofa. 'No. Please, no,' she sobbed, as Gary forced the belt between her teeth.

'Keep her very still, lads,' said Gary, turning her head to one side and advancing on her with the blade once more.

And at that moment Kaitlyn walked into the room.

Gary turned to look, his eyes running slowly, cruelly up and down the girl's thin body. Kaitlyn was shocked into silence by the scene, terrified by the fear she could see in her mother's eyes. She tried to speak but no words came out. Kaitlyn ran over to Angela and held her tightly.

'Well, well, what have we here? I think I might be able to spare you after all, Angela.'

Gary looked back at Angela and saw she was trying to speak. He removed the belt from her mouth. 'Please don't hurt my little girl. Please don't hurt my little girl,' she sobbed. It became a mantra as she repeated it again and again.

Gary smiled, his gold tooth glinting. 'What kind of

a man do you think I am? I ain't no fucking Herbert, am I, boys?' The two men laughed. 'Don't worry, Angela. I'm not going to hurt her, but she is going to help you.

'What's your name, little girl?'

'Kaitlyn.'

'Well, Kaitlyn, I've got a job for you.'

The police and the drug dealers of the Roxford estate had played a game of cat and mouse for years. It was well known in the area that most of the drugs were taken, prepared and sold from the flats on the estate. But with its rabbit-warren-style tunnels, covered walkways and multiple vantage points, it was almost impossible to mount an effective raid because the dealers would always have time to destroy their supplies long before the police got close enough to arrest them.

Chief Inspector Payne had arrived at the Central South-West Division from north London a few months earlier and decided that a change of tactics was in order. Instead of high-profile raids that ended up with nothing to show for all their efforts, he determined instead to launch a programme of high-profile patrols and random stop-and-searches under the 'sus' law that allowed them to search and detain anyone for no real reason.

The first week was a huge success, with more than a dozen couriers and thousands of pounds and thirty packets of drugs being seized. Encouraged by the initial results, the inspector flooded the estate with officers, some in uniform and others in plain clothes. Detectives made a note of the face and name of every potential courier and people were being stopped on a daily basis. The dealers were losing stock and but for the fact that Gary was bald he would have been tearing his hair out. Instead, he took it out brutally on the dealers within the estate.

'Maybe we should kill this inspector,' said Greg, a heavily tattooed thug whose favourite pastime was inflicting pain on others.

Gary rolled his eyes. 'Much as I'd love to, and believe me I'd really, really love to kill him and every other copper on the planet, that won't do any good. If they think his tactics are working they'll just continue them and, worse still, they'll spread them. At the moment the back-up plan is to relocate to another area and base the operation there, but if this pilot scheme works out they'll be doing this on every estate in the country within a year. The only way we can win this one is if we make sure that inspector fails. We need to find a way to outsmart him.'

During the boom times the focus had been on introducing as many residents on the estate as possible to the joys of heroin. Users who had the ability to get others hooked were given considerable leeway when it came to paying their bills on the understanding that this would make sound financial sense in the long run. Once the crackdown began, Gary realised that he would have to call in all the debts in order to maintain his authority.

It was this that had led to him visiting first Rachel and then Angela, but it was only at the latter's home, when Kaitlyn walked in, that the invisible light bulb floating above his head suddenly switched on and he realised just how easy it might be to get around the crackdown after all.

* * *

'Mummy, why's that woman so fat?' Christopher's voice had been just a little too loud and Jane's face flushed with embarrassment, and she pulled him closer as they walked hand in hand along Dorking High Street.

'She's not fat, darling,' Jane explained. 'She's pregnant. She has a baby inside her.'

Christopher's eyes grew wide with astonishment as he stared at the woman's bulging tummy. 'A baby? In her tummy. Did she eat it?'

Jane laughed. 'No, darling, that's where babies come from. They come out of their mummies' tummies.'

Christopher now directed his gaze towards his own mother's stomach. 'Did I come out of your tummy, Mummy?'

There was a slight pause before Jane replied. Part of her wanted to tell the truth but Christopher was too young, too vulnerable. She and Paul had discussed the issue again and again, and decided that

Christopher would not be told of his adoption. Knowing the truth about his troubled background could only cause more harm than good. 'Yes. Of course you did, darling.'

Christopher moved round and raised up his little palm, laying it flat against Jane's stomach. He looked up at her, his eyes full of wonder and as wide as saucers. 'I came out of here?'

Jane could feel waves of emotion building up inside her. As Christopher's fingers touched her, vivid memories of her ectopic pregnancy and the child she had lost came flooding back to her. She had to fight to stop herself from bursting into tears. She placed her own hand over Christopher's, holding it against her body. 'Yes, darling, this is where you came from.' It was a powerful moment that would stay with her for the rest of her life.

'How did I get out? Is there a door?'

'Erm. Well. There's ... you see. Let's just say it's a special kind of magic.' Jane could feel herself breaking into a sweat. It was a terrible answer but it would have to do for now. Before Christopher came into her life she had been unable to understand why parents never took the time to explain things to their children. It had taken only a few months before she had used the phrase 'because I say so' for the first time and now she knew the pressures of parenting only too well. She breathed a silent sigh of relief as Christopher seemed to accept the answer and continued skipping along the street.

'Does Daddy have a baby in his tummy too?'

'No, darling, only mummies have babies.'

'But Daddy's tummy is so big!'

'I know, Christopher,' she said, laughing softly, 'I know.'

Chapter Twelve

June 1981

Kaitlyn clutched her school bag tightly to her chest and smiled politely as she walked past the two uniformed police officers making a slow patrol around the common grassland of the Roxford estate. She moved quickly into the stairwell of block D, then made her way swiftly up to the third floor. She rang the bell of the flat with the dark-blue door secured behind a heavy metal grill and thirty seconds later it swung open.

The man was black, with a raggedy mix of beard and facial growth protruding from his neck and chin. The whites of his eyes were a milky yellow and a powerful stench of marijuana drifted out through the open door. He held out his hand.

Kaitlyn shook her head. 'Not here. I have to come inside. And I need to see the money first.'

The man smirked, then disappeared back into the flat to retrieve the keys to the gate. Moments later Kaitlyn was in the living room. It was dark and dank, the curtains blocking out any natural light. There were at least three other people in the room. She couldn't tell if they were men or women. They were smoking spliffs and shooting up heroin. They didn't seem to pay much attention to her.

Kaitlyn focused on the man who had opened the door as he reached into his sock and pulled out £30 in £5 notes. He counted the notes twice to be sure, then handed them to her, a spliff now hanging out of the corner of his mouth.

Kaitlyn counted the notes herself, rolled up the money and tucked it into the side flap of her bag. She reached into the main section and pulled out a handful of small wraps of paper, spreading them out on the floor in front of her. 'Six bags. OK?'

The man hadn't heard her. Instead, his eyes were focused on the bag she was carrying. She knew straight away what he was thinking: just how many wraps were there inside. Kaitlyn knew: taking away the six she had just sold, there were another eighty-three, more than £400 worth. In fact, there were actually eight-five wraps, but the last two were not for sale. They were freebies and destined for Kaitlyn's mother, all courtesy of Gary's latest arrangement.

'How old are you?' asked the man, his eyes now focused on Kaitlyn's tiny form.

'Eleven.' She was lying, but at her age a year seemed like a long time.

The man threw back his head and laughed. 'Eleven. Fucking eleven.' He used one hand to indicate the others in the room. 'All of us here and one eleven-year-old with a bag full of heroin. Tell me, little girl,

what's to stop me taking that bag off you right now?'
His grin held steady.

Kaitlyn took a deep breath and formed a sentence in her mind. She wanted to get the wording just right. 'Gary says that if you do, he'll cut your balls off and shove them so far down your throat that you'll be fucking yourself up the arse from the inside.'

The grin collapsed. The spliff fell from his mouth, sending a tiny shower of sparks up into the air as it hit the carpet. The man's bottom lip quivered as he struggled to think of something to say. After a silence that seemed to last for eternity he simply reached forward and snatched up the six wraps.

Kaitlyn left the flat with a grin on her face, not caring that the door was being slammed behind her. It had taken just two years but with the help of her friends, she, Louisa, Jacob and Errol were now Gary's biggest distributors.

Kaitlyn was also making money on her own. She had found a way to skim small amounts of the drug off the packages she delivered around the estate. So far no one had found out and just so long as she kept the amounts small and took only a little from each packet, there was no reason why anyone should. To Kaitlyn, it all helped her mother.

But she had been disturbed at the change she had seen in Angela as her addiction had taken hold. Although Kaitlyn herself now smoked cannabis on a regular basis, she was smart enough to know that one drug was far more damaging than the other. More than anything she wanted her mother back the way she used to be. She felt that if only Angela could get clean, they still had a chance to get Chrissy back and be a family once more, and she could make up for what went wrong.

Gary listened to her concerns and did his best to put her straight. 'What you have to understand, Kaitlyn, is that your mum's a user and users are gonna use. That's what they do. And there's not a lot you can do about it. If they don't buy their stuff from me, they're just gonna go out there and get it from someone else. At least the stuff they get from me is good quality, does the job and doesn't give them any kind of problems. They know I'm the best thing that could happen to them. You shouldn't feel bad about what you're doing. You should feel proud.'

Kaitlyn was ashamed that her mother was being classed alongside all the other junkies she and her gang delivered to. She still missed Chrissy so much and remembered vividly the night he was taken away as she had done so many times before. The guilty feeling that it was her fault had not passed with time.

* * *

Paul Tobin returned from the small café with three ice creams and presented one to Jane as if it were a small bouquet of flowers.

Jane smiled graciously, uwrapped the top and plunged it into her mouth.

'You look happy,' said Paul softly. 'I could see your smile from the other side of the park.'

Jane's smile grew even bigger and her eyes turned back towards Christopher, now seven years old, who was squatting in a nearby sandpit and concentrating hard on filling a bright yellow bucket with a small red shovel. They were in the playground of their local park, surrounded by other families all making use of the swings, slides and climbing frames. It was an idyllic scene and one which Jane had always longed to be part of.

Jane sighed contentedly. 'I live for days like this, days when I can put all the worry out of my mind.' Paul took her free hand in his and squeezed it. 'He's a good boy, I know he is.'

Paul nodded. 'I know. I guess this whole thing turned out to be a lot harder than we ever imagined it was going to be. It's obvious when you think about it, but you get so caught up with the emotion of everything you forget that kids who are put up for adoption are sometimes going to have a huge amount of baggage with them, especially when they're more than a few days old.'

Paul had made a huge effort in the months leading up to that Saturday morning to ensure he spent more time at home and helped Jane out with Christopher as much as he could. Although his career was still important to him, he realised he had to slow down at least a little, at least for a couple of years, or he would miss the chance to truly bond with his son, something he was bound to regret in later life. He also hoped that by being around more he could be a calming influence on the boy.

Jane swallowed another gulp of ice cream. 'You don't have any regrets, do you?' Paul lowered his eyes. 'There were times, when Christopher was going through all those night terrors, the bed wetting, the problems at nursery when he was pushing other kids around, a few times when I wondered if we were doing something wrong.'

'But what about now?'

Paul looked up just as Christopher scooped another spade full of sand into his bucket. 'Now he seems like a different boy all together.'

The couple turned to face each other. Paul slipped his arm round Jane's waist and pulled her close. They were just about to share an ice-cream-flavoured kiss when the sound of a woman's desperate scream cut into them. From the corner of his eye Paul could see the large red-headed woman running from just behind them to the centre of the sandpit. 'No,' she yelled. 'Leave him alone, leave him alone.'

Paul's eyes followed the direction the woman was running in and his heart sank. There, in the centre of the sandpit, Christopher was towering over a smaller boy, bashing him over the head with the plastic spade. The smaller boy was in tears and whimpering with pain and fright. Christopher had an angelic smile on his face.

By the time Paul had taken in the scene, Jane was

already rushing towards their son, dropping her ice cream on the way.

The red-headed woman got there first, snatching her weeping child up into her ample bosom and giving first Christopher then Jane a filthy look. 'What do you think you're doing?' she screamed at Christopher. 'He's only little. That's not how you play with little boys.' Then she turned to Jane. 'I suggest you teach your boy how to behave.'

'I'm sorry,' Jane gasped, out of breath after her dash across the park. 'I don't understand, he's normally so good.' But the woman had already stormed off.

By now Paul was also in the sandpit. He bent down so his face was level with Christopher's. The little boy's face gave no clue that he felt he had done anything wrong. He was still smiling and looking around as if he wondered what all the fuss was about. Paul placed his hand gently on his son's shoulder. 'Christopher, why were you hitting that boy?'

Their eyes met. Christopher simply shrugged. 'I wanna go on the swings now,' he said, ducking under his father's grip and running off towards a set of swings at the edge of the play area.

Paul stood up and shook his head. 'It never changes, does it? It doesn't matter how much love we show him, how much time we spend with him, there's always a part of him that we're never going to understand.'

'She was overreacting, Paul,' said Jane. 'This sort

of thing happens all the time, it's just playground stuff. It doesn't mean anything.'

'But it keeps happening. Why does it keep happening?'

'It's just a phase. It's going to be OK.' She took his hand and cupped it in both of her own. 'You'll see, it's going to be fine. He's probably just a bit stressed or something.'

Jane ran off to follow Christopher to the swings, leaving Paul alone in the middle of the sandpit. 'Stressed? What on earth has Christopher got to be stressed about?'

* * *

On Monday morning Kaitlyn left the flat a little later than usual, skipping as she made her way down the stairs of the block on her way to Gary's safe house. At the top of the first flight she saw her elderly neighbour, Mrs Jenkins, struggling with a small bag of shopping. She had managed only a few steps with the bag before she had to put it down to catch her breath, one arm leaning against the wall of the stairwell. Kaitlyn glanced at her watch. She would make time. 'You all right there, Mrs Jenkins?'

The old woman looked up, squinting at Kaitlyn through her thick glasses. She tried to speak but was still too short of breath.

'Don't worry, I'll get that for you.' Kaitlyn bounded down, picked up the bag with one hand, looped her other arm round that of Mrs Jenkins and began helping her up the stairs.

'Do you think they'll ever fix that lift?' Kaitlyn asked as they finally reached the tenth floor. 'This can't be doing you any good.'

Mrs Jenkins stood outside her door, sucking in great lungfuls of air. 'That thing's been broken so long, half the people who live here don't even know there is a lift,' she said with a weak smile. 'Would you like to come in for a cup of tea, love?'

Kaitlyn glanced at her watch again. 'I can't, I'm gonna be late for school.'

'Oooh, they make you go early. When I was your age it was all much later.'

Kaitlyn nodded. 'Listen, Mrs Jenkins, next time you need to go to the shops, just stick the list through our letter box and I'll get it for you, OK?'

'Are you sure?'

'Definitely.'

'OK, Kaitlyn. Thanks, love. You're an angel.'

As soon as Mrs Jenkins was safely inside her flat, Kaitlyn ran back down the stairs. Now she was late and she would have to make up the time she had lost. First she stopped off at one of Gary's safe houses and collected forty wraps of heroin. She was also given a list of addresses and then set off to make her deliveries.

It was a sunny morning with a gentle breeze, which always brought a welcome rush of fresh air to the estate, and Kaitlyn sang to herself as she made her way to block B: 'As I was walking up the stairs I met a man who wasn't there, he wasn't there again today,

I wish that man would go away.' Kaitlyn giggled at the silly words as she walked round the stairwell on the fourth floor. Then something rough caught her round the arm and threw her against the wall.

'What's in the bag?'

The man was tall and broad. Although it was warm he wore a heavy winter coat. His shoes were worn to the extent that you could just make out one of his toes through the end. His shirt was filthy, with a thick black line under the collar. He had a wild, bushy beard and hair to match. There were clumps of white stuff in the corners of his mouth and when he spoke tiny flickers of spittle fell from his lips. He looked as though he'd spent the last few months sleeping on the street, which was exactly what he had done. He was a couple of feet away and she could smell the alcohol on his breath.

Kaitlyn tried to compose herself. Her heart was racing with shock and fear. She pulled the bag a little closer. 'Nothing.'

'Looks kind of bulky for nothing.'

'It's just my school books. Fuck off.'

The man stepped forward and his rough fingers shot out and wrapped themselves round the strap of the bag. 'I just want to take a look. If there's nothing but books then you have nothing to worry about and you can go on your way.'

Kaitlyn struggled to keep control of the bag but the man was too strong. She tried to kick him in the shins but he placed his free hand on top of her head, clamping her in his grip and pushing her back so she was at arm's length. His other hand continued to pull at the bag until it finally came free. Still holding Kaitlyn at bay, the man used his teeth to open the bag and peer inside.

Kaitlyn jumped forward and planted the toe of her right foot hard into the man's groin. He collapsed to the ground, clutching himself and groaning in agony. She felt a tinge of sadness and pity. The man had scared her but he was homeless and desperate. He was probably hoping that the bag contained food as much as it did drugs, which he would undoubtedly have sold to buy alcohol. Kaitlyn retrieved her bag and continued on her rounds before finally heading off to school.

Chapter Thirteen

Paul Tobin kept walking into lamp-posts. He was desperately trying to avoid making eye contact with the people standing on every corner and failing miserably. He was feeling increasingly frightened. What had seemed like a good idea might now be the last thing he did in his entire life. He was convinced he would be found dead in a gutter come the morning. 'This was a bad idea, a really, really bad idea,' he whispered to himself, quickening his pace.

The men he was trying to avoid were lookouts and every now and then they would whistle or give some kind of signal. Around thirty seconds after that a police patrol car or beat officer would go past. Police activity was heavy in the area at this time of night but no one seemed particularly worried. The system they had in place gave plenty of warning and meant the chance of any sales being disrupted was minimal.

It was getting dark quickly. A party started up in a house at the end of an alleyway just as Tobin walked past. Three men in black T-shirts with thick gold chains hanging from their necks like glittery nooses eyed him suspiciously as he hurried past. The music was so loud that Tobin could feel the paving slabs vibrating beneath his feet in time with the beat.

Eager to get off the street, Tobin ducked into a newsagent's and squinted at the bright fluorescent lights. He tried to keep his emotions under control as he noticed that, in place of the traditional counter, there was a large metal grid with a hole just to one side of the till for serving customers. A pit bull terrier sat menacingly on the ground behind the owner, attached to his wrist with a thick leather lead. A second member of staff, an obvious bulge in the waistband of his jeans, stood in the far corner keeping watch. Tobin hurriedly bought a newspaper and made his way back outside.

With his pinstripe suit and Hugo Boss overcoat, Tobin felt ridiculously overdressed. He stood out like a sore thumb and he hadn't even reached the Roxford estate yet. He'd decided on the spur of the moment that he wanted finally to see for himself exactly where it was that Christopher had come from. And at that moment he rounded a corner and saw the monolithic buildings of the estate looming up in front of him.

It was like nothing Tobin had ever seen. It reminded him of a television documentary he had once watched about a team of demolition men bringing down a block of derelict flats in the East End of London. The workmen had gone through the empty building drilling holes to plant the explosives. There was nothing much left, just a shell with a few kitchen and bathroom tiles every now and then to show where things had once been. The Roxford reminded

Paul Tobin of that same estate, but in this case the people were still living there.

The shops were all deserted and the hair salon had been completely burnt out. The first set of flats he passed had had all their windows replaced with mesh grills. Surely no one could be living there any more? The question in his mind was answered when a teen-aged girl with two small, utterly filthy children in tow emerged from the second door, squeezing past him.

There were piles of rubbish in the corners, puddles of urine against the walls. The stench was overpowering. Tobin had seen enough, turned on his heels and made his way back towards the High Street. He had managed only a few metres when a voice called out from behind him, 'You after a bit of business, love?'

She was pale, unwashed and wearing an oversized overcoat. As Tobin turned to look, she opened it slightly, revealing a black halter top and a faded denim miniskirt that barely covered the tops of her bare, battered legs. There was a cigarette in her hand. The skin on the back of her hands and around her eyes was as thin as tissue paper.

Tobin opened his mouth to speak but no words came out.

The woman continued without missing a beat, 'It's ten for a blow job but you have to wear a condom. A fuck is £30 with and £40 without.'

Tobin started to back off at speed. 'I'm ... I'm sorry,' he stammered. He kept walking and did not stop until he reached his car.

'Any luck?' asked Rachel as Angela returned to her usual spot in the shadow of the estate.

'Nah. Think I scared him off. I must be losing my touch. I thought he was a definite. You never get blokes like that, in their fancy suits and wearing a wedding ring, coming down here unless they are looking for a good time.'

'You got that right. And it's always blow jobs they want because their wives won't do it for them. Oh well, I suppose twenty quid here and there every few weeks is a hell of a lot cheaper than a divorce.'

'Funny, though,' said Angela. 'He looked like he had proper money. He could probably afford to go up west, into one of them massage parlour places instead of doing it on the street.'

'But it's the thrill, ain't it, Ange. Blokes like that, they love a bit of rough.'

It took Paul Tobin more than three hours to get back to Dorking. There had been an accident on the A24 and drivers were slowing down their cars and rubbernecking on their way past. They looked on as a team of firefighters urgently tried to cut the top off a car that had been crushed after slamming into the back of an articulated lorry. For once, Paul resisted the temptation to look. He'd seen more than enough horror for one day.

'You're late,' said Jane.

'There was an accident. Traffic was backed up for miles.'

'Heard about it on the radio. How did the meeting go?'

But Paul had already walked through the room without answering.

He went straight upstairs to the bedroom and found the door slightly ajar. He peered inside. Christopher was sound asleep, his mop of tidy blond hair flopping over the pillow. Paul stepped inside and gently kissed Christopher's forehead. The boy murmured as he ran his fingers through his hair and pulled the covers up to cover his shoulders but he did not wake.

'Everything's going to be all right now,' Paul whispered. 'You're going to be safe.' A shadow fell across his face. Jane was standing in the doorway, a look of love and adoration on her face. He stepped into the hallway and embraced her.

* * *

'How about The Specials, "Ghost Town"?' said Kaitlyn, holding up a circle of vinyl. 'You've got to be kidding. No one wants to hear that. Do they?' said Jacob. 'Put on some Bob Marley.'

Kaitlyn was squatting in the centre of Errol's bedroom. Jacob and Louisa sat next to one another on the bed while Errol was on the floor alongside Kaitlyn. Errol shuffled his foot shyly. 'They're all right. I prefer their earlier stuff, though, "Too much, too young".'

'But it's so . . . so seventies,' said Jacob.

'That's on the B-side,' said Kaitlyn, flipping over the record. 'Yeah, let's play that one.'

Jacob groaned.

'Stop fucking moaning,' said Louisa. 'If you don't join in, you're gonna look pretty fucking silly.' Jacob got up to join the rest and within minutes all four were on their feet, holding imaginary microphones, bobbing their heads back and forth and singing their hearts out: 'You done too much, much too young!'

They had spent the morning taking it in turns to play Pacman on Errol's new Commodore 64 computer, which he had stolen from a house two weeks earlier. Kaitlyn had been the envy of them all by achieving the highest score three times in a row. Their gang was by far the strongest on the estate, if the smallest. They had been brought together by chance but had been bonded by the fact that each had a mother hooked on heroin or alcohol and each had somehow been hooked into the world of crime from friendships brought together on the estate.

Louisa and Kaitlyn had cut Errol and Jacob in on their heroin skimming operation, expanding it so they had not only enough to satisfy their own desires but also to sell on a little to like-minded school friends.

By way of return Errol and Jacob had agreed to split the profits of their own fledgling house-breaking and shoplifting ring. The money and drugs were all pooled and divided evenly. The gang soon had enough to buy themselves clothes, records and even to pay to get into the cinema whenever they wanted. All four of them loved the movies and they had embraced video recorders as soon as they became available. Jacob had managed to obtain a nearly new model from the same house as the Commodore, together with a collection of the latest videos, which they spent hours watching.

At five on Sunday afternoon it was time for the *Top 40* – a weekly ritual for the four friends – and Errol tuned in his radio to Radio 1, quickly finding the dry, reassuring tones of BBC DJ Mike Read counting down the hit parade and tapping freely in tune to the new ghetto blaster courtesy of number 34 Newlands Way, Clapham, SW11.

By the time Kaitlyn arrived home a few hours later the door to the flat was slightly ajar with the dimmest of lights emerging from within. Kaitlyn gingerly pushed it open and moved inside, making her way to her bedroom via the living room.

Angela was sitting up in front of the sofa. She was naked from the waist down. She had a needle in her right hand and was tapping the inside of her thigh, waiting for a vein to emerge so she could inject herself with another dose of heroin. She was so fixated on what she was doing that she never noticed Kaitlyn looking at her.

Standing by her was a tall, thin man with the pallor

of a zombie. He was shuffling impatiently from one foot to the other. Kaitlyn assumed that he was waiting for his turn at the needle but as soon as Angela had finished she put her needle to one side and lay on her back, the warm feelings of the heroin rushing into her bloodstream and taking control of her body. The tall man unbuckled his belt and climbed on top. After a little twisting and shoving, he was inside her. Angela's eyes glazed over as the heroin took hold. Most of the time Angela would go out and have sex for money, then spend most of it on drugs. Increasingly, however, she had cut out the middleman and would have sex with anyone willing to share their fix with her.

Kaitlyn glanced over the scene in front of her, taking in every detail in an instant. Once upon a time such scenes might have shocked her but, having grown up around her mother's drug habit, she was now able to put it completely out of her mind. She walked across the living room, stepping over one sleeping body, into the short hallway until she reached the door of her bedroom. Reaching into the back pocket of her jeans, she pulled out a heavy silver key.

On the front of the door there was a faded wooden panel with 'Kaitlyn' hand-painted on the front. To the left, just above the handle, was a large metal bracket held in place by a large padlock. Errol had borrowed his father's tools to fit it at Kaitlyn's request. He had also reinforced the frame with a metal band. It was strong enough to stop both Angela and her clients stealing from her room. Checking over her shoulder to ensure no one was too close, Kaitlyn unlocked the bolt and let herself into her room. Flicking on the light, she clamped the padlock over an identical bracket on the other side of the door, then flopped over to her bed.

Her bedroom was like a time capsule, unchanged since she was a baby. The Beatrix Potter wallpaper Angela had put up when they first moved into the estate was still there, but faded and torn. On a stand opposite the bed there was a smart-looking colour television and next to that a sophisticated ghetto blaster and a large pile of cassette tapes. On the floor beside her bed there was a pile of books including *The Profession of Violence* by John Pearson, a detailed biography of the Kray twins.

Kaitlyn lay on her back. With one hand she picked up a small jar on the bedside table, took off the lid and removed cigarettes, papers and a small chunk of brown resin. Sitting up, she stuck two of the papers together, then licked the side of one of the cigarettes until the paper fell away and she was able to retrieve the tobacco. With one hand she rolled herself a perfect joint, took a Zippo lighter from under her pillow and lit it. She held in the smoke for ages before tiny streams of it escaped from her nostrils. She picked up the copy of the Kray book and read a few pages as she waited for the drugs to take effect. Then, as her head started to fog, she put down the book and flicked off the light so the room was bathed only in the red glow from the end of her spliff as she inhaled.

Slowly the noises from inside the flat and the rest of the estate began to fade and Kaitlyn was able to drift off to sleep.

Chapter Fourteen

August 1982

Errol Gants shielded his eyes from the sun with the flat of his hand and tried to work out just what it was he was supposed to be looking at. At the age of fourteen Errol was already a fully grown man. He was more than six feet tall, with a strong, broad chest that he liked to show off by wearing T-shirts slightly too small for his frame. He kept his hair short, evenly cropped all the way round his head, something which made him look far older and far more menacing. Jacob was shorter but equally stocky. Puberty had seen his once blond hair turn to chestnut brown, while his sparkling blue eyes had become a steely grey. There was no emotion in his stare. He had the face of a poker player.

'So where exactly is this place?' asked Errol.

Jacob pointed a stubby finger and the others squinted as they tried to follow. 'Straight ahead and to the right. Just next to the car repair place.'

Errol, Louisa and Kaitlyn were, like Jacob, lying flat on their stomachs in the centre of a piece of scrubland next to the edge of a railway line. Directly in front of them on the other side of the tracks were the back entrances of a small parade of shops.

'Do you see it now?' Jacob continued. 'A friend of mine works in the car place and told me that the owner of the shop is closing up for a week so he can go back to Pakistan. We can go in through the back entrance late one night. There's gonna be all sorts of stuff there. The back room is his storage area and he'll have weeks' worth of stock.'

'And what are we supposed to do with it?' asked Louisa.

'Sell it, dummy,' snorted Jacob. 'We'll get a fortune for it. There'll be sweets, chocolates, drinks, the sort of stuff we'll be able to knock off anywhere. We could even try selling it on to a few other shopkeepers in bulk.'

Errol was still uncertain. 'You sure he's not going to empty the place out before he goes?'

'No way. He needs to be up and running again the day he gets back. As it is he's well pissed off at having to go.'

'So why's he going on holiday, then?' asked Louisa.

'It's not a holiday. His dad died a few days ago and he's going off for the funeral. He doesn't have any choice but to leave all the stuff there. It's a golden opportunity.'

'What about security?' asked Errol.

'The front door has one of those grid things, it's pretty impenetrable. But the back is wide open. All we have to do is get across the railway tracks and they're not live so that's not going to be a problem.

There's an alarm system but you can see where the wires come out from the box so all you need to do is cut them and you're home free. Once the car place and the greengrocer's on the other side are closed for the night there's no one around.'

The four had come together at the request of Jacob, who believed he had come up with a new money-making adventure. Although the gang were still involved in a number of schemes, their main income, drug deliveries and skimming a little off the top, was making a lot of money for Gary but little for them. They had realised for several weeks that they needed to come up with a series of plans if they wanted to earn really serious money, but good ideas had been hard to come by. Jacob's proposed heist on the shop was the first that seemed truly viable.

Jacob gave the others a few minutes to think things over then asked, 'So, what do you think?'

Louisa rolled over on to her back and looked up at the clouds. 'I think it's fantastic. You're a genius.'

Errol nodded slowly. 'Seems like a great idea. I just hope your bottle doesn't go.'

'You know you don't need to worry about my bottle; it's your bottle I'm worried about.'

Kaitlyn said nothing. She was staring intently at the back of the shop. Jacob looked at her for a few moments. He had already decided that, because she was youngest, she would be a lookout on the night, nothing more. Her opinion really didn't matter, but he might as well seek it. 'What about you, Kaitlyn, what do you think?'

As the youngest member of the gang she was used to running errands and doing the donkey work. Whenever new adventures had been discussed in the past, it was usually without any input from her. She rarely complained, partly as a result of peer pressure but mostly because she had always agreed with the general consensus. This time was different and Kaitlyn felt compelled to speak. She turned and looked at each of the members of the gang one by one, her eyes finally settling on Jacob. 'I think it's a shit idea. You'd be at the police station within an hour.'

'What are you talking about? What makes you think we'd get caught?' Jacob was indignant.

Kaitlyn took a deep breath and sat up. 'Just because you can't see the alarm doesn't mean it's not there. Those wires leading to that box are just a decoy. They would never be on the outside of the wall for that precise reason. The idea is to make you cut them and then go into the building. Cutting the wires triggers a silent alarm, which sounds back at the police station. And that's just one of the problems. I know we can get in over the railway tracks but when it comes to taking stuff out, especially the big bulky boxes of drinks and sweets, we're not going to be able to get them back over the fence. We'd have to go through the front and that means a lot more people around to see what we're up to, not to mention the trouble we'd have getting the grill off the front door.'

No one said anything for what seemed like a very long time. Finally Louisa broke the silence. 'So I suppose you've got a much better idea.'

'Funny you should mention that,' said Kaitlyn.

The first stage of Kaitlyn's plan caused the most objections, all of them from Errol, whose job was to go and get a paper round at one of the local newsagents'. Errol, never much of an early riser, found himself getting up at six in the morning and trudging out in all weathers over to the shop, then spending the next hour walking through the streets around the estate carrying a bag of papers that never seemed to get any lighter no matter how many he'd got rid of.

It took only a week of exhausting rounds before Kaitlyn was ready to put the second part of her plan into operation. While the shopkeeper was distracted, Errol flicked through the delivery book and found two households, the Troys and the Malones, that had cancelled their papers for the following week. Errol made a careful note of the addresses and passed them on to Kaitlyn, who spent the following afternoon checking out the properties.

One was a small terraced house in one of the less desirable streets of the area that had somehow managed to escape the ravages of the blitz. The other, belonging to the Malones, was a large, semi-detached property with a nearly new BMW in the front drive. This, Kaitlyn decided, would be their first target.

By the start of the following week Errol had

managed to liberate three more of the bright orange shoulder bags he used to carry the papers and he passed them on to Jacob, Kaitlyn and Louisa. He had swung by the house on the way to work and checked that the BMW was not in the drive. He had then called Kaitlyn, who was waiting with the others at a nearby payphone, and given her the all clear.

Errol continued with his rounds until he reached the Malone house. Glancing around to ensure no one was watching too closely, he moved up the garden path and rang the doorbell long and loud. There was no reply. He rang again. Still nothing. He took the spare paper he carried in his bag and shoved it half-way into the letter box. This was both a signal to the others who were following behind that the house had passed the final check and also a last-minute precaution. If the family should return unexpectedly or some cleaner or friend go inside to water their plants or whatever, it was almost certain that the first thing they would do would be to take the newspaper out of the door.

The operation was planned with military precision. As Louisa walked by the front of the house with her paper bag draped over her shoulder, Jacob sneaked round the back and smashed a window. Louisa stopped a few doors down and began making deliveries – junk mail leaflets the gang had liberated from the local library – until she reached the Malone house. As she arrived at the front door it quickly swung open and Jacob ushered her inside.

Twenty minutes later it was Kaitlyn's turn to walk up to the front door and deliver leaflets of her own. She reached the top of the path and saw that, as planned, a bag full of jewellery and other valuables was sitting on the doormat. She slipped it inside her bright orange bag and continued on her way.

Jacob and Louisa left the house later and went their separate ways, while Errol continued his rounds as if nothing had happened.

Their first robbery had worked like a dream and the gang ended up with more than £200 of profit after the jewellery was sold. They had also found £30 of cash secreted in nooks and crannies throughout the kitchen. They were careful to ensure they left the place almost exactly as they found it, so the Malones would know something was amiss only when they found the broken window.

That night the gang smoked their joints in Kaitlyn's honour.

Chapter Fifteen

October 1985

The silver BMW 323i took the corner so fast that it clipped the kerb and spent the next thirty feet with only two of its wheels touching the ground, landing with a shower of sparks bright in the night sky.

The police Rover was close behind, sirens blaring and blue lights flashing, but the two officers inside, Bob Marsh and Colin Ash, were getting anxious. The stolen BMW, which they had been chasing through the streets of London for the best part of fifteen minutes, seemed to be headed in the direction of the Roxford estate. Once inside, the driver would be able to vanish into the maze of walkways and balconies, and the chance of them making an arrest would evaporate to almost nothing.

Conditions on the Roxford had always been in slow decline but in recent years, as the drug traders had taken over, they had gone into free fall. Security doors intended to keep strangers out of the blocks had long since been smashed to nothing. The whole shopping precinct had been turned into a bleak no man's land.

The BMW shot forward as the driver floored the accelerator and Ash swore under his breath as he tried to keep up, while Marsh screamed directions into the radio so that back-up would know where to find them. 'He's taking a left, left, left into Mill Road, still heading in the general direction of the Roxford. Now he's doing a right, right, right into Harper Lane. Yep, looks like he's making a break for the estate.'

The lights up ahead were red but the BMW showed no sign of slowing down. A line of three cars were waiting for the lights to turn to green when the BMW overtook them on the wrong side of the road and tore across the junction. He had almost made it when a fast-moving souped-up Escort clipped the rear of the beamer, sending it spinning into a traffic island.

'RTA, RTA,' screamed Marsh. 'We've got contact with another vehicle.' The police car was on its target as the door of the BMW opened and a young black man, blood dripping from a gash in his forehead, clambered out and began running towards the estate. 'He's on foot, he's on foot. We are continuing the pursuit,' said Marsh.

Ensuring there was no traffic coming, Ash took the patrol car across the junction and shot down the road towards the running man. He in turn took a sharp right through a set of concrete bollards and vaulted a wall, which took him to an alleyway leading to the estate's derelict playground.

Ash brought the Rover skidding to a halt, he and

Marsh drew their truncheons and began running after the man. Marsh, a big man but quick on his feet, was running hard, his heavy boots echoing on the grass and then the concrete as he made his way into the centre of the estate. He was the first to arrive at the playground and to begin with he could see nothing, then a shadow of movement close to a wall by his left caught his attention. He made as if he were continuing to walk forward but suddenly dashed to the side, catching the driver of the BMW, who thought he had gone unnoticed and was struggling to go on any further. Exhausted, slightly concussed and with a blinding headache, the driver was in no fit state to offer any more resistance. 'I've got him, Colin,' he called out. 'Help me to cuff him.'

By now residents of the estate had come on to their balconies to see what was going on, many of them descending to the lower level for a closer look. These late arrivals knew nothing of the events that preceded the arrest. All they saw was a big white policeman with a truncheon in his hand, holding on to a much smaller black man who was already bleeding from a deep head wound.

'Look, they're killing him,' called an angry voice.

'We look after our own,' said another.

'Let's get the pig bastards,' cried yet another.

Marsh and Ash had cuffed the man and were dragging him back towards the car when the first missile landed. The half-brick hit the dirt just a few inches from where Marsh was walking. More stones and bricks rained down as Marsh and Ash began to run with their prisoner back to their car.

'Urgent assistance, urgent assistance,' Ash barked into his radio. 'We're coming under attack. There's a hostile crowd on the . . .' Ash never finished the sentence. The rock caught him just under the brim of his helmet and he sank to the ground, blood pouring into his eyes. Marsh left the prisoner and went to the aid of his fallen colleague, dragging him into the car while wincing with pain as stones and bricks struck his back and legs. Locking the doors and squeezing himself into the driving seat, he slammed the Rover into reverse and shot backwards out of the estate, a hail of missiles hitting the windscreen and smashing it to pieces.

Kaitlyn enjoyed playing computer games and watching films with the rest of the gang, but there were some movies she wanted to see over and over again and was almost too embarrassed to admit it to the others. She saved up those films for the nights she wasn't seeing the gang.

They in turn appreciated the fact that every now and then Kaitlyn needed 'thinking time' if she was going to come up with the kind of first-class plans that had helped boost their profits while keeping them well under the police radar.

It was after she had watched *Scarface* for the third time that Kaitlyn went out and bought herself a hardback notebook and a set of pens. Curled up in her bed at night with the video whirring away in the background, the volume turned up high to drown out the noise of the sirens from the streets below, and a joint clutched between the fingers of her left hand, she began to write.

1 Never get too greedy.
2 The market for heroin is going to saturate itself. Heroin addicts make poor customers.
3 Cocaine is the future. Cocaine is where the money is.

Kaitlyn bit the end of her pen for a few moments as her thoughts ticked away. Then she continued:

4 The price of cocaine will fall dramatically if the level of supply is increased. This will open up the drug to a far wider market.

Her note-taking was disturbed by a frantic banging on the door of her home. Kaitlyn glanced at the clock. It was a little after nine. She wondered who it could be and hoped to high heaven it wasn't one of her mother's clients. Filled with frustration and curiosity, she went to the door and opened it.

'Where have you been?' asked Errol.

'What are you talking about? What's going on?'

Errol shook his head slowly. 'I don't believe this. You don't know anything about it, do you? The whole country's going mad. There are riots going on in Brixton, Broadwater Farm in Tottenham and Toxteth in Liverpool. We're gonna have one too. Right here on the estate. Gary's organising it. He wants to get back at the police for all the hassle they've been giving him. Check it out!'

Errol stood to one side and indicated the balcony behind him. Kaitlyn took a few steps forward and looked down. A large crowd had gathered on the green in the middle of the estate. Some were armed with baseball bats and various weapons. Others were carrying bottles filled with clear liquid with pieces of cloth stuffed into the ends. Dozens of Molotov cocktails were ready and waiting. A little further away, a few streets back from the estate, Kaitlyn could see a long, slow line of police vehicles moving forward, the officers carrying shields for protection. They had their truncheons drawn, ready for action.

'Come on,' said Errol enthusiastically. 'Let's get down there before we miss all the fun.'

'No,' said Kaitlyn sharply. 'Not down there, the police are on their way. I've got a better idea. Where are Jacob and Louisa?'

'They're downstairs waiting for you.'

'Tell them to get to the top of block C. Then we'll be able to see everything. If it really kicks off we can always come down later.'

'Great idea. See you up there.'

*

The police were already stretched due to the other riots going on that same evening, and were getting reinforcements from Surrey, Sussex, Hampshire and Kent, and had sent several vans full of officers to the estate to try to finish the arrest of the BMW driver and detail some of those responsible for the attack on Marsh and Ash, but almost as soon as they arrived they found themselves outnumbered by an angry crowd intent on causing havoc and damage.

Over fifty officers in full riot gear with perspex shields held out in front of them tried to advance into the crowd, hoping to snatch a few of the ring leaders, but had to retreat under a hail of missiles. A section of the crowd had begun kicking down one of the low walls bordering the play area and using the loose brick and chunks of mortar as weapons. The officers tried to make it back into the van but the attack was so heavy that they were forced to take cover behind it and then run for their lives. The crowd surged forward and grabbed dozens of abandoned shields, letting down the tyres on the vans and covering the sides with graffiti.

Back-up arrived at the scene and immediately moved into reverse, knocking over a woman as she tried to get out of the way. A split-second later there was a huge 'woosh' as a fire hydrant was broken open, sending a forty-foot gush of water high into the air. Some of the residents had upturned bins and other debris from around the estate to form makeshift barricades. A group of teenagers had managed to push a car into the narrow alleyway between two sets of flats and were dousing it with petrol, ready to set it on fire the moment the police began their charge.

From their vantage point on high, the gang could see the advancing police lines draw to a halt as the officers in command briefed them about their plans for the evening. At the same time the crowds in the centre of the estate became increasingly agitated as they waited for the confrontation.

The four friends sat as they always did, their legs dangling over the ledge of the roof and clouds of smoke rising above their heads from the joints held between their fingers. They alternated between sipping from large cans of beer and smoking their spliffs.

'This is like watching a film.' Errol giggled. 'Only better. Fuck, this stuff is strong. What did you say it was called?'

Jacob eagerly puffed away. 'Skunk. It's this new variety, grown especially to be stronger than the regular stuff. It's amazing, isn't it?' The four friends nodded in agreement.

'From now on, this is the only stuff I'm gonna smoke,' said Louisa. 'I mean, who wants a hamburger when you've got fillet steak.'

'But sometimes you feel like a hamburger, don't you?' said Kaitlyn.

'Trust you to try and get all deep on me. Hey, what's going on down there?'

For the past hour the chanting and shouting had been building up in both rhythm and volume as the crowd grew more and more anxious, but then, suddenly, the noise had begun to die down.

Four pairs of eyes shifted to gaze on the scene below. Gary was in the middle of the square, standing on an upturned dustbin so that he towered above the crowd. He seemed to be explaining something that took lots of hand gestures.

'What's he saying?'

'I don't know, Errol, if you shut the fuck up then maybe we can hear,' said Jacob.

They could catch only the odd stray word – 'disappointed, cancelled, home', nothing more. But no one seemed to be doing anything. The crowd began chanting more and more loudly and eventually Gary got down from his makeshift podium and walked through to the back of the estate.

'What the hell's going on?' said Louisa.

'Don't know, but it looks like he's fucking off for the night,' said Errol.

'But why the fuck would he do something like that? The police are right there, ripe for a good kicking. And nobody wants to give it to them more than Gary,' added Kaitlyn.

As he vanished out of sight a huge orange flash lit up the sky. Someone had thrown a petrol bomb. The flames spread along the ground rapidly, licking at the bottom of the abandoned riot van and making the already nervous police officers surveying the scene even more wary.

Up on the roof, the members of the gang looked at one another. There was no need for words. They all knew exactly what to do.

'Have you got any bottles?' asked Kaitlyn.

'There's a whole bunch of milk bottles down in the flat, and I've got an old T-shirt we can tear into rags, but what are we gonna do for petrol?' asked Jacob.

'We can use anything. Spirits, perfume. Just see what you can find.'

'And while you're at it, why don't you have a look and see if you can find any more of this skunk,' asked Louisa.

'I've got a whole bag back in the flat. Do you want me to go and get it?'

'Do bears shit in the woods? Of course I want you to go and get it.'

'I'll come with you,' said Errol. 'I want to pick up a couple more beers.'

There were a few moments of silence as Louisa watched the scene below. When she glanced over at Kaitlyn she saw she was gazing blankly into space. 'What are you thinking?'

'I've just realised something. For years I've assumed that Gary was the main man in these parts, that he was the one in control of everything.

I don't know why, I just assumed it was that way.'

'But it is, isn't it?' said Louisa. 'He's the one with all the drugs, he recruits all the couriers. He must be the top man, or at least very, very near the top.'

'Nah. What happened here tonight, you can see it on his face. He hates what the police round here do and he'd do anything to get back at them and give them a bloody nose. If he was trying to call it off, then it wasn't his decision, it was someone else telling him what to do.'

'Who?'

'I don't know. But I'm gonna find out.'

'Be careful, Kaitlyn. Top man or not, Gary's not someone you want to fuck about with.'

Another pause.

'Louisa.'

'Yeah?'

'Did I ever tell you about my brother?'

'Eh?'

Kaitlyn made eye contact with her friend and saw that although they were looking directly at one another, she wasn't really seeing anything. Her eyes were virtually glazed over and rolling back in her head as the super-strong cannabis took effect. 'Never mind.'

It was a few moments before Errol and Jacob returned with a selection of makeshift Molotov cocktails. Kaitlyn grabbed the nearest one, lit the fuse and threw it hard into the centre of the advancing police line. The bottle smashed into a thousand pieces with an enormous 'pop' sound and a ball of orange flame engulfed the officers around it.

'Bullseye, great shot,' said Jacob.

'We're cooking bacon tonight,' added Errol. 'My turn next.'

Kaitlyn watched as one of the senior officers back on the ground pointed up at the roof and went off to make a radio call.

'My turn now,' said Jacob.

'No, wait,' said Kaitlyn. 'Wait for the lines to re-form. They'll be a better target then. If we throw too many of them right away they'll keep out of range.'

It took ten minutes for the police lines to move close enough for Jacob's own shot to strike home. All four members of the gang raised their hands in the air and danced with delight.

'My turn, my turn,' screeched Louisa.

'No way,' said Kaitlyn. 'You're too out of it.'

'I'm not. Anyway, I know how to sharpen myself up.'

Louisa reached into her back pocket and retrieved a square of paper, which she unwrapped to reveal a small amount of an off-white powder.

'Is that cocaine?' asked Kaitlyn.

'Sure is. I was going to share it with you all later, but I think the time is right now.' Louisa put a finger in her mouth, then dipped it in the powder, rubbing some on the outside of her gums. 'Oooh, it tingles. Oh, wow, you really ought to try this, Kaitlyn, it's amazing.' The more Louisa dipped, the faster she spoke and the more intense her words became. 'I gotta say, you guys are just the best, you're the fucking best and I really mean that. I mean, no one in the world could have better friends than you guys, you're all fucking brilliant, every last one.'

Within seconds the powder was all gone and Louisa was marching back and forth across the roof with boundless energy. 'Those fucking pigs, they think they can come here and do what they want. Well, I say fuck them, I say let's fucking give it to them.'

Below, the riot was in full swing. Officers in full riot gear had made a series of baton charges, snatching two or three members of the crowd each time, but the numbers were growing far faster than they could make arrests as news of the disorder spread like wildfire. Hundreds of youths from nearby estates were on their way to join them. Television crews had arrived and set up camp to film the bedlam for the late-night bulletins and beyond.

Back on the roof, Louisa marched past the place where Jacob had set down the two remaining Molotov cocktails and picked one up, igniting the cloth end with her lighter. She held the bottle high above her head. 'Come on, then, you bastards. Come on, then, you fucking bastards.' Louisa looked down to the ground to work out where to throw her missile, but just then an enormous gust of wind and noise hit her from behind. The four people on the roof turned to see the huge police helicopter, hovering like a giant beetle in the sky, directly in front of them.

'You are under arrest. Put down your weapons and lie face down on the ground,' said a metallic voice from the helicopter's loudspeaker. 'This is the police, you are all under arrest.'

Kaitlyn, Errol and Jacob dived to the ground – they knew they could always get away later – but Louisa was still standing, staring directly at the helicopter as if she couldn't quite understand or believe what she was seeing. One hand was still high in the air, the flaming cloth was burning fast back towards the bottle. It was only when the flames touched her hand that Louisa snapped back into life. Her hand shook in shock and pain, and a few drops of burning liquid spilled out on to the top of her head. Louisa screamed in agony as her hair became a ball of flame. She dropped the bottle beside her and more flames leapt from the floor to her jeans. The wind from the helicopter blades fanned the fire, which rapidly spread across her whole body.

'Oh, my God, oh, my God,' screeched Louisa, hitting her body with her hands in an effort to douse the fire. Kaitlyn, Errol and Jacob got up and rushed forward to help, but Louisa was moving round in frantic circles, panicking as the flames grew around her.

'Louisa, look out,' screamed Kaitlyn, but it was too late. She had lost her footing and slipped over the edge. Kaitlyn reached the side of the roof just in time to see her friend's fiery body smash into a balcony below with a sickening crunch, before continuing its plunge down into the heart of the crowd below.

* * *

Christopher Tobin rubbed his bleary eyes and let out a long yawn. Paul Tobin whipped round to see his son standing in the doorway, reached out and turned off the television set. 'How long have you been standing there? What's wrong?' he asked, a tinge of panic in his voice.

Paul and Jane were sitting watching the evening news. The lead story had been live coverage of the various London riots including the one at the Roxford estate where a camera crew had managed to capture the horrific image of what appeared to be a flaming person falling from the roof of one of the blocks.

Jane had been shocked by the images – the sheer brutality of the people living in the area and the enormous level of hatred they had for the police. It was a world away from her own experience and something she could never hope to understand. It was the same for Paul, but for the fact that he had been there and seen the conditions for himself. For days after his visit he found himself looking at Christopher and wondering if he had managed to get away from the Roxford completely clean, or whether something from the estate remained in his blood.

Christopher yawned again. 'I can't sleep. Can I stay

up and watch TV?' Jane and Paul looked at one another. There was no need for words.

'Not tonight, darling,' said Jane sweetly. 'There's nothing for you to watch at this time of night. Why don't you go back up to bed and I'll read to you until you feel sleepy. We can finish *Mrs Frisby and the Rats of NIMH* if you like.'

Christopher smiled. He was more than capable of reading the book himself but there was something incredibly comforting about being read to. His mum was particularly good at it, giving each of the characters a different voice and throwing in the occasional funny sound effect. She was much better than the people on *Jackanory*. 'That would be great,' he said, turning and heading back up the stairs to his room.

Chapter Sixteen

An inquest into the death of Louisa Dorothy Briggs was opened and adjourned, two days after her fatal fall and a full week before her remains were due to be buried.

Kaitlyn had never been to a funeral before, at least not one that she could remember. Angela's father had died long before she was born, while her mother had passed away soon after Angela moved on to the Roxford estate. The only person who had died whom Kaitlyn had been close to was Mrs Jenkins, the elderly next-door neighbour she had sometimes helped out with her shopping. Kaitlyn liked her well enough, but losing Louisa was like losing her brother all over again. She had spent many, many hours grieving over the loss of Christopher, but at least she could take comfort from the fact that he was still alive and having a good life with some other family. With Louisa, this really was the end.

Errol dropped the tough-man act for once and cried openly, even in public, over the course of the days that followed. Jacob simply became silent and rarely said a word about what he was feeling, even to Kaitlyn. In many ways Louisa had been the glue that had bound the other members of the gang together.

With her gone, there seemed to be a possibility that everything would fall apart.

The weeks that followed were hard. Kaitlyn needed time to come to terms with what had happened but there simply didn't seem to be any. First the police wanted to question her. Although they could not be certain that she and the others had been up on the roof along with Louisa, they strongly suspected it.

But almost as soon as it began, the police investigation faded away to nothing. When senior officers started probing into the incident they realised they themselves might end up being blamed for the death. Although the pilot and officers inside the helicopter had initially been suspended, they had soon been restored to full duties, adding further insult to those on the estate who did indeed blame the police for Louisa's death.

The night after the funeral Kaitlyn made her way back to her room, reached under her bed and took out a small folder. Inside, there was a picture of her and Christopher as children, smiling and laughing as she danced with him balanced on her hip. Kaitlyn then picked up a picture of herself, Louisa and Jacob that Errol had taken one day on the top of block C. She reached down and ran a finger gently along the outline of Louisa's face. Then she put them back inside the folder, shut it and placed it back under her bed.

The inquest, funeral and short-lived police investigation had all taken place under the glare of the news cameras, the same cameras that had recorded Louisa's fatal fiery plunge. The reporters were everywhere. They would push notes through the doors of flats offering huge sums of money in exchange for pictures of Louisa or information about her life on the estate. A few residents were all too eager to sell their stories and articles about the Roxford soon began to appear. One headline said it was HELL ON EARTH, while another described it as 'the most deprived housing estate in Europe'.

Gary had been furious. Dealing still continued but the heavy police and media presence made it far more difficult. Many casual customers, not wishing to be arrested or filmed, chose to buy their supplies elsewhere.

As life on the Roxford slowly returned to normal, so the dealing continued and Kaitlyn was forced to go back to work. At first she hated the idea, but when she thought about Gary and the fact that increasingly he lived his life away from the estate, she began to see things differently. If she could become a bigger part of the drug operation and take a far larger slice of the profits, she might be able to get her and her mother off of the estate and back to the life they had once known.

Kaitlyn came to realise that Louisa had been the closest thing to a mother figure in her life since Christopher had been taken away and her own mother had sunk deep into the misery of heroin addiction.

Kaitlyn soon began to understand that unless she took drastic action, she would before long lose her mother too.

Kaitlyn arrived for her appointment at the doctor's surgery just as the early morning crowd was starting to disperse. There were, for once, half a dozen empty seats in the tiny waiting room and only a few elderly patients quietly reading newspapers, while coughing or spluttering and waiting for their turn. A silver-haired woman whom Kaitlyn recognised from the estate caught her eye and gave her a smile. Kaitlyn smiled back politely, then turned her eyes to the floor in front of her. She was in no mood to make small talk. Not today.

It was a relief that only a few moments later the nurse called her name and she made her way along the short corridor into Dr Taylor's consulting room. She had seen the doctor perhaps five times in her entire life, always in the company of her mother, for minor ailments. This was the first appointment she had been to alone.

'Hello, Kaitlyn, nice to see you. What seems to be the trouble?'

Dr Taylor was in his late fifties and overworked to the point of exhaustion, particularly since the surgery on the estate itself had shut down, but always made an effort to be kind to his patients. With Kaitlyn having recently turned fifteen he had already assumed that, like other girls of her age who came to him, she wanted advice on contraception and to see if she could go on the pill without her mother finding out.

Kaitlyn shifted forward in her seat. 'Anything I say to you, you have to keep confidential, right?'

'Essentially, yes, but because of your age there are some things I cannot prescribe without the permission of a parent.'

Kaitlyn's brow furrowed with confusion. She had no idea what he was talking about. Then she got it. 'You think I want to go on the pill or something? Don't be daft. I don't want anything from you,' she explained. 'I need some advice. My mum's addicted to heroin and I need to find out how to get her off of it.'

It was, perhaps, the very last thing Dr Taylor had expected to hear. But ever the professional he made notes as he questioned her about how long Angela had been taking the drug, how often she did so and how much she spent on her habit. Finally he sat back and began to dispense his advice. 'What you have to understand, Kaitlyn, is that your mum is being controlled by her addiction,' he told her. 'The reality, I'm afraid, is that no matter how much you love her and how often you tell her, beg her and plead with her to see reason, she will not. She is blinkered and will not listen. When people take drugs they hear what they want to hear and only see what they want to see. She doesn't really notice the hurt and pain you're going through and won't until she stops.

'If you want to save her, the drugs are only half the problem. You have to identify what it was that drove her to take them in the first place and solve that problem. If you don't do that, she'll get clean but she'll just end up right back on them again.'

'So getting her off the estate isn't the answer,' said Kaitlyn.

'It might be part of it, but it won't stop her getting addicted again.'

'So what should I do?'

'There are detox centres, places where they can take your mother in and keep her in a safe, drug-free environment. They'll look after her health, help her through withdrawal and keep a careful eye on what she eats and drinks. At the end of it, somewhere between two and four weeks, she'll come out and she'll be completely clean.'

'That sounds great. When can she go?'

Dr Taylor held up his hand. 'There are a couple of things to consider first. For one, these places aren't prisons, they're just clinics. If your mother doesn't want to go, doesn't want to give up, there is nothing they can do to force her. And if she decides to quit after a couple of days and walk out, there are no bars on the windows to stop her getting away.'

Kaitlyn nodded to show she understood. It was all very well her coming to the doctor and asking for help, but the first step was to persuade Angela that she needed to give up. 'The other thing,' Dr Taylor continued, 'is that there is a huge waiting list. I know a few people at some of the clinics and I can pull some strings, but you're still looking at at least three months before a place comes up.'

Kaitlyn bit her lip. 'As long as that?'

'I can't promise it won't be even longer. There's a huge amount of demand for this kind of service and a woefully inadequate supply. It's a scandal, really. The alternative is to go private, but that's expensive, you're talking several thousand pounds. Tell you what, come back and see me next week and I'll see what I can do for you.'

It was dark by the time Kaitlyn got home and she was completely exhausted. It had been more than two weeks since Louisa's funeral but she still missed her friend terribly. She wandered through the flat, not even knowing if her mother was home, went through into the kitchen to get a drink, putting her heavy bag down on the counter, then went straight to bed. She was asleep almost as soon as her head hit the pillow.

It wasn't until the next morning, just before she set off to work, that Kaitlyn realised she had left her bag in the kitchen. She rushed back to collect it. She had brought back six wraps of heroin but when she looked in the bag they had all gone. Her brow wrinkled in concentration. 'What the fuck?' She knew for a fact that she hadn't sold them and she certainly hadn't left them somewhere. She crouched down on the floor by the side of the kitchen cupboard, checking the lino to ensure they had not somehow slipped out of the top of the bag. Nothing.

She rushed along to the door of her mother's room. She raised her hand as if to knock but immediately thought better of it. She pushed against the door hard but something was blocking it. 'Are you in there? What the hell's going on? Where's my stuff?'

She pushed again, and the chair that was holding the door back snapped in half and it sprang open. Inside, Kaitlyn looked around for her mother. She found her on the far side of the bed, slumped down and asleep, a needle behind her. On the floor were the empty packets of drugs that Angela had stolen and shared with her friends while Kaitlyn had been sleeping.

Kaitlyn could not control her anger. She let out a stream of obscenities and her mother woke up. 'Mum, what the hell have you done?'

'What do you mean what have I done? You're still my daughter, you're still living under my roof. Whatever you bring into this house belongs to me. You should know that by now.'

'You stupid bitch, don't you know anything? That's not my stuff. That belongs to Gary. I still owe him the money for that. What are you trying to do? I'm gonna have to pay for that lot out of my own pocket!'

Angela slapped Kaitlyn's face.

Kaitlyn paused for a second, tears welling up in her eyes. She wanted to slap her mother back but she couldn't bring herself to do it. Instead, she spoke: 'So I'll just tell Gary you took his drugs and shot them all up your arm.'

'You think I'm scared of him. What can he possibly do to me? You can see what my life is like. What can he possibly do to me that I can't do to myself? No one can hurt me more than I already have. If he lays one finger on me, if he comes after me I will tell the police all about his little scheme. You think I don't know what's been going on, the way he's been using all the kids from the estate to run his drugs for him. You think you're so clever, you think you are so grown up. Well, let me tell you, little lady, you don't know nothing.'

Kaitlyn looked hard at her mother. Her youthful good looks had all gone. She could not focus her eyes when she spoke. In fact, Kaitlyn realised there was no point in saying anything in return because her mother was incapable of listening. Angela's relationship with her daughter, just like her relationship with all her former friends, had completely broken down. Her only loyalty now was to the needle. Her life revolved around it.

Later that night Kaitlyn sat in her bedroom smoking a joint, when suddenly the taste and smell of the mix of cannabis and tobacco repulsed her. She took the spliff out of her mouth and cast it out of the window. She'd had enough. She wouldn't be doing that any more. From now on, she wanted to make sure she always had a clear head.

Kaitlyn had returned to the doctor a week after her first appointment and was assured that a place for her mother should be available in around twelve weeks. That only left the problem of how to persuade Angela to attend detox, but Kaitlyn figured she would cross that bridge when she came to it.

As it was, she never got the chance. The weeks went by and Kaitlyn was only too well aware that her mother's condition was getting worse. She was using more and more heroin, far more than the free stuff Gary supplied and far more than Kaitlyn could skim off that which she gave to others. Deep black track marks ran the length of Angela's forearms and cold sores developed on her lips. She now looked so terrible that only the most undiscerning clients came to call at the flat, most of them addicts themselves eager to trade poor quality heroin for sex. As the quality of the heroin went down, so the ailments Angela suffered increased. Once she had injected powder that had been mixed with ground brick dust. The mixture created a large abscess on her calf, which soon burst and bled profusely.

At the end of the three months Kaitlyn returned to the doctor, only to be told that the place he had hoped would be made available to Angela had been taken by someone else deemed more deserving. It would be at least another three months before he would be able to do anything for her mother. But Kaitlyn knew that in another three weeks, let alone three months, her mother would in all likelihood be dead.

Something had to be done. Soon.

Chapter Seventeen

February 1986

Angela slowly undid the paper wrap and swore softly as some of the white powder that she was trying to tip into the spoon spilled out on to the floor. 'Oh fuck,' she hissed, scraping as much of it up with her finger as she could.

She reached into her pocket and retrieved half a lemon, which had already begun to have traces of mould round the edges. She took her syringe and plunged it deep inside the fruit, withdrawing a little of the juice. She then held the syringe over the spoon and squirted some of the fluid on to the powder, using the tip of the needle to mix it until it had all dissolved and left only a cloudy liquid.

When Kaitlyn returned to the lounge, Angela was sitting hunched over a chair, sobbing softly. 'What is it, Mum?'

Angela looked up, clumps of filthy matted hair falling round her face. 'I can't find a vein, they've all gone.'

Kaitlyn smiled kindly. 'Do you want me to do it for you?'

Angela smiled back. It had been years since Kaitlyn

had volunteered to do that and Angela had all but given up asking. Kaitlyn knelt in front of her mother and injected her in the back of the knee. 'Thanks, babe,' said Angela, before passing out into her world of dreams.

Kaitlyn waited a few moments to check Angela was OK, holding her hand in front of her mouth to make sure she was still breathing, then moved into the living room, through the hallway and slipped quietly out of the front door. She made her way up to Errol's flat and knocked gently until he and Jacob came to the door. 'OK,' she said. 'Let's do it.'

Angela woke up five hours later, a dull pain ringing in the back of her head. For a few moments she was confused about where she was but this was such a common feeling that she paid it no attention.

Slowly she realised that she did not recognise her surroundings. This too was nothing out of the ordinary. She had often woken up in the homes of some of the men living on the estate who had paid her for sex or given her drugs in exchange for sexual favours. But there was something slightly familiar about this room. After ten minutes or so the answer slowly dawned. It was Kaitlyn's room. She had passed out and somehow woken up in Kaitlyn's room. Only there was something not quite right about it.

A large wooden panel had been nailed tightly over the window, two big buckets stood in the corner, one full of water and the other empty. Several bars of chocolate had been placed on the floor where the dressing table had once been. Most of the furniture had been removed except for the futon bed, a small side table with a reading light and a stack of magazines.

Soon after she had passed out, Errol and Jacob had arrived at the flat and helped Kaitlyn to drag her mother into the specially prepared room. Now, all three stood guard outside, waiting for Angela to come round. Kaitlyn was determined that her mother was going to kick her heroin habit and that meant going through cold turkey whether she wanted to or not.

It took a few moments for Angela to realise where she was and what was happening. The wave of anger hit her like an avalanche. She tried the handle of the door, gently at first and then more forcefully, beating her fists against it and screaming like a wild animal.

Outside the door Errol turned to Kaitlyn, concern etched on his face. 'Are you sure you know what you're doing?'

'I'm sure.'

There was a moment of silence between the pair, broken only by the sound of Angela's frantic hammering on the inside of the metal door.

'You think she knows that?' asked Errol.

'I've tried telling her but she's not exactly in the mood to listen to anything I say at the moment. I'm sure it's going to be fine. It will peak in two or three days, that's when it will be really bad. But by the end of the week it will pretty much be all over. No one has ever died of withdrawal.'

'So you're gonna keep her locked up for a week?'

'Actually, I'm going to make it two. Even though she'll be clean she's still going to be an addict. The extra week should help her put some distance between herself and the habit. I hope.'

Finally Angela started to scream: 'Kaitlyn. What are you doing? What the fuck are you doing? Let me out of here.'

'You're staying in, Mum,' came the reply. 'You're staying in until you're clean.'

'Let me out of here, you fucking bitch.'

'It's for your own good.'

'Let me out of here right now, Kaitlyn, otherwise I'm gonna give you such a beating. I can't believe you're doing this to me. You fucking stupid bitch.'

'I want to make you better.'

'You're killing me. You're fucking killing me, you stupid cow. What are you doing to me? Why, Kaitlyn, why?'

Kaitlyn turned to Errol. She was more than a little embarrassed and not anxious to share this moment, even with her closest friends. 'Look, she's not going anywhere for a while and I can handle this. Why don't you get a start on the round and come back a bit later.'

Over the course of the next few hours the screams and obscenities got worse, then they turned into desperate pleading. 'Please, please, Kaitlyn, please let me out,' Angela sobbed. 'You can't do this to me.'

'I have to, Mum. Don't you understand? I have to.'

'But I need to go to the toilet. What am I supposed to do?'

'Mum, that's what the bucket is for.'

'You expect me to go in a bucket? What do you think I am, some kind of animal?'

'Mum, it's the only way.'

'You let me out of here right now, you bitch, otherwise I'm going to kill you.'

Inside her makeshift prison cell Angela Wilson was terrified. The few short times she had been forced to go a few hours between fixes had taught her that, from her point of view at least, the agonies of withdrawal were only too real and something she had no desire to experience for herself. She could already feel her body starting to readjust to functioning without the drug. The craving was more intense than ever, strengthened by the fact that she had no idea just how long she was going to remain locked in this room. She could feel her bowels starting to churn, knots in her stomach growing tighter and tighter, pain from her thighs as her leg muscles began to cramp. She knew what was coming, that it was only going to get worse and worse. She couldn't believe her own daughter was going to make her suffer like this.

Gathering up her remaining strength, she flung

herself at the door, pounding with her fists and kicking with her feet. 'Let me out of here, Kaitlyn. You hear me? Let me out of here right now.' Her protests continued until all her strength had gone and she fell against the door and slowly slumped to the floor, the tears falling down her face like rain.

On the other side of the door, Kaitlyn was doing the same.

When Angela was so desperate that she could hold it in no longer she squatted over the bucket and released her bowels. The enormous relief she felt was instantly countered by the dreadful stench that rose up and filled the room. Angela was so disgusted with what she had done that she picked up the bucket and threw it against the door, splashing faeces all across the front part of the room.

Kaitlyn paced around the flat anxiously, listening to the sounds of her mother going crazy inside her cage. She turned up the volume on the television to drown out the noise but it still cut through.

When she had passed a tray of food through the slot, Angela had thrown that against the wall too. Kaitlyn had been careful to make sure there was nothing sharp, nothing Angela could use to harm herself, but still she worried. She wondered whether she was doing the right thing, whether her mother was simply too heavily addicted to heroin ever to be cured. And even if she did manage to get her off the drugs by keeping her locked up for two weeks, what would it do to their relationship? Angela might hate her for putting her through such an ordeal. But the more Kaitlyn thought about it, the more this seemed to be the only way.

She had known too many people who had been prescribed the heroin substitute methadone, only to become as addicted to that as they had been to heroin. The idea of replacing one drug with another seemed like nonsense. The only cure, Kaitlyn was convinced, was not to be taking any drugs of any kind.

Jacob and Errol returned later that evening, but Angela's rage had hardly died down at all. Kaitlyn dared not open the special hatch they had built into the door for fear of what might come flying through. It already sounded as though Angela had smashed the side-table, upturned the bed and thrown the bucket of water at the door.

By the time Jacob and Errol came back the following morning, having made their rounds, no sounds were coming out of the room. Kaitlyn listened hard. Nothing. She pressed her ear up against the door. No sound. As silently as possible she undid the padlock, bracing herself against the door, with Jacob and Errol standing guard behind her just in case it was all a ruse. She placed the lock gently on the carpet and pulled open the door. All three had to hold their noses because of the terrible stench.

Inside, in the far corner on the edge of the futon, was Angela. She was curled up in the foetal position, ghostly pale and shivering in the most alarming way.

Her skin was covered with goose bumps and paper thin. A mixture of food and faeces covered the walls, the bedside table had been reduced to splinters and chunks of mattress had been bitten off. Two large pools of vomit covered the floor just to the right of where Angela lay. She looked up to see her daughter enter the room and tried to speak, but no words came out of her lips. Instead, she retched hard but only a few dribbles of bile emerged. She had been throwing up so hard and so long that there was nothing left inside her. She was going into full cold turkey and felt as if her insides were being ripped apart.

Kaitlyn gasped with shock at the sight of her mother before rushing to her side. With Errol's and Jacob's help she laid her flat on the mattress and began mopping her feverish brow with a wet tea towel. 'It's going to be OK, Mum,' she whispered softly, 'it's going to be OK.'

Over the next few hours, while Angela shivered and sweated, Kaitlyn cleaned up. Every now and then the doorbell would ring and one of Angela's regular clients would come to the door. Jacob and Errol sent them away. Sometimes they had to slip out a blade to show they were serious, but not often. A flex of Errol's bulging muscles or a hard stare from Jacob's dead eyes was usually more than enough to send the punters scampering off.

That night, Kaitlyn held up Angela's head and tipped a few spoonfuls of soup into her mouth.

Almost as soon as the food hit her stomach it came rushing back up, spilling out over the floor. Kaitlyn again cleaned up the mess, then went out of the room, locking the door behind her. She collapsed on the floor, leaning back against the wall, silent tears rolling down her cheeks. Now more than ever she simply did not know whether she had done the right thing, whether her mother would ever be well again.

Her thoughts were interrupted by a knock on the door. It was Gary. 'You gonna invite me in?'

Kaitlyn glanced behind her. 'Mum's asleep in the living room, I really don't want to disturb her,' she lied.

'Fair enough, I don't need to see her anyway.'

'What do you want, Gary.'

'Just giving you a heads up. I need you to go to Glastonbury again. It's gonna be a big one. We're gonna make a fortune.'

The previous year Kaitlyn and the rest of the gang had spent a glorious weekend at the music festival, getting stoned, listening to great bands and above all selling tens of thousands of pounds' worth of drugs to eager festival-goers. The event had proved so lucrative for Gary that he had already planned a follow-up.

For Kaitlyn the idea of going back to the festival was a double-edged sword. She had had the time of her life the previous year but on the other hand it would be incredibly strange to be there without Louisa.

'Do we need to talk about this now?'

'Not at all,' said Gary. 'I was just passing by and thought I'd mention it. It's not long away and I don't want you making any other plans.'

'Don't worry, Gary, I won't.'

After seven days the worst of the symptoms had all but faded away. Angela was still weak, but her appetite was slowly starting to increase. She was eating solids, after a week of nothing but soup, and actually managing to keep most of it down. As the days passed so the colour slowly began to return to her cheeks. She looked human again and increasingly like the mother Kaitlyn had grown up with.

The room remained locked, but mother and daughter would spend hours talking, sitting either side of the door.

'Mum,' said Kaitlyn one day, bending down so that she was almost lying on the floor alongside the reinforced bedroom door.

'Yes, babe.'

'Tell me about my dad.'

There was a long pause before Angela started to speak. 'He was a nice man, a really lovely man. We were both young but he was too young to commit to having children, so it was either him or you. If I had stayed with him I would have had to have an abortion.'

Angela reassured her daughter that from the moment she felt the child growing inside her she knew she could never even consider the prospect of getting rid of her and that, no matter how much of a struggle it turned out to be, she would bring up Kaitlyn to the best of her abilities. She felt ashamed of how it had all gone wrong.

A few hours later Kaitlyn had a strong picture of her father in her mind for the first time in her life. She had often wondered what he had been like, what her life might have been if she had grown up with a father as well as a mother.

'You're not . . . you're not going to try to find him, are you?' Angela's voice was loaded with emotion. This was a man who had hurt her more than anyone in her life. Not physically, not like Steve with his kicks and his punches, but emotionally. She had loved him and longed to be a proper family. When she fell pregnant with Kaitlyn she had expected all her dreams to come true. Instead, they were left shattered into a million pieces.

Kaitlyn could feel her mother's pain, even through the door that separated them. 'No, Mum. Don't worry. I wouldn't do that. He has never been a father to me; he wasn't there for all the bad times. Now that you're off the smack, I have even less reason to get to know him.'

In the hours and days that followed Kaitlyn learned how her mother first came to move to the Roxford estate and how at the time it seemed like one of the best places in the world to be living. Along with Angela's late mother, Kaitlyn's grandmother, they had spent hours putting up wallpaper and decorating Kaitlyn's room to make it just the way she would like it. Then Angela moved on to the way her life changed when she met Steve. At first things were good between them and she truly believed that she had found a way to make a fresh start, but the violence began soon after she got pregnant with Christopher.

Angela regularly burst into tears as she recalled the tender times between mother and daughter in those early days and how the drugs she had taken to dull the pain of losing Christopher had pushed the two of them apart. 'I'm so sorry, Kaitlyn,' Angela sobbed. 'I'm so sorry about everything. I couldn't see it before but now I realise I've really messed everything up for both of us. I've made such bad decisions all my life, about men, about drugs, about how to bring up my kids. I've been a terrible mother. I'm sure Chrissy is much better off without me.'

'Don't say that, Mum,' said Kaitlyn gently. 'I know there have been problems and our life has been far from a fairy tale, but you can't say it's all your fault. Anyone would have been struggling to deal with all the things you have dealt with. And at the end of the day, we're talking now, and that's what's important. Let's just look towards the future, let's work out a way to take control of our lives again and get off this estate. When you think about it, that's the thing that's bringing us down most of all.'

Kaitlyn held up one hand and pressed it against the door. Even though they could not see one another, she knew her mother was doing the same. Each felt as close to the other as they ever had.

'Mum, do you remember when Christopher got taken away and I told you I thought it was all my fault for not stopping him from crying sooner, for getting there a few minutes too late?'

Angela thought for a moment, her mind searching through the horrific memories of her life with Steve to find this specific point in time. 'Yes, I remember. I told you not to be so stupid.'

'I know,' said Kaitlyn softly. 'I know you did. But I blamed myself. I still do.'

'But babe, it really wasn't your fault. There was nothing you could have done. I've spent the last few years blaming myself for not picking up Chrissy when I went to lock myself in the bathroom. But all I wanted to do was stop Steve from hitting you. I wasn't thinking straight. I never imagined he'd go after his own son like that.'

Suddenly Kaitlyn's mask cracked. The shield she had been wearing for so long to guard her from the outside world slipped and she began to sob loudly. 'Oh God, Mum, it's my fault, it was all my fault.'

'Darling, what are you talking about?'

'If I hadn't been so slow, if I'd got there quicker, I could have protected him.'

Angela's voice became firm. She breathed deeply, gathering strength in order to project more powerfully. 'Kaitlyn. Stop it. Listen, stop it and listen to me.

What happened to Christopher was nothing to do with you.'

There was a pause before Angela spoke again. When she did her voice was far stronger than before. 'I'm going to make it up to you, darling. You'll see. Things are going to be good again. I'm going to get my life back, go back to work and start bringing some money in.'

'A job? Steady on, Mum. I don't think you've ever had a job in your life, have you?'

'Yeah, but things were different then. You were a little girl. I always planned to get a job when you were a bit older, when you and Chrissy were old enough to look after yourselves but . . . now that things have changed I guess I can do that a little earlier. I want to get a job and I want us to live in a little place by the seaside.'

'I'd like that, Mum,' said Kaitlyn. 'I'd like that a lot.'

Kaitlyn was smiling as she spoke but in her heart she knew her mother's words were little more than empty promises. Like smokers who insist they can give up any time they want to, like alcoholics who swear they only drink to be sociable, drug addicts were renowned for having an overly optimistic view of their chances of beating their addiction. If Angela had been given her own way she would have come out of her makeshift prison after only a few hours, full of promises that she was now 'cured' and would never again touch smack.

The more positive Angela sounded, the more Kaitlyn knew she was deluding herself. Living in a house by the sea was a wonderful dream but until her mother was well and truly cured, a dream was all it would ever be.

* * *

The headmistress indicated the two leather armchairs in front of her desk before sitting down herself. 'Thanks so much for coming in, Mr and Mrs Tobin, I know how busy you both are and how difficult it is to take time out during the day.'

Paul reached across to Jane and squeezed her hand reassuringly. 'That's OK. We can always make time when it comes to Christopher.'

Sally Baxter eyed the couple carefully. They were both well presented and clearly well educated. She knew that Paul Tobin was a leading architect and that Jane had been a successful secretary before giving up work to become a mother. They were just the kind of parents whose children went on to become doctors, barristers and airline pilots. So why on earth was Christopher turning out to be such a little monster?

Earlier that morning Mr Ellsberg, the mild-mannered geography teacher who was also head of the fourth year, had carried out a random inspection of the first-floor boys' toilets at Irvine Secondary School and noticed smoke rings rising out of one of the cubicles. Marching forward and tugging open the half-closed door, Mr Ellsberg found himself face to face with Christopher Wilson and two other boys, all three of them sharing a single cigarette that Christopher was holding. 'What on earth do you think you're doing?' the teacher demanded.

Christopher cocked his head to one side. 'What does it look like I'm doing? I'm having a fag!'

Christopher's remark earned him cheers from his classmates but resulted in an immediate trip to the office of the headmistress, escorted by Mr Ellsberg.

Now, two hours later, Christopher was sitting outside the office on a chair in the corridor and kept his eyes on the floor in front of him as his parents arrived at the school. Once Paul and Jane were inside, he listened hard and tried to hear what was being said on the other side of the door.

'I can't tell you how disappointed I am about this,' Miss Baxter said. 'If this were some isolated incident, I don't think we would have bothered to ask the two of you to come in but we all know that is not the case.' There was no need for any further explanation. Ever since Christopher had enrolled at Irvine he had been involved in numerous fights, arguments with teachers and several other incidents of bad behaviour. At home, despite living in a quiet cul-de-sac, Christopher had somehow taken to hanging around in the park and on the streets with a group of rowdy older children. Paul and Jane felt they were at their wits' end. Christopher was all but out of control.

'The saddest part of all this,' Miss Baxter continued, 'is that Christopher is clearly highly intelligent and more than capable. When he applies himself he does fantastic work and all his teachers say he could easily be in the top five.'

'Really,' said Paul. 'Top five per cent.'

'Not per cent, Mr Tobin, top five. Christopher is one of the brightest pupils in the school.'

The headmistress remained silent for a moment, allowing the news to sink in. Paul allowed himself the slightest smile. After everything that had happened there had been times when he had almost given up hope for Christopher and had been ready to write him off as a lost cause. Now, here he was, being told his son was practically a genius. Sure there were problems with his behaviour, but Christopher still had potential and that was something worth fighting for.

'What can we do?' asked Paul, leaning forward.

'I wasn't doing anything. You can't do that,' Christopher's voice wailed from the back of the car as he was driven home from school. He had just been told that he would lose his allowance for a month and not be permitted out after 6 p.m.

'We have to do it, Christopher. Don't you understand? You have to be punished. Properly punished. Otherwise it's not going to stop. We give you everything, you want for nothing, yet you continue to throw it all back in our faces. When is it going to end?'

Christopher said nothing for a moment, then sat

back heavily in the back seat, his arms folded across his chest. 'It's not fair,' he mumbled.

'Well, young man, that's just one of the lessons you are going to have to learn,' said Paul, looking at his son's reflection in the rear-view mirror. 'Life is never fair.'

* * *

The day that Kaitlyn unlocked the door of her bedroom and let her mother out was the day that Angela realised she had not seen the world clearly for as long as she could remember. It was as if she had been living in a dream and, now that she was finally awake, she wanted to make the most of all the wonders that she had been missing. That first weekend Kaitlyn took her shopping in the West End. Kaitlyn spent hours sitting in a chair by a waiting room as her mother tried on dozens of outfits, each one more expensive and glamorous than the last. They bought nothing but had the time of their lives.

They ate lunch in a cheap but cheerful Italian restaurant close to Harvey Nichols and then went back to shop some more. In the afternoon they passed a photo booth at Marble Arch underground station, fished out some change and took pictures of themselves together.

For Kaitlyn, having her mother clean again was like starting life anew. They had spent so many hours apart, despite living in the same house, that now all she wanted to do was make up for lost time. That night they found an old game of Twister in a cupboard and began to play, stumbling over one another, rolling around on the floor with tears of joy running down their cheeks. It was the most fun either of them had had in ages.

Those first few days had been difficult, Kaitlyn utterly paranoid that the slightest thing would push her mother back into full-scale addiction, but Angela was remarkably strong. She seemed almost relieved that she didn't have to deal with that part of her life any more and busied herself with so many activities that she hoped she would never go back.

One afternoon, about a month later, Kaitlyn and Angela were sitting on the living-room sofa in the flat together drinking tea.

'I know what would brighten this place up,' Kaitlyn said suddenly.

'What, more windows?'

Kaitlyn groaned. 'Oh Mum, what are you? Ten?'

'What, you think you have to be young to make jokes?'

'Not saying that, just seems that when you get past a certain age, things start to fall apart. And it seems to me that a sense of humour is one of them.'

'I just think you didn't get it. Anyway. What will brighten this place up?'

'A coat of paint. I mean, when was the last time you did any decorating here?'

Angela started looking around, scrutinising the walls and the doors. 'God, it's been ages. Just around the time Chrissy was born. Me and your grandma did it together, though I wasn't much help because I was about eight months pregnant.'

'Well, then it's high time we did it again. What colour do you think?'

'You can't go wrong with Magnolia.'

'No way, too boring. I want to give the place a bit of life.'

'Magnolia's lively. It looks great when the sun catches it.'

'It looks like every other flat in this block when the sun catches it. What is it? Do the council get the stuff on the cheap? It's the only colour they ever use. I want something that's really individual. How about we paint one wall one colour and the rest of them something else? I saw a flat like that once and it looked really good.'

'Where did you see a flat like that? In a fun house at the fair?'

'It was in a magazine.'

The two women giggled and gurgled, but then Angela's face hardened and the tone of her voice became serious. 'Listen, Kaitlyn,' she said. 'I know I'm not one to talk, after everything I've done over the years, but I'm worried about you. When you first got into the drugs stuff it was so that Gary would leave me alone and I knew there was no choice if I wasn't going to get hurt. But all that's changed now. All that changed a long time ago. I don't owe him any money and you don't owe him any favours. But all I see is you getting more and more involved and I don't like it. I don't want it.'

Kaitlyn slowly lit a cigarette and took a long drag on it before passing it over to Angela. 'I'm not saying this because I want to hurt you, but don't you think it's a bit late for you to start being a mother now? I mean, there was all that time when things were going on with Steve and you weren't really there, and then all the time that you've been on drugs when you've been here but your mind, your soul, have been miles away. And now finally I've got you back, but that doesn't give you the right to tell me how to live my life, not when I've done so much of what I've done to help you out.'

Angela said nothing. Without the free drugs Kaitlyn had been given by Gary in return for carrying out her courier work, Angela would never have survived as long as she had.

A week before the Glastonbury festival, Gary was making one of his increasingly rare visits to the Roxford estate. Kaitlyn had proved so effective at organising the distribution of drugs throughout the area and beyond that he was now able to spend far less time on the ground. This in turn meant that he could distance himself from the day-to-day drugs operation and would therefore be more isolated in the event of a police raid. Despite this, he still kept the lion's share of the profits. Life, he thought to himself with a wry smile, could not be better.

His first port of call was the safe house close to

the storehouse where Kaitlyn and the other couriers picked up their drugs each morning. There was little reason for him to attend – Gary simply believed that it was a good idea to show his face every now and then in order to make sure everyone knew who was boss.

The system Kaitlyn had devised meant that the drugs were stored in the storehouse and all the meetings and business discussions took place in the safe house a few doors down. That meant there was somewhere they could all go where, even in the event of a police raid, there would be no evidence against them. While the location of the storehouse changed almost daily, the safe house stayed pretty much the same.

It was while he was visiting the storehouse that Gary made a casual remark about Kaitlyn's mother and her increasing use of heroin.

'Not any more,' said Brian, one of the regular couriers. 'She's off the stuff now. Kaitlyn cured her.'

'What are you talking about?'

'Kaitlyn got her off of it,' Brian continued. 'Locked her up in a room and forced her to go through cold turkey. Reckons they're going to leave the estate and start a new life somewhere. Best of luck to her, don't you think?'

Gary grabbed hold of him and went to strike him but threw him to the ground instead. For all he could think about was the money he was set to lose as a result.

*

The Glastonbury festival of June 1986 was the biggest ever. More than 60,000 revellers attended, 20,000 more than the previous year, to hear hit acts including The Cure, the Psychedelic Furs, The Pogues and Madness.

For Kaitlyn, Errol and Jacob it was great being able to hear so many cool bands but the festival was really about one thing only – getting as many of those 60,000 party-goers to buy drugs from them as they possibly could.

There was no shortage of customers – cannabis was so popular it was almost compulsory and the trio would go from tent to tent offering their wares. Few people had realised the numbers would be so much larger than the year before and, having completely underestimated how much they would need, Kaitlyn found herself having sold virtually all her cannabis and speed by the end of the first day. Traipsing across the field and waiting in line with a stack of change at one of the few public phone boxes, Kaitlyn called Gary on his new car phone and told him the good news. He immediately dispatched one of his workers with fresh supplies and gave Kaitlyn instructions of where to meet the man in order to pick them up.

Later that night, while lying in her sleeping bag inside the tent she was sharing with Jacob – Errol insisted on having a tent all to himself – Kaitlyn could hardly wipe the smile off her face. Since the start of the festival she had already made more money than she could have dreamed of and it was far from over.

The inside of the tent was lit up from the pale glow of the cigarettes she and Jacob were smoking. Then Jacob's soft voice drifted over from beside her. 'It's great this, isn't it?' he said.

'It's wonderful. All that money. Brilliant.'

There was a pause. 'Not only the money,' said Jacob. 'But this. Being here in a tent. Just the two of us.'

Kaitlyn sat up slowly, squinting her eyes to try to see Jacob's face. She could only make out his silhouette and did not know if he was smiling.

She said nothing and the silence continued until Jacob spoke again, his voice hesitant and nervous: 'You know, they say it might get cold later on tonight. I was thinking that, maybe, we should, you know, zip the two sleeping bags together. We'll be a lot warmer that way . . .' His voice fell away into a mumble as his nerves got the better of him.

Kaitlyn reached across and placed her hand gently on his shoulder. 'I think that sounds like a really good idea,' she said in a whisper.

Jacob's eyes grew wide with excitement. 'Really? Great. Well, why don't you . . .'

His words were interrupted by the sound of a zip being undone and a rush of air from the bottom of the tent as the main flaps were opened. A split-second later Errol's head poked into the gap. 'Sorry, lads. Change of plan. I'm kipping here tonight. There's a fucking orgy going on in the tent next to mine. You wouldn't believe the noise they're making – squealing and crying and God knows what. I'm not sure if they're having sex or slaughtering pigs. It's a fucking nightmare. Shift up then, Jacob, I'll come in between the two of you. Oh yeah, and I sometimes snore so I'll say sorry now.'

The next morning the moments of tenderness with Jacob were pushed to the back of her mind as Kaitlyn pondered other matters. Although the work was going well and the money was rolling in, she felt unsettled. She had been anxious about leaving her mother alone for such a long time at such a vulnerable time.

Angela had insisted she go. 'If we're going to get out of here, we're going to need every penny we can get. You can make more at that festival in a couple of days than you can in a couple of months of what you normally do on the estate. You have to go. Please. I'll be fine.'

It had been more than two months since Angela had been clean and, although she had times when she felt life was all too much and that she could really do with another dose of heroin, she had managed to resist.

Kaitlyn had been out overnight a few times but covering Glastonbury properly would mean an absence of at least four days and possibly longer. With no telephone in the flat and Mrs Jenkins the neighbour long since dead, Kaitlyn and Angela devised a system of timed phone calls to a public phone box on the edge of the Roxford. It wasn't always successful. If Angela got there and the box was being used she would have no option but to wait. If Kaitlyn received a busy signal all she could do was keep trying until she finally got through. They had arranged to call one another at 3 p.m. each day but the first two days they simply missed each other.

On the third day Kaitlyn finally got through. 'Hi, Mum.'

'Hello, Babe. How's it going?'

'It's fine. Listen, I'm going to be back in the morning and then we'll start looking for somewhere. Are you going to be OK?'

'Please don't worry, just get on with your work.'

'How are you finding it?'

'It's hard. It's hard but I'm coping. Watching a lot of TV. God, there's a load of shit on during the day.'

Kaitlyn laughed. 'Well, I still think you're better off there than down here.'

'Too many drugs?'

'Too many young people!'

'You cheeky monkey. You wait till you get back here. I'll show you that I've still got a few tricks up my sleeve.'

Kaitlyn replaced the receiver and called Gary just as heavy rain started to fall. She didn't have to worry about whether he would be home – with his new car phone he now toured south London in his BMW, taking calls at his leisure.

'Gary, just to let you know we're packing up and heading back. There's nothing left, it's been a good weekend.'

'That's great, Kaitlyn. But listen, I need you to do me a favour.'

'What?'

'I've got a shipment that's just about to come in any time now and I can't get anyone there. But you're only a few miles away. I want you and the boys to head over, make a meet with the people, pick up the stuff and bring it with you when you come back. It shouldn't take long. A few hours, a day or two at the most.'

Kaitlyn sighed. She was looking forward to getting back home from the festival and this little job would delay her. 'What's in it for me?'

'I'll give you a monkey. I can't say fairer than that.'

The money would be handy for the moving fund Kaitlyn was building. But still there were other issues to consider. 'OK, I'll do it. But I'm worried about my mum. She's expecting me.'

'She's a big girl. She can look after herself.'

'You don't understand. She's . . .' Kaitlyn thought about telling Gary a lie then decided against it. She liked to keep her personal life on a need to know basis and Gary simply didn't need to know about her mother coming off heroin, but under the circumstances she had no choice. 'She's coming off heroin. I'm helping her. I don't really want to leave her on her own for too long.'

'Coming off heroin, eh? Well, that's pretty admirable. How's it going?'

'She's doing well.'

'Tell you what then, Kaitlyn, you do this job for me and I'll look in on her, make sure she's well.'

'You?'

'I have a caring side. Just because you've never seen it doesn't mean it's not there.'

'I believe you although thousands wouldn't. Tell her I'll be back as soon as I can.'

'No problem. Don't worry about a thing. It's all in hand.'

Angela jumped at the sound of the doorbell, moving further into the far corner of the flat each time it sounded. She had no idea who it was, simply that she didn't want to answer. It was only when a slightly familiar voice calling out her name came through the letter box that her curiosity got the better of her and she made her way into the hallway. 'Who is it?' she called out.

'It's Gary. Can I come in? It's brass monkeys out here.'

Angela had seen Gary only occasionally in the past few months. She knew that Kaitlyn worked for him, of course, but he kept a fairly low profile on the estate.

'Wow, Angela,' said Gary, shaking the rain from his hair. 'You look great. Really amazing. I'd heard you'd managed to kick the habit and I just wanted to see for myself. It's really true, isn't it? How long has it been?'

Angela didn't feel particularly comfortable. The last time Gary had been inside the flat he had held a knife to her face and she still bore the small scar just above her cheek. She didn't have much to say but talking about her victory over her addiction was something she wanted to shout out to the whole world. 'Two months and nine days,' she said proudly.

'And you're not tempted to go back to it?'

Angela rolled her eyes. 'Only every minute of every day. But I've got too much to look forward to now. It's like my life is starting all over again, all these new chances and new beginnings. I look at the people I used to hang around with and I can see what I was turning into. I don't want to be like that any more. I've moved on.'

'Well, bugger me. That's incredible, it really is. I take my hat off to you, Angela. I've been in this game a long time and I can count on the fingers of one hand the number of people who have managed to keep off the stuff as long as you have. I just hope it doesn't spread or you're gonna put me out of business.'

'Don't worry, we won't be here that much longer.'

'So I've heard. You're getting out, yeah?'

'That's the plan. We're gonna sub-let at first or do a swap, get away from the estate and the drugs. I just want my life to be the way it was before, before all this happened.'

Gary leaned back against the kitchen counter at a strange angle, his hand balanced precariously on the edge. He was speaking more loudly now, almost shouting for no good reason. 'I'm pleased for you, really I am. But it's a shame too. There's a new batch going around, they reckon it's the best ever, a really pure, sweet high. People are going crazy for it. Cheap too. They call them spider bags. I'm cleaning up. But as you say, you've moved on. How soon before you think you'll be off, then?'

Angela's bottom lip had started to twitch as Gary talked about the spider bags. She had heard about them from the streets too. She took a couple of deep breaths and struggled to compose herself. 'I think Kaitlyn wants me to be clean for six months. If I can stay off the stuff while I'm on the estate, then I can kick it anywhere. She reckons there's no point moving until I'm clean because otherwise the problems will just follow us wherever we go.'

'Clever kid, your girl,' said Gary. 'She's absolutely right.' He straightened up and began walking towards the door. 'I just wanted to say how pleased I am for you. And remember, if you ever need anything, I'll be there for you.' He kept his back towards Angela so that she could not see him smiling.

Angela remained motionless for a few moments,

disturbed by Gary's presence, then moved to the sink to get herself a glass of water. It was as she passed by the counter that she felt something crunch underneath her foot. It was the exact spot that Gary had been leaning over a few seconds earlier. She bent down for a closer look. And there, sitting on the kitchen lino, were two small paper wraps, each with a tiny picture of a spider imprinted on it.

The fifteen kilos of pure heroin had entered the UK via Plymouth earlier that evening. They had been packed into a hidden compartment in the floor of a refrigerated articulated lorry that had set off from Turkey three days earlier. The lorry's main cargo area had been filled from top to bottom with fine tomatoes, a product considered perishable enough to ensure customs officers waved vehicles carrying them through with the minimum of fuss. The vehicle's journey across multiple European borders had been further helped by the fact that the doors of the cargo bay had been given a special seal shortly before departure, which certified that it contained no contraband. The fact that the officials in charge of applying the seal had been paid several thousand pounds to ensure the lorry was not checked too closely was neither here nor there.

Having passed through UK customs without incident, it had stopped first at the warehouse of a major fruit and veg distributor in Newton Abbot, then made its way to the workshop of a lorry maintenance firm a few miles outside Exeter. Here it was parked and left overnight. No attempt was made to extract the heroin. Instead, a close watch was kept on the vehicle and its surroundings using secret CCTV cameras linked to yet another office half a mile away. Years of experience had taught the smugglers that, rather than striking right away, the police and customs both preferred to follow a vehicle suspected of carrying drugs in the hope of catching members of the gang in the act of unloading. Only after twenty-four hours with no sign of any surveillance did the smugglers feel confident enough to remove the heroin. That was when the call had gone out to Gary, who in turn had asked Kaitlyn to go and make the pick-up.

The battered blue Ford Capri bounced along the rough road to the lorry park and Errol brought it to an abrupt halt close to the office building. He and Kaitlyn climbed out and she moved the passenger seat forward to let Jacob out. She took the lead as the trio walked towards the brightly lit concrete cabin.

A stout, wide-bodied man in a heavy overcoat stood guard outside. 'What's your name?' he said in a thick local accent.

'Kaitlyn.'

The man's brow creased as he scrutinised her. 'How old are you?'

'Old enough to know that it's none of your business.'

The man rolled his eyes and nodded his head in the direction of the main door. The gang made their way into the second part of the building. Through the door a thin, weak-looking, middle-aged man sat behind a large desk. He wore an ill-fitting suit and looked deathly pale, almost as if he were a vampire. Two younger men in designer suits were on either side of him, perched on the corners of the desk. Bulges in the waistbands of their trousers under their jackets told Kaitlyn that they were armed, though there was no way of telling if they were carrying guns, knives or coshes. All three were watching a small black-and-white television, which showed an image of the parked lorry.

Kaitlyn didn't like feeling intimidated so she decided to project as much confidence as she could. 'I'm here for Gary's gear,' she said firmly.

'You're early,' said one of the suited men, glancing at his watch. 'We're not expecting you for another couple of hours.'

Kaitlyn frowned. If that was the case then Gary would have had more than enough time to send someone else to make the pick-up instead of her. It had been a long day. Kaitlyn was tired and desperately wanted to go home. The last thing she needed was any more aggravation. 'Is there any reason why we can't take the stuff now?' she asked.

The young man in the suit smiled, looked at the man behind the desk and smiled again, a patronising smile. It was the kind of smile that said she was only a little girl and knew nothing of what was going on with the smuggling gang. 'We're waiting to check it's not being watched,' the man said, turning back to face her. 'There was some suspicious activity in the area a bit earlier; we're just being careful.'

Kaitlyn looked at her watch. She didn't have time for this. She moved close to the desk and scrutinised the television screen. Images from different cameras situated in and around the lorry came into view, changing every few seconds. It didn't take long for Kaitlyn to come up with a plan. 'I think I know a way we can find out if it's clear right away,' she said. The eyebrows of the man behind the desk rose with intrigue as Kaitlyn moved around to where Jacob stood and whispered a few instructions into his ear.

Ten minutes later the television screen showed Jacob walking along the side of the lorry. At first he seemed to be heading directly for the driver's door but then he turned slightly and continued walking towards the rear of the vehicle. To anyone keeping a watch on the lorry, it seemed almost certain that Jacob was heading to the rear doors. In actual fact he was just hiding himself behind the lorry in order to urinate. Ten minutes later, he returned in the Capri to the office building.

'I think we can be pretty sure it's clear now,' said Kaitlyn. 'So it would be great if you could get off your arses and help us load the stuff up.'

One of the suited men scowled and took a step

forward but the man behind the desk held up a hand, silently ordering him to remain still. When he spoke, it was with a strong West Country accent. 'I'm sorry there, missy, we're simple folk here, we'll be getting your things now so that you can be on your way.'

Kaitlyn eyed him curiously. There was something about the accent, something she couldn't quite put her finger on. In any event, she had heard what she wanted to hear.

Angela spent hours pacing back and forth through the flat. As soon as she had found the drugs she had thrown them in the bin but something had made her go back and fish them out. She had sat them on the table in the living room and stared at them, knowing exactly what would happen if she weakened but knowing also that there was nothing she wanted more in the entire world. She had tried going shopping to take her mind off everything but that had been a disaster. As she had walked through the estate, groups of her old junkie friends had called out to her from their hidey-holes in the walkways and corners. Now she felt drawn to them. Shopping helped for a short time but before too long she was recognised by the staff as the woman who had tried to steal from them before and told in no uncertain terms to leave, or the police would be summoned. One of them called her a dirty junkie.

After a couple of hours Angela returned home,

ashamed and more miserable than she had been in months. The reality of her previous life hit her hard and she needed to escape once more. She longed to escape once more.

The journey back from Exeter had been slow and tedious. Traffic on the A303 had ground to a virtual halt after a tanker had spilled its load just outside Andover. Rather than sitting still and getting frustrated, Kaitlyn had told Errol to pull in to the first service station they found to get something to eat and wait out the delay. They had tucked into sausages and chips at the café, spent all their loose change on the arcade machines and Kaitlyn had bought her mum a nice bunch of flowers. By the time they arrived back on the estate it had been dark for a while.

Kaitlyn stifled a yawn as the key turned in the lock of the flat. The first thing she noticed was that there were no lights on. Her mother must have gone to bed, she thought. Kaitlyn, tired and wary, took a single step into the hallway. She could feel a 'mush ing' feeling under her feet as they pressed into the carpet.

Kaitlyn froze. The flat was eerily silent, the only sound was that of a tap dripping in the kitchen. 'Mum?'

There was no reply.

Kaitlyn reached up and flicked on the switch, her eyes blinking rapidly to adjust to the bright light. She glanced around quickly; everything appeared to be as it should until her gaze fell to the carpet beneath her feet. It was filthy, as always, but also stained dark with water that seemed to be coming from the kitchen. She stepped forward cautiously, peering through the half-open kitchen door. The smell was much stronger here, a putrid stench as if someone had left the lid off a rubbish bin for a few days. She saw glistening droplets of water, illuminated by the light from the hallway, spilling over the front of the sink in a series of tiny splashes. And as her eyes followed the falling drops on their short journey to the ground, Kaitlyn finally saw her mother.

Angela Wilson was sitting with her back against the cupboard under the sink, one leg directly in front of her, the other bent so her heel touched the inside of her thigh. Her head was cocked to the right, lolling against her shoulder, her face was bloated, horribly swollen, and ghostly pale where the water had been dripping against it. Her eyes were open but smooth and glassy, like marbles. Her blue lips were parted slightly. One hand rested on her lap, the other loosely on the floor. The hem of her denim skirt had ridden up over her knees, revealing her bare legs. The tops of her shins seemed pale but otherwise normal. The backs of her calves were dark purple with clotted blood. Rising out of her left ankle like a tiny flag was a small syringe.

Kaitlyn took in all the details in an instant. For a brief moment she could not breathe, no air came into her lungs. Then suddenly she gulped in one huge breath and let it out as a long, agonised scream that echoed around the Roxford estate.

It had all happened a few hours after Gary had left the house. The two packets of heroin were still in the kitchen where Angela had left them. There was no trouble finding a syringe – she'd had dozens of them stashed around the house in places Kaitlyn would never have thought to look. And even if she'd found them she would not have been too worried. What good is a syringe without drugs?

It took only a few seconds for the vein in Angela's ankle to swell up. Her mouth became dry with excitement as she plunged the needle into her flesh and gently pressed down the plunger. She leaned back against the sink, slumped to the floor, waiting for the glorious high that she had lived without for so long. She had wanted everything to be the same as it had been before. She had used the same type of needle, the same place in the flat and exactly the same amount of heroin. But having been clean for so long her tolerance had fallen to a new low. As the drug passed into her vein she felt the usual rush and the first steps into her world of dreams.

But this time there was something different. The dream started out the same but soon became darker, more intense, more frightening. Angela tried to wake herself up, to pull back, but it was too late. Her breathing became rapid as her panic rose but then, as the heroin flooded into her system, it became slower and slower.

Ten minutes after Angela took the heroin it had stopped altogether.

Chapter Eighteen

July 1986

She had visited the Roxford at least once a month for the past ten years and was a familiar face to many of the residents, but Margo Kane still hated going there. Angela Wilson's flat was empty, and due to be cleared out and ultimately relet, but now Kaitlyn had gone missing and Margo was desperate to find her. She had last been seen inside the flat when the police arrived to examine the body of her dead mother. Knowing she was under age, they had tried to hold on to her until someone from Social Services could arrive but Kaitlyn had managed to get away and fled into the heart of the estate. Kane was convinced she was still nearby and now she had a lead.

She climbed to the seventeenth floor and rang the doorbell of flat 1716. A good-looking, muscular boy with close-cropped hair opened the door.

'Are you Jacob Collins?' Kane asked.

The boy nodded. 'Are you here about Kaitlyn?'

'Listen, Jacob, I know you're a good friend of hers, but she's very vulnerable right now. You might think you're doing the right thing by protecting her but the truth is she needs proper looking after and that's something I can help with. If you know where she is, you really have to tell me.'

Jacob stared at the floor for a few moments, seemingly thinking over his options. Then he sighed heavily. 'My mate's got a car phone. She called it a couple of days ago and left a message for me, said she was living in a squat down at King's Cross. I'm really worried about her. She totally lost it when her mum died. I'm worried she might do something stupid.'

Kane took out a small notebook and jotted down a few lines. 'Thanks for that, Jacob. I know this must be difficult for you, but it's going to be for the best.'

Kane left Jacob's flat and he shut the front door after her. A few seconds later Kaitlyn emerged from behind the closed door of the kitchen.

'How did I do?' asked Jacob, his face beaming with pride.

'Bit over the top, I thought.'

'It just popped out. I couldn't help it. So what are you going to do?'

'There are a couple of empty flats on the top floor. I'll break into one of those and hide out there for a while. After that, I don't know. If I can get past my birthday they can't touch me.'

Jacob looked over at Kaitlyn. He could see the wetness in the corners of her eyes as she tried to fight back the tears. He knew she was hurting, but there seemed to be nothing he could do to comfort her.

Just a few days earlier, back in the tent in Glastonbury, it had seemed that they were about to embark on a new phase in their relationship. But whatever emotional door had cracked open was now firmly slammed shut. There was a coldness, a remoteness about her that had never been there before. The death of her mother, coming so soon after the death of Louisa, had turned Kaitlyn's heart to ice. The only thing Jacob could do was to wait for it to thaw.

'Kaitlyn,' he said softly. 'I don't want to pretend that I know what you're going through. No one does, not really, no matter what they say. But I want you to know that if there's anything you need, anything I can do for you at all, you only have to ask. I guess I'm saying that you might feel like you're all alone in the world, but you're not. I'm there for you.'

Kaitlyn managed to bring the faintest trace of a smile to her lips as she turned and headed back into the kitchen. 'Thanks, Jacob,' she said. Then, almost as an afterthought she added, 'You're a really good friend.' The words cut into him like a knife.

It was not until a week later that Kaitlyn risked returning to the flat where her mother had died. The flimsy padlock snapped easily when she applied the bolt cutters Errol had lent her. Once inside, Kaitlyn took her time looking around. So many memories — so many painful memories. Perhaps it was just as well that she would not be living here any longer. She moved into her bedroom and sighed with relief when she found her box of photographs and mementoes underneath her mattress. The pictures of Chrissy and Louisa were still there. Now she needed to find a picture of her mother as well.

Just as she was coming out of the flat a man she vaguely recognised as a local on the estate moved along the corridor towards her. He was a tall, middle-aged man wearing a pale boiler suit. At first Kaitlyn had been startled, thinking he might be from Social Services, but she quickly realised he was not.

The man looked her up and down in a way that made her feel incredibly uncomfortable, as if he were mentally running his hands over her body. His gaze finally met her own. 'I was looking for the woman who lives here, the older one.' The man's voice was confident, excited. It was clear what his visits to the estate were for.

'She's not in that business any more,' said Kaitlyn firmly. 'Don't ever come here again.' And with that she slammed the door in his face. As she walked back along the corridor she heard him swear. He pressed the bell a couple more times but eventually left.

Kaitlyn waited for ten minutes, then headed out of the flat, ready to make her way back up to her squat on the top floor. She moved quickly into the stairwell when suddenly something smashed into her. More from shock than anything else she yelled out, 'What the fuck do you think you're doing?'

It was the man who had knocked on the door of

the flat a little earlier. He pushed her back against the wall, eyeing her lustily. One powerful forearm locked against her neck, the other started to massage one of her breasts. 'Are you a whore like your mother?' he hissed. 'Can I fuck you? I'll pay you the same as her. More if you're really good.'

'Fuck off, leave me alone,' Kaitlyn gasped.

'Don't be like that, I know you want it. Come on, let's go back to the flat.'

For a split-second Kaitlyn stopped fighting to get away and stared directly into the man's eyes. She saw them twinkle briefly as if he truly believed she had stopped for his benefit, that the game was over and that he could now do whatever he wanted with her. And in that very moment he made the mistake of loosening his grip.

She needed only a second. The Stanley knife was in her back pocket. In one swift movement the blade had been pushed forward and was in the palm of her right hand, rushing up towards the man's head.

The fountain of blood from his cheek sprayed over Kaitlyn's own face before the man even realised what had happened. His scream of agony, accompanied by his releasing her and reeling backwards, hands clutching at his face, took even Kaitlyn by surprise. 'You bitch, you fucking bitch,' he bellowed, blood running through his clenched fingers now. Then he was away, running, leaving a trail of blood behind him.

In Kaitlyn's world everything that had happened

had been justified and fair. The man had attacked her and she had defended herself with the tools at her disposal, marking him for others to see what kind of man he really was. The police saw it differently and sent a team of officers in full riot gear to search every empty flat. It was only a matter of time before they found her. 'You're under arrest for GBH,' said the officer, smiling. It had been a long time coming but he finally had a reason to slap the handcuffs on Kaitlyn Wilson.

'It was self-defence,' Kaitlyn said. 'He was trying to rape me.'

'Save it for the interview,' the officer retorted.

The two officers sat opposite Kaitlyn in the interview room, looking through their notes and not saying a word. Kaitlyn's solicitor and a representative from Social Services both looked at her and shrugged their shoulders. They would have to wait until the officers were good and ready. It was all part of a silly psychological power game and there was nothing they could do about it.

Finally one of the officers spoke. 'Do you want to tell me what happened in your own words?'

Kaitlyn explained that the man had tried to rape her, that her mother had been working as a prostitute and that he had been one of her regular clients. She explained how he had come to the flat earlier and asked for her mother. She told them how he had looked at her, about the lust she had felt in his eyes. About how she wasn't surprised when she was grabbed from behind and it turned out to be him. She explained how she had taken the knife with her because she felt particularly unsafe in that part of the estate and wanted it for protection, how she resisted using it until she felt her life was in danger. She told them everything she knew they wanted to hear if they had even the slightest inclination to release her on bail and eventually drop the charges. When she finished she sat back and studied the eyes of the men opposite her. They were still as cold as ice.

'Well, that's a great story, Kaitlyn, but then I guess you've had a couple of days in hiding to think one up. I'm impressed. There were times when I was almost starting to feel sorry for you.'

'What are you talking about? It's not a story, it's not something I made up. It's the truth.'

'Really?'

'Yeah. I wouldn't lie about something like this.'

The policeman paused, then shifted his weight forward a little. 'OK. Let's look at it this way, from the point of view of, say, a member of a jury. On the one hand you have the testimony of a young woman. A woman who has been arrested more than four times in the past two years in connection with drug offences, but who miraculously has never been charged, either because she is too young or, dare I say, too clever to be caught with anything on her. Then, on the other hand you have a respectable family man, a father of four no less, who holds down a good job. And let's say this man comes to the police with horrific injuries to his face and explains that a young girl, whom he had often seen hanging around, launches herself at him, demands his wallet and, when he refuses, pulls out a knife and slashes his face. Whom do you think the jury are going to believe? Whom do you think we are going to believe?'

By now Kaitlyn's mouth had fallen open with shock. 'But that's not what happened. It wasn't anything like that. The man's lying. He attacked me. He tried to rape me.'

'And where's the evidence of that? Whom can we talk to that's going to confirm that story? I mean, I've spoken to this guy's wife and she seems like a lovely woman and thinks the world of him. And I've spoken to the people he works for and they all think he's great. And then there's the fact that he has never been in trouble with the police, even worked as a Special Constable a few years ago.'

The policeman paused, shaking his head. 'So whom can I ask to back up your story? Maybe one of your friends from the drugs gang, someone with the same kind of background as you? That's bound to go down well. Certainly no one on the estate, regardless of whether they saw anything or not. You know as well as I do that no one is going to talk to the police, not even if their life depended on it.' He paused for a moment, then lowered his voice. 'Perhaps I should talk to your mother. I guess she'd be more than willing to confirm your story that this man was a client of hers. Oh, but that's right, I can't talk to her. I'm not saying I'm not sorry for your loss, Kaitlyn, but the fact that your mother's now dead doesn't do much for your credibility.'

A split-second later Kaityln had reached across the interview table and clamped her arms round the man's throat. 'You bastard, you fucking bastard,' she screamed. The other officer leapt to his colleague's aid, running to the back of the table and placing his hands on Kaitlyn's shoulder, squeezing her pressure points so hard she almost passed out in agony. The panic button was pressed and within seconds the room was filled with reinforcements. Kaitlyn was pinned to the ground, with her appointed solicitor and social worker asking her to calm down.

The interview continued with Kaitlyn in handcuffs and guarded by several more officers. Only this time Kaitlyn did not utter a single word. Tears could be seen at the corner of her eyes.

It was the same when she made a brief appearance at Horseferry Road Magistrates Court the following morning. When she was asked to confirm that she was of no fixed abode, Kaitlyn shrugged. She felt that even her own solicitor didn't believe her and now she would be going to prison.

A few minutes later she was led out of the station in handcuffs and placed in the back of a van. She was on her way to Holloway.

Chapter Nineteen

'Do you have an ashtray?' Christopher Tobin's eyes darted around the small wood-panelled office as he perched on the end of the sofa, a Marlboro Light clasped between the fingertips of his right hand.

Dr Edmund Manley, who was sitting on the leather chair opposite Christopher, casually looked up from his notebook at the stocky eleven-year-old. 'No, I don't allow people to smoke in here.'

Christopher produced a small lighter from his pocket and lit the cigarette, blowing clouds of smoke high into the air above him. 'Really?' He stood up and walked across to the large desk that dominated the corner of the office, tipped the contents out of the wooden pencil holder and returned to his seat. 'I'll just use this,' he said, flicking his ash into the empty cylindrical container. His eyes were fixed on the doctor. The game had begun and they both knew it.

Dr Manley was a leading child psychologist and had been for more than twenty years. During that time he had seen every kind of defiance imaginable. He had been shouted and screamed at, had books thrown from his shelves and his curtains ripped from the rails. Once a nine-year-old girl had stood on the couch and started urinating. Another time a six-year-old boy had refused to do anything other than stand in the corner of the room and shout 'fuck' at the top of his voice. He would never forget the day that a sixteen-year-old girl with an astonishing case of multiple personality disorder had tried to throw herself out of his window. Or the time the father of a highly disturbed eleven-year-old had tried to punch him after he had told the man his son should be placed in a secure hospital for his own protection. He had seen it all and if Christopher Tobin thought he could get one over on him by simply lighting up a cigarette, he had another think coming.

'Tell me, Christopher,' Dr Manley said calmly, 'why do you smoke?'

Christopher said nothing. There was a long pause.

'Why do you feel the need to smoke in here today?'

Once again there was no answer. Instead, Christopher slouched back on the large, comfortable sofa, enjoying his cigarette.

Suddenly he sat up. 'Wait a minute, have we started? Shouldn't you give me some kind of sign when you're ready to begin? I don't want you to catch me off guard!'

Dr Manley smiled. He knew Christopher's patronising tone and the way he was acting were just his ways of expressing his unease. 'What might I find if I caught you off guard?'

Christopher sighed. 'Is this how it's going to be

for the next hour? I say something and you ask me how it makes me feel, stuff like that.'

'How would you like it to go for the next hour?' the doctor replied.

The room was silent but for the scritch-scratch sound of the doctor's pen moving across his notepad. Christopher didn't want to be the one to break but the longer the silence lasted the more agitated he became. After five minutes he could bear it no longer. 'What the fuck do you want with me?'

Dr Manley didn't look up. Instead, he carried on scribbling on his pad. 'I want you to stop smoking and swearing while you're in this room. Believe it or not, I know exactly what you're going through, the feelings you're experiencing. Alienation, frustration. You're going through what every other eleven-year-old boy on the planet goes through at some stage.'

'Hey,' said Christopher, sitting up again, his eyes bright and alert. 'That's incredible. Don't tell me you've read the Ladybird book of pop psychology too?' He lay back down.

Dr Manley smiled a little. He was starting to like this kid. 'When I was your age I remember spending hours searching through drawers in my parents' bedroom. You know what I was looking for? Adoption papers. I hated my parents so much that I would pray every night to learn that I was adopted so that I could be happy. It was as though I was living in a house with two complete strangers who might just as well have been aliens from another planet. There's nothing unique about those feelings. We all have them.'

Christopher tried not to react, but some of this was starting to sound familiar. Perhaps this man was worth talking to after all. There was another long silence.

'I'll put out my cigarette if you show me what you've written about me,' Christopher said at last. His voice was calm, almost submissive.

'My notes are confidential,' said Dr Manley, still not looking up.

'Then it's a good thing I brought a whole packet with me.'

Dr Manley smiled again, stopped scribbling and looked at Christopher. 'If I show you what's on my notepad, will you stop smoking and swearing while we're together?'

'Yes.'

'OK. We have a deal.'

Christopher put out his cigarette and leaned forward expectantly. Dr Manley flipped the pad round and held it out. On it was an outline sketch of Christopher's face. 'It's a hobby of mine,' he said. He gazed at Christopher, who looked intently at the detailed sketch of himself. 'I do hope we can start to have a sensible, adult conversation. You're too old to play games and, frankly, so am I.'

Just over an hour later Dr Manley led Christopher out of his office and asked him to wait in reception while he spoke to Jane and Paul.

'First of all I want to tell you that Christopher is a highly intelligent and interesting young man. I very much enjoyed talking to him.'

'You got him to talk?' sniffed Jane. 'All I ever get are a few grunts.'

Dr Manley smiled. 'Christopher is a typical teenager in most ways. I'd say the only problem he has is that he's bored, both at school and at home.'

'Bored?' gasped Paul.

Dr Manley nodded, flicking through his notes with one hand and stroking his greying beard with the other. 'Absolutely. It's a classic case of a child who is simply not finding an adequate level of stimulation. Imagine how you would feel if I sent you back to primary school to relearn the alphabet.' Paul Tobin shrugged his shoulders. 'Well, that's how Christopher feels every day. And because he's not being challenged in anything he has to do at school, he is acting up more and more. Also, he knows he is far more intelligent than most of those around him and he worries that this could drive them apart. So he acts up and plays the fool in order to develop a bond between them.'

Paul Tobin pursed his lips and gritted his teeth. He and Jane had discussed sending Christopher to Barrow Hill, one of the top private schools in the area, but instead had chosen to send him to the local comprehensive. At the time it seemed like the best option – somewhere where their son would easily fit in. It was a decision he now bitterly regretted. 'Do you think we should consider changing his school, sending him somewhere like Barrow Hill or even Charterhouse?' Paul asked.

The doctor paused for a moment. 'It might be worth considering. The problem with the school he's at is that teachers have to focus their attention on the lowest common denominator. It's a sad fact that if Christopher does his work and says nothing about how easy he finds it, the teachers will assume his problems lie elsewhere. I think a more challenging environment would do him the world of good.'

There was barely enough room for Kaitlyn to move her elbows. Her knees bashed painfully against the door each time the driver hit a pothole and the rough edge of the hard metal bench she was sitting on cut so deep into her thighs that her feet were starting to go numb.

She was making the slow journey to Holloway prison through the streets of London in the back of a specially converted prison transit van which, instead of having one large space in the back, had been split into two rows of identical high-security cubicles. It was a hot July afternoon, and the air inside the van was thick with the smell of sweating bodies and stale tobacco. The tiny bulb in the ceiling above her offered little illumination and hardly any light was managing to get through the heavily tinted window.

Kaitlyn could hear music blaring out from the radio and a few words of muffled conversation from the two prison officers up at the front of the van, but the main sounds were the gasps and protests of the women in the other cubicles. One in particular seemed to be suffering from a bad case of claustrophobia. 'I can't fucking breathe,' she gasped, banging her fist on the inside of the door. 'I need to get out.'

The response was immediate. 'Yeah, right, never heard that one before,' one of the officers called back before turning up the music to drown out her protests. Kaitlyn bit her lip in anticipation: this didn't bode well at all.

With no way to see out of the cubicles or the window, the only sign that they had finally arrived at the prison was that the van remained still for more than twenty minutes while the guards on the gate sorted out their paperwork. Then Kaitlyn heard the sound of grinding and groaning gears that told her Holloway's heavy reinforced wooden front gate was sliding open to let them in. The van crept forward twenty feet and the gate closed behind them. *This is it*, Kaitlyn thought. *This is my new home.*

After what seemed like an eternity the back of the van was finally unlocked. As the door to her cubicle was opened Kaitlyn looked across to the woman who had been in the one opposite. She was in her late thirties and looked as though she'd been dragged backwards through a hedge. Her blonde hair was plastered to her face with her own sweat. Her make-up had begun to run, giving her huge black panda eyes. She was breathing hard. She looked at

Kaitlyn and the pair managed to exchange weak smiles.

The five prisoners, their wrists sore from the handcuffs that had chafed their skin throughout the journey, were quickly escorted inside to a holding room at the side of the reception centre, a grubby square room with a large two-way mirror all along one wall, bars over the windows and a few wooden benches and cheap plastic chairs. They were told to sit and wait in silence.

It was almost an hour before Kaitlyn's name was called and she was taken through to an adjacent room and made to stand in front of a desk. Behind it was a miserable-looking female prison officer with thinning grey hair and pale skin that was cracked and worn like an old sofa. For the twentieth time that day she barked out a series of questions – date of birth, nationality, religion, dietary requirements – scribbling the answers into a large book and never once raising her head to look at Kaitlyn.

The officer explained that Kaitlyn's property would be sorted into two piles – the stuff she'd be allowed to take into her cell and the stuff that would have to be stored in the prison vaults. She then told Kaitlyn to empty the contents of her pockets and purse on to the desk.

'But I don't have anything,' Kaitlyn explained.

The officer looked up and sighed. 'Look, it doesn't matter what it is, it goes on the desk. I don't care if it's some precious family heirloom or your favourite lipstick. You don't get to decide what you can keep, I do. So it all goes on the desk right now.'

'But I don't have anything, I've got nothing on me at all. Just what I'm wearing and these,' she said, planting a half-empty packet of cigarettes and a small envelope on the desk.

The officer picked up the envelope and opened it. Inside was a picture of Christopher as a baby and one from a photo booth of Kaitlyn and her mother, which they had taken on one of their days out to the West End. The officer sniffed snootily and put the pictures back into the envelope. 'What, nothing else? Not even any money?' she asked. Kaitlyn shook her head and the woman behind the desk did the same. 'Blimey, I can tell it's your first time.'

Kaitlyn then had her photograph taken and was issued with her prison number. 'OK, your number is FE2815. You've no money so that means you've got no spends for the week. You've got your "thirty-nine" right here in your IP and the rest of your prop goes downstairs. If you want to change, just make an App. I'll finish your F-eleven-fifty and you can go back in the holding room. We're pretty full, so you might end up down on the Ones tonight and be on the adult wing, OK? Any queries, just find an SO.'

Kaitlyn didn't understand a word the officer had said. The woman might just as well have been speaking a foreign language. It was clear she didn't give a damn whether Kaitlyn understood or not. She was just going through the motions.

Kaitlyn was then taken to a small room and told to undress so she could be searched. As she waited for her turn, she could hear some of the other girls making a joke of it: 'I didn't know you fancied me,' said one, 'but you must do because your hands are lovely and warm today – I do love a girl in uniform.' They were old lags and knew the score, but for Kaitlyn the whole experience was humiliating and brought tears to her eyes. Was this really what her life had come to?

By the time they had been searched and seen by the doctor in a bid to assess how likely each was to commit suicide, Kaitlyn and the other new inmates had missed the last call for dinner. All they were given were a few leftovers, which they ate off their laps while sitting in the holding room. Kaitlyn fought the urge to throw up as she used her fork to inspect the multicoloured mush in the centre of her plate. It looked as if it had already been regurgitated several times before it had been given to her. She pushed it all to one side and had one of her few remaining cigarettes instead.

Kaitlyn was still smoking when two burly prison officers arrived and started shouting out numbers: 'CF9563, FE2815 and DK6951 follow me.' The voice was deep and firm, and Kaitlyn assumed the two officers were men. It was only when she turned and faced them that she realised they were women.

The small group passed from the reception area through two electronic security gates, which were opened by the control centre, and into the main prison area.

As the last door opened the smell of the prison almost knocked Kaitlyn off her feet. It was awful, the same smell you got if you walked too close behind a refuse van. She held her mouth and nose, coughing and choking against the foul air until she finally had to accept there was nothing she could do but breathe it in.

The corridor they had walked into was so brightly lit that Kaitlyn had to squint. The walls were pale blue, and dull brown cell doors stretched into the distance on either side. The floor was covered with thick green lino, spotted with cigarette burns. Kaitlyn had seen enough gangster films and documentaries to know exactly what to expect – three or four storeys of cells built round a central atrium with wire netting to stop anyone jumping to their death – but the Holloway she saw in front of her was nothing like that.

The prison had first opened in 1851, catering for both men and women. In 1903 it switched roles and became women only and in 1977 the original Victorian 'radial'-style prison was replaced with four five-storey cell blocks designed to be a cross between a prison and a hospital.

As she moved forward Kaitlyn heard a noise like distant thunder rolling towards her. Hundreds of inmates were rattling their cups against windows, kicking at their doors and shouting at the tops of their voices.

'The natives are getting restless,' quipped one of the guards.

'What are they saying?' Kaitlyn asked.

'Nice young girl like you? You'll find out soon enough.'

Soon Kaitlyn began to hear their words loud and clear. The prison's bush telegraph was in full swing and the sinister message going out to the masses was that there were new faces on the block, ripe for exploitation, bullying, manipulation and sex. Over and over again, louder and louder, they were all chanting: 'Fresh fish, fresh fish, fresh fish . . .'

The little group of new inmates started making its way through a series of passageways and corridors on their way to the ground floor cells or the 'Ones', as Kaitlyn would later learn they were called. They stopped at a room marked 'supplies' and were issued with basic toiletries in a brown paper bag, then moved on to one marked 'laundry' where everyone was given one pillow, a blanket and two grubby looking sheets.

They continued their journey and as Kaitlyn descended a flight of stairs she felt a tap on her shoulder and turned round to see another inmate, a tall slim woman wearing a denim jacket and jeans, who was close behind. 'Word to the wise, love,' she said in a soft cockney accent, pointing to the packet of cigarettes in Kaitlyn's hand. 'Don't walk with them on display. You're asking for trouble. Stick one behind your ear and crotch the rest.'

'Crotch?'

The woman looked at Kaitlyn as if she were from another planet, as though everyone should immediately know what she was talking about. 'Yeah,' she said, nodding enthusiastically. 'Crotch it. You know, stick it where the sun don't shine, where the screws don't search.'

Kaitlyn was just about to ask the woman to explain exactly what she meant when her attention was distracted by the sound of a woman's desperate screaming. It was horrific; she was pleading for her life, begging for help and as the group descended the stairs it got louder and louder.

Kaitlyn looked around her: the cockney woman, the guards and the other inmates . . . none of them seemed to take any notice. Then, as suddenly as it had started, it stopped. As they reached the bottom of the stairs and passed through another set of double doors it started up again, along with the noise of other women screaming. Kaitlyn felt as though she were descending into hell.

'Fuck, fuck, fuck, fuck fucking fucker, fuck, fuck fucking fuck.

'Aaaaaaaaaghhhhhhhh!

'Help me, help me, for God's sake somebody help me.

'Aaaaaaaaaghhhhhhhh!

'Fuck, fuck, fuck, fuck fucking fucker, fuck, fuck fucking fuck.'

Kaitlyn was looking around, taking it all in, when

the cockney woman caught her eye. 'Medical wing,' she said. 'Fucking loony bin more like. There's no one sick here, not physically anyway. Don't worry, you'll get used to it. It's the kangas you want to watch out for.'

'Kangas?'

'Kangaroo. Screw.'

The group passed through more double doors into the next wing and the prison officers stopped by a heavy door with a glass slit at eye level and fiddled with a large bunch of keys. On the wall next to the cell was a small blackboard filled with neat writing: PN (Prison Number), FE2815. Name, Kaitlyn Wilson. Religion, n/a. Age, 16. Remand.

The door swung open. 'FE2815 Wilson?'

Kaitlyn jumped and the screw stood to one side to let Kaitlyn go into the cell. The door slammed and she heard the key turning in the lock. She leaned back against the cold steel and took in her surroundings. To her left was the bed: a metal bench bolted to the floor with a stained mattress made from a piece of solid rubber foam about five inches thick but covered in a film of sticky black gunk. Kaitlyn didn't even want to think about what the substance might have been. Behind her, on the left of the door, a small partition blocked off a stainless-steel toilet and a tin sink. The toilet had no seat and no lid. It was caked with filth as if someone had taken handfuls of excrement and smeared them on the inside and outside of the bowl as well as up the wall behind. The sink was just as bad, with years of grime covering its entire surface.

The bed was the only piece of furniture – apart from that the cell was empty. Every square inch of the walls was covered with graffiti recording the names, dates and thoughts of dozens of the cell's previous occupants. To the right of the bed was a window. It was made up of vertical slats and started from waist height rising up to over Kaitlyn's head. Three of the slats were slightly open, letting in a faint breeze. She tried to open them fully but quickly discovered they were jammed solid: she could shut them more but it was impossible to open them completely. There was no way to get enough fresh air to dilute the smell.

Outside the window was a small yard of grass and concrete flanked on all sides by tall, dark buildings holding other cells. She was on the ground floor and peering up she could see only a tiny patch of sky, which looked grimly grey in the last of the evening light. Kaitlyn tried to push her head out to see more but the slats were too narrow. She could get her hand through but that was all. Below, just a few feet away, were piles of rotting food, sanitary towels, old newspapers, and bits of rolled-up toilet paper and old milk cartons – all discarded by the other inmates. Some of the rubbish was moving. Kaitlyn saw a flash of brown and realised there were rats among the rubbish.

Finally she looked back at the main door. That too

was covered with graffiti and there were marks where someone had tried to paint over the messages, only to see fresh ones scratched on shortly afterwards. The side facing the corridor had been covered with a mock-wood veneer but inside it was painted metal. Just below eye level was a long perspex strip, which served as a peephole. To the right, alongside the toilet bowl, was a small hatch that opened outwards and allowed prison officers to inspect the cell more thoroughly without having to come in.

When Kaitlyn had examined every corner she sat on the edge of the stinking mattress and burst into tears. She didn't stop crying until she fell asleep.

Chapter Twenty

By the time the lights came on and the screws started making their early morning rounds, Kaitlyn had snatched only a couple of hours' rest. It had been the longest night of her life.

She dressed sluggishly and by the time she arrived at the breakfast room she found herself at the back of a long queue. Inmates had only a limited time to collect and eat their meals. If they didn't make it for whatever reason, they simply had to go hungry.

By 8.20 Kaitlyn had moved forward only a few paces and she could sense the people behind her getting restless. 'Get the fuck a move on, bitch,' one lag shouted up the line. Ten minutes later she was finally nearing the front of the queue when a heavy elbow smashed into her gut and she was knocked sideways by a tall, shaven-headed black woman pushing her way past. The woman wore blue dungarees and heavy Doc Martens. Her body was more masculine than feminine. You could see the veins in her forearms and the bulge of her biceps through the short sleeves of her filthy white T-shirt. On her left shoulder was a home-made tattoo that read 'Marcia'. She chewed gum noisily, revealing a brief glimpse of a large gold front tooth each time her lips mashed together.

A few of the other inmates looked up from their food but none of them said a word. The blow had left Kaitlyn partly winded and before she could stop herself she had spoken out on instinct: 'Oi, what the fuck do you think you're doing?'

Kaitlyn regretted it even before the last word had left her lips. The big woman spun round and marched over, pushing her face so close that Kaitlyn could smell the stale tobacco on her breath, then letting loose a tirade of insults in a thick Jamaican accent Kaitlyn could only barely understand. She picked out a few words – 'motherfucker', 'bitch' and 'blood clot' – mainly because they were repeated over and over again. Tiny flecks of spittle spurted from the woman's mouth and splashed on to Kaitlyn's face as she spoke. Kaitlyn took her eyes off the woman for a split-second to glance around. The eyes of every other inmate were locked on them.

In that instant Kaitlyn knew that whatever happened at that moment would affect the rest of her time at Holloway. If she backed down or walked away, she would most likely find herself being abused by everyone in the prison. If she turned to the screws for help she would be labelled a grass and considered fair game for anyone.

The heavily built woman leaned forward and pushed Kaitlyn, challenging her to take a shot, then threw a solid punch straight into her jaw. Kaitlyn felt a sharp electric pain shooting up the side of her face. The sound of the blow had been sickening, bone crunching. Her legs buckled but she knew above all else that she mustn't end up on the floor. She had seen the boots the woman was wearing and that would mean the kind of damage that would leave her in the hospital wing for weeks.

She could taste her own blood alongside something small and hard, which she soon realised was one of her teeth. A piercing alarm started to ring, echoing around the room. This was the 'aggro' bell, which sounded throughout the prison at the first sign of trouble and ensured that screws from every wing rushed to the scene and descended on the trouble-makers like a plague of locusts.

A split-second later Kaitlyn sent the heel of her hand surging upwards so that it crashed into the base of the black woman's chin. The uppercut had made the woman bite her own lip so that blood filled her mouth and covered her teeth. She reached her fingers to her lips and exploded with rage when she held them up and saw they had turned crimson.

Kaitlyn's head was still spinning from the first punch as her assailant charged towards her again. She closed her eyes and went in screaming, her adrenalin helping her fight without thought. Then she felt heavy arms locking into her elbows, pulling her to the floor and dragging her backwards. Opening her eyes, she saw the black woman being dragged back in a similar fashion, four equally large female screws having jumped her from behind. The woman was screaming, writhing around like a snake and kicking her feet in all directions in an effort to get away, but the screws were too experienced and had her locked in a vice-like grip. Her eyes focused on Kaitlyn as she was pulled away. 'I'm gonna kill you, you fucking bitch. You wait, I'm gonna fucking kill you.'

The two screws held Kaitlyn hard against the floor – arms pinned behind her back and thumbs bent back double, their knees pushed deep into her back. They also jabbed their fingers into the pressure points in her shoulders and at the base of her neck, sending a wave of intense pain shooting through her body. 'That fucking hurts,' she screamed.

'Serves you right, you cocky little shit,' came the reply. The more she struggled, the worse the pain became and within seconds she had given up all resistance and was being dragged along like a limp rag doll.

The screws dragged Kaitlyn back to her cell and threw her inside. 'I didn't fucking start it,' she protested. 'This isn't fair.' But the screws were in no mood to listen and slammed the door shut behind her. 'What about my breakfast,' yelled Kaitlyn, but they had already gone.

Ten minutes later a brown paper bag with a single slice of dry bread fell through the hole in the inspection slot and landed on the floor.

It was more than four hours before the key clicked in the lock again.

Kaitlyn had spent the time lying on her bed,

massaging the side of her jaw, which ached and felt puffy. She tried examining herself in the shiny plastic circle that was supposed to serve as a mirror, but all she could see was a blurry image of the swelling on the side of her face.

She had repeatedly pressed the emergency call button that lit up a bulb on a large panel in the control room. The duty screws ignored it at first. When someone finally came to investigate, Kaitlyn demanded painkillers and a visit to the doctor's surgery, but her pleas seemed to fall on deaf ears.

The door swung open and a male screw with short cropped hair stared down at her. 'It's lunchtime. You'd better make your way down to the canteen.' He peered at her jaw and his voice softened. 'Then I'll take you to the doctor, check your jaw out. My name's David, by the way.'

He stood to one side to let Kaitlyn go past him but she hesitated and remained on the bed. Even in her wildest dreams she had never imagined it would be as bad as this. She had been in Holloway for less than a day and there was a woman who had promised to kill her. The smell still made her sick and the stifling heat meant she couldn't sleep. She'd always known prison was going to be tough, but she'd imagined that if she simply kept herself to herself and didn't bother anyone, she'd manage to survive. Her lawyer told her that even if she was acquitted when her case came to trial, she could still expect to spend the best part of a year in Holloway on remand and she'd mentally prepared herself for that. But now she wasn't even sure she could survive the night.

David let out a long sigh. 'If you're worried about Marcia, you don't need to be, not for a few days anyway. She took a bite out of one of the other officers. She's going to be in the block for a while.'

'The block?'

'Oh, you'll find out all about it soon enough. But play your cards right and you'll never have to experience it for yourself.'

After lunch and a quick visit to the doctor, which ended with him handing over two aspirin, Kaitlyn was escorted back to her cell to find David waiting for her. 'OK, get your shit together. You're being moved.'

She packed her few possessions, swallowed the aspirin and followed David out of the cell. It was the start of afternoon association and inmates were milling about in the corridors in the wings. Some wolf-whistled as Kaitlyn walked past while others made obscene gestures, flapping their tongues up and down through a V-shape in their fingers.

Kaitlyn's relief at getting away from the noise of the prisoners on the ground floor collapsed the moment she realised that, rather than moving into another single cell, she would be sharing a dormitory with three other women.

'This is it,' David said at last when they arrived at the end of yet another gloomy corridor.

The screw pushed open the door to her new home

and Kaitlyn, clutching all her belongings in two paper bags, walked in.

'I'll leave you ladies to make happy families, then.' David closed the door behind her.

The dormitory was arranged like a small hospital ward. There were two beds on each side of the room with curtain rails round the top, but no curtains attached. To the right of the door was a small area sectioned off by screens, which contained the toilet. To the left of the door was a stainless-steel basin. The colour scheme was drab and dull, a mix of grey and grey-blue with graffiti scratched into the walls.

As she stepped in two women looked up, wondering if the marks on her face were a sign of trouble coming to their cell. One of them was lighting a cigarette. She was standing right in the middle of the room, staring hard at Kaitlyn who stared back in return. The woman had short brown hair and glowing olive skin with bright-green eyes. Her complexion was perfect and she could easily have been a model. She was one of the rare few that didn't have to worry about 'prison pallor'. For most inmates the lack of exposure to natural light meant that after a few months their skin became so pale they almost looked like ghosts.

'I'm Kaitlyn,' she said gingerly,

The woman stared back blankly, slowly looking her up and down. Then she heard a rough voice from behind: 'I'm Julie. You're wasting your time, love – she don't speak English.'

Kaitlyn turned to see a thin girl squatting over the toilet, her knickers and jeans bundled round her ankles and a floppy roll-up hanging from her lips. She stood and dressed herself, flushed the toilet, then gesticulated wildly towards the other girl while putting on a fake Italian accent: 'No speaka de English, eh? Can't understand a word I'm saying, can you, you fucking ugly dago slag.'

Julie took a few steps across the room until she was directly in front of Kaitlyn. She eyed her suspiciously. 'I saw you this morning tickling big Marcia. You're not here to cause trouble, are you? It's bad enough being in this shithole without some cunt bouncing off the walls day and night.' She puffed a cloud of foul-smelling smoke into Kaitlyn's face.

'I didn't start it,' she said softly.

'Whatever. I'll tell you what, Kate.' Kaitlyn didn't bother to correct her. 'My advice to you is to get yourself a weapon and make sure you're prepared to use it. If anyone tries to fuck with you, you need to be able to defend yourself. You're not the biggest and you're not the strongest, so you need a weapon, otherwise you're dead.'

Julie flopped on to her bed and began putting together a fresh roll-up using the contents of a small tobacco tin she retrieved from under her pillow. 'So, what you in for?' Kaitlyn mumbled something about being on remand but Julie set off on a rant about the legal system. She explained she was being done for fraud but that her legal team had 'fucked it up big time' and that she shouldn't have been there at all.

At that moment the door to the cell swung open and a fat woman with sallow skin and dyed fire-red hair marched in. Her pale-blue eyes scanned the room, lingering for a moment on Kaitlyn, then fixing on Julie. 'You been here all the time? I was waiting in the rec room. Who's that?'

'Sorry, Pam, love,' said Julie, standing up and moving towards her. 'That's Kate, she's just moved in with us. Let me make it up to you.' Within seconds the two women were embracing and kissing passionately. Kaitlyn stared wide-eyed at the scene in front of her for a few moments, then tried to find something else to look at. Her eyes moved quickly round the bare room until they met those of the woman who did not speak English, now propped up on her bed, flicking through a magazine.

Kaitlyn turned on her bed so she was facing the wall. She was waiting for the sound of the kissing to stop. Somehow she knew she was going to be waiting for a very long time.

It took only a few days for Kaitlyn to fall into step with prison routine. It helped that, with only a handful of exceptions, one day at Holloway was pretty much the same as any other and by the end of her first week Kaitlyn had learned to ignore the screaming that went on out of the cell windows all through the night. Inmates from one block would try to talk to their friends, shouting to be heard over dozens of other inmates doing the same. More than once in those first few days she had snapped awake, certain she had heard someone call her name. Those noises, combined with the screams from the medical wing and the sound of Julie and Pam having enthusiastic sex under cover of lights out had kept Kaitlyn awake for the first days but now she was finally getting used to it.

The day Marcia was moved out of the block, Kaitlyn was told she was moving again, this time to a single cell in a different wing. It was a relief but Kaitlyn knew it was merely postponing the inevitable. Sooner or later Marcia would catch up with her and at that time the only thing she would be able to do was fight for her life or spend the rest of her time in prison under the woman's thumb.

She thought about the advice she had received – get a weapon and be prepared to use it – and sharpened the end of a spare toothbrush into a point by scraping it repeatedly along the concrete floor while her cellmates were asleep. She kept it hidden in the sole of her left shoe.

Although her new cell was in a different wing, that in itself offered little protection. During association inmates were free to move around the prison at will and, with the staff shortages, the chances of enough screws arriving in time to stop her getting seriously hurt were slim to say the least.

She was relieved to find herself back in a single

cell, this time at the far end of a corridor with a glimpse of a view over north London from her window. By now she had a few meagre possessions. Jacob and Errol had clubbed together and sent in a food parcel, some money and a few clothes they picked up. None of the stuff was ideal and most of it fitted badly, but at least Kaitlyn now had a change of clothes. Jacob had written and promised to visit.

There were only a few minutes of association left when Kaitlyn finished arranging her things in her cell. She had just made her way into the corridor to have a quick look around the new wing when a distant voice made her blood run cold: 'There she is, there's that fucking bitch.'

Kaitlyn stopped and turned towards the sound of the voice. There, pacing rapidly down the long corridor, was Marcia, along with two of her equally violent friends.

The position of Kaitlyn's new cell meant there was nowhere to run, nowhere to hide. The bruise on her jaw had only just started to fade but she knew that this time she would end up with far worse. Taking a deep breath, Kaitlyn crouched down on the floor as if scratching her leg and quickly retrieved the sharpened toothbrush, holding it tightly in her sweaty palm. There was no way she could win this battle, but she was determined to go down fighting.

Just then, the heavy-set figure of a woman in pale-blue overalls stepped out from a side door twenty feet ahead, blocking Marcia's way. Kaitlyn could only see the back of her head as she spoke. 'If you want to get to her, you're going to have to come through me.' The voice was calm, authoritative, and it stopped Marcia and her friends in their tracks.

Who is she? thought Kaitlyn.

'What's this, Diane? Your good deed for the day?'

'Don't fuck with me, Marcia. Not unless you want to wake up dead one day.'

Marcia rubbed the back of one of her enormous rough hands across her nose and sniffed. 'Why are you making yourself busy for her?'

'None of your business. So fuck off and bother someone else instead.'

Marcia took one more step forward. 'And if I don't?' she sneered.

Something about the situation did not make sense. Marcia was a big woman and as strong as an ox. Diane, though solid and formidable, seemed considerably older and well past her prime. Add to that the fact that Marcia had two sidekicks with her and all the smart money would be on her, yet here she was, hesitating.

Diane took a deep breath, inflating her chest to its full size, preparing her muscles for action.

Almost instantly Marcia seemed to shrink in size as the will to fight deserted her like air from a leaky balloon. She twisted on her heel, signalled to her two friends and headed back out of the wing. 'This isn't over,' she spat, as she walked off.

'It's never over, love,' Diane called after her.

Diane waited until Marcia had passed through the double doors at the top of the block before she turned round and looked at Kaitlyn for the first time. Her face was soft and kind. 'Are you OK?' she asked in a firm but friendly voice.

'I'm fine. Thanks.'

'Come on then, fancy some juice? I've got a carton in my fridge.'

Diane turned and disappeared into the door she had come out of. Kaitlyn slowly walked along the corridor until she reached it. The sign above read 'No Inmates Allowed'. Unsure what to do, she stood there for a few moments until the door swung open again. 'Are you coming in or what?' asked Diane, a big grin on her face.

'But it says . . .'

'Oh, please, you haven't been here long enough to have that much respect for authority. Come on.'

The door led to a narrow corridor containing five cells, a small sitting area with a fridge, a television and a sofa. Two more doors led to offices, one marked 'Wing Governor' and the other 'Senior Wing Officer'. There were two toilets, one male, one female, both marked 'Prison Staff Only', and finally a storeroom.

'What is this place?' asked Kaitlyn.

'It's the wing cleaner's annexe,' Diane replied. 'All the cleaners live in these cells, right next to the top kangas. It has to be like that because the storeroom has all the bleach and disinfectant, and if the other inmates could get hold of it they'd use it to top themselves, or poison each other. Come and have a seat.'

Kaitlyn nodded weakly. She waited until Diane sat down on one end of the sofa and perched herself down on the opposite end, stretching her arm to accept the plastic cup of orange juice.

Although she was in a prison, and the senior staff facilities were only a few feet away, Kaitlyn suddenly felt more vulnerable than she had during her entire time at Holloway, even more vulnerable than she had out in the corridor when she first saw Marcia. In prison, there was no such thing as a free favour and Kaitlyn wanted to know exactly what this woman would ask in return.

The time she had spent in the dormitory with Julie and Pam had taught her all she needed to know about the sexual politics of a women's prison and there was no way she was going to fall victim to it herself, not without a fight.

Although Pam was a full-on lesbian, Julie wasn't really gay at all. Pam had spotted her soon after her sentence began and could see how vulnerable she was. Within the space of a few weeks, partly as a result of loneliness and a need for a close friendship in such a terrible place, Julie had come round to Pam's way of thinking, even though she would never have considered herself to be gay. It was a common phenomenon in prison, known as becoming 'nick-bent' – women who were straight on the outside suddenly getting involved with women while in jail.

It wasn't just the inmates who were at it; relationships between the female staff and inmates, female staff with one another, male and female staff and male staff and inmates were all too common, but nine times out of ten sexual relationships at Holloway involved two members of the female sex. More than once this caused all sorts of problems as the nick-bent women were picked up by the genuinely bent women, only to call the whole thing off when they got close to their release date. At least half of all the fights in a women's prison revolved around relationships and Holloway was no exception.

Sometimes, as with Pam and Julie, sex was what it was all about. Other times the tougher of the two women would force the other to become her virtual slave, handing over telephone privileges and food parcels, cleaning her cell, doing laundry and any number of other menial tasks.

'Sorry it took me a few days to get you over here,' Diane said. 'The place is packed at the moment so I had to pull a few strings. I wouldn't take what happened with Marcia personally. She tries that on with pretty much everyone. People don't often answer back. How's your jaw?'

Kaitlyn instinctively reached up to touch the outline of the bruise. 'It's getting better.' Now her mind was racing. Why on earth had Diane gone to all that trouble to get her moved into her wing. Her worst fears were coming true. She took a deep breath. 'Listen, Diane. I don't want to appear ungrateful. But

I think there's something you need to know about me. I'm not . . . look, don't get me wrong, I think you're really nice and I'm grateful that you helped me out but . . .' Kaitlyn couldn't find the words. She stuttered and stumbled, and then went quiet.

Diane stood up and walked over to the door, keeping her back to Kaitlyn as she spoke. 'Don't worry Kaitlyn, I know what you're trying to say.'

'Good, because . . .'

'I've heard it all before. They all say that in the beginning. You'll feel differently when you've had your tattoo. Oh yes, I make all my girls have a tattoo. That way they know who they belong to. Don't worry, I'll be gentle with you.'

Kaitlyn could hear the blood rushing in her ears, feel the bile rising in her stomach. Diane might have dealt with the problem of Marcia but now she was out of the frying pan and into the fire. She stared at the floor, panic rising, her mind racing. She knew she couldn't hide the terror on her face as she pondered what was to become of her in the coming months. Then finally she glanced up at Diane, who had now turned round and was staring at her, a huge beaming smile on her face.

'Jesus, you really believed that shit, didn't you?'

The colour that had drained away from Kaitlyn's face suddenly came rushing back in a huge wave of relief. 'You . . . you were joking?'

'Well, of course I was joking. I can't believe it was so easy to wind you up. Can you play poker?'

'No.'

'Don't worry, I'll teach you. And you'll never be short of people to play with. I'm gonna get so rich off of you. Honestly, you should see yourself. The look on your face was absolutely priceless.' Diane threw her head back and laughed and soon Kaitlyn was laughing too. 'Don't worry, dear,' gasped Diane between chuckles. 'You don't have anything to worry about. I still like men, even if it's been a while since I had one.'

It took a few minutes for the laughter to subside and for Kaitlyn to realise she still needed an answer to the question running through her head. 'So why are you helping me out, then?'

Diane moved back to the sofa and sat close to Kaitlyn, looking deep into her eyes. Whatever she was searching for, it wasn't there and she let her gaze fall to the floor. 'You don't remember, do you?' she said softly, her voice tinged with sadness.

'Remember what?'

Diane waved a hand through the air. 'Oh, it's silly of me. There's no reason why you should. It was all such a long time ago.'

'What are you talking about?'

'I used to bounce you up and down on my knee till you were laughing so hard you'd almost wet yourself.' Diane paused for a moment, then spoke even more softly. 'I was in bits when I heard what happened to your mum. We hadn't spoken for years but I was absolutely in bits. She was a good woman and the

Roxford was a good place to live back then, not the fucked-up shithole it is now.'

Kaitlyn reached out her hand and laid it gently on Diane's arm. 'Who are you?'

When Diane looked up again her eyes were moist with tears. 'Kaitlyn, I'm your godmother.'

Chapter Twenty-one

October 1986

Errol Gants gazed absent-mindedly out of the window as he drained the last of his pint and reached for the long canvas bag at his feet. He had been sitting in a quiet corner of the Spotted Dog public house on the outskirts of Tooting for the best part of an hour and managed to make his one drink last the entire time. Now, finally, he was ready to leave.

The dark wood interior of the old-fashioned pub was thick with cigarette smoke. Most of the tables were occupied, some with small groups of friends enjoying a lively conversation, others by apparent regulars who, like Errol, preferred to drink alone. As he passed one such figure, slumped over a half pint of Guinness, Errol gently tapped the man's heavily padded shoulder. 'Two minutes,' he said softly before making for the toilet. There, feeling a familiar churning in his stomach, Errol threw up into the nearest sink, rinsed it away and splashed cold water on his face. He looked at himself in the mirror, willing himself on, then hurried out of the pub.

Errol crossed the road just ahead of the Securicor van that had parked opposite the pub a few moments earlier. If he had timed it right, and he was sure he had, the guard with the second money box – the first was always empty and used to test the waters – would be emerging any moment. He pulled the scarf up from his neck so that it covered the bottom half of his face and tugged down the peak of his baseball cap to hide his eyes. As the sound of the security lock at the back of the van clicked open, releasing the second bag, Errol reached into his canvas hold-all and took out the sawn-off shotgun, pulling it into his shoulder and pointing it at the guard's startled face in one swift movement. 'Give me the fucking money or you're a dead man,' he hissed.

As soon as Errol's fingers touched the bag, his heart began to beat as the surge of adrenalin hit him. He started running, breathing hard and gathering pace as he reached the first turning off the main road. A split-second after he had arrived at the corner, the stolen Yamaha FZ9 motorcycle screeched to a halt alongside him. Jacob's face was hidden by the full-face helmet and the large padded jacket he wore – the same one he had on in the pub – made him look several times his real size.

As they raced off, Errol couldn't help but smile. They had got away with it. Their first ever armed robbery had gone like a dream.

The two young men had continued to work for Gary soon after Kaitlyn was sent to prison. With few other prospects and a desperate need for cash, Errol and Jacob agreed. As the weeks went by, however, they began to resent the fact that they were getting only a small share of the profits. Like Kaitlyn before them, they too dreamed of leaving the estate and knew the only way to achieve this was to find other sources of income. But the stress of their new occupation meant they paid a heavy price. They had spent the four days after the robbery hiding out in an abandoned flat on the Roxford, never once venturing outside and living off frozen pizza, fish fingers and beer. A radio scanner was tuned to the local police frequency and the television was switched on for each and every news broadcast.

Guns had been placed strategically by the door and windows, and each took it in turn to grab a few hours' fitful sleep while the other kept watch. Two separate getaway cars were also stashed nearby, the keys taped to the upper side of the passenger sun visor. Should the flying squad burst in, so the plan went, one of them would be able to keep the officers at bay while the other made a quick getaway. As the days went by they both became increasingly paranoid about being caught. It didn't help that both Errol and Jacob were snorting increasing amounts of speed, offsetting the effects with strong cannabis joints from Jamaica known as sensimilia.

The canvas bag from the Securicor van robbery had contained more than £3,000. It had also been fitted with an anti-theft device that exploded and covered the money with indelible red dye if the bag was cut or opened incorrectly. Even a small amount of the dye on a note made it worthless. A sure sign the money had been stolen, no one would touch it.

But Errol and Jacob had learned of a sure-fire method for getting round this. They had spent hours making ice cubes, filling the trays again and again until they had enough to fill a bin liner. The canvas bag was then placed in the centre and allowed to cool. The red dye was situated in a small plastic capsule close to the top of the bag. By surrounding the bag with ice it was possible to freeze the dye. Then, when the bag was opened, instead of spraying out and covering the money, all there would be were a few chunks of frozen red paint. The system had worked like a dream and the pristine money had been transferred to an Adidas sports bag, which sat in the centre of the room, ready for a quick getaway.

When they finally felt it was safe to venture outside, they bought themselves some new clothes and hit every pub and club within a ten-mile radius, spending the money like water. Within a few days it was all gone and they found themselves right back at the beginning again. They knew that if they were to get off the estate, they were going to have to do better than this.

Chapter Twenty-two

After three months at Holloway, Kaitlyn and Diane were inseparable. Once word had spread about who Kaitlyn was with, the troublemakers left her alone and on occasion she even found herself being treated with respect. Diane, she quickly learned, was something of a legend in the prison. She had been in Holloway for the best part of fourteen years and no one, least of all Diane herself, was at all sure when or if she would ever get out. When Kaitlyn was just two years old, Diane had been convicted of murdering her husband, Terry, a well-known thief. Their marriage had always been turbulent but when Terry came home drunk one night and started bragging about how the barmaid in his local had been all over him, Diane snapped. She had been sentenced to twelve years for manslaughter and should have been released long ago, but her time in Holloway had not been without incident. Four years into her sentence she had got into a massive fight with a large Nigerian woman serving time for drug trafficking. The battle ended with the woman dead from a brain haemorrhage, caused by Diane, who had smashed her head against the wall.

Diane explained to Kaitlyn that she had been close

to her mother, Angela, and helped look after Kaitlyn when she was young, but that the pair had drifted apart after Diane went to prison. Although she still had plenty of friends on the Roxford estate who kept her informed of every little development, she had not spoken to Angela since the day she arrived at Holloway.

As well as being her godmother, friend and protector, Diane became Kaitlyn's guide to the weird world of the British prison system, advising her that her first priority should be to get a job. The obvious position was for Kaitlyn to join Diane as a wing cleaner. Kaitlyn had quickly discovered that there were two main reasons why inmates agreed to work. The first was the money to spend on treats like chocolate or essentials like shampoo and tobacco; the second and ultimately far more important was for the chance to spend time out of their cells and therefore relieve the constant boredom.

Kaitlyn soon learned that wing cleaners do far more than just clean. Her day started with the cells in the annexe being opened up twenty minutes earlier than other inmates' to give them time to get to the kitchen and serve up breakfast. Afterwards, everyone else would be locked back up while Kaitlyn and the cleaners cleared away the dishes and washed up. It was no easy task. The serving trays were so thick with grease and grime that they could only be cleaned by being immersed in a large industrial sink at the back of the serving area filled to the brim with boiling hot water. It was sweaty, uncomfortable work and the cleaners had to wear special thick black rubber gloves that extended all the way to their elbows so they could wash up without scalding themselves.

After free flow, the cleaners mopped the corridors and the association area, and cleaned out any empty cells to prepare them for new inmates. This was often the worst part of the job. Many of the women who ended up in Holloway had spent weeks, months or even years living on the streets. They came to the prison infested with lice, scabies and all sorts of other conditions, as well as being caked with the most revolting dirt imaginable. It didn't take Kaitlyn long to realise why the prison employed inmates to do the cleaning – no ordinary person would take on such a job, no matter how much they were paid.

Some days were worse than others. In her second week as a cleaner a young girl at the other end of the corridor tried to kill herself. Diane and Kaitlyn were told to go and clean up the cell and arrived to find the blood that sprayed out of her slashed wrists covering the floor, the walls and the ceiling. Another time an inmate with chronic diarrhoea failed to make it to the toilet in time and the resulting stench had made the woman in the cell opposite throw up violently. Quietly, calmly and without comment, Diane and Kaitlyn donned their gloves and overalls and cleared away the mess.

Although the two of them almost always worked

together, they were not the only cleaners in the annexe. There was also Sheree, a slender black woman in her late twenties who made her living as a professional shoplifter. She viewed being caught as something of an occupational hazard and was boastful of the fact that she would be right back at it the moment she was released. Prison just didn't seem to bother her.

Sandra was in her late fifties with greasy grey hair, which she wore pulled back in a ponytail. She spoke with such a strong Irish accent that few could understand her and when she smiled she showed more gums than teeth. She was right at the end of her sentence for benefit fraud and counting the few remaining days before she went home. Diane was in the process of finding a replacement and, despite the nature of the work, there was no shortage of volunteers.

Kaitlyn was lying on her bed peacefully smoking when the door to the annexe was noisily opened by David the screw. 'Here's your new wing cleaner, ladies,' he said cheerfully and walked off.

Kaitlyn recognised her immediately as the pretty foreign girl she had shared a cell with during her first week in the prison. She smiled politely, wondering just how easy it was going to be to work with someone who spoke no English.

Soon after, Kaitlyn took some extra toilet rolls and sanitary towels from the store cupboard into her cell

– yet another of the benefits of being a cleaner was having access to unlimited supplies of toiletries. When she came back out into the hallway the new arrival was sitting on the edge of the annexe sofa reading a magazine. 'Kaitlyn's a very pretty name,' the woman said with a heavy accent. 'It must have really annoyed you when Julie kept on calling you Kate.'

Kaitlyn stopped, turned and looked at the woman, a furrow of concentration high on her brow. 'Fuck me, you can speak English.'

The woman laughed. 'Sometimes I choose to let people believe that I do not. I'm Rosa.' She held out a delicate, slender hand which Kaitlyn took and shook firmly.

'Hi, Rosa.'

Rosa smiled. 'I like to keep myself to myself and pick and choose who else I tell.'

'It's such a great idea. Makes me wish I'd learned Italian at school,' Kaitlyn said jokingly.

'Me too. I'm from Mexico.'

'You mean Julie didn't even get that right?'

Rosa shook her head and laughed. 'I don't think she gets much right, do you?'

'Whereabouts in Mexico do you live, Rosa?' Kaitlyn said while offering a drag from her roll-up.

'It's a little town close to the American border. A lot of people go there for day trips. But we live there so it's nothing special. Instead, we go to San Diego in California for day trips. It takes only an hour to drive there. Have you been to America?'

'I've never been anywhere,' said Kaitlyn. 'Never been abroad.'

'Well, you must, travel is wonderful. You should see the world while you're still young. It's very exciting.'

At that moment Diane arrived in the annexe. 'Ah, I see you've met the new girl. And there was me getting myself ready to do the big introductions.'

'Actually, we met before,' said Rosa. 'We were in a shared cell shortly after Kaitlyn arrived.'

The three women spent a few minutes discussing the benefits of not speaking English in a place like Holloway, then Diane turned to the new worker. 'Hey, Rosa, why don't you teach me a few words of Mexican, help pass the time.' Diane glanced at her watch. 'We've got ages before the next shift starts. Let's begin with the really useful stuff. What's Mexican for fuck off?'

In the weeks that followed the three women became firm friends, working hard and playing as hard as the prison rules would allow. If Diane had become Kaitlyn's new mother figure, then Rosa was the big sister she had never had. The twenty-two-year-old was sentenced to six years for drugs offences and carrying a firearm, after which she would be deported back to her homeland.

Only a few years older than Kaitlyn, Rosa kept Diane and her in stitches with tales of her extended family back in Mexico. Listening to her talk about the mischief her brothers and sisters and many, many cousins got involved in was like watching the best soap opera in the world. Each day, Kaitlyn could hardly wait for the next instalment.

'So he was having an affair with his mother-in-law the whole time,' Kaitlyn gasped as Rosa nodded enthusiastically.

'I've got to go to Mexico,' added Diane. 'It sounds like a wonderful place. Toyboys on tap!'

As the weeks went by the stories got wilder and crazier.

'This time, you have to be kidding, that can't be true,' insisted Diane after another amazing tale.

'Cross my heart and hope to die,' said Rosa. 'You have no reason to doubt me.'

'Bollocks,' said Diane after a long pause.

'I swear it's true. She told it to me herself.'

'You actually know the girl this happened to?'

'Not personally, but her sister is a friend of my cousin.' Rosa tried to keep a straight face, but then all three women burst out laughing.

'OK, this is what we are going to have to do. When you get out, I want you to come to Mexico to visit me. Then you can meet everyone and hear the stories for yourself.'

'Even Juan, the one with three wives?' asked Kaitlyn.

'Oh yes, especially Juan.'

Kaitlyn had a lot of time to think about her life while in prison – where she had come from and where she was going. Stuck to the wall beside her bed were the pictures of Christopher and of her and her mother, two reminders of the past she had left behind. She knew that the only way to get off the estate and make a better life for herself was money and the easiest way for her to make money would be to take control of the drugs on the Roxford. It was the one thing she really knew about and that had been bred into her from an early age. She also knew that at this point in her life she had nothing to lose and everything to gain. She began thinking through her plan over and over again, each time breaking down every section. She worked out whom she would use, where she would buy and how she would control it. Finally, she knew there was only one thing in her way: Gary and his gang.

Her future was taking shape, but first she had to get out of jail. Originally she had intended to fight tooth and nail to prove she was the victim of an assault and acted purely in self-defence, but after a series of long discussions with Diane she took her friend's advice and pleaded guilty. A guilty plea would get Kaitlyn an automatic discount of a third of the time she would have got if she had been found guilty on a not guilty plea. It was, Diane explained, the smart thing to do. 'This has nothing to do with guilt or innocence,' she told Kaitlyn. 'That's something you know in your heart. This has to do with playing the system to your best advantage.' On Diane's advice Kaitlyn also signed up for various educational and business studies courses, all of which would begin after she was sentenced.

On the day of the trial Kaitlyn listened carefully in the dock as her barrister, supplied to her by legal aid, explained that not only was she changing her plea to guilty but that she had been a model prisoner since the beginning of her time in Holloway. He asked for leniency, citing that the death of her mother had made her emotionally vulnerable. Judge Bowen looked directly at Kaitlyn when he sentenced her to five years for her original offence of Grievous Bodily Harm with intent, six months for assaulting a police officer and another six months for resisting arrest, all to run consecutively. He also recommended that she should serve a minimum of four years in prison.

When Kaitlyn heard her sentence she broke down and lost control. 'You fucking bastard, he tried to rape me,' she screamed. The court officers attempted to hold her down while she kicked and screamed. 'Did you fucking hear me, he tried to rape me!' She was grappled to the floor and dragged down to the holding cells below, her yells fading into the distance.

'Diane, can I ask you something?' It had been two weeks since Kaitlyn had received her sentence and she and Diane were mopping a corridor in between smoking roll-ups.

'You can ask me anything, love, anything apart

from how old I am and whether I've ever slept with another woman.'

Kaitlyn's eyes widened for a second but then she focused on what she wanted to talk about. 'You know the estate well, far better than I do.'

'The answer is yes, it's a fucking dump. Sorry, you were going to ask me whether I thought the place was a shithole, weren't you?'

Kaitlyn smiled. 'Actually, I wondered how come you know so much about what goes on there.'

'I still have friends. Sometimes they come and visit. They tell me things. There's nothing more to it than that.'

Kaitlyn nodded. 'Do you know what happened to my mother, how she got hold of the gear? She was doing so well. I know she wouldn't have gone out and got the stuff on her own. I'd warned too many people off. Something about it just isn't right. I think I know who was behind it, but I need to be sure.'

Diane swallowed hard before she spoke. 'Listen, Kaitlyn. You're like a daughter to me. I know you want retribution for whoever is responsible for what happened to your mum, but you've got to be careful. You're only young and you're already doing time. You don't want to end up back here again. You don't want to end up like me. I don't want you to run off and do something rash.'

There was a pause as Diane's words sank in.

'It was Gary, wasn't it?' Kaitlyn said, her voice barely more than a whisper.

Diane nodded. 'That's what I heard. I don't think he meant to kill her, he just didn't want you to leave the estate. He thought if he could get her hooked on gear again you'd have to stay.'

Tears started rolling down Kaitlyn's cheeks. She began sobbing, softly at first but then louder and louder. Within a few moments she was bawling and Diane had cradled her head and tucked it into the hollow of her shoulder, gently stroking Kaitlyn's hair.

'What are you going to do, Kaitlyn?' Diane asked at last.

'I don't know,' she said, sniffing and wiping her tears. 'But I'm gonna make him pay for what he did.'

That night Kaitlyn stroked the worn photograph of Christopher and the picture of her mother as she lay in bed. She wondered how her life would have been if she had been older and more able to look after Christopher. Even now she blamed herself for what had happened, although the older she got the more she realised there was little she could have done to protect him. She still suffered occasional nightmares, vivid visions of Steve and what he used to do to them, especially on the night that Christopher nearly died. He too would have to pay for what he had done, but he was not her main priority. She needed to take her revenge against the man who had killed her mother, then she had to find Christopher. For the time being, everything else would have to wait.

Chapter Twenty-three

August 1990

Christopher Tobin arrived home late in the afternoon to find his mother and father waiting for him. Jane and Paul were sitting at the kitchen table, mugs of tea in their hands and anxious expressions on their faces. As Christopher saw them a fleeting smile crossed his lips before he focused his attention and changed the look on his face to one of pure seriousness. 'Hi, Mum, hi, Dad,' he said casually. 'Think I'll go up to my room and listen to some music.'

Jane and Paul looked at each other as Christopher started to make his way up the stairs. 'Er, Christopher,' his father called out. 'Can we have a quick word?'

'What, right now? Colin made me a tape of the new Style Council album and I wanted to have a listen to it.'

'I'm sure that can wait,' added Jane, 'this won't take a minute.'

'Oh, very well then,' said Christopher, doing his best to appear reluctant. He sat down at the table and looked at each of his parents in turn. 'What is it, then?'

Jane and Paul exchanged glances once more. 'We just thought there might be something you wanted to tell us?'

'To tell you?' Christopher repeated, his face blank. 'Like what?'

In reality Christopher knew exactly what this was all about. He had taken his A levels a few weeks earlier and the letter announcing his results had arrived at the school earlier that day. Paul and Jane were anxious to know how he had done. Paul had taken the afternoon off work especially.

After three months of weekly sessions with Dr Manley, Christopher's mood and attitude had changed dramatically. While not exactly a model pupil, he had truly started to apply himself. The issue of his being bored at school had been resolved by moving him forward by two whole academic years, putting him into a class of pupils two years above him. This meant he had taken his O levels a few months before his fifteenth birthday. It had meant cramming two years' worth of study into a single year but Christopher had relished the challenge and the eight A grades he received had proved he was more than up to it.

What was more remarkable was that Christopher had made the move without alienating any of his old friends who were now stuck below him. He joined the school rugby team, enjoyed the occasional game of cricket and took part in numerous activity weekends as part of the Duke of Edinburgh Awards. A growth spurt that had started at the age of thirteen had seen him become almost six feet tall, with broad shoulders and a strong, sculptured face. Although he did not resemble either parent, he shared his mother's dark hair and his father's piercing blue eyes so the question of his background had never become an issue. He had retained his mischievous sense of humour and love of practical jokes.

Just one year after his O levels he had taken A levels in English, History and Geography. Again it meant completing two years of study in half the time, but for Christopher it was the only way to stop his brain getting bored. He had an unquenchable thirst for knowledge and enjoyed learning new facts and figures more than he ever thought possible. Provided he got the right grades at A level, Christopher knew he'd be able to get into university two whole years early. He had not yet decided what he would study, but those A levels would give him a wide range of options, which was just what he wanted. Paul and Jane were anxious to find out how he had done and he was keen to play with them for as long as possible.

'OK, Christopher,' said Paul with a smirk on his face. 'Stop messing about now. Tell us how you did in your exams. You know this is killing us.'

Christopher put on his best 'confused' face. 'Exams? What exams?'

Jane spoke jokingly. 'You're not too old for a clip round the ear, young man.'

'I'm sorry, Mum,' said Christopher, fighting the urge to laugh. 'I really don't know what exams you're talking about.'

Paul sighed. 'The A levels you took a couple of weeks ago. You know, the exams that will help decide your entire future.'

'Oh, those.' Christopher feigned surprise. 'Are those results due today?'

His parents spoke in unison: 'Christopher!'

He reached into his bag and pulled out a small sealed envelope. 'Ah, that must be what this letter is about. I thought it was a release form for a school trip or something.'

Paul gasped. 'You mean you haven't even opened it yet? I don't believe you.'

The truth was that Christopher had steamed open the envelope hours earlier and carefully resealed it. He knew how proud his parents were going to be of him and he wanted to milk the moment for all it was worth. 'Relax, Dad, you'll give yourself a coronary. I'll open it now.'

Christopher took the envelope between his fingers and held it up to the light, peering at it. 'You know, most parents would be thrilled at the fact their son had taken his A levels two years early. I mean, that's quite an achievement. Two years of study in record time and all that. I guess what I'm saying is that no matter what these results are like, I feel happy just knowing that I had the opportunity to try. And if I fail, then I'll just take them again in a couple of years' time.'

Paul and Jane looked at each other, uncertain of what to say. 'Absolutely,' Paul said at last, stuttering over his words. 'The most, erm, important thing is that you tried your best.'

Christopher smiled broadly. 'Yeah, right. I think you and Mum are even more worried about these results than I am. If I fail you'll probably kick me out and disown me.'

Paul reached across and held Jane's hand as Christopher ripped open the envelope and stared at the little slip of paper inside. 'Oh, dear,' he said softly, his face etched with concern.

'What is it, darling?' said Jane.

'I'm sorry, Mum, I don't know what to say.'

'What is it, son, what's happened?'

'Well,' said Christopher. 'It looks like I won't be here much longer. I'll be at university. Three "A"s.' He jumped up and began dancing round the room. Jane and Paul cheered and did the same, hugging each other and then Christopher as they bounced around the kitchen.

'You sure know how to wind someone up,' said Paul moments later, examining the envelope and inspecting the tell-tale marks left from where it had been steamed open earlier. 'You knew all along, didn't you?'

'Father, I couldn't possibly comment,' said Christopher with a grin.

Paul placed a hand lovingly on his son's shoulder. 'Just for the record, if you can look me in the eye and lie that convincingly, you'll make a great politician, a damn fine lawyer or a world-class poker player.'

'I'll take any one of those over being an architect,' came the cheeky reply.

* * *

Rosa's last week in prison was an emotional one. Diane and Kaitlyn had grown close to her and had no idea how they were going to cope without their daily dose of Mexican scandal. Kaitlyn still had four months of her own sentence to run and was not looking forward to the prospect of spending it without Rosa by her side. 'What will you do when you get back to Mexico?' she asked.

'Shop. It's what I like to do. There is a man, we are supposed to be getting married. He will look after me. How about you?'

Diane put down her magazine and listened in on the two women's conversation.

'I don't have a man, no.'

'Silly, I didn't mean that. I meant what you are going to do.'

'I'm just trying to get through being here, one day at a time. I really hadn't thought about what to do once I get out. I'll probably go back to what I was doing before.' Kaitlyn explained to Rosa how her life had been on the Roxford, about the robberies and the drug trafficking.

'So this is your plan, this is what you will do when you leave here?'

'This is it.'

'But why this? You're a bright girl, Kaitlyn. You could do anything. You could get yourself a real job, work your way up. I know your talents would shine through. In a few years the company would belong to you. Look how much you've learned since you've been here. The way you study all the time in here, the books you read. You must be the smartest girl here. Any company would want to take you on.'

Kaitlyn smiled. 'That might have happened a few years ago, but not now. The system fucked up, they screwed me over. The police, the judges, all of them. How am I supposed to go and get any kind of job now with this conviction hanging over my head? What kind of references am I going to be able to give out about where I've been for the last four years? They made me what I am. And I'm going to live up to their expectations.'

'You feel bitter, even though you might have ended up in prison anyway with the way you were carrying on?' There was a moment of silence as both women absorbed the power of Rosa's words. 'Well, if you insist. In the meantime I am going to teach you something you will not find in any of the books in the library.'

'What's that?'

'How to make men fall in love with you.'

Kaitlyn laughed. 'Why would I want that?'

Rosa gently ran her fingers through Kaitlyn's hair. 'Life has made you hard, being here has made you hard. But underneath it all you are a very beautiful woman. Men like beautiful women. It's still a man's world out there, Kaitlyn, but we have a power the men can never understand. If you make a man think that you want him, that you are falling for him, he will give you anything you want.'

'I don't want to be a prostitute.'

Rosa threw her head back and laughed. 'I'm not talking about sex. Once you give a man sex then you give away almost all of your power. I'm talking about the illusion of sex.'

Kaitlyn leaned towards Rosa, utterly intrigued. 'Please, tell me more.'

* * *

Christopher Tobin was much too young to drink but that didn't stop him being a regular at the pubs and clubs throughout Dorking and Guildford. He was celebrating his exam results but had to be careful that his parents didn't smell the alcohol on his breath when he returned home late on the pretext of having spent the evening watching videos at a friend's house. He loved the atmosphere of the places and the fact that he was surrounded by good friends, all of them doing their best to entertain one another with jokes and stories.

Christopher and seven of his friends found themselves at the newly opened Flutes Wine Bar on Dorking High Street. Christopher noticed the girl as soon as he walked in. She was standing alone at the far end of the bar wearing figure-hugging black trousers over a loose white top. She had long dark hair that fell in tight ringlets on either side of her head. Her skin was pale but smooth and perfect, and she had the most piercing blue eyes Christopher had ever seen. He stood there, in a trance, until a friend slapped him on the shoulder and snapped him out of it. 'Come on, we've found some seats.'

Christopher had grown up into a good-looking young man and he knew it. He had the easy confidence that goes naturally with any combination of a face that is not hard to look at, an athletic body and a quick-witted mind, but still he was worried. Something about this moment told him this was the girl he had been looking for, this was the one. And he was desperate to ensure he didn't mess things up. As his friends chatted, enjoying the beer and joking about with the females within the group, Christopher kept looking over to the girl at the bar. He sat back and tried to think of the best way to approach her. Just then his nostrils were filled with the scent of sweet perfume. He looked up to see the woman standing right beside him, her eyes burning deep into his. He wasn't sure if she'd said anything or if any of his friends had said anything. But this was good, she had come over to see him. She was definitely interested. All he had to do now was play it nice and smooth, play it cool.

'Hi,' he said as casually as he could. To everyone else he looked like a cocky and arrogant young man for he was hiding his nerves well.

'Hello,' the girl replied. Her voice was smooth and silky. It suited her perfectly.

'I saw you looking at me when I came in. I was thinking about giving you my number but as you've decided to come all the way over here to see me, maybe I should just ask for yours.' He smiled his best smile. Around the table his friends fell silent in anticipation of her answer.

The woman smiled briefly and held up a pad and pen that were clutched in her right hand. 'Nice of you to offer, but I came to know what you and your friends wanted to drink. This is business, not pleasure.'

Christopher suddenly felt about two feet tall and his friends burst out laughing. He wished the earth would open up and swallow him. He desperately tried to think of a way to turn the situation into a joke but nothing came to mind. The laughter around him eventually subsided. The girl was still there, smiling, but he was too embarrassed to look at her.

He spent the rest of the evening drinking at a steady pace and by the time he was ready for home he was more than a little drunk. As he made his way out of the bar the girl stopped him. 'You look a bit out of it. How are you going to get home?'

Christopher shrugged. 'It's not far, I can walk it from here.'

The girl smiled and started writing something on her notepad. 'OK, but here's the number of a local cab firm just in case you need it.' She stuffed the piece of paper into Christopher's top pocket and held the door open for him to leave.

It was only when he woke up the following morning and examined the paper as he was putting his shirt into the laundry basket that he realised there were two numbers on it. The first, underneath the name 'Al Cars', was one he recognised as a local cab firm. The second, written in a neat, small hand, was a local telephone number and below it a name: Sarah. And then the words: 'Call me.'

Chapter Twenty-four

November 1990

Kaitlyn hadn't slept a wink but for once she didn't care.

It had been her last night in jail and she felt as though she were about to be reborn. She had seen virtually nothing of the outside world for the past four years and was eager to begin her life over again. She would be starting off on the very bottom rung, but that was good as it meant she had nothing to lose and everything to gain.

Ever since Rosa had left, she and Kaitlyn had kept in regular touch by letter. At first Rosa had written mostly to keep Kaitlyn updated with the goings on in her extended family, but as her release date approached the letters took on a more urgent tone. Rosa wanted Kaitlyn to telephone her the moment she was out of prison, no matter what time of day or night. There were important things she needed to tell her but she couldn't do it by post. It was, Rosa explained, a private matter and she should not tell anyone, even Diane, that she would be making the call. The only clue she gave was that she had something to offer Kaitlyn that would help her to make all her dreams come true. Again and again the letters emphasised the importance of making the call the moment she was released and as Kaitlyn stood just inside the small wooden gate that led to the outside world, finding a telephone box and calling Rosa was the only thing on her mind.

Kaitlyn stepped out through the gate and took a deep breath of chilly autumn air. She didn't mind the cold – she felt as if an enormous weight had been lifted off her shoulders. She had made friends in Holloway and her goodbye with Diane had been deeply emotional. She had agreed to visit her regularly but knew the bond they would have while she was on the outside could never be as close as that which had seen her through the last years.

Kaitlyn's only possessions were the clothes she was wearing along with a few spare outfits, the photographs of her mother and brother, a few of Rosa's letters and £40 in £10 notes – her discharge payment, courtesy of the British government, for leaving prison.

She took in her surroundings for a few moments and then, settling her bag on her shoulder, turned left making her way down Holloway Road towards Seven Sisters in search of a newsagent's and a telephone box. The first place she found refused to give her change for the phone but offered to sell her a phone cards instead. She reluctantly accepted. A few yards further down she came across a red telephone box and stepped inside. The smell of urine and scratched graffiti on the perspex glass didn't bother her. She had spent the past couple of years smelling things that were far worse. She pulled out Rosa's last letter and carefully dialled the number.

'*Hola.*' The voice was slightly slurred and sleepy sounding.

'Rosa?'

'*Si. Quién es éste?*'

'Um. This is Kaitlyn.'

'Ah, Kaitlyn, it's good to hear your voice, even at four in the morning.'

'I'm sorry, I didn't . . .'

'No, no, it's fine. Now listen to me very carefully, Kaitlyn. This is what I want you to do.'

Kaitlyn had used up two £20 phone cards by the time she had put the phone down on Rosa but it had been worth every penny. She had been given detailed instructions of exactly what to do and where to go, and told that she must follow them to the letter. Kaitlyn stepped out of the telephone box and hailed a passing black cab. 'Take me to Edgware Road,' she told the driver and clambered in. Kaitlyn hadn't seen anything of London for four years, so even the bumpy taxi ride was an enormous pleasure. She took it all in as they sped through the London traffic. Passing through Regent's Park, the sights and smells of the city gave her such a heady feeling of freedom that she knew no matter what happened she would never return to prison.

It took a little under thirty minutes to reach the Kasbah coffee shop, just off the main Edgware Road and a stone's throw from Marble Arch and Hyde Park. It was a run-down, smoky place full of men in heavy overcoats. Kaitlyn knew she stuck out like a sore thumb walking up to the counter as she had been told to by Rosa.

'I'm looking for the dentist,' she said to the short, dark-haired woman behind the counter. The woman eyed her cautiously, then indicated a doorway at the rear of the café, blocked off by dangling multi-coloured plastic strips that reached from the top of the frame all the way down to the floor.

Pushing the strips aside with one hand, Kaitlyn saw a narrow set of stairs and began climbing them. At the top her path was blocked by a solid door. She knocked on it gently. Suddenly a small metal panel in the centre slid to one side and a pair of eyes looked through.

'I'm looking for the dentist,' Kaitlyn said.

'Who sent you?' the voice was rough and had a heavy accent Kaitlyn could not place.

'Rosa.'

'What is your name?'

'Kaitlyn.'

The man let out a snort of laughter. 'Not for long.'

The panel slid back and Kaitlyn listened as a series of heavy bolts on the other side of the door were pulled aside before it finally opened. 'Come in,' said the man with a strong Arabic accent, gesturing for Kaitlyn to enter.

The room was large, with faded grimy wallpaper and heavy net curtains on the windows opposite that were blackened with traffic fumes. To the right was a large table, filled with various documents, bottles of ink and rubber stamps. Behind that there was a large laminating machine and a Polaroid camera. To the left was a big desk featuring a powerful spotlight shining down on a drawing board that sat neatly on one corner and a large computer with a gleaming monitor on the other.

Kaitlyn's eyes scanned the room before they returned to see the Moroccan man who had let her in.

He was tall but thin, with a black moustache sprouting from his face, and judging by his stained teeth and smell he had obviously drunk copious amounts of coffee at the same time as smoking the Camel cigarettes that gave off a distinct odour. His eyes were red and tired-looking as if he'd spent hours working at the computer or staring at documents. His fingers were stained, partly with nicotine but also with inks and paints. He held out one hand. 'I am Jamal,' he said, finally removing the cigarette that had been lodged in the corner of his mouth.

'I'm Kaitlyn,' she replied, shaking his hand.

Jamal shook his head and wagged his index finger in Kaitlyn's face. 'No, your name is Monica. Monica Kelly.' He glanced at his watch. 'We've got a lot to do. If you're going to get to the airport on time we had better get moving.' He gently touched her shoulder and moved her towards a stool in a corner of the room in front of a large sheet of plain white paper. As Kaitlyn sat down Jamal reached for the camera and fired off a series of shots.

'Where am I flying to?' she asked, squinting as the flashgun exploded again and again.

'Los Angeles. Rosa will meet you there.'

Kaitlyn had no passport but even had she had one she would not have been allowed to travel to America because of her criminal record. Rosa was one step ahead. Jamal was one of the best forgers in the business and had been ordered and paid handsomely to kit Kaitlyn out with an American passport. It would not be a forgery – the US Immigration Service had some of the tightest security in the world and even the best fakes would fall at this first hurdle. Instead, Kaitlyn was being issued with a genuine US passport on which the photograph would be changed.

Only a small proportion of Americans ever travelled out of their country and there was a thriving market in making fraudulent applications in the names of those who had no plans to go anywhere. The real Monica Kelly would have received $10,000 to obtain a new genuine passport and hand it over to a local gang. Most of the time, though, the customer's photo would be submitted to the passport office rather than that of the genuine person. On this occasion that wasn't possible so a quick change of photos by Jamal, who was well paid for his forgery skills, was arranged and Kaitlyn was ready to travel. It was the perfect scam and officials at the border would have no way of knowing the difference.

'I thought Rosa was in Mexico,' said Kaitlyn, still trying to take it all in.

Jamal nodded impatiently while studying the controls on his camera. 'There are no direct flights to Tijuana from London, but it's only a ninety-minute drive from LA. Also the airport there is really busy. You're going through on fake papers so you want somewhere where the staff are under pressure to rush people through, not some quiet place where they are going to dwell on the details. It's the best route, the one we always use.'

Jamal retrieved the photographs from the camera and waved them in the air to dry. 'This will take me about an hour,' he said, reaching into a drawer for an envelope. 'Rosa told me to give you this. She said you're to go and get some clothes and a bag for the trip. And she told me to remind you that Mexico is pretty hot at this time of year.'

'Where should I go?' asked Kaitlyn.

'Anywhere. Oxford Street is just down the road. Turn left at Marble Arch and Selfridges is a little way down on the left.'

Kaitlyn took the envelope and opened it. She flicked through the notes quickly. It contained £5,000.

Kaitlyn, of course, had never been on a plane before but had heard people complain about the bad food, the lack of leg room and the poor choice of in-flight entertainment. As she sat in her first-class seat on the upper deck of a British Airways 747, she had to ask herself what they meant. It was like the bar of a luxury hotel and with only four of the twelve seats taken there was plenty of space to move around and stretch out – though her seat was so huge there was no real need. The food was some of the finest that had ever touched her lips and would have been even if she hadn't spent the past few years eating nothing but prison slop. She struggled to get used to the fizziness of the champagne but as it was free she kept working at it until she was a little drunk.

After lunch she reclined the seat all the way back and slept like a baby. The twelve-hour flight seemed to whizz by and Kaitlyn almost had to force herself to get off the plane when they arrived. It was only as she descended and caught a quick sight of the cramped economy section, full of grim-faced passengers who had spent more than half a day unable to move around properly, that she realised how spoiled she had been. It was definitely a life she could get used to.

In the taxi to the airport she had spent ages reading a crib sheet that Jamal had given her packed with details about the identity of the woman she was to become. He had also spent half an hour helping her to practise a fake American accent, not good enough to win an Oscar but more than adequate to get her through immigration. She rehearsed a few standard phrases: 'Hi, there, how you doing? Have a nice day' and nothing more.

'Supposing they want to have a bigger conversation with me, or realise something is wrong with the passport and start to question me? I'll lose the accent in a flash.'

'The passport is perfect,' said Jamal reassuringly. 'It has a student visa showing that you spent the last three years studying in London. That explains the accent. Anyway, if they do spot the changes to the passport then no matter how good your accent is you're gonna be totally screwed, so try not to worry about it.'

As it was, none of the details about her home town, the place she had gone to school, her parents or the reason she had travelled to England were needed. The immigration officer glanced at her passport, swiped it through a magnetic stripe reader and waved her through the barrier without a word.

LAX airport was a bustling place but through the crowds Rosa saw Kaitlyn in the Arrivals lounge and the two embraced like old friends.

'Any trouble?'

'None whatsoever,' Kaitlyn replied with a smile. 'I was glad I didn't have a British passport. The queue was enormous.' The pair laughed, clinched arms and walked through the airport chatting rapidly as they made their way into the car park where Rosa had parked her black convertible Mustang GT. 'Nice car,'

Kaitlyn said admiringly as they climbed inside, having stuffed her bag into the boot.

'OK,' said Rosa, still beaming with the joy at seeing her old friend. 'First I'm going to take you on a quick tour of Los Angeles. It won't take long, there isn't really that much to see. Then we drive down to San Diego and we'll have lunch in the gas lamp district – that's a really old part of the town – and then we'll cross the border into Mexico. You're not tired, are you?'

'Not at all.'

The whistle-stop tour of Los Angeles included drinks on the sands at Venice Beach, a drive along Sunset Strip, a quick viewing of the famous 'Hollywood' sign and then a walk along the boulevard where movie stars of the day had left their hand prints in the pavement. Everything Kaitlyn saw was new and different. She couldn't believe the width of the roads, the height of the buildings or the size of the cars.

From Hollywood they headed south on I–10 for the hour-long drive to San Diego. Kaitlyn was astonished to learn that not only was the speed limit just 55mph, but almost everyone was actually sticking to it. 'It's a real pain in the arse,' said Rosa. 'But don't worry, once we're in Mexico I'll show you what this baby can do.' The roof was down, the sun was out and they enjoyed the attention from the male drivers on their trip south.

They arrived early evening and dined on fresh

seafood at the Lobster House that overlooked San Diego bay, then joined the long line of traffic making its way across the border to Tijuana. 'This is a good time,' said Rosa. 'All the day trippers are heading back to the US. If we had come earlier we would be waiting in line a long time.'

They crossed the border and drove into the centre of Tijuana. Rosa parked the car so Kaitlyn could walk along the main street, which had been paved over and blocked to traffic. At one end you could see the huge concrete fence that formed the border with the United States, at the other rows of multicoloured houses on hills stretching off into the distance.

The main road itself was a curious place. Teeming with tourists, it consisted almost entirely of cut-price pharmacies, restaurants, bars and strip joints, and the odd traditional craft stall. Sleazy-looking side roads branching off the main drag were lined with young women in revealing clothes, leaning back and eyeing any male passing them. Rosa smiled. 'For most of the Americans, this is all they ever see. The teenagers come for the beer and the strip clubs, the old come for the cheap medicine and the people in between come for the craft shops. None of this is the real Mexico but don't worry, you will see it soon.'

They returned to the car and left the town centre without incident, weaving through dozens of side streets until they finally reached a stretch of empty road. Rosa put her foot down. Kaitlyn's body was pressed back into the leather seat as the car accelerated rapidly and when she glanced over at the speedometer it was reading 110 and still climbing rapidly. Almost immediately the sound of sirens erupted behind them and Kaitlyn saw flashing blue lights reflected in the windscreen. 'Oh, shit,' she said. 'Now we're fucked.'

Rosa smiled calmly as she pulled to one side of the road. 'You give in too easily. Don't worry about it. Everything is going to be fine.'

The police car pulled in behind the Mustang and a burly officer with a swarthy face and heavy moustache clambered out and made his way towards them. As he approached, Rosa lowered her window and used the tips of her fingers to raise her sunglasses and display her big brown eyes. Kaitlyn spoke no Spanish but she didn't need a translator to work out what happened next. The police officer arrived at the side of the car in a defiant mood, his ticket book already in his hand. One look at Rosa and he blushed deeply, began stuttering and stumbling over his words, then apologising profusely he urged her to continue her journey. Even before the cop had got back in his car, Rosa had gunned the engine and the Mustang was off down the highway. If anything, she was going even faster now.

Rosa said nothing for the longest time. She simply drove and smiled to herself.

It was Kaitlyn who ultimately broke the silence. 'Rosa.' She had to shout to be heard over the noise of the wind rushing past the car.

'Yes, my dear,' came the reply.

'What just happened?'

'Oh, nothing. This is a new car, he didn't recognise it. Now he's just a little worried because he thinks he might not get any money this month.'

Kaitlyn let the words sink in. 'Rosa.'

'Yes, dear.'

'Just who exactly are you?'

'Ah, now that is a story I plan to tell you when we get to my house. But I can tell you something now. I am nobody, but the man I am about to marry is a very important man.'

'What, is he like the mayor or something?'

Rosa laughed. 'Not exactly. He is something far more powerful than that. His name is Benjamin. Benjamin Felix.'

To locals they were 'El Mafioso' or 'Los Traffickers'. From their safe haven north of the border, Americans referred to them as the 'Tijuana Cartel'. Law enforcement agencies around the world knew them as the AFO – the Arellano Felix Organisation – but whatever name they were given, one thing remained constant. The criminal gang run by Benjamin Arellano Felix and his brothers Ramon, Eduardo and Javier was, quite simply, the most powerful, violent and aggressive drug-trafficking organisation in the world. Over the course of a single decade the AFO had turned the freeway between Mexico and the US into a huge pipeline for cocaine, marijuana and amphetamines. The drugs poured across by car, by boat along the Pacific coast and even by secret tunnel.

A month before Kaitlyn had arrived in Tijuana, police acting on a tip-off searched a farm on the US side of the border and discovered a safe under the stairs. They cracked it open but found it empty and were about to move on when someone spotted that the safe floor was too high. It was a false bottom and underneath was a shaft descending to a 1,200-foot tunnel, complete with electric lights and rails, which had borne millions of dollars' worth of drugs under the US–Mexican border. There were at least a dozen other tunnels, as yet undiscovered, dotted along the border.

Despite the gang's audacity, and the fact that it was so well known that it bore the family name, the four brothers remained untouchable. They bought anonymity, bribing politicians and policemen in bulk, at the cost of an estimated $1 million a week. Those they could not buy, they killed. When one official refused to be bribed, the cartel had him executed, knowing his deputy would get the job and accept their money. Benjamin and Ramon led the enterprise. Benjamin had brains and a certain strategic flair, while Ramon, eleven years his junior, was the enforcer – a task to which he was perfectly suited. All the brothers were highly educated, had obtained university degrees and were fluent in several languages. They ran the cartel like a multinational corporation.

*

Benjamin Arellano Felix was a shade under six feet tall and slim, with pale-green eyes that shone out from behind silver-framed circular glasses. His face was smooth and clean-shaven, and he looked much younger than his thirty-six years. He stood up when Kaitlyn entered the room and embraced her, kissing her gently on each cheek. 'I have heard much about you. It is a pleasure to meet you.' She was in the centre of a fantastically plush living room in the middle of a palace that was set within a 1,000-acre estate with everything a young entrepreneur could ever need and want, from a thirty-seat cinema, car museum and a private race track to a hangar housing a private jet and two helicopters.

As Kaitlyn was offered a choice of refreshments, another man walked into the room. He needed no introduction. From what Kaitlyn had heard about him on the journey to the house, Ramon Felix was everything she had expected: tall, powerfully built but with eyes that betrayed his psychopathic tendencies. Brought up in the best tradition of the old school, which meant the men were in charge and the women did as they were told, he eyed Kaitlyn suspiciously as Rosa introduced her.

It soon became clear that Rosa could twist the brothers round her little finger. Part of what had attracted Benjamin to her in the first place was her ability to stand up to him and challenge him. He was used to women falling at his feet but here was one who did the complete opposite. 'I have told the brothers all about you,' Rosa explained as they sat. Ramon remained standing close to the doorway.

'I was impressed with the things Rosa has told me about you, the way you had controlled the drug trade in your area.' Benjamin sat closer to Kaitlyn and all eyes were upon her. Then he looked directly at her. 'More importantly, I'm impressed with your plans for the future. Rosa told me what happened to your mother.'

Kaitlyn swallowed hard at the memory. Ramon was staring at her intently. He had not yet said a word.

'It's a vicious business we are in, Kaitlyn, do you not agree?'

'Yes, it is.' Kaitlyn's voice was calm as she focused hard on what Benjamin was saying.

'When I told Benjamin all these things' – Rosa leaned forward to Kaitlyn – 'Benny came up with an idea. Something that could be of benefit to you and to us.'

'What kind of idea?'

Benjamin took a small bag out of his back pocket and placed it on the coffee table in front of Kaitlyn. 'Do you know what this is?'

'I'm guessing it's cocaine.'

'That's right. And we want you to sell this for us.'

'What, on the Roxford? Are you kidding? The only people who use that stuff are film stars and rock musicians. It's way too expensive in Britain. People on the Roxford have a hard enough time finding £10 to pay for a bag of heroin. There's no way they are going to be able to stump up sixty or seventy quid for a line of coke. No way in the world.'

'A year ago I would have agreed with you,' said Benjamin. 'But the world is changing, Kaitlyn. First, the market for cocaine in America, our main outlet, is almost saturated. There is a little more growth but after that it will reach a plateau. Like any good business, we need to keep expanding in order to maintain our profitability. That means finding new markets. The Colombians are already doing this. They are supplying more cocaine to Europe.' Benjamin stood and crossed the room to get more ice for his drink, his eyes never once leaving Kaitlyn. 'Britain may be only a fraction the size of the US but the price of a kilo of cocaine is much higher there. That means that a smaller number of sales will result in good profits.'

'OK.' Kaitlyn nodded. 'But I don't mix in those kinds of circles. Yet, anyway.'

'You don't have to,' said Ramon. 'We've come up with a totally new product, something that will appeal to the people who are using heroin at the moment and at a price they can afford. It's already taking off in America, in the ghettos and the housing projects, and we want you to help us to do the same in London.'

'What is it?'

'There are many names,' said Rosa. 'People call it wash, cholly, the white lady — but the one name that seems more popular than all the others put together is crack.'

Benjamin took over, his voice heavy with enthusiasm. 'The profit potential is enormous. The drug produces a powerful high that lasts only a few minutes. As soon as it is over, you want more. It is instantly addictive. If it proves successful on the estate, from there it could sweep the country. So what do you think, Kaitlyn? Are you with us?'

'Most definitely, Benjamin.'

'Then call me Benny. All my friends do.'

The following morning Kaitlyn was flown by helicopter to a remote township 150 miles from Tijuana, which served as one of the main packaging plants for the brothers' cocaine operation. A dozen heavily armed guards milled about as Kaitlyn was shown round the warehouse where women and young children worked at weighing and dividing the white powder into smaller bags ready for distribution. She was also given a first-hand demonstration of how to convert cocaine into crack – a simple process needing only some water, a frying pan and some baking soda.

'Cocaine is a profitable drug,' Benjamin explained, 'but converting it to crack will quadruple your profits. You are on your way to becoming an extremely wealthy woman.'

As they left the warehouse, Ramon pulled his brother to one side and hissed in his ear, 'What are we doing with this woman? We know nothing about her except what Rosa has said. This is not good.'

'She checked out. The Moroccan looked into her background even before she left the prison.'

'She has no money and she is a woman.'

'But she has the contacts and the network in Britain, which is the one thing we do not have.'

'Well, she still needs to earn my trust. And if she does not, she will have a very short life.'

By the time they arrived back at the estate Ramon's hostility towards Kaitlyn was greater than ever. The two women lingered by the car as the men walked up towards the main entrance of the house. Rosa could read Kaitlyn's thoughts. 'You'll have to forgive Ramon. He doesn't like strangers knowing our business. Especially women. He thinks they are weak.'

Kaitlyn knew the opportunities that were presenting themselves to her were golden and she didn't want anything to get in the way. The only thing to do with Ramon, she decided, was to face up to him. 'What can I do to make you trust me?' she asked.

Ramon glared at her, then suddenly snapped his fingers. 'Come with me.'

The two of them made their way to the side entrance of the house, which backed on to a series of garages filled with prestige cars. Ramon paused for a few moments, trying to decide which one to take before settling for the bright-red Porsche 911.

Kaitlyn climbed into the passenger seat and ignored Ramon, who rolled his eyes when she snapped on her seat belt. 'If you don't trust me to drive you, how am I expected to trust you as a business partner?'

It took only a few minutes to reach their final destination, a run-down shanty town close to the river that formed part of the natural border with the United States. Ramon drove to the end of a dirt track and pulled up outside a shack built of old breeze blocks and bits of corrugated iron. 'Open the glovebox,' he said softly.

Kaitlyn did and a heavy black revolver came into view.

Ramon looked for her reaction but Kaitlyn didn't flinch. 'OK,' he said. 'In this house lives a man who insulted me two weeks ago. This cannot go unpunished. I want you to take the gun, go into the house and kill the man. I will wait here.'

Kaitlyn turned to face Ramon. She looked deep into his eyes. He couldn't possibly be serious. Could he? 'You're kidding, right; this is some kind of joke?'

'Is no joke,' said Ramon, his face deadly serious. 'Take the gun and kill him. Once you have done that you will have proved your trustworthiness and we can do business.'

She had to think on her feet as quickly as possible. 'But it's broad daylight and we're in the middle of a built-up area. It's too public. The sound of the gun would only bring the police.'

Ramon laughed, reached across and picked up the gun. He leaned out of the open window and pointed the gun up at the sky, then pulled the trigger three times in quick succession. On the street a few people wandering by jumped in alarm but then carried on with their business as if nothing had happened. 'This is Tijuana,' he explained. 'People are used to gunshots. No one will think it is anything out of the ordinary.' He brought the gun back into the car and held it out to Kaitlyn. 'Now do what I say. Go into the house and kill the man. He is tall with no hair. His name is Raul. You will know him immediately. He must die.'

Kaitlyn's eyes were fixed on the gun. She shook her head. 'No, I won't do it.'

'What, are you scared? Are you scared of this?' He dropped the gun into her lap. The smell of gunpowder filled her nostrils and she could feel the warmth of the barrel through her jeans.

Kaitlyn took a deep breath. 'If this man has insulted you, then that is something you need to deal with yourself. I'm not going to execute someone in cold blood on your say-so. If I ever kill someone, it will be because there is a good reason. Not because someone tells me to.'

'This is a test. A test of loyalty, a test of faith. If you do this for me then I know I can trust you, I know that you have guts and courage and balls like a man. I know that you are not a silly little girl.'

'Listen, Ramon, I may be a girl and I may not have

balls but the advantage is I don't have to think with them!'

Ramon laughed. His face suddenly softened. 'Put the gun back in the glovebox,' he said softly. This time Kaitlyn did as she was told. Ramon started the car and they drove back to the house in absolute silence. Kaitlyn had to clench her fists all the way back to stop her hands from shaking.

Rosa was waiting in the driveway when they returned. She walked up to the car and smiled expectantly. 'Well?'

'She didn't do it,' said Ramon. 'She didn't even get out of the car.'

Kaitlyn didn't know where to look or what to say. She got out with her eyes lowered. It took several moments before she finally got up the courage to look at Rosa, who was smiling broadly. 'Well done, Kaitlyn,' she said.

'What's going on?'

'Sorry Ramon put you through that but we had to be sure. I knew you wouldn't let me down.'

Kaitlyn looked round to see Ramon who was walking behind the car to approach them. He too was smiling. 'If we needed someone who will kill for no reason we could find that in less than five paces from the front door,' he said.

Benny came up and put his arm round Kaitlyn. 'Ramon is right. What we need is someone with a few more brains, who thinks before she acts. I know we can work with you, but you have to understand what you are committing to. Our business means everything to us and we will protect it at all costs.'

Kaitlyn nodded. There was no need to spell it out any further. She would be given the chance to work with the gang but if she fucked up, she would be dead.

Chapter Twenty-five

March 1991

Jacob Collins and Errol Gants were right on the edge.

They had been up all night, smoking some of the strongest dope they had ever experienced and snorting lines of high-quality speed known as Pink Champagne because of its reddish tint. Jacob had passed out on the floor and Errol was just contemplating his fourth line of the evening when the sound of footsteps in the hallway made his blood run cold. The flat they occupied on the estate was in a quiet area and almost all the flats on either side of them had been boarded up. No one ever came up this way and that was one of the reasons they had chosen it. Even in his drugged-up state Errol knew this was not a good sign.

Suddenly there was a sharp knock on the door. As quietly as he could Errol reached across and shook Jacob violently awake. Holding a finger to his lips he indicated the door and passed his friend the heavy Webley revolver that had become their favourite weapon. Big and bulky and firing the same round as a .44 magnum, the Webley looked mean enough to scare most people away without a shot being fired.

But if necessary it would take off a man's head at thirty feet.

Errol armed himself with a sawn-off shotgun and moved silently towards the door as Jacob picked up the money bag and made his way to the window. They had chosen the room deliberately because of the small balcony that allowed them to climb across to the fire escape in case of an emergency.

'Who is it?' said Errol once Jacob was in position. The voice that came back through the door was strange: deep and gruff but somehow unreal, as if someone was trying hard to disguise how they sounded: 'It's the council. You're squatting in this flat illegally and I'm here to evict you.' Errol looked over at Jacob and gave him a withering stare. What the hell was going on? 'I've informed the police,' the voice through the door continued. 'They'll be here any minute to assist me.'

Errol signalled at Jacob to move back towards the door. They were going to have to make a run for it but their best chance was to take the council worker hostage. 'I think there must be some mistake,' Errol said, trying hard to keep his voice calm. 'I'm just putting on some clothes.' Using silent sign language, Errol indicated that Jacob should pull the door open rapidly and then grab the council worker and drag him inside. 'Just a minute,' said Errol, turning his head away from the door to make it sound as if he were in the centre of the room. Then he nodded at Jacob.

The door flew open in a flash and, one hand on the trigger of the sawn-off gun, Errol reached round with the other to grab the man by the scruff of the neck. But there was no council worker. Only a face he hadn't seen for a very long time.

'Hello, boys,' said Kaitlyn, eyeing the barrels with a big grin on her face. 'Now what kind of a welcome is that?'

* * *

Paul Tobin was hunched over a drawing board in his study, working on a design for a marble supporting column that was to be the centrepiece of a small housing development and trying to decide the best way to make it stronger without making it an eyesore to the residents. He had spent the day working at home but made little progress and it was now early evening. It was causing him far more trouble than it ought and he really had to fight to concentrate. *I must be tired or going down with flu or something*, he thought to himself. *I should have cracked this by now.*

A few minutes earlier he had heard the doorbell ring but ignored it – Jane was out but Christopher was at home and it would probably be his girlfriend or other friends calling for him. It was only when Christopher coughed that Paul realised his son had entered the room. 'Hello, son, what is it? I'm a bit tied up right now. Can it wait?'

'Dad, I really need to talk to you.'

Something about the quivering tone of the boy's

voice told Paul this was serious. He swivelled round in his chair and gave Christopher his full attention. 'OK, what is it?'

Christopher spoke but his words were mumbled, totally incoherent.

'Speak up.'

'I'm going to have to go out for a few hours. Might not be back for quite a while.'

Paul glanced at his watch. 'No, out of the question. It's nearly six. Mum's going to be home soon and we were supposed to be having dinner together.'

'Dad, I don't have any choice.'

At that moment two tall men in off-the-peg business suits stepped into Paul's study.

'Who the hell are you?' said Paul.

'Sorry to bother you, sir. My name is Detective Sergeant Webster, my colleague is DC McKinley, and we're from Dorking CID. We've just arrested your son on suspicion of theft and deception.'

'Jesus Christ. What the hell's going on?'

'A credit card reported as stolen was used to make a number of purchases,' DS Webster explained. 'We suspect your son of being the signatory.'

Christopher winced at the words. 'Dad, let me explain. I was out with Sarah the other night and she had this wallet that she said belonged to her brother . . .'

Paul held up his hand. 'Stop, for God's sake. Don't say another word.' There were a few seconds of silence as Paul Tobin's face twisted with a mixture of shock and anger. 'You bloody idiot!' he gasped. 'How could you be so bloody stupid?'

The next few seconds were spent in an awkward silence.

'Which station are you taking him to?' asked Paul.

'Harbour Lane.'

'OK. I need to make some calls and get hold of his mother, find a solicitor. Jesus, this is the last thing I need.'

DS Webster placed a heavy hand on Christopher's shoulder and led him from the room. Paul got up from his chair to see them out. 'I can't believe you're putting us through this,' he said as the officers led his son away. 'When Mum hears about this it's going to break her heart.'

* * *

During the time that Gary had known her, Kaitlyn had been something of a tomboy to say the least. He had first seen her at the age of eleven when she was a hard-as-nails kid from the streets who could give as good as she got in any situation. After three years in prison, he had expected her to emerge even tougher. When Errol and Jacob told him she was out and wanted to meet up with him at the local café, he was intrigued, curious, but nothing more. What he saw totally blew him away. Kaitlyn's brunette hair had grown long and had been naturally highlighted by the sun during her visit to Mexico. Her skin was tanned and it glowed. Her eyes were bright and alert, and deepened into a glorious shade of hazel.

'Wow, you look amazing. Have you been away?' Gary asked as two steaming mugs of tea arrived on the table.

Kaitlyn smiled and shook her head, letting her hair fall round her shoulders. 'I wish. Been to the tanning salon. You know how it is when you come out of prison, you just look grey.'

'Well, if everyone who went to prison came out looking as good as you, they'd be queuing round the block.' Gary took a long drink from his mug and ran his eyes up and down Kaitlyn's body. 'So, what can I do for you?'

Kaitlyn looked directly into Gary's eyes, fluttering her lashes slightly. 'I need some work. I'm absolutely broke and being on the estate is the only thing I know, the only thing I was ever any good at.'

Gary shrugged. 'I don't know. Things have changed a lot. You've changed a lot.'

Kaitlyn reached over and gently touched Gary's forearm. 'Surely there's something I could do?'

Gary was suddenly seeing Kaitlyn in a new light and feeling a familiar stirring in his loins. Even if he didn't have any work for her, he would take advantage of the situation to have a little fun. 'Sure, I can sort something out,' he said softly. 'Tell you what. I've got to rush off now, but why don't we have dinner, say tomorrow night?'

'Oh, Gary, that would be great!'

'Yeah. OK. What time shall I pick you up?'

'Shall we say eight? I'll see you at the corner by

the telephone boxes.' Rosa was right about men. She got up and leaned over the table to say goodbye. She could feel Gary's eyes all over her. 'Don't be late because I won't wait.'

Gary wore his best black Armani suit with a black T-shirt and handmade Italian loafers. A Rolex hung from one wrist and a Cartier ring in the shape of a panther adorned one finger. His E-Class Mercedes pulled up outside the estate right on time to find Kaitlyn waiting for him. She wore a silky black dress that showed off the woman she had become. Gary was instantly aroused.

Dinner took place at a fancy Italian restaurant on the south side of the River Thames. They had both been drinking steadily and the conversation had flowed easily. Gary was feeling relaxed and slightly drunk. It was all going according to plan. When they clambered back into Gary's car, Kaitlyn looked across shyly as she did up her seat belt. 'What shall we do now?'

Gary leaned across and kissed Kaitlyn gently on the lips. She responded briefly, then pushed him back. 'Not here. There are people walking past.'

'OK babe. Let's go back to my place, yeah?'

Kaitlyn nodded. Inside she was thinking it was the first time anyone had called her babe since Angela's death. She made a mental note never to let it happen again.

As they made their way up to Gary's luxury apartment only a mile away from the Roxford in the trendy suburb of Clapham, his hands were all over Kaitlyn. As soon as they passed through the door Gary resumed trying to kiss and touch her.

'Shall we have another drink first?' Kaitlyn suggested.

Gary sighed. He hated all the game playing but he knew he had to go along with it. 'Sure, what do you want?'

'Bacardi and Coke.' Kaitlyn took a seat on the leather sofa.

'Coming right up.' As he vanished into the kitchen Kaitlyn opened her handbag to check its contents – paper wrap, syringe, mobile phone. She closed it as soon as Gary returned, placing two tumblers on the coffee table.

'Got any ice?'

Gary groaned and returned to the kitchen. As he did so Kaitlyn slid the contents of the paper wrap into Gary's drink and quickly stirred it with her finger. It had just dissolved when he returned.

'Let's toast the future.' Kaitlyn spoke with a smile on her face. She had been waiting for this moment for two and a half years.

'Fuck the future, let's toast this evening.' Gary raised his glass and they both drank deeply.

Gary put his glass down and eyed Kaitlyn's breasts and the outline of her legs through the dress. He licked his lips noisily, then leaned forward. He placed one hand on her shoulder, the other round her waist and pulled her towards him roughly. Now she was close enough to smell his warm breath, feel his scratchy stubble against the side of her face. Gary nuzzled into her neck, breathing in her perfume as one finger started to trace little circles round her left breast and stomach. His mouth began to move across to her own, his wet tongue forced its way between her lips. He was overeager, clumsy, anything but gentle.

Then suddenly he pushed Kaitlyn back and stared at her. He blinked several times in quick succession, seemingly trying to get his eyes to focus. He held one hand out in front of him and gazed at it, an expression of total bewilderment on his face. 'What the . . .' He never finished the sentence. He pitched forward and collapsed in Kaitlyn's lap.

'Thank fuck for that,' she said out loud, reaching for her mobile. She punched in a number and waited for an answer. 'It's on.'

Gary woke with a start after a bucket of ice-cold water was thrown in his face. He swore and spluttered under his breath, tossing his head from side to side to get the water out of his eyes. He had instinctively tried to reach up and wipe his face with his fingers but for some reason his arms were no longer working. 'What the fuck is going on?' His mind was slow and fuzzy, he felt like he'd been drinking heavily for hours. He blinked rapidly until the final few droplets fell away and he could at last start to see. Looking up, he saw that his hands had been tied to the ventilation pipe that ran along the ceiling of his kitchenette. His feet had also been bound tightly together, the rope cutting deep into the flesh of his calves. His vision was still a little blurry but as he began to focus he saw that Kaitlyn, Errol and Jacob were standing in front of him. Jacob was holding an empty bucket of water, a smug smirk on his face.

Gary shook his arms, struggling to get loose. Kaitlyn looked over at him, then said something Gary could not hear to the two men. Errol and Jacob each flashed a quick glance in Gary's direction and headed out of the room. 'What the fuck's going on?' screamed Gary as he tried to get loose once more. 'What are you playing at, you stupid cow?'

Kaitlyn said nothing. She simply stared deep into Gary's eyes with a look of complete and utter contempt.

Gary tried to kick his legs out in her direction but that put his full weight on his wrists, sending sharp shooting pains along the length of his arms. 'Ah, fuck. For fuck's sake, Kaitlyn, what are you playing at? What's the meaning of this?'

Kaitlyn's voice was calm, her face deadly serious. 'Is that how it's going to be, Gary? You're just going to stand there and play the idiot, pretend you don't know what this is about?'

'I don't know what this is about. You think I owe you money or something? What the fuck is going on?'

Kaitlyn shook her head mournfully. 'I wonder if

that was what my mum said when she found the drugs you left for her.'

Now for the first time Gary saw the syringe clutched in the fingers of Kaitlyn's right hand and the horror of what was about to happen suddenly dawned on him. He swallowed hard. When he spoke again his voice had totally changed. The anger and arrogance were gone. Gary was pleading for his life. 'Listen, Kaitlyn, I don't know what you've got planned but whatever it is, you don't want to do it. You don't want to do it. I don't know what you've been told but it's crap, all of it. I don't know anything about what happened to your mum. I was as shocked as anyone. You know what people around here are like, they say anything. You can't believe a word they say.'

For a split-second a shadow of doubt fell across Kaitlyn's mind. Gary saw it flicker behind her eyes and knew it was his only chance. He pressed on, his words coming in breathless gasps. 'It's that fucking bitch Diane, isn't it? She's been filling your head with all sorts of nonsense. She's always had it in for me. I used to work for her old man before we fell out. She's put you up to this.'

Kaitlyn shook her head. 'No, Gary. You did it. I'm surprised at you. I thought you'd be man enough to admit it, take what was coming to you.' She took a step forward, the syringe pointed upwards at a sharp angle.

Gary saw that it was full of a dirty brown liquid.

Heroin. He began babbling. 'Kaitlyn, babe, listen, you've got to understand. I didn't mean for her to die. It's not like I killed her. She'd been on the drugs for years and she was bound to go back anyway. I just didn't want her to leave. I just didn't want you to leave the estate. You understand that, don't you?'

Kaitlyn said nothing as she moved forward.

'For fuck's sake, Kaitlyn. You can't do this. You can't just kill me in cold blood. We go way back.'

'You're right, Gary. You're absolutely right. It wouldn't be fair for me to kill you in cold blood. I can see you never meant to do my mother any harm. Christ, you probably thought you were doing her a favour.'

Gary nodded. 'Yes. That's it. You thought she was off the stuff but she was always begging for it. She told me to get her those drugs. She went on and on about it. I didn't think I had any choice. I was being torn in so many directions. I was trying to please everyone at the same time.'

Kaitlyn was nodding sagely as she listened to Gary. 'The thing is, Gary, that's exactly what I'm doing. I'm trying to please everyone. Most of all me.'

She moved forward again and grabbed hold of Gary's right arm just below the elbow.

'No, please,' he gasped. 'I'm begging you, please. Look, I've got money. I can give you money. You'll never have to work again. Please.'

Kaitlyn paused. The needle was just inches from

Gary's arm. She looked him right in the eyes. 'You think this is about money? You think you can buy your way out of this? You killed my mother, Gary. There isn't enough money in the world to make up for what you've done.'

Gary tried to move his arm away but the pain was too great. There was nothing he could do apart from watch and swear as Kaitlyn drove the point of the needle through his skin and into his arm. He shut his eyes and the drug started to flood his bloodstream. He could no longer feel the pain in his arms. He could no longer feel anything at all. It was as if he were floating and the ropes that tied him had melted away to nothing. He opened his eyes and saw Kaitlyn directly in front of him. 'You stupid fucking bitch,' he said. His words were drawn out and slurred, as though he were speaking in slow motion. 'You stupid fuck,' he said again and again, his voice growing softer each time.

Kaitlyn moved her ear closer to Gary's mouth. His voice was only a whisper now, the swearwords barely audible. It became softer and thinner until there was nothing left of it, just the sound of breath passing back and forth over his lips. Soon this sound also became softer until it stopped and there was only silence.

Kaitlyn moved back and looked up at Gary's face. His eyes were still open but now they were glassy and soulless. He was dead.

*

311

While Kaitlyn emptied the drinks tumblers and put them in her handbag for later disposal, Errol and Jacob loaded and checked the automatic guns they had picked up from Benny's and Ramon's London contacts. Kaitlyn slipped into the change of clothes Jacob had brought her, then loaded her own gun like a professional. She had spent hours practising with a variety of weapons while in Mexico. Now at last she had a chance to put the theory she had learned into practice. Everything had been planned to perfection. Gary's safe house, where the youngsters came to collect the drugs they ran through the estate, was run by Big Dave and Tommy. Errol kicked down the door and Kaitlyn and Jacob went inside, guns drawn. Big Dave's and Tommy's hands shot into the air.

'Gary no longer looks after the estate. We do. You either work with us or against us.'

Dave spoke first: 'What's happened to Gary?'

'You'll find out soon enough,' said Kaitlyn, waving the barrel of her gun in his face. 'You might even get to join him. Now, what's it going to be?'

From that night on the distribution of drugs was transformed on the estate. Instead of having runners they had two main safe houses, one run by Tommy, the other by Big Dave. Both men were taught how to manufacture crack, which they sold through a tiny hatch in the main front door. Business boomed almost instantly, crack took off like wildfire. On all four blocks on the estate there were lookouts positioned, so that if the police launched a raid, the safe houses could be abandoned at a moment's notice. Kaitlyn put Errol in charge of distribution and Jacob in charge of security. Now nothing could stop them. Benny was right – she was going to make a lot of money.

* * *

Detective Sergeant Karl Marshall was the eldest son of Jamaican immigrants who had arrived in the UK as part of the great Commonwealth migration in the early fifties. His father, Bernard, had expected great things. He had been working as a panel beater in a garage in the heart of downtown Kingston when the recruiter from England arrived. He and his fellow workers crowded round as the man showed brochures about the life they could expect if they moved to Britain. There were plenty of jobs on offer but the one that caught Bernard's eye was that of London Underground guard. It sounded so glamorous. After all, they had guards at Buckingham Palace. The photograph on the cover of the brochure showed a man only a few years older than himself directing passengers on to a sleek-looking silver train that ran – though it hardly seemed possible – beneath the city streets. The man wore a smart uniform and a peaked cap. The money sounded good too – at least ten times what he was earning in Jamaica. Although he understood the cost of living would be higher, he would surely still be living like a king.

It didn't take long for Bernard's hopes and dreams to be smashed. He had expected to be respected as a guard for the transport system. Instead, he was forced to work ludicrous hours in filthy conditions, despised by passengers and racially abused by his fellow workers. His salary would have made him a wealthy man back home but in London he was only just scraping by. He found lodgings in a tiny bedsit conversion in Hackney. The single room, with its fold-down bed, hotplate and sink for washing and cooking (there was a separate toilet down the hallway) was filthy even by ghetto standards. He couldn't believe he was paying as much as he did for the place.

Bernard's room was right at the top of the house, an exhausting climb up four storeys. The only good thing about it was the woman who lived in the basement bedsit, another Jamaican called Norma who was also working for London Transport but would soon leave to become a nurse. Slowly Norma and Bernard became friends and then lovers. By the time she finished her nursing training they were married and their eldest son, Karl, was born. Two more sons followed and from the moment they arrived Bernard swore they would not end up making the same mistakes he did. He ruled his boys with a rod of iron and pushed them to strive for success in every field.

Karl was setting a fine example to his younger brothers, joining the police straight after university and getting on to the fast-track programme. He found himself battling racism and prejudice every day, both within the force and outside it – but his father had prepared him well. There had been hard times but under the guidance of Detective Inspector Rooney, Marshall had blossomed into a fine officer and a credit to the force. The investigation into the murder of Gary was being headed up by Detective Inspector William Rooney, a thirty-year veteran of the south London murder squad just a few months from retirement. His greying hair and hangdog expression made him look so much like a cartoon character that he avoided television interviews whenever he could. When *London Tonight* asked for a talking head to make the appeal on camera, Rooney gladly passed on the baton to a more media-friendly member of his team and DS Marshall was more than happy to accept it.

Gary Taylor had been hanging from the heating pipes in his kitchen for seven days when his body was finally found by the police. They had been called after neighbours complained about the smell coming from the apartment. What they found inside made them want to throw up. His own dead weight had pulled his arms out of their shoulder sockets, all the blood from his body had pooled in his legs, making his calves swell to twice their normal size. His head had started to decompose rapidly and there were maggots crawling around inside his mouth, feasting on his rotting tongue.

The post-mortem found that Gary Taylor had enough heroin in his system to kill five grown men.

The first stage of the investigation did not go well. A canvass call to all the addresses and occupied flats close to the one where the body had been found revealed that no one had seen anything out of the ordinary. Marshall, who knocked on a fair few doors himself that day, sat in a pub round the corner from Southwark police station with Rooney and shared his concerns over a pint of Guinness. 'It's like trying to get blood out of a stone, Guv,' he explained between sips. 'Nobody has seen anything.'

Rooney nodded. 'Why do you think I'm taking a back seat on this one?'

'You mean it's not just because your face is more suited to radio?'

Rooney shot Marshall a withering look, which slowly changed into a sly smile. 'You wait till you've got thirty years on the job. I'm telling you now, you won't be pretty any more.' Marshall laughed. 'The reason I'm taking a back seat is that this is a no go,' Rooney continued. 'You're wasting your time. None of these people saw anything. Even if they did they knew he was a small-time drug dealer. They'd be too scared to say anything.'

'But we could move them. Put them into witness protection.'

'These people don't want witness protection; they just want to get on with their lives.'

'So what do we do, then? Give up?'

'No. Go and make some noise, lean on a few sources. If you get nowhere, get a big file full of all the information and you stick it in a drawer somewhere. Maybe one day you'll have the chance to do something with it. Just don't hold your breath.'

Two weeks later Marshall walked into Rooney's office with a big smile on his face, both arms behind his back.

'What are you looking so happy about, Marshall?'

'You know that Taylor case, the one you said we'd never get anywhere with?'

'Yeah. Don't tell me you've got someone in the frame.'

'Not quite, but I do have a list of suspects.'

'I'm impressed.'

'Knew you would be. Wanna see the list?'

'Of course.'

Marshall brought his arms round in front of him and let the telephone directory he had been holding fall on to Rooney's desk with a loud thump.

Rooney stared at it. 'This your idea of a joke? It's not that funny.'

'Just trying to make a point, Guv. You can go through the telephone book, pick any name you like and chances are they'll have a reason to hate the man. Taylor made some enemies over the years. A lot of enemies. He controlled drugs on the Roxford but he was greedy. He'd switch between suppliers whenever a better offer came along. Pissed a lot of people off. He used to work for the Bowers, you know, that East End firm, but fell out with them a couple of years ago. I think he had some dealings with the

Fergussons too. He's been around the block a few times and picked up more enemies each time.'

'So what are you saying?'

'I want to keep a few men on it in case something comes up, but we've got no forensic, we've got no witnesses and we've got no leads. Unless someone walks into the station and confesses, I don't think we've got a hope in hell of putting this one to bed.'

Chapter Twenty-six

Paul Tobin had been sitting in his favourite armchair for more than an hour. It was something he liked to do when he returned from work feeling stressed and exhausted. Half an hour with his body sunk deep into the supple brown leather, sometimes with a small glass of twenty-year-old single-malt Irish whiskey in a tumbler by his side, always made him feel like a new man. It had worked almost every day of his life for the past ten years. But no more.

Ever since Christopher's arrest, the rage had been building up inside him like nothing he had ever experienced. The chair might just as well have been a hard wooden bench, the whiskey water.

For years society had pondered the question of nature versus nurture. Do people turn out the way they do because of some predetermined path they have to follow or are they a product of their upbringing? Paul Tobin had always believed the latter. Despite all the disadvantages Christopher had experienced in the early months of his life, he and Jane had given the boy absolutely everything a child could want: the best school, a loving home, a chance to experience all the good things in life.

Christopher had taken it all and thrown it back

in their faces time and time again. He had got into trouble at every school he had ever attended, smoked and drank long before he was old enough to, almost got himself expelled on numerous occasions and finally ended up in therapy. Then, just when Paul thought they had finally turned the corner and that he could see the light at the end of the tunnel, Christopher had become a criminal.

He recalled how, three years earlier in a moment of blind panic, he had confessed the truth about Christopher's background to Dr Edmund Manley, the child psychologist. The doctor's words still reverberated round his head: 'You have to understand, Mr Tobin, that every teenager feels alienated from his parents. The difference with Christopher is that this feeling of alienation may well be seated in the fact that he has partial memories of his life before he was adopted by you and your wife.'

'But he was only eighteen months old,' Paul had replied.

'Medical science has been studying the mind for hundreds of years but we still understand only a fraction of how it actually works,' the doctor had said. 'Some of the difficulties Christopher is experiencing could be the result of childhood trauma, others will say this could have happened to any child. Your son is certainly not the first boy from a wealthy, privileged background to end up in therapy, I can assure you of that. Sometimes it is the children who are given everything that end up sinking the lowest. Most children aspire to become more successful than their parents, to earn more and live better lives. That's easy enough if you grow up on a council estate in south London. It's a bit more difficult if your parents are millionaire businessmen, successful writers or artists. Some children follow in their parents' footsteps, others rebel. The trouble is there's no way of telling which ones will do what.'

Paul had hesitated for a long time before asking the question that had been spinning round in his mind: 'Dr Manley, in your professional opinion, should I tell Christopher that he is adopted?'

Dr Manley had looked over his thin spectacles while scratching his beard and studying Tobin carefully. 'Perhaps that's a question you need to find the answer to yourself. Why don't you tell me the reasons you think you should and those why you shouldn't.'

Paul had taken a deep breath. 'I've seen where he came from and I know the way people in those places live. It's hard to escape that kind of life. This is a boy who likes the company of the bad kids, hanging out in the toilets and smoking cigarettes. If he discovers he has a link to a world of drugs and violence, I'm worried a part of him might be drawn to it. I also think it could be traumatic to learn that his mother is not his real mother, that his natural father tried to beat him to death when he was young.'

Dr Manley had nodded sagely. 'And what are the reasons you think he should be told?'

'So that he knows how lucky he is, so that he knows how much we have done for him and sees the golden opportunity he has been given in life. I guess I feel that if he were aware of what he was rescued from, he'd see the value of the lessons I try to teach him.'

Dr Manley had laughed.

'What's so funny?' Paul had asked.

'I'm sorry, it's just that the last argument you made, it's the same that all parents have, regardless of whether their child is adopted or not. We all want them to appreciate what we've done for them, to know of the sacrifices we've made and how much better off they are than other children. But it's part and parcel of being a parent. If a child grows up with a loving family in a comfortable home, that child almost inevitably takes it for granted. They know no better.'

'So you think I shouldn't tell Christopher the truth?'

Doctor Manley had looked directly into Paul's eyes. 'What I'm saying, Paul, is that it can be easy to blame adoption when things go wrong and congratulate yourself when things go right. I think you need to look into yourself and find the real answer you're most happy with. And the one that is in Christopher's best interests.'

Paul Tobin remained in his chair until he could bear

it no more. He rose up slowly, feeling his age more than ever. He moved over to his desk, pulled out the middle drawer, the same drawer that Christopher had been rummaging around in a few months earlier while looking for a stapler. The drawer came out smoothly and he kept tugging until it was completely away from the desk. He took a step back and turned it upside down. A small brown envelope was stuck to the bottom, covered with a sheet of clear plastic. Sitting back on the chair, Paul pulled the envelope away and opened it. He spread the yellowing papers on the desk in front of him, smoothing out the folds. He traced his fingers along the words at the top of the first sheet: 'Official Certificate of Adoption'.

Earlier that week the police had submitted a file to the Crown Prosecution Service on Christopher's case and it was now up to them to decide whether he would be prosecuted. The CPS had received submissions from Christopher's school and Dr Manley, as well as Paul and Jane, but there was no knowing which way their decision would go. Christopher had been bailed to return to Dorking police station the following month and that was when they would find out what was going to happen.

Paul sighed deeply. For years he had planned to tell Christopher about his adoption one day. He had been waiting for the right moment, a time when the troubles of Christopher's past were well and truly behind him. But that moment had never come. Now Paul knew there was nothing else to be done. Under no circumstances should Christopher find out the truth about his past. He must never know.

Paul placed the documents in the mouth of the shredder and switched it on.

Chapter Twenty-seven

May 1991

It was the part of the job Jacob hated most. He had spent all day visiting banks across London, waiting in long boring queues while clerks counted up the money he was paying in. They called it 'smurfing'. Banks had to report any transaction where they suspected money may have come from criminal activities and were on the alert for anyone paying in large sums of cash on a regular basis. The problem was, smurfing was boring and time-consuming. To be on the safe side, £40,000 would be split into six or seven smaller bundles. Each one had to be paid into a different branch of a different bank around London, just to ensure there was no suspicion. And each visit to the bank had to be accompanied by a different cover story. Banks were only too well aware of smurfing and knew there were people out there trying to get round it. At first the scheme had worked well but as the amount of money increased so did their chances of being caught.

Kaitlyn hated to admit that the money she was making was fast becoming a problem. Each and every week drug sales from the Roxford generated thousands of pounds in cash, mostly in £5, £10 and £20 notes, and the amounts coming in were increasing daily. Even when all the couriers had taken their cut, even when brown envelopes stuffed with cash had been handed over to the bent police and customs officers who had become an integral part of Kaitlyn's operation, there was still a huge amount of cash left over. The sheer volume of cash made the operation extremely vulnerable.

Regular consignments of money were being shipped back to Mexico in order to pay for the next order, which was always larger than the last. With strict regulations on the amount of cash you were allowed to take out of the country, Kaitlyn's cash couriers were forced to adopt the same methods to take out the money that they used to smuggle in the drugs. They used suitcases with false compartments, body suits with wads of cash sewn into the lining. Some of them even took wads of rolled-up bills, placed them inside condoms and swallowed them before boarding their flights to South America.

During her time in prison, Kaitlyn had planned not just to make a lot of money but also to leave the estate. Although she, Errol and Jacob were now on the road to riches, Kaitlyn knew that if she was truly going to change her life for ever she needed to find a way of getting more cocaine into the UK and to get larger amounts of her cash into the banking system without arousing any suspicion.

She had come up with the perfect solution and couldn't wait to tell the others.

*

Jacob was exhausted when he got back to the Roxford after a long day of smurfing and decided to relax the way he knew best. Moving to the kitchen of his flat, he took out what looked like a regular can of baked beans, unscrewed the bottom and removed his hidden stash. He had followed Kaitlyn's rule about not taking any drugs for as long as he could, but with so much around him all the time he saw no harm in the occasional smoke. That night, one joint turned to two and then three. He was listening to the Happy Mondays, his eyes were closed and he was settling back on his sofa. There was a tiny smile on his face. Jacob was young, good-looking and richer than anyone he knew. Pretty soon he would be out of this dump and living like a rock star. He was on his way, he thought, blowing a huge cloud of smoke into the air.

The album had just come to an end and he was enjoying the silence, wondering what to put on next, when there was a sharp knock at the front door. Jacob glanced at his watch. It was 8.30 p.m., far too late in the evening for a police raid. They only ever came at dawn and he had done nothing to draw attention to himself of late.

Then he heard a voice calling his name: 'Jacob, are you there?'

It was Kaitlyn.

Jacob's heart froze. He looked about the living room, at the billowing clouds of sweet-smelling smoke above his head. He felt like a naughty schoolboy all over again. A part of him longed to see her and let her in, but he knew he could not. She would never forgive him for putting the entire operation at risk by getting stoned. He did not move, he did not respond and a few minutes later he heard the sound of footsteps walking away. Kaitlyn had gone.

The news that Kaitlyn could not wait to tell Jacob as she made her way home that night was that she had decided to use the money they were making to buy into a nightclub and in turn use that to launder their profits. The more she thought about it the better the idea became. It would also give Kaitlyn, Jacob and Errol the chance to pass themselves off as employees of the club, open bank accounts and obtain credit cards of their own. After seeing a few going concerns that really didn't cut the mustard, Kaitlyn realised that she would be far better off starting from scratch. And that was when she came across the Palace.

Kaitlyn first heard about the Palace Nite Spot from a friend while at the hairdresser's. It had been shut down for the best part of a year due to lack of funding and there was little doubt the place had seen better days. It was a run-down building on the corner of Borough High Street, which led a short distance up to London Bridge and into the City, and going south to the Elephant and Castle and into Balham and the Roxford. It was a large building, like a warehouse but with little soul or atmosphere. It had started life as a cinema in the early sixties but declining audiences had seen it converted into a snooker hall at the start of the eighties.

The owner of the Palace was a forty-five-year-old one-time entrepreneur called Jonathan Green. He had come into the nightclub business five years earlier full of confidence and high expectations, but was by this time a broken man, and each week he fell deeper and deeper into debt. And now his life was in danger. When money had become tight, Green had turned first to his bank who were happy to extend his credit in the mistaken belief that the good times of the early days would soon return. As the months dragged on the bank grew increasingly concerned. Desperate not to lose everything and eager to avoid bankruptcy, Green turned to a loan shark linked to a local underworld family known as the Bowers. Falling behind with payments to the bank was one thing. Falling behind with payments to them was quite another. The burly man who arrived at his door and gave him forty-eight hours to come up with the first instalment had left him with a broken thumb as a 'reminder'. It was his policy, he explained, to start with the smallest bones first and work his way up from there.

Kaitlyn explained her terms simply enough. All Green's debts would be settled and he would continue to be paid while the club was shut down for three months and completely refurbished. It would then reopen under Kaitlyn's strict guidelines. She would be given the title of Marketing Executive, a job that came with a generous salary. Errol would be Head of Security and Jacob would be Musical Director. The headquarters of the smuggling organisation would move out of the Roxford and into a meeting room above the club.

'Are you sure you know what you're doing, taking this place on?' Green said wearily.

'Quite sure.'

'I mean, we've had a lot of trouble.'

'Nothing that the calming touch of a woman can't solve, I'm sure.' She focused on the sweat pouring down his face and spoke confidently: 'Don't worry. I'll make it work.' Kaitlyn held out her hand for his. 'I'll have my lawyer draft a contract within twenty-four hours.'

Chapter Twenty-eight

Christopher Tobin arrived in the car park of Dorking police station in the passenger seat of a car driven by his solicitor, Tom Symons. In the weeks since his arrest he had felt as though an increasingly heavy weight was bearing down on him and now that the actual day had arrived when he was to learn whether or not he was to be charged, he felt as though he was being completely crushed. His parents had volunteered to go with him but he had adamantly refused. It was partly because he could not bear the pain he had caused them, partly because he had turned seventeen a month earlier and, in the eyes of the law, was now an adult, but mostly because he feared the worst – that he might be placed in custody there and then. Though he had said nothing to anyone, Christopher had known all about the credit card Sarah had stolen and had been a willing participant in the fraud.

It was, in fact, just one of a number of scams that Sarah had introduced him to in the weeks after they had started going out with one another. As their relationship had progressed he had realised he was just as attracted to her love of danger and involvement in criminality as he was to her looks and personality. If anything, the more he got to know her, the more the illegal activities she was involved in excited him. She would obtain scores of stolen credit cards from a range of sources including bent postal workers, muggers and house burglars. She would have only a limited time to use the cards, buying up all the high-value goods she could before the owners realised they were stolen and had them blocked. A well-dressed and highly presentable woman, whenever she went out on her shopping sprees she would attract little suspicion from store staff. If they ever became concerned about the validity of a card Sarah would remain calm, protest that her 'husband' must have cut her off again and storm out of the shop. More often than not, however, she was successful.

Her purchases – video recorders, portable televisions and pieces of fine jewellery – would then be sold at bargain basement prices for cash. She would also occasionally put smaller sums through the wine bar where she worked – it was one of the main reasons she had taken the job. Whatever she made, she would receive a third of the profits, the rest of the money going to other members of the gang.

She had confessed everything to Christopher almost as soon as he questioned how she managed to have such a glitzy lifestyle on such a modest salary. A few months on, when Sarah was accidentally given a card in a man's name, Christopher was more than willing to try out the scam for himself.

A few days later Sarah had been arrested. A credit

card company had grown suspicious at the large number of stolen cards being used to buy expensive bottles of wine at the bar and called in fraud investigators. Sarah was soon uncovered as the culprit and a search of her belongings found dozens of stolen cards, including the one Christopher had used the week before. With the wine bar manager's help, it was only a matter of time before the police tracked him down.

Sarah had been in custody ever since and Christopher had not had a chance to talk to her to find out what she had told the police. He had no idea whether she had implicated him more fully or, out of some kind of loyalty, had kept quiet about his true role. His fear was that if he tried to lie his way out by saying he knew nothing about what was going on, he could land himself in even more hot water.

Tom, the solicitor, looked far younger than his thirty six years. Up close you could see the first specks of grey in his mop of thick black hair but from a distance he looked only a few years older than Christopher. Tom found a parking spot at the front of the station, applied the handbrake and switched off the engine. He had a winning smile and relaxed manner that instantly put Christopher at ease. A week or so earlier they had met to discuss strategy. Although the charges were potentially serious, Tom had explained, Christopher had excellent mitigation and with any luck they would be able to walk away without too much damage being done. He showed

Christopher a letter he had drafted to the Crown Prosecution Service outlining many of Christopher's academic achievements and previous good character until that point. Most of the text was straightforward enough but every now and then there were a few legal terms or references.

'Are you throwing in these phrases to make yourself seem extra cool?'

Tom chuckled. 'Only a little. Is it working?'

Christopher shook his head mournfully and Tom's smile grew wider. 'I'll try harder next time. Actually, it's just the way the law works. It's nothing to do with what's written down in the books, it's all about what happened the last time someone was in a similar situation. Half the trials I get involved in, you spend more time doing research on precedent than you do on the facts of the actual case. It's crazy.'

'So on that basis,' said Christopher, 'what do you think will happen here?'

'I can't make any promises,' said Tom. 'There are plenty of variables that I can't control. Worst-case scenario, they'll do a formal interview under caution and then charge you. But that's worst-case scenario.'

'Well, that's the scenario I'm most concerned about.'

Tom smiled warmly. 'I know, Christopher, but try not to worry.'

'Easy for you to say. You're not the one who might be going to prison.'

Tom opened the car door and he and Christopher

climbed out. Then Tom placed his elbows on the roof and leaned across with a smile. 'Hey, have you ever heard the story of the optimist and the pessimist who go on a round-the-world cruise?'

Christopher shrugged. 'No.'

'Then let me tell you. These two guys, one an optimist, the other a pessimist, go on a round-the-world cruise, but halfway round the world the ship hits an iceberg and goes down. They end up side by side in the ocean, each of them clinging for dear life to a little bit of wood. So then the optimist keeps smiling and says, "Don't worry, we're going to be rescued" but then the pessimist looks all sad and says, "You're crazy, we're going to die." Now this conversation goes on for a while, back and forth until eventually' – Tom paused for dramatic effect – 'they both drown.'

Christopher frowned. 'I don't understand. What's the point of that story?'

Tom grinned. 'The point is that it makes no difference to the outcome of an event whether you're an optimist or a pessimist. But if you're an optimist, the time you spend waiting to find out is a lot less painful.'

Christopher smiled, then chuckled, then broke into a full-blown laugh. 'Good one. I'll try to remember that,' he said as they headed up the stairs towards the police station.

Jane Tobin was in the kitchen loading up the dishwasher when a sudden shudder passed through her body. *Somebody just stepped over my grave*, she thought to herself. The tingling sensation persisted and she was gripped by a sense that something was wrong.

As though she were walking underwater she moved through the house, out of the kitchen into the hallway and along towards the front door. And that was when she saw the dark shadow through the glass. She stood, frozen on the spot, for a few seconds as the shadow grew larger. Then, her heart starting to race, she saw the shadow reach into a pocket and fumble for a key. She ran forward and threw open the door. 'Christopher,' she gasped.

'Hello, Mum.'

She turned round. 'Paul, Christopher's home.'

Paul made his way downstairs as quickly as he could, eager to hear the news. 'Well, what happened?' he asked, gasping for breath.

Christopher looked at each of his parents in turn, a smile creeping across his face. 'It's OK, they're not going to charge me.'

Jane's hands clutched at the air with joy. 'Oh, thank God, thank God for that.'

Paul embraced his wife and his son. 'That's such a relief. I'm so happy.' Then he turned away quickly. He didn't want Christopher to see the tears in his eyes.

An hour later they were all sitting round the kitchen table drinking their second pot of tea and Christopher had taken them through every detail of what had happened at the police station, what Tom had said and how the officers had reacted. By the time he had finished all three of them had huge beaming smiles on their faces.

'So, now you can move on with your life,' said Paul. 'Any clearer idea of what you're going to do?'

Christopher smiled. 'You'll be pleased to know I've finally made up my mind,' he said. He could see the anxiety building up on their faces and decided to put them out of their misery as soon as possible. 'Don't worry, I'm going to university.'

Both Jane and Paul looked relieved.

'And I'm going to study law.'

Chapter Twenty-nine

July 1993

It was a few minutes past midnight and the dawn of a new Saturday when Jacob walked up to the edge of the safety rail and looked over. The dance floor at Lush – as the Palace was now known – was three-quarters full and the sea of scantily clad bodies seemed to jump and jerk awkwardly under the flash of the powerful strobe lighting. Lush had been open for more than a year and had been a storming success right from the start. Kaitlyn had come up with plans that utterly astonished Jonathan Green, Errol and Jacob. Lush was to be a Gothic wonderland full of flame-throwers, contortionists, half-naked male and female dancers suspended in cages, and podium dancers who gyrated to the thumping dance beats all night long. They hired the hottest DJs in town and the club soon became a regular hang-out for anyone who was anyone or wanted to be someone.

Kaitlyn knew what Lush was for: to help launder the money from the Roxford and her expanding drug empire. She had fitted out two floors but one was always closed to the public. The club was licensed to hold 1,500 people but only 750 were ever allowed in.

As far as her bank manager and accountant were concerned, Monday through Saturday the place was packed and the drinks flowed all night.

As Jacob's eyes flicked from one part of the crowd to another, they suddenly alighted on a tall, slender woman sweeping across the dance floor so smoothly that she looked as if she were floating. Kaitlyn wore a shimmering sapphire dress with a split well above the knee and a pair of matching high heels. Her long brunette hair flowed behind her as she moved.

The sound of someone calling his name snapped him out of his trance. He turned to his left to see a pretty young girl in a crop top and a pair of tight hot pants standing beside him, smiling shyly. Jacob had slept with her twice or possibly three times, but had been so drunk he hardly remembered it. She saw him as a way of getting free drinks and her name on the guest list to all the best parties; he'd seen her as an easy lay, though the novelty had long worn off and he had no intention of repeating the experience.

'Hello, Jacob.'

'Miranda. You having a good time?'

She nodded towards the cigarette in his hand. 'I'd be having a much better time if I hadn't just run out of cigarettes.'

Jacob smiled and held out his hand.

Miranda took the cigarette and placed it in her mouth, then she moved closer to where Jacob stood, leaning on the rail so that her cleavage all but spilled out of her top and her bottom stuck out behind. 'Busy night.'

'It'll get busier. It's still early. People are only just coming out of the pubs and making their way over to us.' Jacob was only half concentrating on what he was saying. He could no longer see Kaitlyn on the dance floor and his eyes darted around as he searched for her, finally finding her at the far end of the long bar, throwing her head back and laughing as she spoke to a tall, muscular man in leather trousers and a black T-shirt. She looked genuinely happy. Contented. Comfortable.

The man was leaning forward, cupping Kaitlyn's chin in his hand as he whispered something into her ear that sent her into fits of hysterics. Kaitlyn stepped back as she laughed hard, then playfully slapped the man's chest, her palm resting flat against the curve of his shoulder.

'I like your shirt,' said Miranda, her hand moving to stroke the material on his forearm.

Her touch lingered a bit too long and Jacob turned and scowled at her until she removed it. 'I'm a little busy right now,' he said at last.

For a few moments Miranda didn't know what to say, looking at Jacob's intense expression as he returned to scanning the dance floor below. 'Maybe I'll catch you later,' she said softly.

'Yeah. Maybe,' came the reply.

Jacob scurried along the walkway to the other set

of stairs and raced down to the ground floor. He recognised the man Kaitlyn was talking to. It was the man she had left the club with two weeks earlier. He had seen them driving off in the small hours of the morning. They had done the same thing just a few days earlier.

Like Jacob, Kaitlyn had been involved in a number of short-term relationships and having your pick of the crop was one of the fringe benefits attached to running a club, but Kaitlyn had never seemed interested in anything more than a one- or two-night stand. As far as he was aware, she had never had what anyone would describe as a serious relationship. Something about the way she behaved around this man seemed different and that had to be a bad thing. Jacob's heart was pounding in his chest as he moved closer to the bar.

He was only a few paces from her and still he didn't know what to say – he just needed to say something. 'Hey, Kaitlyn,' Jacob was breathing hard.

'Hey, Jacob.'

He waited for her to introduce him to the person beside her or say something, but she didn't. Instead, she fixed him with a stare, waiting to hear what he had to say.

Jacob looked around and shuffled his feet. 'Busy night. Good crowd. Looks like the bar's going well.'

'Did you want something, Jacob?' asked Kaitlyn, a touch of impatience in her voice that instantly made Jacob uncomfortable.

'I think we're running a little short on cocktail mixers.'

Kaitlyn's eyes widened in surprise. 'OK, get Johnny to deal with it.'

There was an awkward pause. Jacob stared hard at the stranger who stared back.

'Anything else?' she asked, trying to break his stare.

Jacob struggled to think of an issue he needed to talk to Kaitlyn urgently about, but when nothing came to mind he simply shook his head slowly.

'OK,' said Kaitlyn, looping her arm through that of the man in the leather trousers. 'I'm just popping out for an hour or so. I'll be back before things get really busy.'

'Are you sure that's a good idea?'

Kaitlyn smiled. 'Don't worry, if you can't handle it you can always give me a call.' She flashed a look at the man beside her and grinned, 'Of course, I can't promise my phone will be switched on!'

As Jacob watched her walk away he tried to tell himself that his concern was purely professional, that he was worried about the effect a proper relationship might have on her ability to run the club, let alone their real business, but he knew he was only fooling himself. Jacob had seen Kaitlyn transform from a hard-nosed tomboy friend to a sophisticated, clever and beautiful young woman. Every time he thought about her his mind raced on about how their life could be together. His real concern was that he had found himself feeling an emotion he didn't even know he possessed. Every time he thought of Kaitlyn with another man, Jacob found himself torn apart with jealousy. That night, at home alone, he smoked his first crack cocaine.

Chapter Thirty

September 1993

Daniel Pilgrim had always striven to do the right thing, no matter what the cost.

In his first job as a data clerk for a small accounting firm in south London it had been he who had reported that another member of staff had set up a programme to steal money from the accounts of dozens of clients. The thief was sacked and Daniel promoted, but none of his colleagues ever trusted him again. After months of being frozen out of every social occasion he decided to leave.

A few years later he found himself teaching English in a secondary comprehensive school in Catford. He enjoyed the work and the chance to interact with young minds, even the ones who did nothing but swear and throw chairs, but drew the line when one of his married colleagues began an affair with a sixth-form student. This time he didn't even bother to wait for his colleagues to turn on him. Daniel Pilgrim left the same day he reported the affair to the headmaster and the girl's parents.

His sense of morality and belief that he was acting in the best interests of everyone he came into contact with stayed with him through several more careers until he took a change of direction and set up South London Investigations, a private eye agency with a long-time friend and ex-copper called Julian Thomas. Much of the work involved serving papers on fine defaulters and those who had missed appointments at magistrates courts, but every now and then he would have a visit from a woman convinced her husband was having an affair and get the chance to follow the person for several days in order to procure incriminating evidence.

Although Daniel and Julian had been friends for many years, their business relationship soon began to fall apart over differences in their approach to work and within two years Thomas moved abroad, leaving Pilgrim to pay him off, thereby gaining the freedom of his own business. Pilgrim now had some of the best contacts within the force, thanks to Thomas, and it was his ability to get the kind of information often within a few hours' notice that made him extra valuable. That was how he came to be working for Errol Gants, the person who would ultimately introduce him to Kaitlyn Wilson.

He had been surprised at just how easy it had been to turn, how little it disturbed his sleep and how much more exciting his life had become as a result.

That first job had been easy. Pilgrim had to find an address to match the number plates of a certain Ford Granada. It took less than twenty minutes and cost him £60 to his usual police contact. The payment he received from Errol was £500. Pilgrim, being Pilgrim, at first protested he was being given too much but Errol insisted the amount was correct.

Pilgrim thought little of it until two weeks later when a story about a second-hand car dealer who was rumoured to have a connection to the south London underworld caught his eye. The man had emerged from the house he shared with his wife and children in the early hours of the morning, to be hit with a hail of bullets from semi-automatic guns. The guns – the police believed at least three separate weapons were involved – were pointed out of the side window of a Jaguar which, according to eyewitnesses, had spent most of the night parked nearly opposite the house. Bullets pierced the man's stomach and chest, one of them severing his spine and tearing out a kidney. He took only minutes to bleed to death. The burnt-out stolen car was later found twenty miles from the scene of the murder.

Daniel's blood froze in his veins as he read the words. For the name of the man who had been killed was the name that Pilgrim had given to Errol Gants a few days earlier. Any lingering hope that this was anything more than a ghastly coincidence was shattered later that morning by a brief telephone call.

'Pilgrim?' Gants's voice was harsh and humourless.
'Yeah.'
'I have a message from my boss.'
'Er. OK.'
'The message is – never forget you're expendable.'

Pilgrim desperately tried to think of something brave to say in return, but was relieved to find the line had already gone dead.

The call from Errol was nothing unusual as he was now Pilgrim's biggest client. This time he was asked to come along to a club called Lush in order to discuss a business proposal. Pilgrim was nervous, to say the least, especially since Errol's most recent comments. Panicked thoughts raced through his mind. 'I haven't done anything wrong. I haven't told anyone anything.'

An hour later Pilgrim arrived outside Lush, to be greeted by two large, smart-looking, heavily built men at the entrance. He'd never been to Lush before but had read about the place in the papers. It wasn't really his scene and he was glad it was daytime. One of them radioed up and within a few minutes Errol came out of the door to greet him.

'Hey, Errol, what's happening?'

Errol escorted him up to the office on the top floor. 'Got a special job for you.'

'What is it?'

'The boss will talk to you.'

As he climbed the two flights of stairs Pilgrim couldn't help but smile. It would be the first time he would meet him. This had to be a good sign; he was moving up in the estimation of the organisation. Perhaps he'd get a pay rise too.

At the top of the stairs a big heavy door blocked

his way. There was clearly some kind of meeting going on. He could hear the sound of muffled voices, nothing distinct. The thickness of the wood made sure of that. Outside the door two small plastic chairs were sat against the wall next to a coffee machine and a small pile of clubbing and nightlife magazines. 'Wait here.' Errol pointed towards a seat as he went in the room. Pilgrim made himself a coffee, sat down and began flicking through a copy of *The Face*.

The large meeting room had been decorated like a luxury lounge. There were sumptuous high-back Knoll sofas facing each other with a coffee table in the middle. Lamps were positioned around the room to give a warm ambience. In one corner was a desk and in the middle a large oval table. Round the table sat Errol, Jacob, Jonathan and Kaitlyn. The conversation moved back and forth, details of shipments, distribution problems and rising overheads. It was the kind of scene that would have been repeated in boardrooms across the country, but in this instance the commodity was drugs.

Twenty minutes later Pilgrim had flicked through the magazines and had nervously downed three coffees when the door opened.

'Come in.' Errol escorted Pilgrim in as Jacob and Jonathan left the room. Pilgrim was confused, to say the least. He had assumed the boss was going to be a man.

'This is Daniel Pilgrim. You wanted to see him.'

Kaitlyn smiled, her beauty putting Daniel instantly at ease. 'Please. Come in and have a seat.' Then, turning to Errol: 'I'll see you later.' They smiled as Errol closed the door behind him.

Jacob hated seeing Kaitlyn in the company of another man, especially someone he didn't know. What on earth was going on? Was this some kind of boyfriend she'd picked up? He waited downstairs to speak with Errol.

Kaitlyn sat down on the sofa and gestured for Daniel Pilgrim to sit opposite her. She studied him for a few moments before she spoke. He was happy just to stare back. 'Errol tells me you come highly recommended, that you're a top private eye.'

'Kind of him to say so.'

'And you've never worked for the police? Most of them do, don't they?'

'That's the usual thing. A copper does his thirty years and then sets up his own agency. A lot of people find that a problem. They're the people who come to me.'

'You've done a lot of good work for us over the last year.'

'Thanks.'

There was a pause. Kaitlyn's eyes looked deep into Daniel's, searching him out. 'I have a special job I need you to do for me. Strictly confidential. I hope I don't have to explain what that means. I know you've done things for us in the past that have been – how shall we put it? – of a delicate nature but the details of this job must stay between you and me alone. They don't leave this room.'

Pilgrim swallowed hard. Just what had he got himself into? A vision flashed into his head of him standing over a dead body, a bloody knife in the palm of his hand. He'd never killed anybody in his life and he had no plans to start. Just how on earth was he going to get out of this?

Kaitlyn could see the nervousness in his eyes and moved to calm him. 'Don't worry, it's nothing difficult. I just need someone I can trust, someone who can be discreet and in the kind of business I'm in those people are few and far between.'

Daniel's shoulders relaxed and he sat back in his chair. 'What do you want me to do?'

'I need you to find someone.' She reached into a briefcase on the floor beside her and pulled out a slim manila envelope. She ran her finger across it and slid it over the table towards Pilgrim. 'His name is Christopher.'

Pilgrim's fingers trembled as he opened the envelope. Inside was a picture of a baby boy, not more than eighteen months old.

Chapter Thirty-one

April 1994

It was the Easter break at Durham University, and Paul and Jane Tobin looked forward to spending time with their son. Christopher, not surprisingly, had other ideas. While taking full advantage of home cooking and the fact that someone else would be making his bed and tidying away his dirty clothes, he intended to spend as much time with his old friends as he possibly could.

Of the small group of friends he had grown up with, Christopher was the only one to go to university. Although they sometimes took the piss and called him 'professor', it had never been an issue and he was as much one of the lads now as he ever had been. And while Christopher enjoyed the intellectually stimulating conversations he had with his chums at university, there were times when he found it all a bit pretentious and longed to let his hair down and have a good old chat about football and birds over a couple of pints of beer.

There would be no drinking this night, though. Christopher had asked to borrow his father's new car – a 5-series BMW – for the evening to ferry him and his friends to a particularly fine pub on the outskirts of Dorking. Paul had reluctantly agreed on the basis that his son promised that not a single drop of alcohol would touch his lips all evening. Christopher had borrowed the car twice before and on both occasions Paul had made himself almost sick with worry all night long. 'I promise, Dad,' said Christopher earnestly, snatching the keys from the hook in the hallway and making his way out of the door. 'Not one single drop of alcohol will touch my lips. I'll be using a straw.' And then he was gone.

Despite teasing his father, Christopher was true to his word and drank only orange juice and Coca-Cola as his friends downed as many pints of high-strength lager as they could in the shortest possible time. Christopher didn't mind too much – it would be his turn to get plastered the next time they went out drinking. His only concern was the worry that he looked as much of an idiot when sober as his friends around him looked when drunk.

The evening finally came to an end and Christopher led his worse-for-wear friends out to the pub's car park. One in particular, Peter, was in such a state that he needed to lean on Christopher's shoulder to prevent him falling over. 'Remember,' said Christopher sternly. 'If anyone feels like throwing up you have to do it now, not inside the car.'

Peter's glazed eyes scanned the area in front of him. 'What car?' he slurred. 'It's fucking vanished.'

Christopher had called the police but they told him

there was little they could do. A fancy car like that had no doubt been targeted by a highly organised theft ring. Within a matter of days it would have been shipped out of the country or stripped down and sold off as parts. The chances of seeing it again were practically zero.

When Christopher arrived home in a taxi an hour or so later, all he could give his father were the car keys and a police crime reference number to enable him to proceed with the insurance claim. Inside, Paul was in pieces but he did his best to put on a brave face. 'It's not your fault, Christopher,' he told him. 'It's just one of those things. I'm not going to hold it against you.'

Christopher had already headed back to Durham a few days later when Jane went out one morning to collect the milk, leaving Paul in the kitchen fixing breakfast. As Paul loaded the toaster, he heard a sudden scream and the sound of breaking glass. He dashed outside. Jane was standing in the doorway, rooted to the spot, with broken glass and a trail of spilt milk spreading round her feet. Her jaw hung open with shock and her eyes were fixed in the distance. Paul followed her gaze and soon he too was paralysed with shock, staring at the sight in front of him like a rabbit caught in the headlights of a speeding car. There, in the middle of the driveway, gleaming like new, was Paul's car. 'Well, bugger me,' he gasped.

This time the police arrived in person. The young

officer shook his head as he filled his notebook with Paul's answers to his questions.

'I do feel terribly embarrassed about this,' said Paul. 'I really don't understand it at all. I hope you don't think I've been playing some silly game. My son's quite a serious boy, you know. He's studying law at Durham University. I hope you don't think this is some kind of practical joke.'

'Not at all, sir. I really wouldn't worry about it too much. I've actually seen this kind of thing before.'

'Really?'

The young officer moved closer. 'Let's just say that sometimes young lads out on the town get a bit rowdy and crack a wing mirror or scratch some paintwork on Daddy's new car. Rather than putting their hands up for it, they make up some cock-and-bull story about the car being nicked, but actually send it off to a garage to get it fixed. A couple of days later the car turns up, good as new, and everybody's happy.'

Paul smiled. It was just the sort of cunning scheme he could imagine Christopher coming up with. And so long as the car wasn't damaged and his no claims bonus was safe, where was the harm in it?

* * *

Daniel Pilgrim knocked on the door of Kaitlyn's office at Lush and walked in when he heard her call out his name.

'How did it go last night?' she asked.

'Like clockwork. We found the gang who had

stolen the car. Well, I say gang, bunch of amateurs, just kids, really. They had it stowed in a garage a couple of miles away, ready to break up for parts so we got there just in time.'

'Are they gonna give us any trouble?'

'Nah. We paid them off, gave them what they would have made if they'd sold it and told them to steer clear of the Tobin house in the future. They were pretty cocky at first, but when they saw the guns my boys were carrying the main man almost shat his pants. They understand they are dealing with a pretty heavy firm. They don't know exactly who, of course, but the last thing they want to do is rock the boat. Christ, they even cleaned the car, inside and out, before they gave it back.'

It had taken Daniel Pilgrim just under four months to track down Christopher and Kaitlyn's world had revolved around the life of her brother ever since. She still smiled at the memory of the day when a triumphant Pilgrim had walked into her office late one evening and placed the folder containing the results of his investigation on her desk.

She had waited until he had left the building before using her trembling fingers to open the file at the first page. Even if she had not known that the file was all about Christopher, she would have recognised him right away from the full-page black-and-white picture that greeted her. She had not seen her brother for more than eighteen years but in her eyes he had not changed one little bit. Every line, every dimple, every curve on his face had been burned into her memory. 'Oh, Chrissy,' she had whispered, tracing the outline of his face with the tips of her fingers, tears of joy flowing freely down her cheeks.

There were more pictures spread throughout the file, some recent, others copies of school class shots that Pilgrim had managed to obtain. Then there were pictures of the Tobins, their home, their car and the office where Paul Tobin worked.

There were also lengthy biographies of each member of the family. The one of Christopher stretched to more than sixty pages and carried an impressive amount of detail. As she had read, Kaitlyn almost felt as though she had been there alongside her brother for each part of his journey through life.

She had laughed out loud when she read about his troubles at school, whistled ruefully when she came to the section about his sessions with Dr Manley, smiled as she scanned paragraphs about his first girl-friends and frowned with genuine concern when she got to the part about his troubles with the police.

Pilgrim returned a week later with a list of potential venues where Kaitlyn could 'accidentally' bump into Christopher if she wanted to meet him. Alternatively, she could approach him direct and set up a more formal get together.

'I don't want to meet him,' Kaitlyn said firmly.

Pilgrim was taken aback. He had assumed the whole point of his months of work was to enable Kaitlyn to be reunited with her brother. It had indeed been Kaitlyn's original plan but the more she looked into the files that Pilgrim had prepared, the more she realised it would be a terrible mistake. It wasn't just that Christopher was studying law and that she was a career criminal, though the irony of the situation did not escape her. It was also the fact that it was clear that Christopher had no idea that he was adopted, no memory of his former life.

Kaitlyn had looked into the background of the Tobins and seen that they were good people who had spent years struggling to have a child of their own before finally welcoming Christopher into their lives. His childhood, for the most part, had been happy and secure. He was now a gifted student making his way in what would undoubtedly become a glorious career. To appear in his life at a time like this could only do more harm than good. Instead, she would have to be content with watching him from a distance. With the wealth and power Kaitlyn had accumulated she was able to look after Christopher in a way she had failed to do that night on the Roxford estate. The events of that night still haunted her and she was determined to make sure that nothing bad would ever happen to Christopher again.

Ever since that day, Pilgrim's job had been to keep a discreet eye on Christopher. He employed a small team of surveillance agents who kept watch over him twenty-four hours a day, whether at university, at home or out with his friends. The agents themselves had no idea of the connection between Kaitlyn and Christopher – to them he was just another job – and they were swapped around on a regular basis so that Christopher never got suspicious.

One female agent managed to get work in a popular student bar that Christopher frequented, another actually enrolled at Christopher's college and became quite friendly with him. By reading transcripts of their conversations and details of his movements, Kaitlyn felt that in some small way she had become a part of her brother's life once more. And for now, that would have to do.

Part Two

Part Two

Chapter Thirty-two

September 1999

'Hey, Christopher.' William Taylor poked his head round the door of the small office and smiled. 'What are you doing right now?'

Christopher was sitting behind a large dark wooden desk piled high with box files and papers. He had obtained a first class law degree from Durham and remained in the historic city for a further year to take the Bar Vocational Course, the first step to becoming a barrister. After that he moved to London to undergo his pupillage at the chambers of Edward Wallace-Aitken QC.

Two years on from that he was finding the work incredibly challenging but knew deep down he had made the right choice. Not only did he enjoy everything about being a barrister, he loved the fact that with nothing more than a trip to court he could see exactly where his own future lay. Much of the meagre free time he had was taken up sitting in on trials and watching the country's top barristers at work.

'Not much,' Christopher replied. 'I'm looking through the papers for the Hackney case.'

'That's weeks away.'

'I know, means I've got even more time to get ready.'

William shook his head as if to say that Christopher really needed to get a life. 'Come on, grab your coat.'

'Where are we going?'

'Old Bailey, Cardy's about to start his closing.'

Of all the barristers that Christopher admired, one stood out above all the rest: James Cardy QC. Cardy, like Christopher, had studied law at Durham, graduating in 1952 with first class honours. After a pupillage in London he had plied his trade as a criminal barrister on the relatively obscure northern circuit. He had become a QC in 1971 but it was not until 1979 that he cemented the reputation that saw him become one of the most sought-after lawyers in the business.

He was defending Graham Metcalf, a former leader of the Liberal Party who had been charged with conspiracy to commit murder. From his opening address to his masterful cross-examination of the main witnesses, Cardy handled the case brilliantly. But he saved the best for last. In his closing address he told the jury that during his time as a politician, Metcalf had won millions of votes from the people of Britain, but now came the twelve most precious votes of all. He then paused and pointed to each member of the jury in turn: 'Yours and yours and yours . . .'

Metcalf was acquitted and Cardy had never looked back.

William and Christopher arrived at the Old Bailey just as the jury were about to return from their lunch break. They entered the court and spoke to the usher, asking if it would be OK for them to sit in on the case. As she pondered the question, James Cardy came into court, walked over and introduced himself.

William had met the great man before and smiled warmly when Cardy remembered him. Christopher was almost speechless. It was like meeting a Hollywood movie star or a member of the royal family. He desperately wanted to ask a really intelligent question, something that would show Cardy what he was made of, but all he could think of was: 'Have you finished your closing speech, then?'

Cardy cocked his head slightly sideways and looked at Christopher through his gold-framed glasses. 'Oh, yes,' he said softly. 'Some time ago.' He could see the young man was intimidated so he carried on, offering some friendly advice. 'This job we do, it's a lot like playing chess. You have to plan several moves ahead. I love it when you have witnesses under cross-examination and you know you're shifting them into a corner from which they will not be able to escape. One minute they're feeling confident, the next it's checkmate. It's exactly the same with a jury. You have to take them somewhere where the only option is for them to vote the way you want them to.'

Ten minutes later Cardy stood up to deliver his closing argument. Christopher shut his eyes and held his breath. He wanted to make sure he didn't miss a single word.

'Ladies and gentlemen of the jury, it was the great American President, Abraham Lincoln, who said you can fool some of the people all of the time and all of the people some of the time, but you can't fool all of the people all of the time. Dare I say to you, members of the jury, are you all fooled?'

Two hours later Cardy's client had been acquitted of all charges and Christopher was more in awe of him than ever before.

Chapter Thirty-three

Kaitlyn had been to Mexico so many times she had enough frequent-flyer miles to travel to the moon and back. She would visit Rosa and her family as much as possible during the cold winter months and knew she was always assured of a warm welcome. She also flew regularly to the Caribbean and to Europe, opening up an ever more complex network of off-shore bank accounts that helped disperse the vast wealth her drug business continued to generate. Even pouring all the profits the clubs made back into refurbishment and hiring new, hugely talented DJs, she couldn't spend the cash fast enough. She was well on her way to being a legitimate multimillionaire.

During the summer Rosa would pay the occasional visit, passing through London as part of a whistle-stop tour through Europe's major banking and gambling centres including Geneva, Monaco and Liechtenstein. Things were good. Even Ramon was impressed with the way Kaitlyn handled the business. No longer did they have to deal with large sums of money either. Kaitlyn had the money in the banking system and as such, transferred it electronically to the AFO accounts. She had lowered the risk to the business and herself.

* * *

Christopher Tobin took a deep breath and pushed open the door to the courtroom. He glanced around quickly. A few junior clerks, a couple of journalists and the court bailiff were already there. It didn't matter how many times he walked into a courtroom, something about the atmosphere always took his breath away. But on this day he was even more breathless than usual.

Christopher had been rising up the ranks in dramatic fashion. While most new barristers expect to spend years acting as junior counsel on big cases, Christopher was already handling the big prosecutions on his own. His big break had come during a high-profile murder case in which he assisted Edward Wallace-Aitken. The day before the closing speech was due to be given, Wallace-Aitken was involved in a car crash and badly injured. The trial had already run for months and cost hundreds of thousands of pounds. The judge was reluctant to adjourn and even more reluctant to declare a mistrial. When Christopher suggested he take over the judge agreed, provided both the defendant and his solicitor were also in agreement. It took Christopher more than three hours to persuade all those involved that he was more than up to the job. They finally gave in and he was given his chance. The closing argument was brilliant – easily the match of anything James Cardy had come up with throughout his career. The client was acquitted and Christopher was propelled into the big time.

For his next job Christopher had undertaken the defence on a case that, so far as most of his colleagues were concerned, was completely unwinnable. Thirty-five-year-old Alvin Tuite had broken into the house of his ex-girlfriend, who had dumped him a week or so earlier, and found her twelve-year-old sister there. Neighbours heard screams and called the police. By the time they arrived the schoolgirl was dead and Tuite had gone on the run, only to be captured a few weeks later after a massive manhunt. Tuite claimed the death was accidental but it soon emerged that he had a prior conviction for sexual assault against a minor. The Crown's case was that he had deliberately broken into the house in a bid to sexually abuse his ex-girlfriend's sister as an act of revenge. When she fought him off, he killed her.

However, there was no evidence of any attempted sexual assault and the girl's extensive head injuries were consistent with her having fallen hard down the stairs, which was exactly what Tuite said had happened after he startled her.

The case had been even all the way through. Though Christopher had fought to keep details of Tuite's previous conviction – some ten years earlier – out of the case, it had emerged during Tuite's own spell in the witness box. The revelation had turned the tide of opinion against him. If Christopher was going to win, it would all be down to his closing argument.

Half an hour later he rose and faced the jury. 'Ladies and gentlemen. There are cases where the accused person has a record or a history that might inspire a jury with revulsion against that person's character. This is one of those cases. As a jury, your job is the most difficult of all. What you are charged with today is the task of separating from your minds the natural revulsion you feel against behaviour which nobody would seek to condone or commend. I am not here to condone, still less to comment on, the conduct of the man who is currently sitting in the dock. I am not here to cast one single stone against the person in the dock who got there through a mixture of folly and self-indulgence. That is because this person is a victim of circumstance.

'Who among us does not have a past? Who among us can truly say they have never regretted a single decision? Who among us can say that, with the benefit of hindsight, our lives would have followed exactly the same path? Ladies and gentlemen of the jury, to hold this man's past sins against him would be unjust. Don't we all deserve the benefit of the doubt?'

The jury was mesmerised by Christopher's words. He felt like a famous actor delivering a classic monologue in a packed theatre. There was absolute silence in the courtroom as he spoke, every pair of eyes was locked on to him. He could see it in the jurors' faces. He knew he had won them over.

Two hours after being sent out by the judge they returned with their verdict. Tuite was acquitted of all charges and walked out of court a free man.

'Excellent closing speech,' his junior said to him as they left the court to celebrate Tuite's acquittal. 'Shades of Rattenbury and Stoner I believe?'

Christopher smiled. He had indeed taken the inspiration for his closing speech from the 1935 trial of Alma Victoria Rattenbury and George Percy Stoner who had been charged with the murder of Alma's husband, Francis. The powerful closing speech by her barrister had seen Rattenbury acquitted of all charges on the basis of her mental state. 'You know that and I know that,' he said with a grin. 'But there's not a snowball's chance in hell that anyone on the jury did.'

Paul Tobin stared again at the blank sheet of paper but nothing seemed to be happening. He had no ideas. His mind was completely empty. The only thought running through his brain was that his great hero, the American architect Frank Lloyd Wright, had once designed an entire building from scratch in the space of three hours. Not only that, Lloyd Wright had begun drawing only after the client called to say he was on his way to inspect the plans.

Tobin looked at his watch, back at the blank sheet of paper and prayed for a miracle. There was still a week to go before the first meeting with his client but he didn't hold out much hope of getting anything done. He chewed hard on the end of his pencil, tasting the bitter lead against his tongue. The electric desk fan was blowing a gale; nevertheless his office was stiflingly hot. The sound of the intercom buzzer finally snapped him out of his daydream.

'I've got Mr Schnider on line three for you, sir.'

Tobin sighed. He couldn't make sense of it all. His world seemed to be falling apart. 'Tell him I'm busy, Sandra. Tell him I'm on the phone and I'll call him back.' Tobin picked up the notebook he had started keeping with the names of his clients and details of the work he was doing for them. It was increasingly necessary for times like this. For some reason Tobin simply couldn't remember who the hell Mr Schnider was. It was a problem he'd first noticed several months earlier. Forgetting names, forgetting meetings and an increasing difficulty concentrating on work. He had begun writing everything down and relied more than ever on his secretary, but now even that back-up system was falling apart.

There was no great mystery about why all this was happening. He was tired; he had been working too hard. He had been staying up late to finish other projects and that was why he was struggling so much. He had also been a little unwell recently; he was just recovering from a cold and knew he had been stupid to carry on working right through it; that he should have taken a few days off. But he was so worried about getting behind that he did not. Now he was paying the price for that rash decision. Yes, that was the reason he had been staring at a blank page for the past three hours, he tried to convince himself. That had to be the reason.

He stood up to fetch a glass of water from the nearby water cooler and immediately stumbled. It was a feeling he'd never experienced before, a combination of dizziness and something akin to drunkenness. It was as though he'd stood up too quickly and spun round too fast, all at the same time. He managed to raise himself upright and made his way across the office to the water tank, using one hand to steady himself along the way. For a few moments he couldn't remember what he was doing there, then he took a plastic cup, filled it and raised it to his lips. The cool water went into his mouth and immediately dribbled out. It took three more attempts and all his concentration before he finally managed to swallow.

He'd been having similar problems for a while and had seen several doctors, none of whom was able to come up with a satisfactory diagnosis or to provide any medication that relieved the symptoms. The more time that went by, the more worried Paul became. He confided in Jane but they both decided that, until they knew exactly what it was they were dealing with, they would not say anything to Christopher.

Paul Tobin cancelled his appointments for the rest of the day and went straight home.

The moment he arrived, Jane knew something terrible had happened. It wasn't just that he was home in the middle of the day; it was the look of complete and utter despair on his face. 'There's something wrong with me, Jane, something seriously wrong, and I just don't know what it is. And I'm scared.'

* * *

Knocking on doors to tell someone a loved one had been killed; viewing child pornography in order to get a conviction: these were two of Karl Marshall's least favourite things. But top of the list was witnessing a post-mortem. The pornography happened only rarely and while he had done his fair share of death knocks when he had been lower down the ranks, nowadays there was always someone else there to do it for him. But that still left the post-mortems.

He'd never managed to get used to the smell of rotting flesh or the sight of pools of congealed blood. The way the bodies bloated up with gas that then escaped with an evil 'hiss' as the pathologist made the first incision. Information about how the victim died had to be obtained as quickly as possible, which meant the officer in charge of the case simply had to be there. He had now perfected his own personal system. He would hover around the outside of the pathology lab and go in at the very last minute, early enough to get the information he needed but late enough to avoid seeing any of the gore. His timing was now so perfect it had become something of a joke among the department's staff.

'What have you got for me, doc?'

Nick Reynolds, the Home Office pathologist,

was washing his hands at a large sink as Marshall walked in. 'Hey, Karl. Wasn't expecting you for at least another fifteen minutes. I haven't even started stitching him up yet. You must be losing your touch in your old age.'

'Very funny. What's the verdict?'

'Not a lot, to be honest. Death occurred forty-eight hours ago, can't be more specific than that at the moment. He didn't have much of a last meal, just some snack food and a couple of pints of beer.'

Dr Reynolds moved down the body that lay on the steel table in the centre of the room and Marshall fought hard to stop the bile rising in his stomach. There was a gaping Y-shaped incision in the centre of the man's torso and all his organs sat in a tray alongside him.

'When I first saw the body,' Dr Reynolds continued, 'I thought that whoever did this had gone to a lot of trouble to make sure we couldn't identify who this person is. See here how the jaw has been smashed in, that was done with a hammer. The teeth are in pieces, which means I can't do anything with dental records and the rest of the face is such a mess I don't think you'll be able to identify him that way either.'

The car had been destined to be crushed until some kids playing in the local scrapyard found the body in the boot.

Reynolds picked up the dead man's arm and lifted it towards Marshall. 'See here,' he said. 'This is unusual. The hands are intact but the fingers have been taken off, right down to the knuckle. I'm guessing they're a lot easier to dispose of than hands.'

'So no fingerprints, which means we have no idea who this guy is?' said Marshall.

'I didn't say that, I just said the killer had tried to make it difficult. At least I think he did. I'm not sure now. He messed up. Forensics managed to get a print off the inside of his belt buckle, the kind of place that only the victim would have touched. My problem is that I think a killer who went to that much trouble would know something like that.'

'So what's your theory?'

'Looks like a revenge killing. Whoever did it wanted to send a message.' The doctor pointed at the chest of the dead man, whose body was covered with severe discoloration due to the bruising. 'His lungs are filled with blood, which indicates that his face was smashed in while he was still alive.'

'I wouldn't be surprised if the killer had taken photographs and sent the fingers along as proof of death,' Karl said while observing the doctor's findings.

'There are wood fibres around his body and face, which suggest he was attacked with a blunt object. My reckoning is a baseball bat. Here, look.' The doctor showed Karl the long lines of bruising round the dead man's body. 'You're dealing with some pretty sick people here, Karl.'

'How long before the fingerprint comes back?'

'It's being run as we speak. If this guy is in the system – and I have a sneaking suspicion he will be – it will only take a couple of hours. But I have something for you before then anyway. I might not know who he is right now, but I know where he was before he died. Take a look at this.' Reynolds picked up the man's hand just above the severed fingers and held it palm down towards Marshall.

'I don't see anything,' said the detective.

'Exactly. Invisible to the naked eye. That's why they missed it. Now be a good chap and switch off the lights for me.'

As the room was plunged into semi-darkness, Dr Reynolds picked up a special portable wand which emitted ultraviolet light. The doctor waved the wand over the back of the victim's hand. 'Now do you see?'

Marshall moved forward and peered down at the man's hand. There, printed in a special luminescent ink, was a copy of the logo for the hottest nightclub in town: Lush.

Chapter Thirty-four

Paul and Jane Tobin clutched hands as they sat in front of the large oak desk belonging to Dr Douglas Sax, a consultant neurologist at the Royal Surrey County Hospital in Guildford. For months Paul had been subjected to dozens of tests in an effort to find out what was wrong with him. Now, at last, Dr Sax believed he had found the answer and had called the couple in right away.

'Sorry to have kept you waiting,' said Dr Sax as he entered the room, shutting the door behind him. 'The last appointment took me a little longer than I expected. Can I get you anything? Tea? Coffee? Water?'

'No, thanks,' said Jane, speaking for both of them. No matter what happened, she had already prepared herself for the worst. She had secretly been reading up on Paul's symptoms – the loss of balance and co-ordination, the slightly slurred speech, the clumsiness – and come to two conclusions of her own. Now Dr Sax was going to confirm one or other of them, she thought.

The doctor sat behind his desk, resting his elbows and touching the tips of his fingers together. His face was incredibly serious. 'Have you ever heard of Huntington's disease?' he said at last.

Paul and Jane looked at one another, then back at the doctor, shaking their heads.

Dr Sax turned his gaze directly to Paul. 'It's never been mentioned by anyone in your family?'

Paul shook his head more vigorously. 'I've never heard of it at all. Is that what you think I have?'

'That's what the test results indicate . . .'

For a few brief moments Jane felt an enormous sense of relief wash over her. She had been so certain she was about to hear the words 'Parkinson's' or 'Multiple Sclerosis' that having those two conditions ruled out had to be a good thing. Her relief lasted only as long as the brief pause before Dr Sax continued. '. . . And I can't lie to you, Paul. The prognosis isn't good. It isn't good at all.'

* * *

Business was excellent and Kaitlyn couldn't have been happier. The Roxford, where it all began, accounted for only a tiny percentage of her overall drug sales these days. She now imported at least fifty kilos at a time, whereas her rivals were bringing in a few kilos here and there, using human couriers on small inflatable boats making midnight runs across the channel. Kaitlyn's drugs were magnetically sealed against the side of large cargo ships and dropped into the North Sea. They were then collected by fishing vessels and trawlers. They would use satellite navigation to pinpoint the exact whereabouts of the cargo and electronics to signal the inflatable air pouches to open and bring the goods to the surface to be caught in the fishing nets. Then they were packed in ice and sent to London, hidden among fish deliveries. Kaitlyn had lost some shipments to faulty equipment but none to customs. The money rolled in and her empire expanded. She now owned four nightclubs and three bureaux de change as well as several other businesses. What she couldn't launder she shipped out of the UK to foreign banks. Every six weeks she made an instant £1 million profit without even seeing the drugs.

Kaitlyn was sitting alone in her office above the club, tapping her fingers impatiently on the desk.

At last the door opened and her secretary came in. 'Detective Inspector Marshall to see you, ma'am.'

Kaitlyn sprang out of her chair. 'Come in, Mr Marshall,' she said, reaching out to take his hand. 'How are you?'

'I'm fine, Ms Wilson. I'm sorry I'm a little late.'

'I didn't notice,' Kaitlyn lied. 'Can I get you something to drink?'

'No, thank you. I don't like to drink when I'm on duty.'

'I understand. You don't mind if I have one, though, do you?'

Marshall had no time to reply, the premixed vodka and tonic was already hitting the bottom of the ice-filled glass. 'Take a seat,' said Kaitlyn and Marshall turned to have a look around the office. It was large, the biggest he had ever seen, and filled with a variety of expensive antiques and paintings. A bank of security monitors sat to one side; two computers adjacent to one another; the large teak desk with the soft leather swivel executive chair behind. 'Nice place you've got here,' he said softly.

'Well, I spend a lot of time here so I like to make sure I always have everything I need. Now, what can I do for you, Mr Marshall? Is it Mr Marshall or is it Detective, I never know?'

'Detective Inspector.'

He had been late on purpose, of course. Marshall had no reason to believe Kaitlyn had anything to do with the death, but could not rule out some problem at the club. These sorts of disputes between dealers were known to break out at this kind of venue. At the same time few venues were willing to do much about it. Sure, they all made a lot of noise about their anti-drug policy but in most cases that amounted to little more than a few signs in the toilet and behind the bar. In practice the clubs knew they had to keep the drugs coming in unless they wanted the punters to stay away. The chances were Kaitlyn would be able to help far more than she would be willing to, so Marshall wanted her rattled. He had sat outside in his car for twenty minutes. If she was hiding anything, he would be able to see it in her eyes. As he sat down Kaitlyn looked directly at him. Her eyes were dead. No emotion, no clues. He had nothing here. He was wasting his time.

But there was something. Something inside him stirring. He couldn't help but be attracted to this

successful and beautiful woman. There was something alluring about her. It was incredible.

'So what's this all about, Detective Inspector?'

'Did you know a man called James Lyons?'

Marshall watched her carefully as he showed her a
police photo of the victim. Again the eyes gave nothing away.

'No. Should I?'

'He was a small-time drug dealer and a regular
visitor to your club.'

'And now he's dead.'

Marshall raised his eyebrows. 'I never said anything
about him being dead.'

Kaitlyn took a long sip of her drink, using the
pause to maintain her composure. Of course Lyons
was dead. He had been ripping her off for months,
coming into the club and dealing drugs supplied by
another clan. He had failed to pay attention to any
of her warnings, so ultimately she had ordered the
hit herself, using one of her top operatives. The job
had been carried out with the usual high level of
efficiency, which meant no one could possibly trace
it back to her. The link to the club was unfortunate,
but of no great consequence. Marshall clearly had
nothing to go on. He was on a fishing expedition.

'You didn't have to say anything about him being
dead,' Kaitlyn said at last. 'When you mentioned
Lyons you were using the past tense. And you're a
DI, you wouldn't be here unless he had been killed
or something.'

Marshall nodded. 'Yes, you're right. He was murdered, found a couple of miles from here. He had the stamp from your club on the back of his hand. I understand you use different stamps for different nights.'

Marshall produced another photograph, a close-up of the dead man's hand. The picture showed the missing fingers but only just. Marshal wanted to shock her. 'This is the one.'

Kaitlyn didn't even blink. 'I believe that was Wednesday.'

Marshall turned a page in his notebook. 'Do you allow drugs into your clubs, Ms Wilson?'

Kaitlyn sat back in her chair. 'Are you going to give me a lecture on the evils of drugs? You really don't need to bother. I do what I can but you know what the club scene is like. You know the people down there on the floor wouldn't be dancing their arses off all night unless they were on coke or ecstasy or sometimes both. We catch dealers, we throw them out, we confiscate their drugs and we either throw them away or hand them in to the local station. You can check if you like.'

'I already have.'

'So you know we do what we can.'

'But this man, James Lyons. He never came up on your radar?'

'You'd have to ask the security team. I don't really know anything about it.'

'Who's the Head of Security?'

381

'His name is Errol Gants. All our people come highly recommended, Detective Inspector, and are all fully licensed by Westminster Council.'

Marshall didn't respond as he copied the name down in his notebook before continuing, 'Do you think we'd be able to look at your surveillance footage for the last forty-eight hours?'

'You're welcome to, but they won't do you any good.'

'And why is that?'

'Because all the cameras point behind the bar. They are there for my benefit, to ensure the staff don't steal from me. I'm afraid they won't be any use to you at all.'

*   *   *

Like any good barrister, Christopher Tobin knew experts in a wide range of disciplines that he could call on for advice on any subject. If one of his cases relied on a defence of duress, he knew the criminologist Professor Lindsey Cox who had written authoritative papers on witness intimidation and would happily give her opinion; if it involved a crime of passion there was the psychologist Dr Russell Kennedy who had spent years delving into the mind and was a master at explaining what drives sane people to murder. And if the case involved anything to do with medicine there was Dr Kerry Prior, a senior research fellow at the Hospital for Tropical Diseases in central London.

It was already getting dark as Christopher Tobin

made his way along Tottenham Court Road into the hospital complex and thence into the library. There, tucked into a quiet corner behind a table piled high with textbooks, was Kerry. 'I knew I'd find you here,' he said with a smile. 'Don't you ever stop working?'

Kerry's grin lit up the corner of the room. 'I tried it once, I didn't much like it. Anyway, this isn't really work, more like recreation; I find this stuff really interesting.'

Christopher leaned across the table she was sitting behind and picked up the nearest book from a small selection she had spread out in front of her. '*Pterygium and Corneal Warpage Management in Adolescents*,' he said, reading the title out loud. 'Hey, wasn't this on last year's Booker shortlist?'

'Very funny. Is there actually a point to you being here? The pubs opened half an hour ago, you know,' she said in a friendly but sarcastic tone.

'I'm aware of that, so we need to be quick. Have you got a minute?'

'Sure.' Kerry pushed the books to one side, rubbed her tired eyes and yawned while Christopher sat down beside her.

'I went home at the weekend and my dad was acting funny and so was my mum. I think he's got something wrong with him, some kind of illness but neither of them is saying anything to me yet. I know he's been having loads of tests but the doctors had failed to come up with anything until now.'

'What do you think it is?' said Kerry.

'Something bad, I know that much. I think they're worried about stressing me out because I've got some big cases coming up, but I want to know what's going on. I overheard something about Hunter's Syndrome, something like that, and I wondered if you knew what it was.'

'Well, I think it's highly unlikely your dad has Hunter's Syndrome, not unless you're adopted or something.'

'Why?'

'Because it's a form of dwarfism.'

'Ah. Mind you, my dad's not the tallest man in the world.'

'Most of those who have it end up being hunchbacks and have these distorted gargoyle faces. It's pretty sad, really, most of them tend to die long before they become teenagers. I think I've got pictures of it here.' She searched through her books and opened the page to show Christopher several stages of the disease. Christopher's eyes were focused on the deformed figures of children and adults.

'If your dad had Hunter's Syndrome, you'd have known a long time ago and you probably wouldn't be here anyway. It has to be something else.'

Christopher scratched his head. 'I was sure she said Hunter's. Is there anything that sounds like that, something that might fit?'

'Well.' Kerry reached behind her to a bookshelf and ran her finger along a line of medical encyclopaedias. 'There's Ramsey Hunt Syndrome, that's a form of shingles you sometimes get after chicken pox.' Christopher shook his head. 'Or there's Tolosa Hunt Syndrome,' Kerry continued. 'That causes pain behind the eyes. You need a long course of steroids to get rid of it.'

Christopher was surprised at her knowledge. 'Jesus, is there anything you don't know?'

Kerry kept looking through the encyclopaedias. 'Oh yeah, lots of stuff, but I'm sure I'll get round to it eventually.'

'I'm sure you will. I think we were closer with the dwarf thing. There was no word before it. It was hunt something. Hunting, hunton . . . wish I could remember.'

Kerry turned back to Christopher, her face deadly serious. 'Not Huntington's disease?'

Christopher snapped his fingers. 'That's it, that's the one.'

'Are you sure, are you sure that's what was said?'

'Positive. Huntington's. It's all coming back to me now.' The self-satisfied smile on Christopher's face dropped away when he saw the haunted look in Kerry's eyes. 'What's wrong?' he said softly.

'You've never heard of Huntington's?'

'No. Should I have?'

'If it's what your father has, then yes, you should have.' She paused for a moment, seemingly unsure whether to continue. Her next words hit Christopher like a lightning bolt: 'It's hereditary.'

*

Christopher Tobin never did make it to the pub. He spent the rest of the night at the library, reading up about Huntington's. He learned that the disease is caused by the degeneration of brain cells. Normally passed down from parent to child, there is a fifty–fifty chance that the offspring of someone suffering from HD will go on to develop the disease themselves. It causes the sufferer to lose his or her intellectual faculties, to become emotionally disturbed and to lose control of the body. For those who inherit the HD gene there is no escape. Sooner or later they will go on to develop the disease. The early symptoms include mood swings, depression, irritability or trouble driving, learning new things, remembering a fact, or making a decision. As the disease progresses, concentration on intellectual tasks becomes increasingly difficult. Huntington's causes complete physical and mental breakdown, robbing people of their faculties and their dignity. It takes away their ability to walk, to talk, to dress and feed themselves. It renders them incontinent. Before it kills them it can also take their minds.

How quickly the symptoms develop and how fast they progress varies enormously from person to person. Some first show deterioration when they are in their twenties, others in their eighties. For those at risk there is simply no way of knowing when the disease will strike. Christopher read that, although it is a hereditary disease, more than half of those who go on to develop it had no idea it was in their family.

An effective test for the defective gene was only developed in 1986 and before that, many of those suffering from Huntington's were misdiagnosed as having other conditions. Others simply died before they had a chance to develop any symptoms, masking the disease for future generations.

Christopher thought back through his own family background. His great-great-grandfather had been killed during the First World War, his great-grandfather during the second. Paul's father had died of a heart attack at the age of fifty-seven and, although he had become all but incoherent in the last year of his life, doctors put this down to the early onset of senility rather than anything else. Christopher realised with horror that this terrible disease could have been in his family for generations and that no one would have known.

A few hours earlier Christopher's life had seemed as though it was just beginning. Now all he could think about was how it was going to end for his father. And for himself.

* * *

Back at his office, Detective Inspector Marshall flicked through the file on his latest case, then picked up his phone and dialled the extension for Detective Sergeant Steven Brown, his favoured assistant. 'Do me a favour. Look into the files on Kaitlyn Wilson. There's something about her that doesn't quite add up. She's hiding something.'

Chapter Thirty-five

Misha Borostrova killed his first man at the age of nineteen. He had joined the Blue Berets, the Special Forces division of the Soviet army, and was immediately dispatched to Afghanistan as part of the disastrous Russian campaign to defeat the Mujahedin rebels. As a member of the army's elite, Misha was given the opportunity to study, learning both languages and engineering skills. He was allocated the best equipment, fed the best food and rewarded with the best pay. Most of all, Misha's time in the army taught him how to kill. He learned how to take life by hand, by dagger, pistol, rifle and landmine. During the seven years he spent in Kabul hardly a day went by when he didn't kill someone, or watch one of his fellow soldiers die in agony.

Once the war was over Misha returned to his native Moscow and expected to be treated like a hero. He had done his duty to the motherland and felt sure he would be rewarded for his service. Instead, he found the only work he could get was on the assembly line of an electrical factory, for a tiny salary.

After the wild life he had lived in Kabul, he simply couldn't cope with it. He became a hitman almost by chance. He and a friend were involved in a fight on the housing estate where he lived on the outskirts of Moscow. Misha killed a man by stabbing him in the throat. His friend, also an ex-commando, had just been released from jail and told another ex-con about Misha's skills. The ex-con was an enforcer for the Moscow Mafia. Misha found he had a new job.

He needed little persuasion. His first job had been a thirty-five-year-old man from Uzbek who had ripped off his business partner in a cocaine deal. Misha never knew his name, only his address. He arrived there late one night, knocked on the door and shot him at point-blank range with a Makerov pistol and silencer. Misha watched, fascinated, as the man's head exploded before his very eyes and his lifeless body fell back into his hallway. Although he had no qualms about killing in this way, Misha felt bad that he knew neither the man's name nor the reason he had been asked to kill him. From that day on he made a vow that he would kill only those he truly believed deserved to die. In Afghanistan, he had thought he was doing God's work.

Then, when the Russian Mafia set up an operation in London, he moved there too. He had killed two men from Moscow before branching out and offering his services to other gangs.

He was sitting in a small office above an east London gymnasium surrounded by burly men, three brothers and their father, but Misha felt no fear. He had stared death in the face so many times it no longer concerned him. Besides, he was here for business.

'We will pay your usual fee,' the man smoking a cigarette on the other side of the table said. 'Plus a hefty bonus if this can be carried out within the next fourteen days.' The man pushed a photograph, face down on the table, across to where Misha was sitting.

He turned the photograph over. He could not disguise the look of shock on his face.

'Something the matter?' asked the man with the cigarette.

'It is a woman,' Misha said softly. 'I don't kill women and I don't kill children. I only kill men.'

'This woman, she is special. She is like a man. In any case a life is just a life. I don't see how it makes any difference.'

Misha shook his head firmly. 'This is not right. I would die before I killed a woman.'

'This is important, Misha. That's why we wanted you to take this job. Nothing must go wrong with this hit and we know that you are the man who plans everything down to the very last detail. We will be willing to pay you five times your usual rate.'

Misha leaned back in his chair, his fingers still resting lightly on the portrait of the woman in front of him. 'Tell me', he said, his voice soft and steady, 'exactly why it is that this woman has to die.'

* * *

Christopher Tobin locked the door of his silver-blue Vauxhall and looked around him. It didn't matter how many times he arrived at work at Lincoln's Inn Fields, something about it always made him smile.

There was a real sense of history, knowing of all the famous barristers and lawyers who had filled the chambers where he now worked. He made his way across the cobbled stones. Most of the other inhabitants had already arrived and parking spaces were few and far between.

He had noticed two men sitting in a black Porsche when he had driven towards his parking space. He would not have paid them any mind but for the fact that the car was one he hoped to own himself before too long and the fact that the driver's eyes had flashed with recognition when Christopher had driven past. The man had recognised him, but although something about his face seemed familiar, Christopher had no idea who he was. There was, he decided, nothing unusual about people waiting in their cars until their appointment with their barrister came up, but something about these two made Christopher feel incredibly uneasy.

He continued across the road and entered the interior of the red-brick terraced building that housed his chambers along with those of fifteen other barristers. Position mattered little in this area – one block was pretty much as good as another so far as most people were concerned. Some of the chambers charged vast fees to those who stayed there. Here he paid twenty per cent of his earnings, roughly the average for the area. Although Christopher had worked hard and his profile was rising fast, he still had a long way to go before he made it into the big money league. Most of the other barristers in the chambers earned far more than he did and he knew that unless his earnings took a significant upward turn soon, he would be in the position of having to justify himself to the rest, as he would be seen as not pulling his weight.

Ignoring the small, stuffy lift, Christopher climbed the four flights of stairs to his office, taking them two at a time. Ever conscious of the fact that he spent long hours sitting behind his desk or on a bench in court, he did his best to keep in shape and took every opportunity to exercise. His heart was beating faster and his breathing heavy as he stepped into the hall-way, the sound of his secretary's fingers clattering against a keyboard there to greet him. 'Hello, Sally,' he said, returning her beaming smile.

'Good morning, Mr Tobin. I see you took the stairs again.'

'What can I say? It's cheaper and quicker than going to the gym.'

Sally was pretty, with a nice smile. Her naturally blonde hair hung just above her shoulders in a style that managed to be both smart and fashionable. She dressed well, skirts just above the knee, sensible shoes and neatly pressed blouses. More than once Christopher had caught himself watching her from the corner of his eye as she crossed the room and wondering what the future might hold. They had yet to move beyond mild flirtation but there was no reason to think it wouldn't happen. After all, finding yourself happily married to your former secretary was a Tobin family tradition.

They both laughed. 'Is Ryan in yet?' he asked, becoming serious. 'I wanted to talk to him about the Basset case.'

'He's got someone with him. I'll let him know you want to see him as soon as he's free.'

Sally worked not just for Tobin but for two others in the chambers – a way of keeping their costs down. As he made his way to his office, Sally waved a piece of paper at him. 'This gentleman wants to see you this morning, Mr Tobin.'

'What? You know I don't have time to see anyone, not without an appointment. Who is he?'

'I tried to tell him that, but he insisted. He had another man with him. They were quite intimidating. They said they needed to speak to you right away.'

He took the piece of paper from her and unfolded it. His earlier sense of unease had been correct. 'Did one of them have dark hair, dark complexion, in his early thirties?'

'Yes,' said Sally, looking at him curiously.

'They're downstairs waiting in a car. When they come up again – and I'm sure they will any time now – tell them I can give them ten minutes.'

A few minutes later the two men entered his office and made their way across to the battered but comfortable brown leather sofa. Close up, Christopher could see that the man whose eyes he had met was the younger of the two, heavy-set and mean-looking. He wore blue jeans with a V-neck sweatshirt over the top and sand-coloured Kickers boots. The other man was smaller, wiry-looking with small, round-framed glasses and a badly trimmed moustache. He looked like an accountant.

The younger man shook his hand. His grip was hard and dry. He was short and stocky, his hair black and crinkly, cut short. His features were dark, as if he had spent a lot of time in the sun. When he spoke there was a heavy south London accent. 'Do you know who I am?'

Christopher squinted at the man as he indicated that the pair should sit down and returned to his own seat. 'Forgive me, your face does look familiar, but I can't quite recall the name.'

'The name is Fergusson, Ron Fergusson. I'm in a little bit of bother and I was hoping you might be able to help.'

Christopher could have kicked himself. Of course. Ron Fergusson was a member of one of the most notorious criminal families in London. The clan owned a gymnasium in the East End but their real wealth came from a mixture of sophisticated armed robberies and more recently drug trafficking.

'Sorry to turn up without an appointment,' Fergusson continued. 'It's just that I don't have a lot of time to spare and I need to get a decision as quickly as possible. I'm in court in two weeks and I've had to sack my brief cos he's a wanker. I want to appoint you to defend me instead.'

Christopher was taken aback. 'Well, I'm sure you realise that as a barrister I am not able to work for clients directly. Instead, you need to find a solicitor and that solicitor will approach me and see if I want to be appointed.'

Fergusson pointed at the man beside him. 'This is my solicitor right here. So that side of things is all taken care of.'

Christopher took a deep breath. 'Still, this really is highly irregular. And if the case is only two weeks away, that hardly gives me any time to prepare. It's ridiculous, asking to change your barrister at such short notice. I don't think the judge would consider that valid grounds for an adjournment, not unless there was some issue about a conflict of interest.'

Fergusson shook his head. 'Nah, nothing like that. I just don't like the bloke. Ugly fucker. One of them types with the one big eyebrow that goes all the way across the middle. Nah, I don't want to be looking at that from the dock. I hear good things about you. I thought you'd be able to do a better job.'

Christopher sat back in his chair. 'I see. Well, I'm flattered, really I am, but I just don't think . . .'

Fergusson jerked his heavy elbow into the ribs of the man beside him, who suddenly came to life. 'Mr Tobin, we realise these are unusual circumstances and we would be taking that into account when it came to the matter of your remuneration. My client has authorised me to offer a sum of three times your usual fee.'

Christopher felt a flush of excitement run through him as the hairs on the back of his neck started to bristle. He had to force himself to keep breathing steadily as his mind raced through the calculations of how much he could earn. Surely it was madness to take on such a case, but at the same time if he did and if he won, it would propel him into the big league. Christopher planted his elbows on the desk and pushed the tips of his fingers together. 'OK, Mr Fergusson. You have my full attention.'

* * *

Kaitlyn hated taking precautions but knew she had no choice. The word on the street was that some of her rivals in the drug business were less than happy with her. One gang in particular, headed up by the Bowers, were causing her particular concern. They had approached her with the idea of forming a partnership and she had laughed in their faces. 'Why would we want to partner up with you lot?' she had told them. 'We have all the power, we have all the property, we have all the drug routes in and out of the country, and we have a rock-solid distribution network. What could you possibly offer us?'

It was a mistake. Kaitlyn had known that at the time, but there was simply no way she was going to let all the hard work she had put in to build up the business to this point go to waste. Had she agreed to their proposals, she would eventually have been forced to step down from the board of several of her companies and see a huge slice of the profits diverted into the pockets of others. But having turned down the idea of a friendly merger, Kaitlyn was now alive to the danger posed by the threat of a hostile takeover.

She still ran the most successful drugs gang in the country but others were snapping at her heels, wanting to take over her business the same way she originally took over from Gary. She knew the matter would only ever be sorted out with extreme violence and that in the process she personally would become a key target.

Chapter Thirty-six

Ron Fergusson hadn't exactly been caught red-handed, but he might as well have been. He had been filmed on CCTV at Heathrow airport parking outside Terminal 1 and escorting a young man through the departure area. A few hours later that man, Pete Kennedy, had flown to Brazil for a ten-day holiday. On his return, sniffer dogs in the baggage area went crazy when they came across his case. It was secretly opened and found to be stuffed with four kilos of high-quality cocaine.

Rather than arrest Kennedy there and then, customs officers hurriedly assembled a surveillance team with the idea of following him back to wherever the drugs were destined to be delivered and therefore catch some of those higher up the chain. The officers on the team were stunned when Ron Fergusson turned up in Arrivals and greeted Pete with a warm hug, taking the bag from him and making his way towards the car park. The vintage Jaguar that Fergusson drove didn't even make it out of the car park before it was surrounded by armed officers. He and Kennedy were both arrested. Kennedy immediately pleaded guilty to possession with intent, but refused to implicate Fergusson in the plot. Fergusson exercised his right to silence. Freed on bail, he was now facing a charge of conspiracy to import narcotics and looking at a stiff sentence if he went down.

Although Fergusson had a considerable reputation throughout the underworld, he had no criminal record to speak of. This was the reason he was ultimately given bail. Having lost that battle the Crown Prosecution Service insisted the jury should be given protection throughout the trial. 'It's outrageous,' Christopher told the judge during the opening legal arguments. 'We all know that there has never been a case with a protected jury where the defendant has been acquitted. It puts an incredible bias on the case and I object to it most strongly. My client is not being tried on his past reputation but on the charges here today. If this is to be done fairly, then the jury should not receive protection.'

The judge listened carefully to Christopher's many points but dismissed them all. 'I find in favour of the Crown, Mr Tobin,' he said. 'You make the point yourself that your client has a reputation and so does his family. Members of his extended family are likely to attend this court in order to show him their support. Should they become overenthusiastic in this role, they might find themselves, shall we say, scrutinising the jury in order to decide which way the case was going. In order to avoid this action being misinterpreted, I want the jury kept out of sight and given round the clock protection. That is my final word on the matter.'

There was a short adjournment before the case proper began and Christopher returned to the robing room seething with anger. The jury would be picked up from their homes every morning, given a police escort on their way to court and have armed guards outside their homes throughout the trial. It would leave only one impression in their minds – that they were dealing with a criminal so dangerous that he posed a threat to their very lives. Under those circumstances there would be no way they would let him walk the streets, no matter how flimsy the evidence. Fergusson was going down and there was nothing Christopher could do about it.

Unless. Christopher's mouth suddenly curled up into a smile as an idea shot through him. It was risky, and it was unconventional, but it just might work.

Minutes later they were in court and the prosecution went through their opening speech. When it was Christopher's turn he said only a few words. 'Ladies and gentlemen of the jury, my client is innocent of the charges against him. As the case progresses, I will show you exactly why this is. Thank you.'

Fergusson glared at him from the dock. Christopher Tobin was supposed to be the best young barrister around and he wasn't even trying. If he went down for this case there would be hell to pay.

Christopher saw the look on Fergusson's face and asked the judge for a moment to consult his client. He walked over to the dock and whispered, 'You'll have to trust me. We need to turn around your past and reputation to our advantage. No matter what I say, you have to trust me and believe I am doing this in your best interests.'

The prosecution case was solid, if mostly circumstantial. There was the footage of Fergusson arriving at the airport, the footage of him picking up Kennedy and the fact that the flight had been paid for using a credit card in Fergusson's own name. When the prosecution rested it was almost lunchtime.

'Do you want to wait until after the break to begin your case?' the judge asked.

'No need, Your Honour. The defence has but one witness and he will not be in the witness box for long.'

'Very well. Do carry on.'

'Thank you, Your Honour. The defence calls Ron Fergusson.'

As Fergusson moved to the witness box, Christopher turned to face the jury. 'Ladies and gentlemen of the jury, I am here to tell you today that my client is a bad man. A very bad man. He is prone to violence, he has a temper that would scare the bravest of men. He is handy with his fists. There are many tales of his exploits, people who have been hospitalised by his violence.'

In the public gallery members of the Fergusson family were looking shocked. One of them drew his fingers across his throat as Christopher briefly glanced up.

Christopher swallowed hard and continued, 'You will have heard that my client has no previous convictions. Well, that is only because he has never been caught. I can tell you here and now that he has been involved in numerous armed robberies, protection rackets and frauds. He is part of one of the most notorious criminal families to emerge from the East End in the past thirty years.

'It is for this reason, members of the jury, that you are under protection. That in itself shows just how serious a threat this man represents.

'But there is one element of this which you must be aware of. For all the violence, for all the robbery and other crimes that my client will freely admit to, he has never once been involved with drugs. That is something he and his family are firmly opposed to.'

At last Ron Fergusson could see where Christopher was going with this and twisted his craggy features into their most sympathetic form before turning to face the jury for the first time. 'Mr Fergusson,' said Christopher, 'can you tell me something of your attitude towards armed robbery.'

Richardson sniffed deeply. 'Nothing wrong with it as far as I'm concerned. Taking a gun and asking someone for money, that's just going out to work. No one has to get hurt if you do it proper. And all them banks are insured anyway. It's not as if anyone loses out. At the end of the day all the money only belongs to the Queen and she don't need it anyway, does she?'

A ripple of laughter worked its way through the jury. Christopher smiled. They had taken the bait and all he needed to do now was reel them in. 'What about your attitude to drugs, Mr Fergusson?'

'Can't stand them,' Fergusson said. 'I think they're evil. The people who traffic in that stuff are sick. I've got kids, three of them, and I don't want them anywhere near that stuff. People say you can make good money from it but I don't care about that. I want to be able to hold my head up. I can do that if I'm an armed robber, I could never do that if I was a dirty drug dealer.'

Now Fergusson was getting into his stride. 'You see, with the armed robbery, if you do it right, nobody gets hurt. Scared a little, yeah, maybe. But no one gets hurt. I've never shot anyone. No need. I'm no killer. But that drug business, no matter how you do it, people get hurt. You've got kids taking pills and ending up dead, good little girls ending up as dirty junkies and overdosing in some squat. You've got schoolkids smashing into cars and breaking into houses to get enough money for their next fix and teenagers with guns shooting each other over bits of turf. I'll be an armed robber until the day I die. It's in me blood. But drugs, nah, I could never be a part of something like that.'

Twenty minutes later Christopher had finished and the barrister acting for the Crown Prosecution Service was sitting open-mouthed at his table.

'Your witness, Mr Jones,' the judge told him.

Jones rose slowly and shut his mouth at the same time. He had planned somehow to discredit the witness, but now he had nothing left. 'No questions, Your Honour.' And he sat down.

The jury had been back from lunch only half an hour when the call came out over the court tannoy system that they had their verdict: Not guilty.

Fergusson was almost crying with joy. 'Mate, I don't know whether to kiss you or stab you. You're a fucking genius.'

That night Christopher went out drinking around the clubs and pubs of the East End as the guest of honour of the Fergusson family. There was a lot of drinking, a little dancing and more raucous jokes than he could possibly remember. Of all the nights out he had ever had – celebrating getting his degree, passing his bar exams, winning his first case, even losing his virginity – this was far and away the best.

* * *

Jacob knocked on the door of the office for the third time before giving up and simply pushing it open. Kaitlyn was inside behind her desk, staring down, her brow deeply furrowed with intense concentration. She had not even heard him open the door.

He took a few steps forward but it was only when his shadow fell across the desk in front of her that she looked up with a start. 'What?'

'I've knocked three times. What's going on? Are you OK?'

'Yeah. I'm fine. I was just reading.'

'Rick's gonna be here any minute.'

'OK, I'll be there. Sorry, I was miles away.'

'What's got you so hooked?'

Kaitlyn laid down the magazine in front of her but Jacob was still too far away to see what the article she was reading was about. 'Oh, the usual stuff, make-up and boys,' she said with a cheeky grin. 'You know what us girls are like. Give me thirty seconds to powder my nose and I'll be ready.' She stood up and moved quickly towards the door of her private bathroom, vanishing inside.

Jacob waited until the door clicked shut behind her, then stepped over to her desk, picking up the magazine. It was a copy of the European edition of *Newsweek* and the page was open at a short article about the way the popular American television show *Sex and the City* had influenced the clothes-buying habits of a new generation of women. Jacob grinned and flicked the magazine over. The other side featured the start of a separate article about 'people to watch' in the coming year.

At that moment the door to the private bathroom opened and Kaitlyn emerged. Jacob turned to face her. 'Don't tell me you're planning to use this as justification to get an increase in your shoe budget.' Kaitlyn's expression was one of confusion so Jacob held up the article. 'Honestly, it's in one ear and out the other with you, isn't it?'

Now Kaitlyn smiled. 'Come on, we don't want to keep Rick waiting.'

Jacob replaced the magazine and headed towards the main door. Kaitlyn glanced back over her shoulder as they left. The article about 'people to watch' was sitting face up on her desk. The third entry, like the others, had a small picture and a mini biography of the subject. The name at the start of the entry was Christopher Tobin.

Chapter Thirty-seven

The meeting had dragged on for more than three hours and Kaitlyn had hated every minute of it. In many ways being the head of a large criminal gang was a lot like being the head of a multinational corporation. There were problems with distribution overseas, suppliers of raw materials were paying late, transportation links were breaking down because of inclement weather. Some days it seemed that everything that could go wrong was going wrong. In the early days she had been a hundred per cent hands on, fully involved in every aspect of every single shipment. Now she was so far removed from it as almost to feel as though she wasn't involved at all.

That was precisely the idea. When, as occasionally happened, shipments were intercepted or someone on the fringes of the organisation she had taken so long to build up was caught and interrogated, they could say or prove nothing that would point the finger at her, even had they wanted to. She had ensured that there were numerous levels of what she liked to refer to as 'insulation' between her and the actual products that were dealt on the street. Even those workers employed directly by the organisation had little idea who was at the head of the table.

But at the same time this isolation took away much of the excitement that had been present in the early days and this, as much as anything else, had been the driving force. For the first time in her life Kaitlyn could understand why ageing armed robbers went out to try to do one last job, even when they'd made more than enough from jobs before. It wasn't to do with the money. If that were all it was about there were other legitimate careers you could go into where the money would be almost as good and a damn sight more regular than robbing banks. No, it wasn't about the money at all, it was about the thrill of getting away with it. Remove that and all that was left was the money. Kaitlyn had more than she could ever spend and it had been that way for as long as she could remember, for so long that she was all but bored with the way her life had become. Getting her hands dirty, going back to work at the coalface wasn't an option. For the first time she started to think the unthinkable. She was ready to give it all up.

She had been so lost in her thoughts that she hadn't realised the meeting was coming to an end and that Jacob had spent the last ten seconds staring at her, waiting for her to give permission to wind things up. 'Sorry,' she said softly. 'Any other business?' She looked round the table and saw there was none.

Jacob leaned towards her. 'There is one thing but it's private, I'll wait till everyone else has gone.'

'What is it?' she asked when she and Jacob were the only ones left in the boardroom.

'Pilgrim wants to see you.'

The discomfort was obvious on Kaitlyn's face but Jacob misread it. 'How is it going between you two? Not well?'

'What are you talking about?'

'You and Pilgrim. You're seeing him, aren't you? All this time you've been spending together.'

Kaitlyn laughed. 'No, not at all. He's been working for me.'

'On what?'

'It's nothing, Jacob. Nothing that affects anything we do. It's a private matter.'

'I'm one of your oldest friends. We've been through hell and high water together. You know I'd do anything for you, but you still feel the need to keep secrets from me.'

'If you're such a good friend, you'll understand why some things are best left in the dark. Tell Pilgrim to come on up.'

'I wasn't expecting you today,' Kaitlyn said as Pilgrim entered the office and made his way to a seat. 'Has something happened to Christopher?'

For the past ten years Pilgrim had found regular employment doing little else but keeping tabs on Christopher Tobin. As one of the only people in the world aware of the connection between the famous barrister and London's top criminal mastermind, he made a good living keeping Kaitlyn updated on the brother she could never approach.

Pilgrim shuffled uncomfortably in his seat. 'I'm having a few problems. I've run up some debts. Gambling. A couple of years ago I had this amazing winning streak, I was cleaning up. Everything I touched turned to gold. Then, I don't know what happened, it all fell apart. Since then I keep waiting for my luck to change but so far it hasn't. I'm up to my neck in debt, bookies, moneylenders, credit cards. You name it. I've got some real heavies coming down on me.'

Kaitlyn nodded slowly. 'The world is a pretty small place. If you like, I'll have words with the people who are putting you under pressure. Get them to ease up, give you more time to come up with the money.'

Pilgrim let a snort of laughter escape from his nostrils. It was a horrible sound, right out of a farm-yard. 'I guess you could do that.' There was attitude in his voice, an arrogant, sneering attitude that Kaitlyn had never noticed before. 'Yeah, I guess you could do that, but I was really hoping you might be able to clear all my debts for me.'

'Why on earth would I do that?'

'Listen, Kaitlyn, you've treated me well, you've always been fair and square with me and I really appreciate that. But I'm not stupid. I know what goes on here. I've got ears, I've got eyes. And I've got a heart. I know that at least five men whose names and addresses I have supplied to your organisation have been murdered in the past three years. I know what goes on.'

'So what? You're part of it all.'

'Maybe. But a lot of people are going to be pretty surprised to learn that one of London's leading criminal barristers has a sister who just happens to be one of London's leading criminals.'

'Are you trying to blackmail me?'

'Blackmail is such an ugly word, Kaitlyn. Do you mind if I call you Kaitlyn? I just think that after all I've done for you, after doing such a good job of tracking your brother down, I think you might have treated me a little better.'

'You were paid for what you did. You were paid well.'

'Not well enough, I don't think so.'

Kaitlyn leaned forward. Her nostrils flaring with anger, she slammed her hand down hard on the table in front of her. 'You've got a real fucking nerve. You know what I'm capable of. Do you know the risk you're taking?'

'I'm not stupid. I've got insurance.'

Kaitlyn leaned back in her chair, stiffening slightly. 'What are you talking about?'

'A file, photographs, copies of documents. Everything official to back up what I've said. And there's more, copies of all the material I've given you over the years. I've put it somewhere safe; somewhere you'll never find it. With instructions to hand it in to the police if anything ever happens to me.'

'You lied to me.'

'You've given me a nuclear bomb, you can't blame

me for wanting to have some protection. I know you don't fear going to prison or being caught. It's always a possibility in this line of business. But imagine the effect it will have on Christopher. It could be devastating. I don't think he'd ever work again. Think of the shame, the scandal. Think of all the cases he's prosecuted, the enemies he's made. Your enemies. I really think you should consider my offer,' Pilgrim said.

* * *

Misha Borostrova was waiting for the right moment to strike. Sometimes it took hours, sometimes days. The important thing was not how long it took, but to make sure that he never struck before the time was right. That was the kind of mistake that would cost him his liberty. Or his life.

He had been waiting in the street outside the club for the past four hours and only now had his target finally come in sight. He waited until the woman climbed into a black taxi. Years of practice had taught Misha how to follow a car from such a discreet distance that the driver would never know. It helped that he knew exactly where the vehicle was going and did not need to keep her in sight the whole time. All he wanted was the right opportunity.

It came a few minutes later when the vehicle pulled into a petrol station and the driver got out. Misha pulled his own vehicle on to the forecourt, stopping so the woman sitting in the back of the taxi couldn't see him. A quick glance to make sure there were no prying eyes, and Misha was out of his car and across the forecourt in a flash. His gun was in a holster on the left side of his jacket and he held it against his chest as he ran to stop it smashing into his ribs. His head was inside the back of the taxi before the driver even had a chance to turn round and stop him. 'Kaitlyn,' he said softly.

She turned round and saw the stocky Russian standing opposite her, a mixture of alarm and worry on her face. 'Misha. What are you doing here? What's wrong?' Kaitlyn signalled to the driver that everything was OK and with that Misha took his hand away from the gun holstered inside his jacket.

He leaned into her and spoke even more quietly: 'We need to talk. We need to go somewhere private. Follow me.'

Ten minutes later Misha pulled his 5-series BMW up into a side road that formed part of an old industrial estate. As Kaitlyn's black cab pulled up alongside, Misha threw open the passenger door, inviting her to join him.

'What's going on?'

'Two days ago I picked up a contract to kill from a gang in East London. You were the target. I thought you might want to know. Oh, and don't worry, I didn't take the job.'

'Why not?'

'For two reasons. First I have worked for you in the past and you have always treated me very fairly.

You were my client before these other people, the Bowers. That gives you priority. The second is that I have never killed a woman. It is something I am not willing to do. It is out of courtesy that I wanted to tell you this.'

Kaitlyn nodded thoughtfully. 'You'll be paid well for this.' She knew it was the Bowers even before Misha had mentioned the family name. There was no one else it could possibly be. Now all she had to do was decide what to do about it.

Jacob Collins had been in bed with Miranda when Kaitlyn had called. His on-off girlfriend was hugely pissed off that he rushed out of the room as if his trousers were on fire, but she knew she couldn't question Jacob too closely. It was about the source of his wealth and influence, which was part of the deal of getting to be with him at all. The sex had been rough, frantic and far short of satisfactory, mostly thanks to the huge amounts of cocaine Jacob had been snorting earlier in the evening. As Miranda lay alone in the bed, she wondered if this was all her relationship with Jacob Collins would ever amount to. She gave him everything and there had been some good times, but for the most part the whole thing just made her miserable.

As Jacob made his way across London in the small hours, he realised that he and Kaitlyn had been so busy recently and the gang had grown so large that they had hardly ever spent any time alone. Errol was in

Jamaica visiting relations, which meant that whatever she had planned for later that evening would involve just the two of them. It had to be something important, something she could trust no one else with.

'We need to take out one of the Bowers,' she explained when they met up at the Lush office. 'And we need to do it tonight.'

Jacob was stunned. 'Are you sure this is a good idea?'

'Positive. They tried to take out a hit on me last night.'

All his protective instincts came to bear. 'Are you all right?'

'Fine. They hired the wrong guy. Misha.'

Jacob couldn't help but laugh. They had come across Misha early in their drug-running game and he had quickly proved himself a reliable enforcer. When James Lyons, a dealer from the Bowers clan, had started frequenting Lush on a regular basis, taking business away from their own dealers, it was Misha who was hired to execute him, even going so far as to carry out the grisly task of cutting off the man's fingers in order to send them to the Bowers as a warning not to mess with Kaitlyn and her colleagues.

An uneasy peace had reigned for a few years but now it was all set to blow up again. A quick, decisive strike against the enemy before they had a chance to realise what was happening was the only way to prevent a full-scale war.

*

Misha had known only one thing about George Bowers, head of the family, but it was enough. Bowers had a weakness for young prostitutes and regularly hired girls from the Pretty Pimlico agency. They would arrive by taxi at the porter-protected entrance of his penthouse flat in a mansion block in a quiet east London cul-de-sac and make their way upstairs, where for £250 per hour he could do pretty much whatever he wanted to them. Speed was of the essence so the plan had to be thrown together in no time at all. It was considerably less than perfect but Kaitlyn knew that the consequences of not taking immediate action would be far worse.

George Bowers was not just the father figure, he was also the head of the gang. None of his sons had anything like the same amount of brain power or business acumen. If they could take him out, the rest of the Bowers clan would be left in disarray.

Kaitlyn stood in front of the mirror and examined herself. She was wearing high heels, red stockings with full suspenders. Over the underwear she wore a sleek, figure-hugging black dress that was slit open at the back right down to the base of her spine and finished just above her stocking tops. She wore no bra. Carefully she applied her make-up, using far more than usual to raise her cheekbones and lengthen her face. She finished off the outfit with a bright-red wig and a pair of sunglasses. There was a good chance Bowers would recognise her if she took off the wig and the sunglasses, but she had no intention of removing any item of her outfit. Nothing at all.

Misha had told Kaitlyn that Bowers liked his girls to arrive just after 8 p.m. They usually stayed until between 10 and 11 p.m. Bowers would spend a couple of hours sleeping and then, in the early hours of the following morning, would order a takeaway and settle in front of the television.

Kaitlyn climbed into Jacob's waiting car. His eyes had almost popped out of his head as she had crossed the street. 'Wow, you look incredible.'

Kaitlyn smiled. 'Let's just hope that George Bowers thinks so.'

'Of course he will, you look fucking knockout. Fucking dynamite.'

Kaitlyn looked across at Jacob. His pupils were wide open, fully dilated and there was a fine dusting of white powder round the end of his nostrils. 'Are you OK, Jacob? I need you to be a hundred per cent for this.'

Jacob brushed the back of his hand along the underside of his nose. 'I only did a line, just to keep me sharp. I'm OK. Really.'

Kaitlyn frowned. She hated to work with people who were under the influence of drugs. It made them unreliable and overly paranoid. In an ideal world she would have abandoned the job, or at least got Errol to take her instead, but Errol was in Jamaica and there was no one else she could trust anywhere near as much as Jacob. The hit had to be tonight. Jacob would have to do.

The pair set off in silence and stopped at the top of the cul-de-sac where Bowers lived. It was just before 7.30. All they could do was wait.

Twenty minutes later a minicab appeared at the top of the road. Jacob had parked at an awkward angle and only a few inches of space remained on either side of the cab. As the driver slowed right down, Jacob appeared at his window and put a gun to his head. 'Don't be a hero, mate,' he said softly. Then, turning to the scantily clad woman in the back, 'This is the end of the journey for you, love. Fuck off out of it.'

A few seconds later the same minicab was making its way down to the bottom of the cul-de-sac and pulling up outside the Bowers home. Jacob was behind the wheel, a baseball cap pulled down low over his eyes, and Kaitlyn was in the back. As he parked, one of Bowers's bodyguards peered through the driver's window. 'Never seen you before, sunshine. You new?'

'Yeah,' said Jacob, putting on a warm East End accent. 'It's me first night, mate.'

Any further enquiries were abandoned when Kaitlyn quickly got out of the car. The way she looked, the smell of her perfume and the wicked smile on her face were enough to completely captivate the two guards outside the house. Jacob was totally forgotten.

Kaitlyn was led inside and, after the rather burly porter had taken a quick glance into her tiny handbag to make sure she was not armed, placed in the small private lift that opened out directly into the middle of the penthouse flat where George Bowers lived. He was there to greet her, smiling approvingly at her outfit and her figure. His hands guided her across the room, lingering a little too long on her buttocks for Kaitlyn's liking. She made a mental note that she would make him pay for that later.

George Bowers was a red faced man in his late fifties. He had an enormous barrel chest and short, squat legs. In his youth, around the time of the Kray twins, he had developed a reputation as something of a brawler, but those days were long behind him now. Today he got his kicks from fine women and fine wine, nothing more taxing than that.

Bowers smiled so widely that tiny white bubbles of spittle started to form in the corners of his mouth. He rested his hands on top of his huge belly for a moment, then reached up and started to unbutton his shirt, all the while staring directly into Kaitlyn's eyes.

Part of her wanted to turn away but she forced herself not only to keep looking but to give Bowers the impression that she really liked what she saw. She knew only too well that the most successful working girls were the ones who made every man feel as though he was special, different from the rest. That was how she wanted George Bowers to feel. She wanted him to feel that way for the rest of his life.

As his shirt slid to the floor and his white, sparsely

haired belly came into view, George Bowers reached down and began to unzip his fly. Kaitlyn ran her tongue seductively over her lips as he looked at her, then opened her bag and pulled out a small lipstick holder. She lowered her sunglasses so they were perched on the end of her nose and walked, hips swinging, towards Bowers's now naked body. He reached up in an attempt to grasp her shoulders and pull her towards him, but she slipped to one side, tracing one delicate fingertip along the top of his shoulder and across the back of his neck. Bowers shut his eyes and shuddered with anticipation. He'd been sent a good one this time. He'd be sure to remember to give her a substantial bonus.

She was directly behind him now, her hips pressed up against his naked buttocks. He could feel himself starting to get aroused. Her left hand was flat against his chest, toying with his hairs. Then suddenly the hand whipped up and locked over his mouth, pulling him back and off balance. At the same time he felt something cold and hard enter the back of his neck. He tried to scream in agony but his cries were dampened by the hand clamped over his lips.

A spatter of blood fell across Kaitlyn's face and she blinked furiously to get it out of her eye. She pushed harder with the tiny lock knife that had been hidden inside the lipstick case, twisting the blade and feeling it cut through cartilage and splinter bone. George had stopped struggling so much now. Bubbles of blood were seeping out of the corner of his mouth and through her fingers. Kaitlyn finally relaxed her grip and George Bowers fell to the floor. Dead.

Kaitlyn waited a full hour and a half in Bowers's flat before making her way back into the lift. She had spent the time getting the blood off her face and clothes, and ensuring that she left no forensic evidence behind. She had a mental checklist in her mind and ran through it one item at a time, wiping every surface she had touched and erasing every trace of her presence. Using a strength she did not know she had, she had somehow managed to drag Bowers's body over to the bed, cleaning up the trail of blood afterwards, and tucked his bloated figure under the covers. Now, at last, she made her way downstairs. 'Think I wore the poor bugger out,' she said with a cheeky grin to the porter. 'Left him sleeping like a baby.'

Kaitlyn felt a wave of anxiety pass through her as she stepped past the two guards on the pavement outside. Jacob should have been there waiting for her, ensuring she spent as little time as possible at the scene of the crime, but he was nowhere to be seen. She glanced at her watch.

'Want me to call you a cab, love?' said one of the guards. The last thing she wanted was to make small talk. Every second she stayed in the lobby was a second lost, a second wasted. Kaitlyn was just about to answer when the road in front of her was lit up by the lights of a car. Soon Jacob appeared once again behind the wheel of the borrowed taxi, looking even more wild-eyed than before. He executed a three-point turn and Kaitlyn climbed in. 'Where the fuck have you been?' she said as they sped out of the cul-de-sac.

'Sorry, lost track of time.'

She decided to let it go. Kaitlyn had been getting increasingly worried about Jacob in recent weeks. She knew he'd been taking cocaine occasionally but now it seemed to be a regular thing. He was starting to let himself go, to make silly mistakes. In short, he was turning into a liability. She had known Jacob almost all her life and she hated to see him like this. She knew she had to do something to help sort him out. Rehab perhaps? The longer she waited, the more difficult it would be. She decided to have a proper talk to him about it the following day.

They were back in Jacob's own car now, had crossed into central London and were heading south on the A23 towards an abandoned warehouse on an industrial estate on the outskirts of Croydon. It was a place Kaitlyn had used before: somewhere to burn clothing and destroy any other remaining evidence.

They drove in silence, Kaitlyn watching the street signs and roadside trees speeding past. Suddenly she glanced over at the speedometer. 'You're going too fast,' she said softly.

'Relax,' said Jacob. 'There's no one around.'

At that moment two bright flashes of light erupted

behind them. Jacob's foot hit the brake but it was too late. 'Fucking speed camera,' he hissed. 'I fucking hate those things.'

Kaitlyn said nothing.

Chapter Thirty-eight

August 2004

Jane Tobin swung the mouse across the computer screen and clicked on the link to the next web page. A headline appeared in bright yellow and she read the text underneath out loud.

On 10 April 2001, the Upper House of the Netherlands Parliament passed legislation whereby the termination of life on request and assistance with suicide will not be treated as a criminal offence if carried out by a physician and certain criteria of due care have been fulfilled.

Ever since Paul had shown the first signs of the disease he had had to face the fact that his career had come to an end. He tried to stay with the firm for as long as possible but finally it took only a few weeks before he was forced to give up, no longer able to produce anything of value. At first he simply moped about the house, watching television and reading. Then, as the disease progressed, he found he could no longer remember what he had read the day before, or even a few minutes before. His speech became increasingly slurred. He also knew he was set to become more and more depressed.

Looking back, the early symptoms had been there for a while, but Paul had ignored them, attributing them to fatigue and general ageing, anything rather than illness. Now that he had accepted something was actually wrong with him, his deterioration quickly accelerated. Within a matter of months he had lost the ability to speak. At first he would try to write down his requests but then he lost control of his arms. He was wasting away before Jane's eyes and watching it happen was almost more than she could bear.

There had been so little time to discuss what they should do, how they should act. Paul wanted to stay at home rather than be moved into a hospice, she knew that much. But did he want to go on living like this? Did he want to die in agony or did he want to have the choice and freedom to take his own life and stop his suffering?

Jane had spent all day surfing the Internet for information about euthanasia. It was only the sound of a key in the door that snapped her out of her trancelike state and she quickly flicked back to the BBC home page.

'Hello, Mum,' Christopher said as he came into the kitchen towards her and embraced her. 'How's Dad?'

'No change. The doctors say he'll go on getting worse but that it will happen in fits and starts.'

Christopher looked at his mother, trying to gauge

from her expression whether now would be the right time to break the news to her. He decided it was. 'Mum, I've been thinking about this a lot and I've decided to get myself tested.'

'Tested? What are you talking about?'

'There's a blood test you can take to find out if you have Huntington's or not and I need to know.'

Jane's face was a picture of confusion, her mind was still swimming with Paul and his needs, and thoughts of the uncertain future she now faced. 'What are you talking about?'

'The test. I want to have the test.'

'For Huntington's? But why on earth do you need to be tested? You don't have Huntington's, darling.'

'I need to be sure. It's a fifty–fifty possibility. I can't just rely on convincing myself that I don't have it.'

'Christopher, you don't have Huntington's.'

Christopher stared hard at his mother. Something about the level of certainty in her voice didn't make sense. 'How can you be so sure? How can you possibly know?'

In that moment it dawned on Jane that the secret she had been keeping, a secret that had been so lost in the mists of time, now had to be revealed. She reached over and took Christopher's hand, opening out the flat of the palm and moving it down so she could hold it flat against her stomach, and broke down and cried. 'Christopher, you are our son and I love you more than words could possibly say. You will always be our son.' She pressed his hand into the flesh of her stomach. 'But you didn't come from here.'

Christopher held his mother tight but his mind was racing.

Jane Tobin was sobbing hard into his chest. 'I'm so sorry, son, I'm so sorry.'

Christopher held his mother away from him. 'I don't understand.'

'Christopher. You're adopted.'

It was as if the world suddenly stopped spinning on its axis. There was no movement, colour drained from the room around him and the only sound was the echo of his mother's voice: 'You're adopted, you're adopted, you're adopted.'

A thousand questions flooded into Christopher's mind. There were waves of despair, followed by anger, followed by an intense feeling of loneliness. All at once everything fell into place: the notion that he somehow didn't belong; the feeling that he was so very different from his mother and father; his troubled childhood; the resentment at the world that had built up inside him for so long. Now, at long last, he knew why.

But who was he? What was he really like? Why was he given up for adoption in the first place? Christopher felt dizzy as his mind swam. He was still in a daze when he heard his mother, her voice etched with concern, calling out his name again and again, felt her fingers touching his arm.

He stood up abruptly. He could feel tears of both joy and pain welling up inside him. 'I have to go.'

'Please don't.'

'I have to.' Jane continued sobbing in the kitchen while Christopher walked through to the hallway. He walked past the sitting room, where his father sat on the sofa unable to move with the television switched on in front of him. He looked at the man on the sofa and reached out to stroke his hair as tears started to fall from his eyes.

* * *

Errol Gants threw up his hands in frustration. 'I've tried talking to him but he won't listen. I've known the man since we were four years old. If he won't listen to me, I don't know who he'll listen to.'

Kaitlyn nodded in agreement. They were talking about Jacob and the fact that he was becoming increasingly addicted to cocaine. It had always been a cardinal rule within the gang that drugs were strictly off limits. In Kaitlyn's eyes anyone with an addiction was a liability because their first loyalty would be to the drugs, not the gang. Lesser members of her criminal organisation had been kicked out after their own habits had been discovered. It was only the fact that Jacob was part of the inner circle that had enabled him to remain within the gang for so long. But something had to be done. 'We need to take action,' she told Errol. 'Things are getting really heavy now. The Bowers are all over the place but it's only a matter of time before they get themselves back together and try something. I need everyone to be at their best. I don't want to see the whole thing go belly up for something as stupid as a line of coke.'

Errol scratched the end of his nose and ran his fingers through his dreadlocked hair, the tips of which had now been dyed blonde. He'd spent a month in Jamaica visiting relatives and had enjoyed the sunshine and relaxation. Now, back in London, he felt all the stresses and strains returning instantly. 'Maybe we should cut him loose. Pay him off and set him up somewhere where he can't do any harm.'

Kaitlyn shook her head. 'He knows too much. The Bowers would track him down and use him to get back at us. The only way for him to be safe, and for us to be safe, is for Jacob to be one hundred per cent loyal to the organisation. It's all or nothing.'

Chapter Thirty-nine

September 2004

Daniel Pilgrim kissed his wife goodbye and got into his car to head for work. He had managed only a few hundred yards when he was brought to a halt by a large van that had skidded across the middle of the road, blocking his path. This was no accident; Pilgrim knew he was in a trap. He immediately threw the car into reverse and tried to back up but he was too slow. Another car skidded into position behind him and there was no way out.

His hands shot over to the glove compartment where he kept an illegal can of CS spray but no sooner had his fingers touched the release button than the whole passenger side of the car was showered with glass as a man in a balaclava wielding a baseball bat smashed through the window. Pilgrim was quickly dragged out of the car, a hood was thrust over his head and he was manhandled into the back of the van that had skidded to a halt in front of him and whisked away. He was made to lie face down on the floor and the last thing he remembered was a tremendous pain as he was hit on the back of the head. Then everything went black. Another figure in a balaclava jumped into Pilgrim's own car and shot off at speed.

When Pilgrim came to and the hood was removed he found himself in an unfamiliar room with an unfamiliar pain in his legs and running along the length of his arms. He had been stripped to the waist and was tied firmly to a hard wooden chair. His eyes took a few seconds to find their focus but when they did he could see Kaitlyn, Errol and Jacob standing directly in front of him.

'You and I are going to have a little chat,' said Kaitlyn, speaking in a soft tone.

'You can't do this. I've got insurance. You won't let anything happen to me.'

'Funny you should mention that. It's exactly what we want to talk to you about.' Errol bent down so as to speak an inch from his face. His dyed blond dreadlocked hair made him even more menacing than usual.

'What are you going to do with me?'

'Me and my friend are going to make you talk,' said Jacob as Kaitlyn walked out of the room.

Errol reached over to a nearby table and picked up a builder's hot-air gun, the type used to strip paint by heating it until it bubbles and melts.

Pilgrim's brow crinkled in terror. 'I'm not saying anything. You might as well let me go.' His frightened voice quivered.

'This is going to make you talk. I'm going to start with your eyeballs. Then I'm going to move to your ears. I'm gonna melt your fucking brain. So you tell me where the files are.'

*   *   *

The offices of Parental Research Services sat perched above a dry-cleaning store in the middle of Tooting High Road. It was, according to co-owner Michael Highfield, cheap, centrally located and, most important, handy for getting their suits dry-cleaned. As for the danger from the fumes, Michael was convinced it was no more dangerous that actually working in a dry-cleaning store. His colleague, Patrick, was less convinced but the offices were the only ones they could afford. They had both dreamed of being private detectives. Michael in particular, having seen *The Maltese Falcon* and *The Big Sleep* as a young man, had visions of spending hours tracking down missing daughters of aristocrats, getting involved in shootouts and picking up women.

The reality was somewhat different but after a career in the police force Michael soon realised that a niche market existed. He had always enjoyed tracking down missing people and now he wanted to help others. He himself had been adopted as a child and realised it put him in the ideal position to empathise with others who wanted to find their true parents.

Christopher Tobin stood outside the front door of the agency and looked at the leaflet he had downloaded from the Internet.

Parental Research Services
Every year we carry out hundreds of successful tracings
on behalf of adopted persons who are seeking to trace
their birth mother or father. We have the experience and
expertise to find out whether your natural mother married,
divorced, remarried, became a widow and we do not
consider a case closed until we are able to provide the
current whereabouts of the person you are seeking or a
close living relative. We can begin our searches by knowing
just the basic details: your date of birth and your original
birth name.

Christopher had always felt there was something
odd about his relationship with his parents. The feelings of alienation from his parents he had had while
an adolescent had been dismissed as those of every
teenager, but now at long last he knew why he didn't
fit in. He had learned about his adoption the hard
way and whatever way you looked at it the same
question kept coming into his head: 'Why?' He also
needed to know why Paul and Jane Tobin had never
told him. He began to look at his parents in a different
light, not as parents but just as people who looked
after him for as long as he could remember. He still
loved them – that he was sure of – but he needed to
fill the gap of why his biological parents didn't want
him. He took a deep breath, pushed open the door
and made his way inside.

Michael gave him a hearty handshake and directed

him to a comfy chair in the corner of the room. 'What can I do for you, Christopher?'

'I've recently learned that I was adopted and, having thought things over, I've decided I want to trace my natural parents.'

Michael nodded and reached for a pad and pen. 'OK. Just so I can give you an idea of whether we can help you, tell me what kind of information you have. Do you have copies of any of the papers, your original birth certificate, the name of the agency involved?'

Christopher shook his head. 'All I know is that I was born on 4 October 1974 and that my birth name was Christopher, as it is now.'

Michael whistled through his teeth and doodled on the pad in front of him. 'That's not really very much to go on. Don't you have any paperwork?'

'Nothing at all. My father destroyed it all years ago.'

'That could make it difficult and time-consuming. And that in turn could make it expensive,' said Michael.

'It's not really a question of cost. I'll pay any price. It's a question of getting results,' he explained.

'I understand, but while we have a fantastic track record, there is no guarantee that we will be successful.'

'I know that. I still want you to go ahead. I don't just want to find out who my parents are. I want to find out the reasons I was adopted. Is that possible?'

'If we can get hold of the files from the local authority, the details should all be there. I want to tell you right now that once we take on a case we never give up regardless of how long it takes or how many enquiries we have to make and in any case your outlay will be restricted to the initial amount charged.'

'Sounds good,' said Christopher.

'Now, before we can go any further, there's a bit of small print I need to go over with you.' Michael cleared his throat. 'If you were adopted before 12 November 1975 you're required by law to receive counselling before being allowed access to the information. This is needed because some natural parents and adopters may have been led to believe that their children would never be able to trace their original names or the identity of their parents.

'If you were adopted after 12 November 1975, you're not legally required to seek counselling but we would advise it. If you do decide to try to find your birth parents, it's really important that you think things through and talk to someone about it.'

'I understand,' said Christopher.

'I do have to warn you, Christopher, that if we succeed, you may find the whole experience somewhat unsettling. Right now you probably feel that you are unable to get on an even keel again until you have found your natural parents. Be prepared for an emotional roller coaster and confide in a good friend for added support if you can. Beware of how easy it can be to idolise the image you have of your birth parents, thinking they are a million times better than your adoptive parents. If you do this and then try to trace them you will be setting yourself up for a fall as no one can live up to such dreams. Be realistic.'

Christopher nodded slowly.

'How do your adoptive parents feel about this?' asked Michael.

'My dad's not very well. That makes it all harder. My mum's a little hurt, but she understands that I need to do this.'

'It's a pretty common reaction. So far as they are concerned, they have been your parents for the past thirty-odd years. When you go out looking for someone else, they can't help but see it as a rejection. Give your mum time, she'll come round.'

The last piece of information Michael had to impart was the hardest for Christopher to hear. He had to accept that there was a good chance he might never find out the truth about his real family.

'I know that,' said Christopher. 'And in some ways a part of me hopes you don't find them. I don't have much information, but I know there were a lot of problems when I was growing up.'

Michael leaned forward, pen poised above the notepad. 'Tell me more.'

'Well, it's difficult because my dad's illness makes it hard for him to communicate, which means I can't confirm anything. But my mum's told me everything she knew about my real parents, which to be honest

436

is hardly anything at all. According to my mum, my dad always believed I'd been born on the Roxford estate in south London.'

Michael frowned. 'The Roxford. Why do I know that name?'

'It was in the papers years ago during the riots. Some girl died when she fell off the roof of one of the blocks.'

'That's right,' said Michael. 'There were all sorts of articles saying what a terrible place it was.'

'And I know I was attacked, quite badly, by my father, I think. I'd been in hospital for almost three months before I went to foster homes and eventually got adopted.'

Michael continued nodding as he scribbled across his pad. 'Well, it's not a lot to go on, but it's a starting point. I'll see what I can do.'

Daniel Pilgrim's screams could be heard for miles around, which made it all the more poignant that there was no one to hear them. It didn't take much torture for Pilgrim to give the details of the safety deposit box where he had placed the documents that would incriminate Kaitlyn and it took even less for him to give up the combination to the safe in his office where he kept copies. By this time Pilgrim was in so much agony he would have sold his own children. Jacob only had to switch on the hot-air gun for Pilgrim to explain that the safe – to which his secretary had access – also contained the letter that was to be passed on to the police in the event of his death.

Errol produced a pad of paper and a pen, and untied one of Pilgrim's hands. 'I'm going to go to your office right now and empty the safe,' he explained. 'I need you to write down the alarm codes and safe combination so I can get into your office. I'm sure I don't have to tell you what will happen if you don't.'

Pilgrim winced with pain as he flexed the fingers of his hand. He hurt all over, and the smell of his burning flesh filled the room. He knew that it didn't matter what happened now, they would kill him anyway. 'You won't get away with this, you know,' he gasped to Jacob as Errol took the paper and made his way out of the abandoned warehouse on his way to the private detective's office. 'They'll get you for what you've done.'

Jacob smiled. His face was a picture of evil. 'Come now, Daniel, you're gonna be dead soon. If you want people to remember you, your last words are going to have to be a lot better than that.'

It was almost dark by the time Kaitlyn returned to the warehouse. Pilgrim was drifting in and out of consciousness – a combination of the extreme pain and exhaustion – but Jacob was wide awake, pacing up and down the warehouse floor like a caged animal.

The moment Errol had left the warehouse Jacob had taken a couple of hits of cocaine. He'd never liked Pilgrim and he was looking forward to killing him. He'd always believed the detective had been having an affair with Kaitlyn – they had spent far too much time together for his liking – but now Pilgrim was going to be put out of the picture for good.

Jacob's mind was racing as Kaitlyn walked into the room. It wasn't just the drugs. It was the buzz of being part of yet another murder. It was the buzz that went along with being part of the most sophisticated criminal gang in the whole of London. Jacob felt on top of the world, invincible. Bullet-proof. Tonight he was a king and could do anything. And at that moment he decided that this was the night he would finally tell Kaitlyn the things he'd wanted to say for so long. 'Kaitlyn. There's something I've been meaning to tell you. I mean, ask you. Well, it's a bit of both.'

Kaitlyn was looking around the room, making a mental note of all the things they would have to wipe down or burn to ensure there was no trace of them ever having been here. Her mind was focused on the task in front of her. This was no time for small talk, this was a time for action. 'What is it, Jacob?'

Jacob stood and grabbed Kaitlyn's arm. 'You need to listen to me. I don't want you to be concentrating on something else while I say this.'

Kaitlyn stood up straight and stared directly into Jacob's eyes, taking in the intensity of his words. 'What is it?'

'I . . . I want to be with you, Kaitlyn.'

She didn't mean to do it, but somehow before she had a chance to stop, Kaitlyn laughed. 'It was the outfit, wasn't it? I had no idea you were into tarts.'

Then she looked at Jacob's face and realised this was no joke. 'Oh, my God, you're serious, aren't you?'

'Yes. I've fallen in love with you.'

Kaitlyn paced around, totally flustered, completely thrown. Daniel Pilgrim was going to be dead in a couple of hours and she was trying to make sure they didn't get caught for it. This was the last thing she expected or needed. 'You can't be serious. This can't be happening. I mean, come on, you're virtually family to me. We've known each other for ever. Sorry, Jacob, it just won't work.'

'But do you even want it to work? Do you have any feelings for me at all?'

'Jacob, I love you, I love you as a friend. You're one of the few people in the world I feel I can trust and rely on. There's a special bond between us, everything we've gone through, everything we've achieved. You know I'd die for you, but I can't be with you in that way.'

Jacob turned and started to walk away.

'Jacob, you can't leave.'

'You can't stop me. I'm out of here.' Jacob felt completely rejected. After all the things he had done for Kaitlyn and the sacrifices he had made, this was how she treated him. He felt sick to his stomach. His head was buzzing. He needed another line of cocaine and he needed it right now.

Kaitlyn called after him, 'But look at everything we've achieved, how far we've come since those days on the estate.'

'It doesn't mean a thing to me if I can't have you to share it with.'

'What will you do?'

'I'll set up on my own. Do my own thing. I can't do the friends thing any more if you're not interested in taking it further. There are plenty of people out there who want to work with me. Plenty of business for me to do.'

He walked quickly towards the door of the warehouse and was almost there when Kaitlyn suddenly called out, 'Jacob. Wait.'

She walked over to where he stood, her hair glowing in the light behind her. When she came to a halt, her face was just inches from his and Jacob stared deep into her beautiful eyes. 'Don't go.' Her voice was calm and sympathetic, barely a whisper.

'There's nothing for me here.'

Kaitlyn reached up and touched the side of his face with her fingers. He felt an electric shock of delight run through him. 'You really love me?' she asked.

Jacob nodded. 'I've never loved anyone but you.' He reached up with his own hand and ran his fingers gently through her hair, feeling the soft strands between his fingertips. It occurred to him that in all the time he had known her, he had never touched her like this, never been so close to her.

'And the only way to make you stay is for us to be together?'

'If I hadn't said anything, maybe we could have

carried on. But now that you know how I feel, I'd be better off on my own. There's no other way.'

Kaitlyn smiled and moved a little closer. Their bodies were touching now. Jacob felt as though he could no longer get enough air into his lungs to breathe properly. He felt his face flushing, his heart racing. This was everything he had been dreaming of for years and so much more.

Kaitlyn felt it too. Ever since the death of her mother she had been all but dead inside. There had been plenty of relationships, plenty of men, but she had never once let anyone get close to her. She had lost Louisa and then her mother in the space of a few months. Before that she had lost Christopher. She had become convinced that anyone she cared about would be taken away from her.

In the years that had passed she had done her utmost to keep her emotions under control, not to let them get in the way of the business. She had convinced herself that sacrificing a normal life with a husband and children of her own had been worth it. But did she still believe it?

For here was Jacob, a man who knew her better than anyone. A man who had been there for her through thick and thin, especially after the death of her mother. A man who, one dark night in Glastonbury around the time her mother was taking her fatal overdose, she had been seconds away from being truly intimate with.

Jacob was offering her all the things she had denied

herself for so long. All she had to do was say yes. 'Are you sure, Jacob? Are you sure this is what you want?'

'Totally sure.'

Kaitlyn dropped her eyes. 'I was afraid you might say that.' There was a sinister tone in her voice.

Jacob's fingers tightened round her hair. He followed her gaze down and saw the barrel of a snub-nosed .38 Smith and Wesson in her palm, pointed directly at his chest, just in time to see a spurt of flame erupt from the end of the barrel. Jacob staggered back, his eyes wide with shock, blood spurting from his mouth and his ruptured stomach.

'I'm so sorry, Jacob,' she said, taking a step forward and aiming the gun directly at his head.

Two more bullets embedded themselves in Jacob's brain, sending an arcing fountain of blood across the room. He fell back, dead.

Kaitlyn fell to her knees. For the first time in as long as she could remember she started to cry.

She was still crying as she walked to the other end of the room, picked up Jacob's gun from the table, stood ten feet in front of the unconscious Daniel Pilgrim and blasted him twice in the stomach.

By the time Errol returned, Kaitlyn had adjusted the scene to suit the scenario she wanted to paint. She had untied Pilgrim's body and placed Jacob's gun in one of the outstretched hands. She had taken her own gun, cleaned it and placed it in Jacob's dead hand.

'Jesus! What the fuck happened?' said Errol as he entered the room.

'I don't know. Pilgrim must have broken loose and got hold of one of Jacob's guns. Looks like they both fired at the same time.' The images of what she had done were still floating around in her mind. She had to fight to suppress them. The last thing she wanted was for Errol to know the truth. She had to stay strong, no matter how hard it was. 'Did you get the stuff?' she asked.

Errol was too shocked to speak.

'Errol, did you get the stuff?' Kaitlyn said again.

He nodded and handed over a padded envelope. He could not take his eyes off his dead friend. He wanted to go over to him but he knew deep down that they had to get away from the scene as quickly as possible. This was bad, this was really bad and it threatened to bring the whole organisation crashing to the ground.

Errol looked over at Kaitlyn. He could see the track marks on her face where she had been crying. He reached out and put a hand on her shoulder.

She looked over at him her bottom lip quivering, then she shrugged off his hand. 'Look, Errol, I'm every bit as cut up about this as you are. I can't fucking believe this has happened, but we've got to stay focused. We've got to get out of here. Right now.'

* * *

At first Christopher called on a daily basis, then every other day, then weekly. As the days went by with little or no progress, the frustration he felt at not knowing his true origins grew ever more powerful.

'How's it going, Michael?'

'Nothing to report I'm afraid, Christopher.'

'Sorry to keep on badgering you like this.'

'It's not a problem, I fully understand. I get this a lot. I only wish I had more news for you. Sometimes these things just take time.'

Christopher put the phone down. It had been more than six weeks and the agency was no closer to finding his family. He had to wonder if they ever would. Not knowing what else to do, he threw himself back into his work in a bid to take his mind off it all.

* * *

Detective Inspector Karl Marshall arrived at the office of Assistant Commissioner Jackie Barker two minutes early for his midday meeting. He knew it wasn't going to be good. He'd had a bee in his bonnet about Kaitlyn Wilson for months and had devoted way too much of his time and budget to pursuing her. None of that would have been a problem if he had a single scrap of evidence to show for all his effort, but there was nothing.

The murder of James Lyons was still unsolved and although there was a tremendous amount of anecdotal evidence pointing towards Kaitlyn's involvement in the drug trade and high-level organised crime, there was nothing concrete enough to allow them to apply for a search warrant, let alone press charges.

Marshall had been told to focus on other cases but had somehow always managed to swing his resources round so they focused on Wilson instead. Now he was about to get his wrist slapped.

It was an open secret that Barker was gay and it didn't stop her from using her feminine charms to wrap men round her finger. Although they knew she was only playing with them, it seemed to work regardless. 'Hi, Karl. Have a seat. How are things?'

'I prefer to stand. Things are OK,' came the cautious reply.

They talked about the shift system, the lack of overtime and staff shortages. Ten minutes later they had discussed a variety of topics, the tension building up inside Karl the whole time until he reached the point where he felt he was about to burst. That was when she told him he could go.

Karl was totally confused but tried his best not to show it. He walked over and reached for the doorknob.

'Just one more thing,' Jackie called after him. 'What the fuck is going on with the Kaitlyn Wilson case?'

Karl turned round, moved back into the office and this time took up the offer of a seat. Barker had been one of his strongest supporters. If she decided to pull the plug on him it meant there was nothing more to be done. 'In a nutshell, we're in a world of shit. I think she has spies in every office, fingers in every pie. We can't make a move without her being two or three steps ahead. She runs a tight ship. Even if one of her couriers is going to Tesco's to pick up shopping they'll follow all the same procedures as if they had £20 million's worth of cocaine in the back of the car.'

Barker looked thoughtful. 'You know this op's costing us a fortune and that we can't go on this way, don't you, Karl.'

He nodded sheepishly. 'You want me to rein it in?'

'Not just yet. I want you to change tactics. I want you to step up the surveillance but I don't want it to be covert. I want it high profile. I want you to use marked cars.'

'Marked cars? Why?'

'If they see a car when they wake up in the morning and then they see that same car at lunch and again in the evening, they're not going to know what we've seen and what we haven't.'

'This is a waste of time. She knows we're out there. She isn't going to do anything.'

'She knows we're out here but she can't do nothing. She still has a business to run. She isn't going to be able to stop just because we're around. I want to keep her under as much pressure as we can. If we do that and we keep on doing that, sooner or later she's going to make a mistake.'

* * *

At first Miranda Plummer had merely been frustrated. After that she became angry about being ignored. It was only when two days had gone past and she had still not managed to get hold of Jacob Collins that she found herself becoming extremely concerned. It didn't help that no one at Lush seemed to know exactly what to say about where Jacob had gone. Some said he was working away from London, others that he had gone abroad on a special job for the company. There had been plenty of times in the past when Jacob had vanished out of the country at the drop of a hat for a few days at a time and she had asked no questions. But during those times there would be the occasional phone call, or at the very least she could rely on him replying to the odd filthy text message. It was the fact that she had heard nothing that made her feel anxious.

She had seen the reports on that morning's news programmes about two bodies being recovered from a south London warehouse and her concerns had grown even deeper. She had been queuing up for more than half an hour at Southwark police station before she finally got to make her initial report of Jacob having gone missing.

'To be honest, madam,' the officer had said wearily, 'he's a grown man. He's not married, he doesn't have any kids. If he wants to pack up and head off somewhere, it's really no concern of ours.'

'No, no, you don't understand,' said Miranda. 'This just isn't like him. I don't think he's gone away some-where. I think something has happened to him. Something terrible.'

*

Detective Chief Inspector Alvery had a huge smile on his face as he made his way across the room to the desk of Detective Inspector Karl Marshall. 'How you doing, Marshall?'

'Up to my ears. Not like you to show the slightest bit of concern, though. Why do you ask?'

He dropped the thick file on to Marshall's desk.

'You've got to be kidding me,' said Marshall. 'I can't. I'm chocker.'

'You're a lot less busy than some of the people here. And what's more, there are some people doing real police work, not chasing ghosts.'

'The Wilson case is not a joke.' Karl Marshall spoke in a defensive tone.

Alvery pointed to the file he'd placed on Marshall's desk. 'You'll like this one. It's a double murder. Private detective in south London and a gangster by the name of Jacob Collins. We found the two bodies last night.'

Marshall was suddenly alert: 'Did you say Jacob Collins?'

Within an hour Marshall was on his way to see Nick Reynolds, the Home Office pathologist.

'They put you on this case too?' gasped Nick when he saw Marshall. 'What is it, have all the other detectives in London gone on strike and you've taken on all their cases?'

'It sure feels like it sometimes. So, what you got for me?'

'Pretty standard stuff. With one of them, Pilgrim,

you're looking at prolonged torture followed by two shots in the stomach. Mid range. Snub-nosed .38. Good gun for this sort of work.'

'And this is standard stuff?' said Marshall.

'For me it is, yes. But I don't get out much.'

'Tell me about it, you weirdo,' Reginald smirked.

'Anyway, victim would have bled to death in about an hour.'

'Nice.'

'The other one, Collins, three shots this time. The first at close to point-blank range, the second two in the head from a few feet away. But this is where it gets interesting. If I were some amateur the obvious conclusion would be that Collins pulls a gun on Pilgrim and shoots him twice in the stomach. Pilgrim manages to fire back and hits Collins in the chest, that sends him reeling back and Pilgrim finishes him off with a couple of head shots.'

'But you're saying that's not what happened,' said Marshall.

'That didn't happen at all. The angles and distances are all wrong for one thing, but what really gives it away, even to the world's worst pathologist, is that they were holding the wrong guns. The one in Pilgrim's hand was the one that killed him. Same goes for Collins.'

'You mean someone else shot them and then placed the guns.'

'You catch on fast, Karl.' Nick Reynolds wagged a finger in the air. 'But that's not all I have for you.

Take a look at this.' They moved to a different part of the lab and Reynolds flicked through some files sitting on a table until he found what he was looking for. 'Here you are,' he said, holding a close-up photograph of Jacob's right hand up to the light. 'You see what we have here?' Reynolds traced a line with his own fingertip and suddenly Marshall saw it. Two strands of long, wavy hair were sticking out from under the fingernails. 'Now the really interesting thing', said Reynolds, 'is that when we examined the hairs, we found they were speckled with gunpowder residue and blood splash. Those hairs were there when he was shot. There were no signs of a struggle, but I have no doubt that he touched the head of whoever shot him seconds before it happened.'

Marshall could feel his heart pounding in his chest. 'Did you manage to get a DNA match?'

'Sample, yes, match, no. Only one of the hairs had enough of a root for a test and we got a full profile, but there's nothing on the record. Of course, if you have a suspect in mind and you can get a sample, then I can tell you if you've got the right person.'

Marshall scratched his chin thoughtfully. 'I have someone in mind. Let me see what I can do.'

* * *

Kaitlyn looked terrible. Her hair was a mess, her make-up was all over the place. An ashtray full of cigarette butts sat beside her. She was under clouds of smoke. She was chain smoking and tapping her fingers on the desk. In all the time she had been operating, things had never been more difficult. The police were everywhere, following her night and day, and making her life impossible. It was easy enough to lose unmarked cars. The drivers always had to worry about being spotted by being too obvious so a sudden U-turn in the middle of a road or circling a roundabout a few dozen times soon got rid of them.

The marked cars were different. Because they were not worried about being seen, they were right on her bumper every time she took a trip in her taxi. Uniformed officers were also a constant presence outside the club and occasionally inside. The drug dealers had been unable to ply their trade and customers had left Lush in droves as a result.

They were outside her house when she emerged first thing in the morning, they were on each and every street corner on her way to work and they were there again when she went to bed at night. She even saw one of the officers hunting through her bin. She knew it was just a new campaign of high-profile harassment and that it couldn't last for ever, but it was driving her crazy all the same.

She had issued a series of formal harassment complaints to the police through her lawyers but they had little effect. The police insisted that, because one of their key workers had been executed in a gangland-style attack, such a high police presence was necessary to reassure the public. It was a lie, of course, but one which Kaitlyn's best lawyers were unable to act against.

'What is it?' she snapped. 'Can't you see I'm busy?'

The secretary looked sheepish. It took an age before she finally spoke. 'I'm sorry to bother you. It's just that Detective Inspector Marshall is here to see you.'

Kaitlyn rolled her eyes. 'Oh, for fuck's sake. Tell him I'm not available, tell him he'll have to come back later.'

At that moment the door behind the secretary burst open and Marshall walked in, several other officers following close behind.

'What the hell's going on?' Kaitlyn demanded. 'This is an outrage. You can't do this. You can't just walk in here like you own the place . . .'

Marshall approached Kaitlyn's desk and slapped down a piece of paper directly in front of her.

Kaitlyn looked down at it and she let out a snort of defiance. 'You're wasting your time, you know.' Kaitlyn's eyes fixed on Marshall. He stared back deeply and he could see that he had got to her, that he had made her nervous. He was going to enjoy this. He took a deep breath. 'Kaitlyn Wilson, I am arresting you for the murder of Jacob Collins.'

Chapter Forty

It had been more than five months since the arrest of Kaitlyn Wilson. She had spent only a single night back in Holloway prison – a place she had sworn she would never go back to under any circumstances – before being granted bail. Finding herself back behind bars was even more traumatic than the prospect of losing everything she had worked towards. Her bail conditions restricted her movements, but that suited Kaitlyn just fine. Her assets had been frozen pending a full investigation into her finances and she spent the months before her trial keeping as low a profile as possible. Having had her name splashed across the papers on a daily basis for the first few days, she had now virtually vanished from public view.

Kaitlyn Wilson was the last thing on Christopher Tobin's mind when he received a telephone call asking him to attend a meeting at the headquarters of the Crown Prosecution Service in London's Ludgate Hill. For a defence barrister to be invited to the heart of the opposition was unusual, to say the least, and Christopher's first thought was that he must have done something terribly wrong and that he was on his way to a high-level bollocking. He was in for a surprise.

Upon his arrival Christopher was led immediately to the office of the Head of the CPS, Brian Stockley. After the usual greetings Stockley came straight to the point. 'We have a major case coming up. It's the result of a long investigation,' he said while handing Christopher a file. 'It's going to be one of the highest-profile trials there have been in this country for many years.'

'Sounds interesting.'

'It will be. We'd like you to be involved.'

'I'm confused. Are you saying you want me to defend this person?'

'We don't want you to defend. We want you to prosecute.'

'I don't really do many prosecutions.'

'Exactly. You have a reputation as one of the top defence lawyers in the country. You defend people who are innocent. You have a skill. But in this case there is no doubt; this is a woman who has peddled misery and carried out murders across the country.'

'A woman.'

'That's right.'

'Do you really want me or is this just a ploy to make sure this woman doesn't hire me to defend her? I don't really need to think about it. I can tell you right now, I'm not interested. I'm not going to be a pawn in some political game. I'm sorry, Brian, but the answer is no.'

'She's already instructed James Cardy for the defence.' Stockley looked for Christopher Tobin's reaction when he mentioned Cardy's name. He knew that Christopher was ambitious and he also knew that with a high-profile QC defending they needed someone just as good to prosecute. Christopher had everything going for him and Stockley was aware of it. He handed Christopher a large file. 'Just take a look and let me know what you think by the morning.'

Christopher returned to his chambers and kept eyeing Kaitlyn's file on his desk. In his mind he began to think about the possibilities of winning a case over the great man himself, James Cardy QC. If he decided to take the case, the opportunity of going up against Cardy would be the main reason.

It was while Christopher was still contemplating the case of Kaitlyn Wilson that Sally knocked on the door of his office and told him a certain Detective Inspector Karl Marshall was waiting to see him.

'What can I do for you, officer?'

'I need to speak to you about the Kaitlyn Wilson case.'

'Not you as well.'

'I'm sorry?'

'Nothing, it's just you're not the first person to talk to me about that. I had the CPS asking if I wanted to prosecute.'

'And are you going to?'

'I don't think so. I prefer to work for the defence.'

'I see. Well, our investigation is still going on. But we've come across some material that is a bit disturbing and pertains to you.'

'To me. How?'

'Can you think of any reason why Kaitlyn Wilson would want to do you harm?'

'No, of course not.'

Marshall reached into his briefcase and pulled out a slim manila envelope.

Christopher looked on intrigued as the detective opened it and removed a series of photographs, which he proceeded to spread out on the table in front of him. The first, taken with a telephoto lens, showed Christopher getting out of his car just outside his home. The others followed in quick succession, Christopher locking his car door, Christopher walking up the driveway of his home, Christopher opening the door of his home and so on. 'What does this mean?'

'I'm hoping you can tell me.'

'Have you been taking photographs of me? Am I under surveillance? What the hell's going on?'

Marshall leaned forward. 'These photographs were found during a search of Kaitlyn Wilson's private residence. We're not certain, but we now believe they were taken by a private detective by the name of Daniel Pilgrim. Pilgrim himself was murdered in a brutal gangland killing. His body was so badly burnt he could only be identified by the few teeth that hadn't been pulled out.

Christopher sat back in silence and took in what he was being told.

Marshall paused for effect, then continued, 'I can't pretend that we know everything, but one thing we do know at the moment is that for some reason he had been tracking you, finding out where you lived and putting together a catalogue of your movements.

'I suspect it was something to do with the Richardson case that you defended recently. He's a pretty heavy character, as you know, and perhaps someone was pissed off that he was acquitted, wanted to take revenge against you. To be honest, we just don't know why these pictures are here, but we felt you ought to be informed.

'I should tell you as well that we found photographs of other men and women, some of whom have subsequently been murdered. There seems little doubt that Pilgrim was providing information for serious criminals, Kaitlyn Wilson among them.'

When Marshall departed Christopher was left outraged. All the time he had worked so hard to bring people the best defence they could have and this was how he was treated. The time he had spent in the company of criminals meant nothing, it was all completely hollow, and he could see that now. He therefore had a second reason to take the case – to show the gangsters that he could not be intimidated. He reached for the phone and punched out a number. 'Brian? It's Christopher. About the Kaitlyn Wilson case. I'll take it.'

Chapter Forty-one

November 2005

The build-up to the trial of Kaitlyn Wilson was an extraordinary event. In the immediate aftermath of her arrest dozens of prominent figures from the music and club world had been talking to newspapers and chat shows about how they could not possibly believe that someone like Kaitlyn, one of clubland's most loved and charismatic characters, was involved in anything like what she had been accused of. But as journalists had started to dig into her background the support had begun to fall away. While the papers were restricted on what they could actually print because of the forthcoming trial, the implication was clear that this leading businesswoman had a dark side and strong connections to the underworld.

Even though she had entered a not guilty plea, Christopher was certain – and the evidence supported the notion – that she had personally murdered Jacob Collins and at least ordered the killing of Daniel Pilgrim. That was his justification for taking this case. This was a woman who deserved to go to prison. And if he had taken the job as her defence barrister, he would have been sure to lose.

It had been months since Kaitlyn first learned that Christopher Tobin would be leading the prosecution. She knew her little brother was completely ignorant about his past, but she also knew that this would play to her advantage. If all else failed – the bribery, the threats, the intimidation – she would arrange for their connection to be 'revealed' by the press and the trial would collapse. So long as she ensured the proceedings were as high-profile as possible, she could argue against a retrial on the basis that all the facts of the case were simply too well known. But such a move would cripple Christopher's career and she was determined to use every other possible strategy first.

She wore a plain navy-blue suit and looked clean and fresh for her trial. To onlookers it would be hard to believe she was capable of murder. As she was led into the dock by three prison officers her heart was racing and there, seated below her, was Chrissy. He could feel her presence and turned to face his sister for the first time. As he turned her eyes never left him. Christopher sensed something but he didn't know what. He felt as nervous as the first time he was lead barrister in a case. He turned back and tried his best not to look. But he couldn't help himself. There was some kind of attraction, something emotional or psychological, that he simply couldn't explain. He had to work hard to concentrate on his job.

The case began with two weeks of legal argument in the absence of a jury. Christopher stuttered and stumbled over his words in the first few days as he put forward a series of submissions to Mr Justice McDonald who was hearing the case.

'Are you quite well, Mr Tobin? You seem to be having a little trouble with your diction,' said the judge after a particularly garbled attempt at making a point.

'I'm fine, Your Honour. I think I just have a frog in my throat.'

'May I suggest,' interjected James Cardy, 'that my learned friend seems to have the contents of an entire rock pool inside his throat.'

A ripple of laughter echoed through the court-room.

Oh, great, Christopher thought to himself. *The case hasn't even started yet and Cardy's scoring points off me already.*

Christopher soon settled into his stride and after two weeks of submissions they were ready for the jury to be called. It was late in the afternoon, so the judge decided to adjourn proceedings until the following morning. After court that day Christopher checked his mobile phone and saw he had three missed calls from Michael from Parental Research Services. He checked his voice-mail and heard

Michael's increasingly urgent tone asking him to return the call. He knew the only reason he would ever call would be if he had news about Christopher's parents. But here he was, fighting the most important case of his life. He needed his full concentration just to get through. There was a lot of work to go over before the morning with his team and there was no way he could even entertain the idea of speaking to Michael at the moment. The truth about his family would have to wait. He deleted the three messages and switched off his phone once more.

Although Kaitlyn had seen Christopher on television several times, read interviews in various magazines, newspapers and even browsed through several websites dedicated to his exploits, seeing him in the flesh was something she had been completely unprepared for. All she could think of was that night back on the Roxford estate, locked in the bathroom and listening to Steve battering her brother half to death. She remembered beating her fists against the door of the bathroom, the anguished screams and sobs, the horrible sucking sound that Christopher made during the ride in the ambulance. She recalled the day that her mother had told her they would no longer have Christopher living with them; the hours she had spent looking out across south London wondering where Christopher was and what he was doing.

And now here he was, standing just a few feet in

front of her. He had no idea who she was and there was no way she could tell him.

The press gallery was packed. The case was attracting huge attention, partly because of the defendant but also because it would be a battle of wits between two of the highest-profile barristers in the country.

Michael was getting desperate. He had been trying to call Christopher all night and all morning, and knew he now had no choice but to get back to London as quickly as possible and see him in person.

After a tricky start, the investigation had progressed quickly. Michael had spent hours scouring through local newspapers published the year before, the year and the year after Christopher had been adopted. During that time he had found six cases where fathers had appeared in court on charges of assault. Victims were never identified in such cases but using his contacts at the police, he learned that two of them had involved grown women and one a three-year-old girl. Of the remainder, one of the boys was aged nine. It left only the case that took up a single paragraph in the crime column of the *South London Press*.

Steve Brooks, 35, an unemployed resident of the Roxford estate, appeared at Horseferry Road Magistrates Court this morning on a charge of assaulting a minor. He was remanded in custody for seven days.

Michael had used every trick in the book to track down Brooks, following his progress through the legal system in and out of various prisons, until his release in Manchester. Michael eventually found Steve in a drying-out clinic for homeless alcoholics and drug users, and got the whole terrible story straight from the horse's mouth. It was then that Michael had discovered that Christopher had a half-sister. Not only that, but Social Services had decided to leave her in the care of her mother, splitting up the family.

When Steve told Michael the name of the little girl involved he could hardly believe his ears. 'She's famous, that girl,' Steve slurred, his brain irreparably damaged by his years of addiction. 'I should have played my cards right. I'd be living in the lap of luxury right now.' Whenever Steve bragged about Kaitlyn everyone thought he was a dreamer, an old homeless man high on drugs and meths. No one realised he was telling the truth.

The case was all over the newspapers and television broadcasts. The country had been obsessed with it for the past week and in a few hours' time Kaitlyn Wilson would be stepping into the witness box for the first time. Not only did Christopher have a sister he did not know about, he was about to cross-examine her at the Old Bailey.

Christopher was used to people trying to stare him out in the courtroom. Whenever he had worked on defence witnesses for the prosecution, they would scowl at him from the stand, evil thoughts running through their minds. But this was different. It wasn't just that he was prosecuting for the first time in many years, it was something about the look that Kaitlyn was giving him, something that said much more than merely the hatred and despair he had become accustomed to. He tried to convince himself it was only because he had rarely acted for the prosecution and that he had to get used to playing the enemy of the accused rather than her best friend.

He swallowed hard as he stood up at the podium and stared Kaitlyn Wilson straight in the eye. 'Ms Wilson. Exactly how much money have you made from the drug trade?'

Cardy jumped up from his seat. 'Objection.'

The judge placed an elbow on the bench and rested his face in his cupped hand. 'Mr Tobin,' he said wearily. 'I know for a fact that you have done a great deal of preparation for this case, which I'm assuming means I have no need to remind you that your client is on trial for charges of murder, not of drug trafficking.'

'With your permission, Your Honour,' Christopher said, 'I am pursuing this path because I believe it shows motive for the murders. Although no specific charges are being placed, there is a great deal of circumstantial evidence that suggests the murder was the result of the deceased's involvement in drug trafficking. It is therefore only natural to assume that the accused also has some involvement.'

There was a long pause as the judge considered this. 'You may proceed,' he said at last. 'But I want you to be careful about this line of questioning. There should be no assumption of guilt on charges that have not been heard in a court.' He turned to the jury. 'Ladies and gentlemen, when it comes to hearing testimony in this case, there are bound to be many unproven allegations bandied about. I want you to focus on the facts and I will endeavour to ensure that counsel do the same.'

Christopher gave the judge a small bow and continued, 'Ms Wilson. Is it true that drugs are sold in your clubs?' He waited until the last two words before he resumed staring at Kaitlyn. She looked furious. He knew he had got to her.

'Drugs are sold in all clubs,' she said flatly.

'I'm not concerned with all clubs, just Lush.'

'We do everything we can to prevent drugs . . .'

'Answer the question, Ms Wilson. Are drugs sold in your club or not?'

'Not if I can help it . . .'

'It's a simple question, Ms Wilson. The answer should be equally simple. Yes or no?'

'But . . .'

'Yes or no?'

Kaitlyn folded her arms and stared hard at Christopher, slowly shaking her head. She had waited so long to have her little brother back in her life, she couldn't help but laugh at the fact that her dream had come true under the most bizarre of circumstances.

She wanted to turn to the jury and say, 'I used to change his nappy, you know,' or, 'I saw him take his first steps and speak his first words.' He was so handsome, so clever. He'd done so well for himself. Despite everything that was going on, she felt incredibly proud of her little brother. 'You've done so well, little Chrissy,' she muttered under her breath. 'You really have.'

Across the courtroom Christopher Tobin stared up at the woman in the witness box. He knew he'd got her rattled. Her body language said it all, the way she had folded her arms like that. Another few hours and she'd be eating out of his hand. She'd muttered something about him 'doing well', which he took as a compliment, but then she'd said something that sounded like Chrissy. No one had ever referred to him by that name, but at the same time there was something oddly familiar about it.

Christopher sucked in a breath and composed himself. 'Yes or no, Ms Wilson?'

'Yes, Mr Tobin. There have been times when drugs have been sold in my club, but not by me and not by any of my staff.'

Christopher tried to cut her off but she carried on. 'And that will be the same in any club in the country. We are under siege. There are dangerous organised criminals out there who know only too well the vast profits they can make by selling drugs in clubs. My staff have been threatened by these people . . .'

'And what better way to fight back than to get

involved in the trade yourself,' said Christopher triumphantly.

'Objection,' screamed Cardy.

'Sustained,' said the judge. 'Mr Tobin, I do hope you have not already forgotten what I said a few moments ago. Otherwise this is going to be a very long and very difficult trial.'

Chapter Forty-two

Michael jabbed at the buttons of his mobile phone once more, only to have the signal die as his train passed through a tunnel. He swore under his breath, waited until the signal had been restored and tried again. This time the phone rang but, like so many times before, it rang until Christopher's voice appeared on the answering machine.

'Christopher. It's Michael. Again. You've got to call me as soon as possible. It's really urgent. I've found out about your family and I need to tell you about them right away. It affects the case that you're involved in at the moment. You have to get back to me.'

Michael put away the phone and looked at his watch. It was nearly the end of lunchtime. There was no way he was going to make it into court before the start of the afternoon session. He tried to ring again but the battery on his mobile died halfway through the call. In desperation he turned to the man sitting across the carriage from him. 'Excuse me, do you have a mobile I could borrow? Just for a few seconds. I'll pay you for the call.'

The man looked doubtful so Michael pulled out his wallet and started taking out bills. 'I'll give you

... er ... £10 if you let me use your phone for two minutes. Just two minutes. And it's another mobile I'm calling. You can check. My battery's gone and I'm desperate.'

The man eyed Michael's wallet suspiciously. 'Make it £30,' he said with a smirk, 'deal.' Michael threw over the notes and snatched the phone from the man's hand.

At the end of the lunch break Christopher switched on his phone to check his messages. The confrontation with Kaitlyn had left him strangely unnerved and he couldn't understand why he was having such a hard time in court. Perhaps he had taken on too much too soon, heading up such a big case and going face to face with Cardy. He would have to pull his socks up if he wanted to pull this one off and he knew it. He saw the three messages from Michael but erased them immediately without even listening to them. More than ever, that call would have to wait. He was about to turn off his phone when it started ringing. This time the number was one that he did not recognise and almost out of instinct he answered it.

His heart sank when he realised it was Michael's voice. 'I'm sorry, Michael, I really can't talk now, I'm just about to step back into court. We're going to have to leave this until after the trial. I know I was the one who was begging you to get results but I just can't deal with it now.'

'Christopher,' said Michael. 'You don't understand. It's Kaitlyn. She's your half-sister.'

Twenty minutes later Christopher switched off the phone. He could hardly breathe. He knew that no matter what, nothing would ever be the same again. It was enough of a shock to find out that he had a sister he never knew about. He also had to deal with the fact that his sister was one of the biggest criminal masterminds in the country and a ruthless killer. And here he was, trying his hardest to send her to prison for the rest of her life.

The phone had been placed back in his locker for only a fraction of a second when there was a knock at the door of the robing room. *What now*, Christopher thought. The door opened and the court usher stood staring at him. 'Sorry to bother you, Mr Tobin, but the judge wants to see you in his chambers. He says it's extremely urgent. He wants you to go there right away.'

Chapter Forty-three

Christopher's feet seemed to be getting heavier with every step as he approached the chambers of Judge Gordon McDonald. If somehow the judge had learned what Christopher himself had just found out, it would be the end of his career. He knocked on the heavy door and heard the judge's soft Scottish tones calling for him to enter. Christopher pushed it open and stepped inside.

The first thing he saw was James Cardy QC, sitting in a high-backed armchair, sipping on a glass of neat whisky with the smuggest smile on his face that Christopher had ever seen. Cardy didn't need to say a single word for Christopher to know what was happening. This case was over. It was worse than he could possibly imagine. Not only was he going to lose the case but Cardy was going to make a real meal of it. Christopher scanned the room and found the judge standing by the window, smoothing out the creases of his robe with his hands.

'Ah, come in, Christopher,' said McDonald. 'Mr Cardy has discovered something that puts a slight question mark over the rest of the trial. It's something we need to discuss right away to decide how to proceed.'

Cardy grinned. 'Out of fairness to you, I thought I'd bring it up here, in chambers, initially. I didn't want the first mention of this to be in open court. I'm sure the press are going to go absolutely crazy for the story once it gets out and we all need to decide how best to deal with it.'

Christopher nodded slowly. It suddenly occurred to him that having his half-sister as the key defendant in a major murder trial didn't just reflect badly on him but on the whole judiciary. No doubt questions would be asked over previous trials he had worked on. After all, if one of the country's biggest crooks was his sister, how could he be seen as an impartial voice for the defence in any other case involving a leading gangster?

'I really don't know what to say,' Christopher said. His voice was weak and quiet, with none of the projection he used out in the courtroom. 'I've only just found out myself. I'm a little stunned, to be honest.'

The judge raised an eyebrow. 'You already know?'

Christopher nodded. 'I received a phone call in the robing room just a few minutes ago.'

The judge glanced at his watch. 'Damn, that means the press might get hold of it in time for the lunchtime news. If they print anything I'll put whoever is responsible in contempt of court.'

Christopher felt like crying. Everything he had worked on for so many years was about to come crashing down around him.

Then something occurred to him which made him feel a thousand times worse. He was replaying the events of the past few days in his mind when he recalled the time Kaitlyn had called him Chrissy. Something about the name had struck a chord deep within him and now that he had learned Kaitlyn was his sister the distant memories were starting to come back to him. He began to think of a little girl giving him food and smiling. He didn't know whether it was for real or his imagination running wild.

Christopher was so lost in his own thoughts that he didn't even realise the judge had been speaking to him. 'I'm sorry,' he said.

The judge smiled. 'I know this is distressing for you, especially considering your position, but I think you'll agree we have no option but to abandon the case.'

'Yes, I see. I agree of course.'

'In the light of the revelations about the contamination of the evidence there is simply no way we can proceed.'

Christopher nodded. Then his brow wrinkled with confusion. 'Contamination?'

'Good grief, Christopher, what do you think we've been talking about for the past ten minutes? The fact that the integrity of the chief medical officer who found the hairs on the body of Jacob Collins can no longer be guaranteed. There were at least six or seven points on the journey between her office and the police laboratory where it was not properly accounted for. The whole defence case has been that these hairs were planted deliberately in order to bolster a strong case. While there is no evidence to suggest it was so, the usual procedures were not followed. Dr Midsun has admitted going back and changing the records at a later date. She says this was because she made a genuine mistake but under the circumstances it's simply too suspicious.

'Then, to add to concerns, there is the rather dubious matter of how the prosecution actually came to find a DNA sample in order to match it to the hairs. Are you actually aware of the sequence of events?'

Christopher shook his head.

'I should hope not. It seems Mr Marshall took it upon himself to ask one of the officers on routine patrol in the vicinity of Ms Wilson's home to look through her bin and extract a number of cigarette ends. Honestly, if that doesn't constitute an illegal search, I don't know what does. Mr Marshall has been overzealous in his attempts to get this woman and now he is paying the price.'

Christopher was desperately trying to take in all the information.

'We could proceed and I could direct the jury to ignore that evidence, but I'm not prepared to sit in judgement on a case only to have it overturned by the court of appeal in six months' time. No one wants that to happen. I'm going to declare a mistrial and leave it to the CPS to see if they want to run through this whole thing again.'

Christopher's jaw dropped open and it was the judge's turn to frown. 'You didn't know about this at all, did you? You said you'd received a phone call a few minutes ago.'

Christopher shook his head. 'I'm sorry, sir, I thought you were talking about something else.'

'Something else that would lead to the collapse of the trial?' asked Cardy suspiciously. 'What on earth could that be?'

Waves of relief had been sweeping over Christopher but now he felt himself tense up. His eyes flicked between the judge and James Cardy. He was on the spot and needed to come up with an answer fast. 'I was having a little personal problem. It's nothing, really,' he said shyly. 'My father is very ill, he's taken a turn for the worse. I wanted to spend some time with him. That's all.'

James Cardy was looking at Christopher strangely. Years of working in the courts had given him a sixth sense about when people were lying and when they were telling the truth. Just by looking at Christopher he knew he was lying. But he said nothing.

Minutes later the two barristers were heading out of the judge's chambers, ready to face the court and tell the world that the biggest criminal trial of the past decade was about to collapse because of police incompetence.

'I'm sorry about your father,' said Cardy.

'Thanks. He's been ill for some time now. It's just something I've learned to deal with.'

Cardy nodded. 'It's a shame about this case too. You know, if I were anyone else I'd dare say you would have won the case. You were doing very well out there. You're good. Very good.'

Christopher's face lit up with a broad smile. As far as he was concerned, this was the ultimate compliment. 'I'll get my chance, I'll beat you yet,' he called out after Cardy, who was walking down the corridor.

'Not in this lifetime, dear boy. I'm getting out while I'm still young enough to enjoy my retirement. This was always going to be my last case. It's like my father used to say, leave them wanting more.'

Chapter Forty-four

January 2006

Kaitlyn had been in her office at Lush for less than ten minutes when the phone rang. Her secretary was nowhere to be seen. She, like many of the staff, had decided to leave when Kaitlyn had been arrested rather than find themselves implicated in some massive criminal conspiracy. Kaitlyn hesitated. She usually had her calls fielded to make sure they were not from the press or anyone else she did not want to speak to, but somewhere deep inside her an instinct told her to pick up the phone. She did so and placed it gently against her ear.

She said nothing and eventually a voice on the other end of the line broke the silence. 'Hello?'

She recognised it at once. 'Chrissy.'

More silence. Then at last Christopher spoke: 'I don't know why I'm calling you. I'm so angry, I'm so confused. I just don't know what to say.'

There was a long pause before Kaitlyn said, 'I think we should meet.'

They met in a small café in Harlesden, a place where they were unlikely to bump into anyone they knew.

As the only non-locals in the place, it was quickly obvious that the venue had been a perfect choice.

That first meeting was terrible for both of them. For a long time they said nothing. There were no words either could think of. Instead, they just stared at one another, remembering as much as they could. Then Christopher's anger burst out. He accused Kaitlyn of playing games with his career, of being an evil, manipulative cow who clearly was the criminal mastermind the police said she was. He demanded an explanation for why she had done the things she had done to him, but Kaitlyn couldn't find the words to reply. 'Just tell me what the hell you think you were doing,' he said again and again. 'What were you playing at?' Christopher became even more angry when Kaitlyn responded with nothing but silence. He told her that she was the sort of woman who would trample over anyone in order to get her way, even her own flesh and blood.

Kaitlyn sat and listened to Christopher's words, each one cutting through her like a knife. Tears welled up in her eyes. Then Christopher rose and stormed out of the café. Part of her wanted to follow him but she felt as though all the energy had been drained out of her. For so long she had wanted her brother back in her life. Now that it had finally happened it was a complete disaster.

Over the next few days she tried to contact Christopher again but he refused to take her calls. A week later he approached her once more. Still wary and untrusting, he finally agreed that they should meet again.

Slowly they began to talk. Kaitlyn told her brother all about the life they had led together on the Roxford estate, the fun they used to have and about how she used to look after him and was the only one who could stop him crying. With tears in her eyes she recounted the events of the terrible night when Christopher almost died and the painful weeks that followed when she learned he would never ever be coming back.

When she began to tell him about their mother and the drugs, he held up a hand to stop her. 'Kaitlyn, I don't know if you should be telling me this. I mean, how can you trust me? I don't even know if I can trust myself.'

Kaitlyn smiled. 'I know that whatever I tell you you're never going to be able to use anyway. There is no way in the world you want anyone to know about our relationship.'

'You're right.' Christopher nodded. 'I can never tell anyone about us, you know, not if I want my career to carry on.'

'What about me, what about my career?'

Christopher paused. 'Which career? The best club boss in London or the largest drug supplier to the capital?'

She smiled again and began to tell him a little of the operation she ran. She left out many of the details but told him how Gary gave their mother the drugs that would lead to her fatal overdose, and her own killing of Gary. One day she might tell him everything, but there was no need to do that right away. It would be too much for him to take in.

'You know, Chrissy, it's only now when I look back that I realise I've been a bit of an idiot about all this.'

'What do you mean?'

'All I ever wanted to do was get off the estate. I never wanted all the responsibility I've taken on. I never wanted to do all the terrible things I had to do. I want to change my life. I want a new future. And I want you to be part of it.'

'So where do we go from here?'

'I don't know, Chrissy.'

Christopher drifted off to thoughts about his childhood and the life he had left behind. He wondered how things would have turned out if he had stayed on the estate with his sister. When he looked up at Kaitlyn again, returning from his vivid daydream, her eyes were once more wet. There was something she hadn't told him. He had no idea what it was but he knew he would have to wait to find out.

They had met regularly since then and went to dinner at least twice, sometimes three times a week until they felt comfortable in each other's company. Both of them explained about their hopes and dreams. The bond between them soon became stronger than anything they had ever known and they were constantly on the phone to one another, laughing and joking.

They had been seeing each other for just over two months, usually in Alfred's bar and restaurant on Shaftesbury Avenue, when one evening Christopher arrived early and sat drinking a gin and tonic, staring at the buses and taxis moving back and forth. When Kaitlyn was thirty minutes late he called her cellphone. It instantly hit the answerphone, which suggested it was switched off. Christopher felt something was wrong and a chill ran through his body. In the short time he had known her Kaitlyn had never been late.

*   *   *

Thirty minutes earlier Kaitlyn's taxi driver had spotted the police car right away. It was a dead giveaway. The dark grey Vauxhall Cavalier had no stickers in the back window, no ornaments hanging from the mirror and carried two large men. She allowed herself a small smile. She was aware that she had got to them when she had been released from the court case and the evidence that had emerged as part of their murder investigation pointed to her being one of the biggest drugs traffickers in London. She had covered her tracks well and knew that gathering evidence against her in this area would be a mammoth task. Still, though it might take a while, the evidence would eventually surface. She knew she had to get out while she still could.

The grey Cavalier would not, of course, be working

alone but once she realised she was being tracked it was a simple enough job to find the two or three other cars that would be part of the surveillance team. She had encouraged her drivers to use anti-surveillance techniques for so long that they were part of their normal driving routine. Most of the time it was just a precaution, but every now and then she knew she was being followed. It would take her at least ten more minutes to get to the restaurant but she had no choice. Being in a black taxi helped enormously. It made the job of the police so much harder because there were so many of them around.

Kaitlyn's driver lost the first car going round the roundabout at the bottom of Waterloo Bridge, the second, a dark-green Ford Granada, by pulling an illegal U-turn as they emerged from the Kingsway underpass and the third, a navy-blue VW Passat, by pulling into a multi-storey car park in Poland Street. To be extra safe shey took a long route to the restaurant from there, driving up Baker Street and being sworn at by other drivers by pretending the taxi had stalled at every set of green traffic lights. Then, just as the lights changed, the driver would put his foot down and the taxi would rush forward, narrowly avoiding being hit by the cross traffic. It was a last-ditch manoeuvre to ensure Kaitlyn was not being followed as any car behind her would find its way forward instantly blocked.

At the top of Baker Street her taxi did a loop round Marylebone Station, then headed back towards

Shaftesbury Avenue where the restaurant was. She had spent so much of her time looking out for the three cars that she hardly noticed the powerful motorcycle that had been following her for the past half-hour. Although individual cars were easy to spot in the side mirror, motorcycles could slip in and out of traffic as well as in and out of view. They also kept their headlights on, meaning all a car in front could see would be a beam, not a make or model. It was even impossible to work out what the rider was wearing.

Kaitlyn wasn't the only one hoping she would be able to lose the police cars. The man on the motorcycle had also noticed the three vehicles following her. Once the last had been left behind the rider spoke into the mouthpiece of the hands-free mobile phone attached to his helmet. 'It's a go on Marylebone Road, I repeat, it's a go on Marylebone Road.' Seconds later a second, even more powerful motorcycle had roared alongside the first. This one had two passengers, both dressed all in black with deeply tinted full-face helmets. The solo rider pointed up ahead to where Kaitlyn's taxi was moving slowly in the traffic. The rider of the bigger bike flicked a switch so that his headlight went on to full beam, then pulled hard at the throttle sending the bike shooting forward.

The first thing Kaitlyn saw from her seat in the back of the taxi was the blinding flash of the headlight in the wing mirror as the bike pulled up alongside.

The light dazzled her eyes so much that she could barely see the pillion passenger pulling something dark and heavy from the folds of his leather jacket and pointing it at her head.

By the time her driver realised what was going on it was too late. He tugged the steering wheel hard to the left, hoping to crash into the bike, just as the first bullet tore into the flesh of his thigh. The hot, searing pain made him cry out with agony and sent the car reeling the other way into the central barrier. More bullets burst into the vehicle and shards of shattering glass ripped into the driver's face. Blood streamed into his eyes as he fought to control the car. The taxi smashed into the barrier and came to a halt. Kaitlyn scrambled to her feet and tried to reach the door handle, but the release light was still illuminated and she was trapped. Two bullets hit her square in the back. Two more slammed into her brain and she slumped back against the seat. Dead.

Christopher emerged from Alfred's having waited an hour and feeling something was terribly wrong. He jumped into the nearest black cab and decided to head straight home to Maida Vale, but the taxi soon got stuck in the most awful traffic jam. 'Must be some kind of accident,' the driver said as they ground to a halt just before the Marylebone Road underpass. 'Too late for me to turn off, I'm afraid. Looks like we're stuck for a while.'

Christopher looked at the meter. The fare was

already eight pounds and he'd travelled only a short way. Pulling a £10 note from his wallet, he told the driver to keep the change and opened the door to step out.

He could walk a little way from here, get past the jam and then get another cab to take him home. He made his way with the evening crowd along the main road, crossing over Great Portland Street when he saw dozens of flashing blue lights up ahead. This, he thought, must be where the accident was. As he got closer he saw several police officers in bright yellow fluorescent jackets diverting both traffic and pedestrians along a side road. Three police cars were blocking off the main part of the road and two ambulances had driven up on to the pavement. The mangled wreck of a London taxi lay sideways against the central barrier and several men and women in white forensic suits were milling about, erecting a tent over the car. Even from a distance Christopher could tell there was something odd about the way the car had crashed. There was damage on the side that had hit the barrier, of course, but the window on the passenger side had also caved in and there were pockmarks all along the door. He had taken three more paces before he realised the pockmarks were bullet holes, two more before he saw with a gasp that the taxi was the one Kaitlyn used and only half a step further before he knew for certain that his sister was dead.

Chapter Forty-five

February 2006

In complete contrast to the way she lived her life, the funeral of Kaitlyn Wilson was a quiet, low-profile affair.

Rosa had returned from Mexico to pay her respects, Diane got special permission to leave Holloway for a couple of hours and a few other well-known figures from the underworld also showed up. Staff from Lush and some of her other clubs came to pay their respects. Even Detective Inspector Marshall was there, keeping an eye on the crowd to cast a discreet, watchful eye over the underworld figures who attended.

Christopher realised he must stay well out of sight. Only a handful of people knew the truth. So far as the public at large were concerned the only link between Christopher and Kaitlyn was that he had been the prosecutor in her recent murder trial.

Christopher found it hard to make sense of it all. He had spent only a few months with his sister until she had been brutally murdered. Until his father had become ill he had never truly believed there was anything missing in his life. Once he found out he had been adopted, he knew there was. And now that

Kaitlyn was dead he could feel the agonising hole she had left behind.

Two weeks later Christopher, who had taken a break, had yet to take on another case. He felt as though his heart was no longer in his work and the idea of spending time with professional criminals just made him feel sick. The excitement of the past had all but faded away.

That afternoon he received a call from Roger Brunswick of Brunswick and Moon, Solicitors. Christopher had done work on behalf of their clients before, and instantly recognised the man's voice and cut him off almost as soon as he started speaking. 'I'm sorry, Roger, I'm really not looking to take on any new cases at the moment. I'm having a bit of a sabbatical.'

The man on the other end of the line did not miss a beat. 'Actually, Christopher, I'm not calling to instruct you but rather because someone has instructed me.'

'What are you talking about?'

'All I can tell you, Christopher, is that this is a most unusual situation and one that demands the highest possible level of discretion. Under the circumstances, I think it might be best if you came to my office at your earliest convenience.'

An hour later Christopher found himself sitting in Roger Brunswick's office overlooking Fleet Street in central London.

'I don't want to shock you, old chap,' Brunswick began, 'so I'll just get this over with as quickly as possible. I know about your sister.'

'But . . .'

'It's OK. You know I have to respect my client's confidentiality, even if she is dead. And I have known you too long to cause you any problems. Anyway, let's just say it would not be in my interests to reveal anything more.'

The man did not need to say another word. Christopher knew only too well what his sister was capable of.

'The reason you are here is because I have been instructed to tell you that upon your sister's death you are required to go to the reading of the will. This will take place next Tuesday at the offices of Allen and Turner, Attorneys at Law.'

'Attorneys at Law?' Christopher spoke in a surprised voice. Lawyers were lawyers everywhere in the world. Only in America and parts of the Caribbean did they become attorneys.

Brunswick continued reading the instruction: 'Yes, Attorneys at Law, 1528 Harbour Drive, Grand Cayman.' Kaitlyn's lawyer explained that everything had been prearranged. A first-class ticket had been booked in his name and various solicitors and accountants would be there to greet him on his arrival.

Christopher was intrigued as he went home and packed his bags.

*

The twelve-hour trip to Grand Cayman was smooth and trouble free. On landing, Christopher was met at the Owen Roberts International Airport by a limo driven by a heavy-set, well-dressed black man who introduced himself as Big Al. The driver made small talk about the weather and Christopher's first visit to the island. It seemed, from the way Big Al was talking, that he had already heard of him. It was a forty-five-minute journey to Cayman Kai, an exclusive area where only houses, not hotels, are allowed to be built.

Christopher fished out a pair of sunglasses from his bag as they made their way across the island. Even though the windows of the limousine were slightly tinted, the blazing sun was still shining through.

'Here we are,' said Big Al as they turned into the driveway of a large plantation house. Christopher could hardly believe his eyes. The building was set within its own grounds and was perched on the edge of a low cliff overlooking a small cove. The pristine and incredibly private beach curled round on the left and the right like pincers. Palm trees flapped gently in the wind and the sound of waves crashing against rocks could be heard on the wind.

Inside the house a group of neatly dressed members of staff took his bags, escorted him into the lounge and fixed him a drink, snacks and supplied cool wet face towels to mop his brow.

Fifteen minutes later a tall black man in a well-cut

Italian suit appeared in the doorway. 'I do apologise for being late, Mr Tobin. I am Alvin Turner of Allen and Turner, Attorneys at Law,' he explained. 'I had planned to meet you at the airport but your flight actually arrived a little early. I trust you have been made comfortable.'

'More than comfortable,' said Christopher, still in awe of his surroundings. 'This is a wonderful house, but I'm sure I would have been just as happy in a hotel. Does your firm maintain this property just for the use of its customers?'

Turner's brow creased as he struggled to understand the question. 'I don't follow, Mr Tobin. What do you mean?'

'I mean who owns this place?'

There was a pause. 'Well, technically speaking, the bank does own the property at the moment but once you sign the paperwork this property, and all the others in the portfolio, plus the liquid assets, will be transferred to you as per the will.'

It was as if someone had sucked all the air out of his lungs. Christopher struggled to speak. There were so many questions running around his head he did not know where to start. 'The other properties?' he said at last.

'Why yes, Mr Tobin. This was Ms Wilson's principal residence when she was in Grand Cayman but there are others in and around Rum Point and Cayman Kai, some overlooking Snug Harbour, one at the bottom end of Seven Mile Beach and a few dotted around the yacht club. There are, I believe, twenty-six villas in all, as well as a number of other developments.'

'I see,' said Christopher. His mind was whirling almost out of control.

'The full list is available at our firm's head office along with other possessions. Would you like to see them now or would you like more time to relax?'

Christopher stood up. 'I think I'd better see them now. Right now.'

The office of Allen and Turner was a plush, three-storey, mirror-windowed building in the centre of Grand Cayman. After being introduced to the numerous staff and executives, then having a formal reading of the will and signing all the papers, Christopher was taken to the basement.

Alvin Turner led him into a private room and switched on the lights. On a desk in the centre of the room was a small wooden box, the size of a pet's coffin. 'These are the possessions of your sister. These are the things she wanted you to have.'

The man left the room so that Christopher could study the contents of the box alone. At first it seemed to make little sense. There were various notebooks, journals, photographs and diagrams. He opened one of the books at random. It was full of dates, places and times. Another was full of flight details. Yet another contained the names of various ships and the dates and times they had travelled from one country to another. A book labelled 'accounts' was simply full of long numbers with little indication of what they related to.

Some of the photographs were of men and women whom Christopher did not recognise, others he knew as high-ranking figures from the world of international organised crime. Then there was another envelope stuffed with photographs, separate from the rest. He opened it and was astonished to see photographs of himself, all of them taken in the past ten years, of the day he won his first case, the day he graduated from university, the day he came out of the hospital when his father had been diagnosed with Huntington's. He gasped as he realised that Kaitlyn had been there in the background the whole time, part of every moment of his life, yet he had never known.

At the bottom of the box was a handwritten letter from Kaitlyn addressed to him. With trembling hands he opened the envelope, took out the three sheets of paper and began reading. He saw that it was dated the day after the last time he had seen her, just a few hours before she had been killed. He fought back the floods of tears and started to read.

Dear Christopher

The view from the big blue chair at the back of the house is perhaps my favourite view in the whole world. I had hoped and dreamed that one day I would be able to share it with you, but the fact that you are reading this letter means that my dream will never come to be.

Don't mourn my death. Anything that has happened to

me is as a direct result of the choices I made in my life. I always knew the risks I was taking and I have always been ready to face the ultimate consequences.

There are many things I have done for which I feel great shame and remorse. I have caused huge pain to others and their families in the pursuit of wealth and in a bid to maintain my liberty. The fact that you are reading this letter can only go to show that, in the long run, none of it was worthwhile, none of it meant anything.

All my life I envied you, Christopher, even more so once I tracked you down and found out about the life you were living. All I ever wanted was to get out of the estate, to make a better life for myself. And that is just what you have had the chance to do, though it almost cost you your life. Now my way of doing the same has cost me mine.

That is why, Christopher, I sought you out. I wanted to be sure there was always one thing in my life that I could be proud of. The downfall of everyone who becomes successful, no matter what line of work they are involved in, is that they become greedy and do not know when to stop. Christopher, promise me you will never fall into that same trap. Know your limits. Get out while you can.

The more he read the more astonished Christopher became. He realised that the police, the Crown Prosecution Service, no one had any real idea about the scale of Kaitlyn's operation. Although it was widely assumed that she was a major figure in international drug trafficking, the scale and size of her enterprise were simply staggering.

It all fell into place now. This was what she had been trying to tell him just before she died.

The notebooks, journals and diagrams that filled the rest of the box explained in intimate detail exactly how everything worked. They gave details of safety deposit boxes, secret bank accounts, laundering techniques and drug routes. There was an electronic diary that contained names and contact numbers for major drug traffickers everywhere in the world, listing those who could be trusted and those who could not. None of this information was known to the police or any of the international law enforcement agencies. None of the assets mentioned had ever appeared on the list of properties and other items drawn up by the Assets Recovery Bureau.

Christopher realised he was sitting on an absolute goldmine. He could use the material to guarantee prosecutions against the world's biggest drug barons that would stretch on for the rest of his career. It would be the ultimate coup, the single biggest operation against organised crime anywhere in the history of the world.

Or he could use it to simply carry on from where Kaitlyn had left off. He would be rich and powerful beyond his wildest dreams, with access to tens of millions of pounds. The choice was his. She was handing it to him on a plate and all he had to do was decide which way he wanted to go.

*

Later that afternoon Christopher relaxed in the big pale-blue easychair at the back of the plantation house and looked out at the view. A large crest of white water was crashing over the pale-yellow sand. The shadows of the casuarina trees were dancing along the beach. He could see now why Kaitlyn had chosen this place. It was paradise. It was beautiful. It was the kind of place he imagined he might end up in after a long and successful career. But why wait until he was retired and too old to enjoy it? It was somewhere his parents could see out the last of their days in comfort and security. He could have it all now. It was just what Kaitlyn would have wanted.

Making up his mind what to do would be the biggest and most difficult decision of his entire life. There was no sense in rushing it.

For the next few days Christopher ran through each of the different scenarios in his head, while making the most of his time on the island. He hired a jeep and went exploring the outermost reaches of the island, played golf with Big Al, tried his hand at sport fishing for tarpon and went snorkelling off the coast of Parrot's Reef. He changed his return flight to make it a week later, then changed it again to make it a week later still.

He took a scuba-diving course and went out on boat trips to explore the Trinity Caves and Orange Canyon. Deep under the water, among the spectacular multicoloured fish, elephant-ear sponges and arrow crabs, he felt a million miles away from the stresses and strains of his life back in London.

But it was while he was sitting under the shade of a large palm tree close to the plantation house, eyes closed with the sound of the waves crashing on the beach filling his ears, that he finally made the decision that would affect the rest of his life, ensuring nothing would ever be the same again.

Christopher walked back into the house and dug around in a drawer until he found a pen and a pad of paper. It was then that he began writing.

Dear Martin
It is with deep regret that I am writing to inform you that I will no longer be practising law . . .

Christopher sighed and paused, unsure of what to say next. Then there was a noise from outside the window. Christopher looked up. A young local boy, aged around six or seven, was running bare-chested into the waves, his black cut-off trousers flapping in the wind as he went. He waved his arms as the cool water hit him and made a gurgling, laughing sound that brought an instant smile to Christopher's lips. Within a few moments, the young boy had been joined by two more children of a similar age, a boy and a girl, and all three were eagerly running through the surf and playfully splashing one another.

Christopher put down his pen, stood up and grabbed a towel. He had started the letter and it would take only a few minutes to finish it. Right now, he was going outside to enjoy himself. Everything else could wait until tomorrow.